Merry Christmas,
Mom,

these store "you
hung for awhile!"

Love,

Const

ALFRED HITCHCOCK'S

MYSTERY
BY THE
TALE

ALFRED HITCHCOCK'S
MYSTERY
BY THE
TALE

CASTLE

Grateful acknowledgment is hereby made for permission to reprint the following :*A Habit for the Voyage* by Robert Edmond Alter, copyright © 1964 by H.S.D. Publications, Inc., reprinted by permission by Larry Sternig Literary Agency; *Waiting for the Coroner* by Gary Brandner, copyright © 1979 by Davis Publications, Inc. reprinted by permission of the aurthor; *Jambalaya* by Douglas Craig, copyright © 1964 by H.S.D. Publications, Inc.; *Number One Suspect* by Richard Deming, copyright © 1962 by H.S.D. Publications, Inc., reprinted by permission of Ruth Deming; *A Murderous Slice* by Marguerite Dickinson, copyright © 1964 by H.S.D. Publications, Inc.repirnted by permission of the aurthor; *The Sheriff's Rainy Day* by Elijah Ellis, copyright © 1965 by H.S.D. Publications, Inc., reprinted by permission of Scott Meredith Literary Agency, Inc.; *Small Town Justice* by Leo R. Ellis, copyright © 1964 by H.S.D. Publications, Inc., reprinted by permission of Larry Sternig Literary Agency; *Dream of a Murder* by C.B. Gilford, copyright © 1965 by H.S.D. Publications, Inc., reprinted by permission of Scott Meredith Literary Agency, Inc.; *High Tide* by Richard Hardwick, copyright © 1963 by H.S.D. Publications. Inc., reprinted by permission of Scott Meredith Literary Agency, Inc.; *The Mark of Cain* by Allen Lang, copyright © 1965 by H.S.D. Publications, Inc., reprinted by permission of the author; *Man with a Hobby* by Carroll Mayers, copyright © 1965 by H.S.D. Publications, Inc., reprinted by permission of Wayne Hamilton; *$16,940.00* by Larry Niven, copyright © 1974 by H.S.D. Publications, Inc., reprinted by permission of Kirby McCauley, Ltd.; *Blood Will Tell* by Arthur Porges, copyright © 1964 by H.S.D. Publications, Inc., reprinted by permission of Scott Meredith Literary Agency, Inc.; *Bertillon's Odds* by Talmage Powell, author; *A Piece of the World* by Jack Ritchie, copyright © 1965 by H.S.D. Publications, Inc., reprinted by permission of Larry Sternig Literary Agency; *Tight Fix* by Harold Rolseth, copyright © 1964 by H.S.D. Publications, Inc., reprinted by permission of Larry Sternig Literary Agency; *The Park Plaza Thefts* by Ernest Savage, copyright © 1978 by Davis Publications, Inc., reprinted by permission of the author; *Crime Buff* by James H. Schmitz, copyright © 1973 by H.S.D. Publications, Inc., reprinted by permission of Scott Meredith Literary Agency, Inc.; *Obligations* by Beatrice S. Smith, copyright © 1975 by H.S.D. Publications, Inc., reprinted by permirsion of Ann Elmo Agency, Inc.; *Something for the Club* by Pat Stadley, copyright © 1962 by H.S.D. Publications, Inc., reprinted by permission of Larry Sternig Literary Agency; *The Zigzag Line* by Don Tothe, copyright © 1965 by H.S.D. Publications, Inc., reprinted by permission of Janet Van Derveer; *Some Lucky License* by Charles Willeford, copyright © 1965 by H.S.D. Publications, Inc., reprinted by permission of the author; *Ley de Fuga* by Brad Williams, copyright © 1962 by H.S.D. Publications, Inc., reprinted by permission of John Schaffner Associates, Inc.; *Diminishing Wife* by Michael Zuroy, copyright ©

Contents

Frank Sisk

Stately Ruins

"If you want to know the truth, Ed," said Miss Muldoon quite seriously, "I'm trying to get through the rest of my life as fast as possible."

Edwin Coleman, M.D., appraised the trim old lady on the other side of the desk with sympathetic blue eyes in which there was a trace of amusement. "When the hell did you start on that tack, Peg?"

"Soon as a drop of whisky failed to take the winter chill out of my bones."

"Physically, you know, you're right as rain."

"And just as damp in spirits. I'm down in the dumps, Ed."

"You've been down before and bounced up."

"It's the old bounce that's finally gone. A few weeks ago when I celebrated—which is hardly the word—my seventy-third birthday I was struck by the fact that everything in life has become dreadfully boring and repetitious. It's as simple as that, Ed."

"That's not nice, Peg. You have a birthday and fail to invite me to the party."

"You wouldn't have come anyhow. My fat young cousins were present."

"The Sheehans? Well, they're fat, all right, but I'd hardly call them young."

"At my age anyone under fifty's young. But they came, all five hundred pounds of them. And without invitation. Just chanced by with a chocolate cake from the three-day-old bakery and a bottle of cooking sherry."

"Sounds jolly."

"If you fancy a pair of corpulent vultures." Miss Muldoon veiled her pale green eyes with delicately thin lids as if trying to banish such distasteful images. "They grasp at any occasion to check out the state of my health, among other things. Terence, you may recall, pretends to be in the real estate business, though God only knows whether he's ever completed a transaction. Well, Terence spends part of each visit estimating aloud what my house and land would fetch on the rising market. And his sister Maureen—a cousin I find it increasingly hard to kiss—takes inventory more or less covertly of all the valuables in sight. The sterling, the porcelain china, the cut glass." She unveiled her eyes with a sign. "It's obvious that they can hardly wait for my will to be probated."

"So they're in your will, are they?"

"Largely out of respect for Father's wishes. He was a great believer in blood being thicker than water, may his soul rest easy with that sentimental nonsense."

"Didn't your father remember them in his own will?"

"Of course. Enough to whet their appetites. In fact, Father was practically the sole support of his sister, my Aunt Liz, and those two spoiled brats after her husband died at the height of his career as a three-bottle man. Then when Liz herself died, the brats by that time being full-grown oafs, Father bought the house they'd been renting and gave them the deed outright."

"All in all, the Sheehans seem to have fared well by the Muldoons," Dr. Coleman said.

"And they'll fare better when I'm boxed and put away," Miss Muldoon said with a certain proud severity.

"You resent them and yet you provide for them."

"They're an ill-favored pair, sir, but mine own."

"Sometimes, Peg, I don't understand you at all."

I was paraphrasing the Bard."

"I know that. What I mean is—"

"When you're my age," she continued on a doleful note, "without chick nor child and all your old friends pushing up daisies, you grow grateful for any bit of attention, even if it's wholly selfish. You're like a person, say, crossing a burning desert, delirious with thirst. You welcome the circling vultures because you know as long as they circle up there you're still alive."

"A fine figure of speech," the doctor said, smiling. "It's none of my business, Peg, but do you plan to leave your entire—" He stopped, visibly embarrassed. "I'd better keep my mouth shut."

Miss Muldoon awarded him a pert grin. "No, they don't get it all. I haven't left out your favorite charity."

Coleman's favorite charity was the Institute for the Deaf and the Mute. He had been spending a lot of his own time and money in strengthening the institute's endowment fund ever since his only son, aged nine and born deaf, had stepped off a curb into the path of a fire truck because he failed to hear the siren.

"It's a worthy cause," the doctor said.

"I know it and Father knew it, but I'm going to do better by you than Father. You'll be pleased when the time comes."

"I can assure you, Peg, that's a distant day. Now if you'll take a bit of advice from a friend not too much your junior, I suggest you get away from that old mausoleum you live in. A few months abroad should perk you up. Ireland's lovely this time of the year, especially from Tralee to Dingle."

"I'll think about it. Meanwhile, I'd like you to write me my prescription again . . ."

Miss Muldoon was nobody's fool.

She knew the prescription that Ed Coleman had been scribbling for her these last few years wasn't a powerful tranquilizer—*Never more than one before retiring, then only when natural sleep impossible*—but just a harmless placebo.

Sugar and spice, she thought as Herbert helped her into the back seat of the Chrysler sedan, and everything nice. That's what an old lady's capsules are made of.

Well, she now had a special use for them.

Herbert slid behind the wheel, then turned his homely fist of a face toward her.

"O'Hara's Pharmacy, Herbert."

"Yes, ma'am."

The air-conditioned car glided smoothly from the parking lot of the Community Medical Building and proceeded at an even thirty-five MPH, no more or less, along five blocks of a sun-filled avenue bordered by fine old apartment houses and fancy new condominiums—high-priced frontage, as Terence would have described it.

O'Hara's once-modest facade was somewhat garish, in Miss Muldoon's opinion, since Junior had taken over from the old man, but that was the sad way of the world.

Herbert assisted her from the car.

Junior himself was on duty. His rapidly thinning red hair and ever-thickening eyeglasses were steadily transforming him into the spit and image of his old man who nowadays was rocking his life away on the porch of a convalescent home, probably dreaming of past magic with mortar and pestle.

"Good afternoon, Miss Muldoon," said Junior with an ingratiating smile. "My, aren't we looking fit today."

"I doubt that I am and I know you aren't. In fact, Junior, you're looking downright waxy."

"That's what the wife's been telling me. Guess I'm due for a vacation."

"Overdue. But before you take off, please fill this prescription."

"Certainly." He took the blank she handed him, scanned Dr. Coleman's scrawl, and nodded his head. "Be ready in a jiffy."

A few minutes later he emerged from the pharmaceutical compartment with a small brown phial which he dropped into a paper bag. "The label spells out the doctor's warning, Miss Muldoon. Never more than one capsule in any twenty-four hour period. You'll be sure to heed it, won't you?"

"Of course. How much?"

"Five seventy."

The price of sugar is surely skyrocketing, she thought, but if Ed Coleman and Junior O'Hara were going to maintain a fiction, she supposed they must also maintain a logical price for it.

As the Chrysler entered the long driveway and headed for the old carriage house, which back in the twenties had been converted into a three-car garage, Miss Muldoon found herself glumly agreeing with the doctor's assessment of the old place. It really was a mausoleum.

In her father's time it always wore a coat of gleaming white paint. For the last decade its color had been Quaker grey because grey concealed dirt and didn't need to be scraped down and repainted every four years.

Now, however, with the wide pilastered proch, the two upstairs balconies that jutted out beyond tall front windows, the towering cupola, and the railed widow's walk, the house somehow resembled the midsection of a battleship.

"Shall I put the car away, ma'am?" Herbert asked.

"Yes, I won't require it again today."

He brought the car to a gentle stop at the trellised walk leading to the side door and helped her out.

"Oh, Herbert," she said as he released her arm. "While I think of it. I want you and Agnes to come upstairs to my sitting room in ten minutes or so. It's time we arranged your holiday. Do you realize it's already the sixth of June?"

"So it is, am'am."

Agnes, the housekeeper, was Herbert's wife. Together they'd served Miss Muldoon diligently for the last eight years. From the start there had been mutual agreement that they were to have paid leave during the last three weeks of June. They used this time to visit their married daughter in Sandusky, Ohio, where they devoted considerable energy to spoiling an endless proliferation of grandchildren. They always returned with an air of consummate pride and utter exhaustion.

Miss Muldoon usually spent the same interval poking around Boston, which vied with Dublin as her favorite city.

This year, however, she had different plans.

She ascended to the second floor by way of the front staircase, and by the time she reached the top, she told herself for the hundredth time in as many days that it might be a good idea to have to small elevator installed.

Agnes and Herbert left on the tenth of June. An hour after their departure Miss Muldoon phoned her gross young cousins, the Sheehans. Old habit made her think of them as "young" despite the fact that Maureen was pushing fifty and Terence was close behind. But when they'd arrived in the world, hungry for all its goods, she was already well into her twenties.

Maureen answered the ring with an indistinct utterance.

"This is Cousin Margaret," Miss Muldoon said. "What's the matter with you, Maureen?"

"Jush a mome."

"What the devil ails you?"

"Nushin." Sound of a gulping swallow. "Sorry, Margaret. I was eating a doughnut."

I might have known, Miss Muldoon thought. "I called to ask a favor, Maureen."

"A favor?"

"Yes, a favor."

"A favor?"

"You know what a favor is, don't you? You've been on the receiving end of enough of them."

"What kind of a *favor*, Margaret?" She spoke the key word with a hint of fear.

"Don't fret, Maureen. It's not going to cost you a penny, just a bit of your time."

"Whatever you say, Margaret."

"Well, I'm not feeling up to snuff. A touch of fever with migraine. And as luck would have it, Agnes and Herbert are off on their annual holiday. So I wondered if you and Terence would care to come over and pamper me for a few days."

Would they care to come over? In less than an hour they arrived like an avalanche in their bulging Peugeot.

Miss Muldoon met them at the side door. She led them, suitcases in hand, up the creaking rear stairs and assigned each of them a back bedroom with bath.

"You'll have as much privacy here," she said, "as if you were in your own place. My own quarters, as you know, are at the front of the house. I'll try to be as little bother as possible."

"But we're here to help," Maureen piped. Though she weighed nearly two hundred pounds and possessed forearms that could have belonged to a butcher, she spoke in a high girlish voice. "That's what we're here for, aren't we, Terry?"

"Absolutely right, Sis." At two hundred ninety-five pounds and over six feet, Terence looked like a bullock too long at the feed pen. A shock of white hair accentuated the pinkness of his bovine face. "That's what we're here for, Margaret. And it's the first time we'll be staying overnight in a coon's age."

"Not since Uncle John died," Maureen added, unable to hide a faint note of resentment.

"Ten years?" Miss Muldoon questioned the time lapse with bland incredulity. "It seems only yesterday. Father was adoze in his study over the works of Yeats."

"A sainted man," Maureen trilled reverently.

"A hothouse flower, more like it," Miss Muldoon countered.

"A free-handed man," said Terence ponderously, then added with the sudden dazed expression of one beaned by a clown's bladder: "A hothouse flower? Your *father?*"

"I was referring to Yeats. In his latter years he found temperatures under ninety intolerable. I'm told he wrote some of his best and final work in steam baths."

"Yeats?" Maureen's wishy-washy eyes sought her brother's for edification. "Did we ever meet him?"

"Once at a wake, I think," Terence replied.

"Make yourselves at home," Miss Muldoon said, terminating the conversation. "I've a letter to write before dinner."

It was a few minutes after six. At ease on the chaise longue in the sitting room, Miss Muldoon was enjoying a second glass of very good sherry when a discreet knock sounded on her bedrooim door.

Rising, she went to the half-open door of the sitting room. Just up the hall Maureen prepared to knock again.

"I'm in here," Miss Muldoon said.

"Oh, yes. It's about dinner, Margaret."

"I'll settle for a dish of soup."

"Any special kind, Margaret?"

"I'm not fussy tonight, Maureen."

"There's a good variety on the pantry shelves. Terry and I thought we'd have oxtail."

"That'll suit me fine."

"I'll bring you up a bowl in a few minutes, then."

"That's not necessary, Maureen. I'll be coming down."

"But, Margaret, if you're not feeling well—"

"I'll feel the better for a trudge down the stairs."

The Sheehans, both of whom were competent in the kitchen if nowhere else, had done well for themselves.

Following the soup, which they finished in a trice, they figuratively rolled up their sleeves and dug into a repast that would have foundered Falstaff—thick sirloin steaks, mounds of mashed potatoes drenched in brown gravy, clumps of asparagus dressed with hollandaise, and a huge Waldorf salad, supplemented by hot buttered rolls and drafts of dark German beer.

Still toying with her soup, Miss Muldoon commented, "Well, you seem to have found everything."

"I had trouble finding the freezer." Terence tore the words from the process of mastication. "Back of cellar once. Up front now."

Miss Muldoon said, "It's a different freezer from Father's."

"Thought so. Smaller."

"More efficient."

"Stocked well." Terence buttered his fifth or sixth roll. "Margaret, while I think of it." He bit the roll in half. "Studs."

"What?"

"Studs." He took a great swig of beer. "Joists."

"Yes?"

"Near the freezer, above it."

"Yes?"

"Riddled with termites."

"Herbert said as much recently."

"Dangerous, Margaret."

"I imagine so."

"Should do something about it. Maintain the property properly. Maintain its value."

"Thanks for the advice, Terence. I'll do something."

"Sooner the better."

For dessert the Sheehans treated themselves to king-sized sundaes in Waterford glass finger bowls.

"How much Waterford do you actually have, Margaret?" Maureen asked, watching Miss Muldoon pour herself a cup of tea.

"Too much."

"Nobody could have too much. Oh, I just love it. It's so solid and heavy, even the salt and pepper shakers."

"And expensive," Terence mumbled, spooning ice cream into his face. "Those two decanters from Uncle John. I priced them at Hungerford's. Hundred fifty each."

"And that was years ago," Maureen said. "I bet they're much higher today, with inflation and all."

Miss Muldoon decided to dangle bait. "What I ought to do is pick out some of the more useful pieces—wine glasses and sweetmeat jars and such—and let you both have them now."

A gleam of avarice shone in Maureen's ordinarily vapid eyes. "Why, Margaret, that would be marvelous."

"After all, you're going to get the whole kit and caboodle one of these days."

Terence licked whipped cream from his slavering lips. "Sure, we could choose the items now, while we're here."

"Not so fast," Miss Muldoon raised a thin but authoritative hand. "All in my own good time."

"Oh, of course, Margaret, of course," Maureen said hastily.

"If you'll excuse me, I'm going to retire." Miss Muldoon rose, started for the hallway door, then stopped and turned with an air of uncertainty. "I think I'll take a little sedation tonight. Now where did I put those capsules?"

The Sheehans remained dumb.

"I probably left them in the bathroom off the kitchen."

"I'll go see," Maureen said, hoisting herself from the chair and waddling off through the service door.

"Don't tell me. Margaret," said Terence, and accusatory ring in his voice, "that you have to take stuff to make you sleep."

"Rarely."

"Myself, I sleep like a log."

And eat like a hog, Miss Muldoon added silently.

Maureen returned. "Is this it?" She held out the brown phial. "From O'Hara's?"

"Yes, thanks." Miss Muldoon snapped off the cap and tilted a single capsule into her palm. "One does the trick." Replacing the cap, she handed the phial back to Maureen. "I'll be obliged if you'd return it where you found it. I don't like having it handy. At my age, I might absent-mindedly take an extra capsule, and that could be curtains."

Miss Muldoon, while not subscribing to the aphorism on the relative thickness of blood to water, didn't really expect the Sheehans to be the ones to disprove it. Not that she underestimated their greed and stupidity, but she'd always seen in them a clumsy instinct for self-preservation. They had been heirs presumptive for so long that they'd never risk their status on a reckless gamble that might make them heirs in fact.

The next morning at eight her bedroom door resounded with two courteous taps.

Miss Muldoon was already wide awake. Propped up in bed, she was frowningly engrossed in the *Prose Works of Jonathan Swift*, one of her father's favorite books, which she'd been trying to appreciate most of her life. "Come round through the sitting room," she called out. "The bedroom door's locked."

There was a muffled response. A moment later Maureen, bearing a heavily laden tray, filled the sitting room entrance, her round face wreathed with a cheery smile that never reached her dull eyes. "Did you sleep well?" she asked.

"Quite well, thank you."

"We thought you'd enjoy a good breakfast. Last night you pecked like a bird."

"That looks like enough for the Cork militia."

"Scrambled eggs with mushrooms. Muffins and marmalade." Unfolding the legs of the tray, Maureen began to place it across her cousin's lap. "And a pot of coffee."

"Don't put it here," Miss Muldoon snapped. "I can't bear eating in bed. Set it over there on the bureau."

Maureen looked like a child who had been slapped. "You mean you don't want breakfast?"

"I didn't say that, Maureen. I simply don't want it in the bloody bed with me."

"You *will* eat it then?"

"As soon as I wash my face and put in my teeth."

Taking an unspoken cue, Maureen reluctantly withdrew.

Miss Muldoon eased out of bed and into a pair of old slippers. Going to the tray, she lifted the silver lid. With a fork she nibbled the eggs.

As sweet as candy.

She poured a cup of coffee and sipped it black and sugarless.

Like syrup.

Silly devils, she thought. They couldn't wait.

An hour later Miss Muldoon, fully dressed, found the Sheehans in the dining room. They were lingering over the remains of what must have been a sumptuous repast if one were to judge from the number and variety of dishes on the table.

Her presence plainly surprised them. Their stupefied eyes traveled as one to the tray she was carrying.

Terence finally managed speech. "How are you feeling, Margaret?"

"Right as a trivet."

Maureen blinked as if witnessing an unwelcome vision. "Did you enjoy you, uh, your, uh ..."

"Eggs?"

"Yes."

"I avoid them. Too much cholesterol. And I never take coffee. Tea's my drink—tea and, on occasion, whisky."

"You should have told us," Terence said in a tone of reprimand.

"You should have known," Miss Muldoon said, feeling wicked and very much alive.

She went to the kitchen and deposited the tray in the sink. Then she stepped into the bathroom and checked the medicine cabinet. The brown phial was still there—but empty.

"I've imposed on you long enough," Miss Muldoon said after lunch.

The Sheehans mumbled protests in unison.

"But I must impose upon you once again."

The Sheehans tried not to look apprehensive.

"I'd be obliged," she continued, "if you'd drop me off at the Community Medical Building on your way home."

"*On our way home?*" Again the Sheehans spoke together, with shared astonishment.

"That's what I said."

"But we thought—"

"I appreciate your concern for my health, but last night's sleep really restored me back to normal."

"But we planned—"

"I have an appointment with Dr. Coleman in thirty minutes."

Terence drove. Maureen sat in the front seat, her bulky shoulder against his.

Miss Muldoon, in the rear, felt the Peugeot overflowing with flesh and grumpy silence. The Sheehans were obviously confused and boiling mad.

As the car neared the Community Medical Building, Maureen ventured in her paradoxically girlish voice, "I've been remembering what you said about the Waterford glass, Margaret."

"Yes?"

"Are you still going to—"

"Of course." Poor fools, set on salvaging something.

"But when?" grumped Terence.

"In a couple of days."

Almost palpably taut hamstrings loosened.

Dr. Coleman said, "Damn it all, Peg, if you aren't a new woman."

"An old one, Ed, with a new lease."

"Good as new."

"Speaking of old, though, it's the house. Termites are devouring the foundations. And in the name of Father, I want to remedy the damage they've done. Don't you have carpenters at the institute?"

"We teach all crafts, Peg. The best carpenter is a young lad I use myelf—Brian Healy. Deaf and dumb but a veritable genius with hammer and saw."

"Is he free to do some work for me?"

"Not free, but non-union."

"I'll pay him union wages with a bonus to boot if he reports to work in the morning."

"He'll be there. But what's the hurry, Peg?"

"I want to visit the Old Sod with an easy conscience, Ed."

"Erin go bragh."

Brian Healy, a freckle-faced youth with tight knots of red hair, studiously perused Miss Muldoon's written instructions, then looked at her.

"Do you understand, Brian?"

Brian nodded and went to work.

Three days later Miss Muldoon phoned the Sheehans and told Maureen, who answered the phone, that a box of Waterford glass was packed and waiting for them.

"I suggest you pick it up soon," she said, "because I'll be going abroad as soon as Agnes and Herbert return."

"Oh, glory," Maureen chirped, "we'll be over tomorrow morning."

And so they were, all five hundred pounds of them.

Miss Muldoon led them upstairs to her bedroom and pointed to an old steamer truck with leather handles at either side.

"There you are," she said.

"The trunk itself is an antique," Maureen cooed. "We don't know what to say, Margaret. Do we, Terry?"

"You grab one handle, I'll grab the other," Terence said.

"Glory, it's heavy," Maureen said.

"Damn heavy," grunted Terence. "Which way do we go?"

The juxtaposition of bureau and bed prevented them from taking it through the bedroom door.

Miss Muldoon said, "I'm afraid you'll have to go through the sitting room."

Jointly they hoisted, Maureen seeming to take somewhat more of the trunk's weight than Terence. Their gasps of exertion were constant and unified.

They jockeyed their burden across the threshold and stood breathing heavily for a moment—but for a moment only. Then, before they could take another step, came the excruciating screech of wood strained to the breaking point. Next, the lumpish twosome, still holding the trunk by its handles, dropped precipitately from sight. From the floor below, which was the front parlor, they sent up a magnified howl abruptly overridden by the sound of more wood being rent asunder.

Two days later Dr. Coleman was on the phone. "Well," he said in his dry professional voice.

"I'm quite well, thank you," said Miss Muldoon.

"Tell me what went on over there, Peg."

"An unfortunate accident Ed."

"You've conned the police, obviously, and the insurance investigator, but don't try that line on your old family physician. Brian, remember, is one of my boys."

"And a fine boy he is."

"Truthful, too. And he's told me in so many vagrant words—sign language to you—that the job you set him doing had nothing at all to do with repairing damage done by termites."

"Didn't he tell you he cut away the affected joists and studs?"

"He did, and he says you had him saw nearly through a number of them not at all affected. *Nearly* through."

"That was simply to facilitate the work of the mechanics when they come to install the elevator."

"So Brian informed me—which was the first I ever heard of this elevator."

"It's been in the back of my mind for a long time. While Brian was here I decided to go ahead with the project."

"Oh, Peg, you're a plausible biddy. But please answer me one question. How did those overweight cousins of yours happen to be carrying a trunk full of books across that weakened part of the second floor?"

"They were giving me a helping hand, Ed, transporting some of Father's treasured Irish tomes to the cellar."

"But why didn't you warn them?"

"I was asleep at the time, in the downstairs den."

"At eleven in the morning?"

"That's right. I hadn't slept a wink all night, so after breakfast I decided a nap was in order."

"And I suppose the Sheehans arrived without your knowing it and went right upstairs to take care of the trunk."

"Exactly."

"And you didn't hear them until they plunged through two floors to the cellar?"

"No. And you can believe me, Ed, when I tell you it was the fault of those capsules you prescribe for me. I took one just before I lay down and as usual it put me out like a light."

At the other end of the phone the silence went on and on and on.

Ernest Savage
The Small Hours

I don't know what time it was in Zurich when Henry Taylor called me from there, but it was a quarter to one in San Francisco and I'd been asleep for an hour. "Lance has been kidnapped," he told me bluntly. "I want you to go out to the house."

I swung my legs out of bed and planted my feet on the floor. He'd sounded only mildly perturbed, but it could have been the connection. "And what do I do when I get there?"

"Put a cap on it—if you can. But it may be too late, Sam. Mrs. Jason called the Belvedere cops before she called me."

"When did Mrs. Jason call you?" My feet were cold; I was waking up.

"She hung up about five minutes ago. It seems Millie—the maid—was knocked unconscious by the kidnappers and she called the cops reflexively."

"How can I put a lid on it? And why should I?"

"Because I'm asking you to! For one thing, that jerk kid of mine could have done it himself—I wouldn't put it past him—and for another I don't have to tell you it would hurt the company. I don't need any more bad publicity right now, Sam, so please do what you can." The "please" came out like a tooth.

I was silent. I didn't like Henry Taylor; he had all the flaws that go with fifty million hard-won bucks, and few of the graces. But I liked his son Lance, despite the name, and I didn't think it was likely he'd arranged his own kidnapping, tempting as it might be to devil his father.

Taylor spoke again. "Mrs. Jason said the note the kidnappers left said we had only eight hours to come up with the money or he'd be dead."

"How much money?"

"I don't know—the note didn't say. Get out there, Sam, for God's sake, and do what you can for me. I'll be in touch later." He hung up before I could ask him why he didn't take the next plane home; but on reflection, I didn't really want to know.

I'd been to the Taylor place three times before—to play tennis with him. He owns the two best red-clay courts I've ever seen. I've also been fishing with him on his yacht. But it doesn't mean we're friends. I'd done a job for him, and it was a case of one thing leading to another. Besides, I'd play tennis on a red-clay court with the Archfiend himself.

The chief of the Belvedere police force and one uniformed cop were there when I arrived. They'd been there about an hour and had worried frowns on their faces. The chief, who introduced himself as Howard Parks, had wanted to bring in the FBI, but a call from

Taylor—after he'd talked to me—put a stop to that. Taylor had told him to let me handle it, and he seemed glad to. He and his aide comprised about a third of the Belvedere force and their principal duty was to keep the pristine little town they served clear of undesirables. They were bouncers more than they were cops.

In the kitchen, Parks introduced me to Mrs. Jason, who was seated tiredly at the table in the center of the big room. I said to her, "Tell me what happened."

It was her night off, she said, and she'd gone to a movie in Sausalito, getting back at midnight. She'd found Millie, the maid, unconscious on the kitchen floor and had seen the note Scotch-taped to the refrigerator door. She'd brought Millie around with cold compresses and had made the phone calls. She'd gotten about that far in her recitation when I sensed something missing.

"Where's the dog?" I asked her. Taylor had a Doberman guard dog and every time I'd been here before, his barking, it had seemed to me, was damn near continuous. The question opened her eyes and she said she didn't know—it *was* funny she hadn't heard him.

Parks and I went out to his run to look and found him dead. Poisoned meat, probably, tossed over the six foot chain-link fence. Taylor kept him thin and voracious and he'd probably wolfed it down in a gulp. Even dead he looked dangerous.

On the way back we went through the eight car garage and I snapped on the lights. A Daimler, a Rolls, a Jaguar XJ, and a Porsche were side by side, then two blanks, then a beat-up VW bug about ten years old. It didn't look as sassy there as they usually do.

"Mr. and Mrs. are in Zurich," Parks said. "The cook and the head gardener—they're married—and the chauffeur are all on vacation. Mrs. Jason says Mrs. Taylor is having neurological surgery of some kind in Zurich and they gave everybody a vacation for two weeks while they're gone—everybody except Mrs. Jason and the maid."

Millie was laid out on a chaise longue in the sunroom. She was whimpering. Mrs. Jason had rigged an ice pack on a good-sized lump on the back of her head. There was blood, some still fresh. I asked Mrs. Jason if she'd called a doctor and she said Millie didn't want her to.

"You have a family doctor, don't you?"

"Yes."

"Call him."

Millie's eyes were red from crying, the fear in them still high. She had a round pudgy face, a small pursed mouth, and a receding chin. A patch of old acne scars emblazoned each cheek. Her eyes were her best feature, even red and full of fear. A blanket was pulled up to her chin. The eyes watched me.

"Where's your room?" I said.

"On the third floor."

"Don't you want to go to bed?"

"No!" Firmly. "I don't want to be alone."

"Can you tell me what happened?"

She said she and Lance had been drinking cocoa at the kitchen table and watching Johnny Carson on the kitchen TV. Carson was introducing his second guest when they heard the dog raise a ruckus. Lance went out to investigate and a minute later she followed him. That's all.

Mrs. Jason had returned from phoning the doctor and was standing behind me looking stern. "One of her slippers," she said. "was just outside the kitchen door. She must have been dragged back into the kitchen. I found her on the floor by the table."

The note was still taped to the refrigerator door. It was composed of letters clipped from magazines and newspapers. It read: "You will receive instructions shortly for the payment of ransom for the return of your son. You will have exactly eight hours to comply with these instructions starting at midnight today, the 18th, so be prepared! Otherwise Lance is lanced."

I asked Mrs. Jason to make a pot of coffee. The eight-hour thing had puzzled me from the start. The eight *night* hours.

"Funny damn thing, isn't it?" Parks said. "We got six hours and change left and we don't even know how much they want. Or where to take it, or nothing!"

"Except they'll kill him," the uniformed cop said.

"Yeah, except that." Parks was gloomy. One of his priceless charges was in jeopardy and everthing he lived for was on the line.

I asked Mrs. Jason for Taylor's phone number in Zurich and she said it was written on the blackboard over the kitchen phone. I was just about to dial when the phone rang. It was Charlie McDermott, Taylor's executive V.P., and he asked for me.

"This, is Train," I said.

He said he'd gotten a call from Taylor in Zurich about forty-five minutes before, ordering him to go down to the office in the Trans-America building and get all the cash they had in the vault and bring it out to me at the house. He was at the office now and wondering what the hell it was all about. Taylor hadn't told him.

"How much you got?"

"Seventy-seven thousand in even numbers, but what the hell's it—"

"Bring it out."

I didn't need to call Taylor now. He was smart and quick, whatever else he was. He'd realized it was the dead of night in California and the only money available for ransom would have to be on hand. And the kidnappers would realize that, too. I hung up the phone and stared at the blackboard for a while. They needed ketchup, soda crackers, and more cocoa.

I'd begun to consider the possibility that it was Lance. Certainly it was an inside job, or one remove from an inside job, but my God—*that* kid? He was an artist and he had his room and a big studio in a second floor wing of the house. One day, after I'd whipped his old man at tennis and Lance seemed to want to kiss my feet for it, he'd taken me up there to look at his stuff, and I'd liked it. He had a watercolor there that I would have been glad to take home with me, but he was into oils then and about twenty of them dominated the room in a display of savage color that galvanized the eye. Wild. Fauve wild. But extorting ransom money from his old man? It was too far out of character, I told myself.

I asked Mrs. Jason to sit down at the kitchen table with me and Parks when the coffee was done and asked the uniformed cop to go hold Millie's hand until the doctor arrived. She didn't want to be alone, she said.

"Mrs. Jason, when did the Taylors leave for Zurich?"

"Last Sunday, five days ago." She sat like a plebe at West Point, shoulders back, chin tucked in. She looked competent.

"Do you always go to the movies on Thursday night?"

"Yes. Almost always. They change the bill on Wednesdays."

"Did the cook and the chauffeur and the gardener all leave on Sunday?"

"Yes. The cook and the gardener are married—I got a card from them today from Tijuana. I mean yesterday."

"Are they Mexican?"

"No. They're American. Mr. and Mrs. Jefferson."

"And the chauffeur?"

"Charles. He has people in Seattle. He drove up there in the station wagon."

"Is your husband around, Mrs. Jason?"

"I'm divorced."

"How about Millie? Any family?"

"She has a brother in medical school at Berkeley. I know of no other family."

"Where's your husband, Mrs. Jason?"

"I—he's in Oakland, I believe."

"How long have you been divorced?"

"Four years."

"How long have you been here?"

"Six years next month, but we were separated three years before the divorce."

"It's a long day's drive from here to Tijuana," I said, "but a man could make it in a day, couldn't he? Do the Jeffersons know you always go to the movies on Thursday?"

"Yes, I suppose they do. There's something else I suppose you should know, Mr. Train. Mr. Jefferson was in prison once, many years ago."

"For what?"

"I'm not sure. I think it was extortion."

"Here in California?"

"I think so."

"What's his first name?" Parks barked. He was bristling.

"Peter. And his middle name is Lemuel."

"He live here?"

"Yes. They have an apartment over the garage. So does Charles."

Parks got up and went to the phone. "I'll find out," he said. Mrs. Jason and I looked at his big broad back as he dialed furiously.

"Is there anything else I should know?" I said to Mrs. Jason.

Her eyes flickered some. "Yes, there is. My ex-husband worked for Mr. Taylor's company until two months ago. He was fired for falsifying invoices and stealing things from the Oakland warehouse."

"And—?"

"He phoned me and asked me to intercede on his behalf with Mr. Taylor and I did, but Mr. Taylor refused to reinstate him."

"Why should he have? Wasn't he guilty of theft?"

"Yes, he was and he admitted it, but he promised to repay everything he'd stolen. He had some kind of a gambling debt, he said."

"Was he mad at Mr. Taylor?"

"Yes, I believe so."

"Has he ever been here?"

"Not as far as I know."

"Does he know you have a Doberman?"

"I have no idea—but most people in Belvedere have Dobermans."

"Does he know you're out every Thursday night?"

"I don't know how he could."

"Do you think he did it?"

"No. I—"

"What?"

"I don't think he has the guts," she said flatly, and I grinned at her.

"We'd better check on him, though, hadn't we?"

"I suppose so." She said it with a little sniff.

"Mrs. Jason, Millie said she was having cocoa and watching Johnny Carson with Lance when this happened. Are they friends?"

"Yes, I think Millie is the only friend Lance has in his house."

"Including you?"

"No, excepting me. But they are quite close. She listens to him."

"Does she have any other friends?"

"Not that I know of."

"How long's she been here?"

"Longer than I. Nine years, I believe."

"Do they treat her well, the Taylors?"

"Mr. Train, they hardly know she's alive. She serves the food and she cleans the place and they hardly know she's alive. Except Lance."

"She's a lonely woman, then?"

"We're all lonely here."

The front doorbell rang just then and I told Mrs. Jason I'd answer it while she gave Parks the data on her husband. It was the doctor, a jacket zippered over his pajamas, a bag in his hand, his grey hair askew under the brim of his hat. He was no happier at being rousted out in the middle of the night than I'd been.

The cop had been good company for Millie. Her eyes were dry now and the two of them were watching some garbage on all-night TV. Her nice eyes showed fear again when the doctor, a little roughly, I thought, examined her head. I left them alone and beckoned the cop to come along to the kitchen.

Parks was pretty upset. He'd put out a pickup order on Mrs. Jason's husband and wanted to order an APB on the Jeffersons, but thought better of it when he said it out loud. What worried him was the swift passage of time, the lack of instructions, and his own vulnerability.

"Look," I told him, "if they want their money they'll have to tell us how much it is and where to take it, won't they? Relax, chief, the only thing we can do now is wait—unless you want to search the grounds."

"That's not a bad idea, but God, Train, it's two thirty and unless we pick up Jason and beat it out of him where the kid is, he'll be dead at eight o'clock. And if Mr. Taylor's son gets killed, there'll be seven kinds of hell to pay around here. I'm supposed to keep the peace in this community and by God, if Mr. Taylor hadn't asked me directly not to, I'd call the FBI right now. Or at least the sheriff. We need men, lots of men! He's probably buried in some box in the ground with eight hours' worth of air or something, and if we—"

"Chief, why don't you have your man look around outside? And maybe you and I can look around the house, just in case he's upstairs in bed. You're obviously a man of action."

"Good idea! Irv, you check the outbuildings and the grounds. Take a flash and—"

"My God, chief," Irv said, "there's thirty acres enclosed by fence alone! Hell, it's a quarter mile down to the road from here!"

"Just go do it! Start with the garage and the buildings around the tennis court and the pool and look for fresh-turned earth. Maybe he's dead already."

"Why would they—?"

"Just go do it, Irv! That's an order!"

Mrs. Jason offered to come with us, but I asked her to stay with Millie so she wouldn't be alone when the doctor was through with her. Lance's pictures were what interested me most and we went directly to his studio, Parks checking his watch about every thirty seconds. The studio was lit by banks of fluorescent lights suspended from the high ceiling, and when I flicked them on, the whole room came alive with color. There must have been forty canvases of various sizes on display. A window seat ran the full length of the south wall, and paintings were resting all along its padded length as well as leaning against it from the floor. The effect was stunning, but didn't do the kid's work justice because the eye couldn't isolate any one piece from the rest. There was a quality of defiance in the place, as though Lance was saying, "Look, damn it! I'm an artist and I *work* at it!"

There was a big canvas on the easel and the corner of it I touched was still tacky. There were twice as many pictures showing as there had been the last time I was here.

The chief said, "Does he sell this crap?"

"You don't like it?"

"Do you?"

"He's good," I said.

"Nuts! No wonder the old man and him are on the outs. I'd throw him out the house if he was my kid."

And maybe that's it, I thought. Maybe Lance has gotten his notice and needs money to go on his own. It was the only thing that could drive him to extortion—his art. He and Millie. If he did it, then she was in it with him. But it faded as I looked at it. He was a gentleman in the root sense of the word. He had his mother's slender patrician face and long supple hands. Those hands couldn't have raised that lump on the back of Millie's head, even if his mind commanded it. He was a tiger with a paintbrush, not a blunt instrument.

I asked the chief to search the rest of the house and went back down to the kitchen. The doctor was having coffee. He said, "Is it true Lance was kidnapped?"

"It looks that way." I sat down.

"Who are you? Or isn't it any of my business?"

"I'm Sam Train. I'm a private investigator. How's Millie? That's your business."

"Don't get sharp with me, Mr. Train. I've had it with this family. I couldn't care less what they *or* you think. Millie is an hysteric. The last time I saw her at my office it was for an imaginary female illness. She's a frustrated old maid at thirty-three."

"Have you given her a sedative?"

"No. She refused it."

"What do you mean you've had it with this family, doctor?"

"Look, I've made more house calls here in the last six months than I have for all the rest of my practice put together. This is the first time it's been for anything of substance."

"What were the others for?"

His head snapped up from his cup of coffee. I thought he was going to tell me it was none of my business, but he was beyond normal discretion. "Mrs. Taylor," he said. "Dear Loretta. She's in Zurich right now to have her face lifted when what she really needs is a husband who's home now and again and a pile of dishes to wash every day, and maybe a garden to grow. I'm telling you, Train, riches are a curse!

That woman is useless and she knows it and she can't live with it. Every second night she wakes up screaming and clawing the walls and hollering for ol' Doc Binning! Well, ol' Boc Binning hereby quits!"

"Can a doctor resign from a patient?"

"This one can!"

"How about Lance? Anything wrong with him?"

"No. He's a good kid. The last time I saw him—a few months ago—was for a sprained wrist and he gave me a painting in lieu of a fee. He didn't want to use his old man's money. And I like it, too, that painting. I don't know what the hell it's supposd to be, but it looks good on the office wall, jazzes up the place. Maybe it's even therapeutic. No, he's a good kid, Train, and I hope you get him back." He stood up abruptly and jammed his hat on his head. "Good night. I can see my own way out. God knows I've done it often enough."

Millie was fighting sleep. She and Mrs. Jason were still watching TV and Millie's eyes were sagging shut every few seconds. I stood in the doorway watching her for a while before going in and sitting on the edge of her chaise longue.

"Why don't you go upstairs to bed?" I said.

The simple question shocked her eyes wide. "I don't want to! I don't want to be alone, I don't want to be asleep."

"Eventually you'll have to be, Millie."

"I'll get her some coffee," Mrs. Jason said, and got up. "I could use some myself."

I moved a little on the edge of the chaise and she fussily pulled her legs to the far side. A slight blush rose in her acne-scarred cheeks. An old maid at thirty-three, Binning had called her. A sad little woman with lovely sleepy eyes. "Do you like Lance, Millie?"

She closed the eyes and swallowed. "Yes." Her voice was husky, almost inaudible.

"Do you think we'll get him back?"

"Oh, I hope so! Oh, yes, I hope so!" She turned her head aside and I put my hand gently on her cheek and pressed it back. Her sigh was almost a shudder.

"Have you any idea where he is, Millie?"

"What?" Her eyes were wide open again, big and dark. "Oh, no—no, I don't!"

I couldn't fathom her. She'd been hurt and badly frightened, and yet she refused rest. Did she fear sleep all the time or just tonight? She was homely and squat and unloved and lonely and maybe in sleep these horrors always roved her mind. An hysteric, Binning had called her; but even hysterics have to sleep. Could she and Lance, out of their mutual frustrations, conceivably have worked up this ploy? Two shy gentle people—?

The door chimes sounded and I looked at my watch. It was almost

four o'clock. It could be McDermott with the money and I wondered
what had taken him so long. Mrs. Jason went to let him in.

"Millie," I said. "Tell me about your brother. Are you close? Is he a
friend?"

"Robert's at school."

"Yes, I know, at Berkeley. Does—?"

"Train!" It was McDermott standing in the doorway. He was fully
dressed, tie neatly knotted, topcoat, hat on, briefcase in hand. I'd met
him a few times in the work I'd done for Taylor and had formed no
opinion; but I was forming one now. He'd used his quarter-deck voice
on me. I got up.

"What took you so long, McDermott?"

"I went home and got dressed. It looks like my day is beginning
early. I've got an eight o'clock breakfast conference. Fill me in."

We went to the kitchen and had coffee and I brought him up to date.
He asked good questions in a take-charge sort of way, but it was just
habit. He knew Lance and shared Taylor's opinion of him, total
disdain. Taylor had told me McDermott was an import-export genius,
and maybe he was, but he had the terse automated quality of most top
executives I'd known. To like him would be to like a machine that
worked a little better than other machines. He had eighty-seven
thousand dollars in the briefcase. He'd found another ten after he'd
phoned. It seemed like a lot to have in the office, but Taylor'd explained
that to me once. He bought a lot of people in the course of a month's
work and he needed the ready cash. The people market is all cash, no
credit. Taylor said it was all routine.

"It's more than the kid's worth," McDermott said, "but it's a hell of a
lot less than they'll probably ask for."

"I doubt it," I said.

He glared at me. "Now what, Train? We just wait?"

"Yes."

Parks had been sitting with us. He grunted. He'd made a drink with
some of Taylor's whisky and he downed it. McDermott looked at him
with scorn.

Mrs. Jason knocked on the frame of the kitchen door. "Millie's
asleep," she said.

"Good!"

"I left that TV on. Would you gentlemen like more coffee?" She too
looked at Parks with scorn. I grinned at him; he was having a bad
night.

We were all sitting looking at each other when the phone rang and
Parks got up so fast to answer it he knocked over his chair. He listened
for a minute, then said, "What?" He hung up slowly. "Well, I'll be
damned!" he growled.

"Well what?" McDermott barked.

"It was Western Union with a telegram for anyone at this number.

It said, "Go look in the doghouse,' The guy said it wasn't signed."

"Guy?" I said.

"Yeah, guy." He went through the kitchen door and McDermott and I followed him outside.

Parks fished it out of the doghouse with a stick while I held the flash for him. It was an attaché case. Parks put the stick through the handle and carried it back to the house. He put it on the kitchen table and looked at me, red-faced.

"We gotta check it for prints."

"What we've got to do," I said, "is open it. There won't be any prints on it, chief."

It was closed by two snap catches with push-button releases. I pressed them and the case opened like a book. There was nothing inside but a note taped to the lining of the lid with the same cut-out letters and figures as before. "Put $50,000 in used bills in this case. Have the maid deliver it in her car. Have her stop at the phone booth at the corner of 14th and Main in Belvedere at precisely six A.M. She will receive further instructions then. Make no attempt to follow her."

Parks sighed deeply.

"Poor Millie," Mrs. Jason said.

"What the hell!" McDermott said. "Fifty thousand! Chicken feed!"

We decided to let Millie sleep for another half hour. It was about fifteen minutes from the house to the corner of 14th and Main, so she'd have to leave no later than twenty to six—if she could be made to leave at all. She looked peaceful sleeping on the chaise, her pudgy face untroubled by the dreams she feared. Mrs. Jason said she couldn't do it, couldn't be made to do it, but I wasn't so sure.

Parks got a call from the Oakland police advising him that Jason had moved from his fleabag room a week ago and they were tracing him now. Then Parks sat Mrs. Jason down at the kitchen table and questioned her about where her husband might have gone, but got nowhere with it. He was overmatched. You hire a bouncer for a chief of police, you get a bouncer for a chief of police. McDermott left for his office to practice being a genius before his conference and I sent Irv out to hunt for the blunt instrument that had coshed Millie. I wanted to be the one to waken her, and at five twenty I went into the sunroom to do it.

The TV was still on and I left it on. Somebody—for the love of heaven—was selling cars as though it were the middle of the afternoon. I sat down on the edge of the chaise and shook Millie awake and told her what she had to do.

"No!" she said, and began shaking her head violently. "No! no! no!"

"You want Lance to come back alive, don't you?"

"No, I won't do it!"

"You've got to, Millie. Those are the instructions. Nothing will happen to you."

She didn't cry, she just kept shaking her head, but she was listening to me and a few minutes later she said, "All right," and began to cry, her fine dark eyes lost tears again. I asked Mrs. Jason to help her get ready and told her to be sure Millie had pencil and paper in case she had to take notes.

Mrs. Jason confirmed my guess that the lonely old VW in the garage was Millie's and I backed it out and pointed it down the drive toward the road. McDermott had counted out the fifty thousand before leaving so he could take the change with him, and Parks and I put the money in the attaché case and put the case in the car. At twenty to six she was as ready as she would ever be and took off, still snuffling.

Her car had disappeared down the drive when I told Parks I was going to follow her. He didn't protest.

I knew the town well enough to take a back route to the corner of 12th and Main. I parked my Dart there and got out and took a position at the corner of a building facing Main. A milk truck was the only moving vehicle on the road at that hour and I thought maybe Millie had gotten lost, but a minute later she showed up in the distance and drove slowly to a point alongside the prescribed booth and stopped. The dawn sun was just pinking the tops of the hills to the west and visibility was perfect. Millie sat in her car for a while and then got out and stood by the phone booth door, blowing her nose. Then she stepped into the booth and took the phone off the hook. I hadn't heard it ring from where I was, but it was exactly six.

She was in there for three minutes—a long time, it seemed to me. A chauffeur-driven Rolls passed me, heading for Sausalito and the bridge. A pickup rattled by, going the other way, the driver giving me a cold eye. Millie came out of the booth and leaned on her car. She seemed to be crying violently and I thought maybe she'd gotten instructions that were beyond her. But after a moment she wiped her eyes, got in her car, made an illegal U-turn, and headed my way.

I jumped back into the Dart and hunched down until I heard her pass, and then following her, three blocks behind. We were alone on the road leaving town and I doubled the distance between us, just keeping her in easy sight. She seemed to be wobbling around, crossing the divider line in the center of the road and then raising dust from the shoulder every few hundred yards. She was going slowly, probably peering through tears.

She turned left on Upland Hills Road, heading east. The road climbs and twists for a few miles and then levels out on the Uplands Plateau and goes fairly straight. She was still wobbling all over the place, but it didn't matter, there was no traffic at all. It was six twenty.

We drove for about seven miles before she slowed suddenly and pulled to the shoulder of the road and stopped. I'd let about a quarter mile build up between us and closed it a little before I found a place to turn off and get behind some trees. I got my binoculars from under the seat and ran back up to the road. I was in time to see her carry the attaché case into the trees on the left of the road, disappear, and return in about five minutes. Her VW was parked alongside a CURVE sign, the only sign between her and the turnoff. You couldn't miss it.

She got into her car and cut sharply left, trying to turn around. For a perilous moment she was broadside to anything that might have come around the curve, but nothing did. She backed and filled twice on the narrow, high-crowned road before heading back my way, coming fast.

I ducked back into the trees and watched her pass. She was bent over the wheel, her nose an inch from the windshield and pushing the old bucket as fast as it would go. Two minutes later I was parked by the CURVE sign myself and crossing the road into the trees.

It took me twenty minutes to find the attaché case. It was in a narrow ravine that fed into the drainage ditch alongside the road. It was open and empty. I clambered down the steep slope and got it, lifting it by one finger on an inside corner. Now it might have fingerprints that meant something, but again I doubted it.

There were a dozen places a man could have hidden while Millie brought the case into the woods, put it down, and left. And a dozen ways he could have gotten out of there without being seen. The trees trailed up a slope and around the shoulder of a hill. Where they ended, I had no idea and no intention of finding out. There seemed to be no marks or traces around that mean anything. And no sign of Lance.

I went back to the Dart and put the case on the front seat, wondering why the man had bothered to transfer the money from it to something else before taking off. The probable reasons didn't seem adequate.

It was ten after seven when I headed back toward Belvedere and twenty to eight when I parked near the kitchen door of the Taylor house. Millie's VW was back in its corner in the garage. I sat there for a minute looking at it while Chief Parks, following by Irv, came trotting out of the house and over to where I was.

"Well?" Parks said, and then testily ordered Irv to go back into the kitchen and wait for the phone to ring.

"Well nothing," I said, and gestured toward the attaché case. "It was empty when I found it. Where's Millie?"

"She went to bed."

"What did she say?"

"She said she'd done what she was told to do—and then she went to bed. Where's the boy, for God's sake? It's quarter to eight, Train!"

"I know what time it is." I got out and stretched and yawned. Parks glared at me, red-eyed with fatigue and worry.

"He's dead," he said. "They killed him."

"I hope not, Parks."

"You *hope* not!"

"Come on, let's go take a look at Millie's car."

"Why? You think he's in there, for God's sake?"

"No, but I think the money is."

"What?"

We found it under the floorboard on the passenger side. A foot-square hole had been cut in the steel floorplate and a shallow metal box crudely welded beneath it. The piece of metal cut from the floorplate had been used as a lid for the hole. Covered by the worn carpet, you'd have no reason to think anything was there. The hole was packed solid with money and was one of the reasons he'd asked for only fifty thousand. You couldn't have gotten much more into it. And it was the reason Millie had been driving all over the road. That and tears. She'd been transferring the money from the attaché case to the box from the moment she'd left the phone booth. And she'd done a good, neat job, even though she probably knew she was being followed. He'd probably told her she would be.

Parks looked stupefied. "So where's the kid?" he said.

"He'll probably come lurching in any minute now—with a knot on his head too." I felt dead tired.

"They did it together, didn't they?"

"It looks that way, except for one thing, chief—" But he wasn't listening. He was pounding a meaty right fist into the palm of his left hand.

"By God," he growled. "I'm going up there and take that broad by the—"

"You go to her in any way, Parks, and I'll deck you. We'll go up together."

She wasn't in her room. Her bed hadn't even been turned down. And she wasn't in her bathroom, either. But there was a little brown bottle in the bottom of the washbasin and it was empty. I sniffed it, but got nothing. It could have held about thirty capsules. There was no label on it. I left the room on the run.

We found her in Lance's studio—and Lance, too. She'd removed the pictures from the window seat, stacking them carefully against the wall, and then lifted the lid of the seat before the capsules took effect and she fell to the floor. She'd wanted Lance to have more air. He was laid out in the bottom of the window seat like a corpse, his hands folded across his chest. But he was alive, breathing softly through his mouth. Why in the name of God, I thought, did they put him in there?

Millie was in the fetal position, her black maid's dress way up around her thighs. It would have embarrassed her terribly.

"Call the emergency squad," I told Parks. "Make sure they bring a stomach pump!" He moved.

Millie was still alive. I picked her up and tried to get her legs to work, but they wouldn't. Then I carried her into the shower stall in Lance's bathroom and turned on the cold water full blast and held her under it, her head draped over my shoulder. I held her there for five minutes, jiggling her up and down and hollering in her ear, but it didn't work.

She was alive, but not coming back. I figured she didn't want to come back. I took her in and put her on Jason's bed, just as Parks returned with Mrs. Jason. I told Mrs. Jason to dry Millie and keep slapping her face and she set to it at once while Parks and I returned to the studio and lifted Lance from the window seat to the floor.

He had a knot on the back of his head about like Millie's—enough to knock him out, but not for eight hours. He began to stir, rolled his head and groaned, just audibly. He would be all right. He was coming up, not going down like Millie. I pulled up his sleeves and looked at his skinny arms. There was a small red dot on his left bicep that would have been where the needle went in. He'd been doped, expertly. I wiped water from my face and hair and stared at him. Why in the window seat?

The emergency squad was there in about twenty minutes, and gone five minutes later. The young paramedic in charge said he didn't like the looks of Millie, and he seemed to have care in his eyes. I asked him to do this best. They took both Millie and Lance in the one rig.

"Well, I guess everything's gonna be all right," Parks said when they'd gone. "The kid's gonna live."

"Yeah," I said.

I dried myself as best I could with a couple of Lance's towels and then went back to his studio and stared into the open window seat. Millie had insisted that he be put in there—it was the only reasonable explanation. He was her best friend; perhaps in her way she loved him. She would have insisted that he remain in the house—it was the price of her collaboration, and if she died it would be the cause of her death.

I went down to the kitchen, Mrs. Jason was sitting at the table drinking coffee. She looked at me tiredly as I picked up the phone to call Doc Binning. He was still at home.

"This is Train," I said. "Did you prescribe barbiturates for Millie Whelan?"

"Of course I didn't!" he snapped.

"Well, somebody did!" I snapped back, and hung up before we could get into another argument. Mrs. Jason was looking at me curiously and I told her that I'd just wanted to make sure.

"Is she going to live?" she asked. There was care in her eyes, too.

"I doubt it. But you can call Mr. Taylor and tell him Lance'll be all right. Not," I added, "that he gives a damn."

"I'll wait a while," she said with a small glint of satisfaction in her eyes. "But perhaps we should nofity Millie's brother Robert."

"Do you know where he lives?"

"No. But the university would have his address."

"Have you met him, Mrs. Jason?"

"No, but—"

"But what?"

"He's called her fairly often lately. I've spoken with him on the phone. I think he's been asking her for money—for his schooling."

"Does she give it to him?"

"I think so, Mr. Train, but she doesn't have much to give. Mr. Taylor doesn't believe in—"

"I know what Mr. Taylor believes in, Mrs. Jason, and what he doesn't believe in. Does Millie have any estate, do you suppose?"

"Oh, I doubt it. But perhaps her brother would like to know he'd have her car if she—she died."

"I think he's arranged for that already," I said.

At home I took off my wet clothes and put on a robe. Then I made myself a pot of instant coffee and sat down and phoned every Western Union office within twenty miles of Belvedere. Not any of them had a record of four A.M. telegram for anyone in the Taylor house.

Parks was still in his office when I phoned him. He sounded to me about the way I must have sounded to him. Beat. "Chief," I said, "when you took that call from Western Union last night, was there the usual background noise of a Western Union office? You know, teletype clatter, voices, etc.?"

"Yes."

"No doubt about it?"

"No. Why?"

"A moment on that. Any report on Millie?"

He yawned noisily. "Hang on a minute, I'll check."

I put the phone in my lap and thought about her. If she lived, it would be possible, just barely possible, to put a lid on the whole thing. Except for the hospital records on her and Lance, it was still a private affair and could be kept that way. But no, no it couldn't. I shook my head in a rage of helplessness. I'd grown to respect her through the night. She'd done a dangerous thing, against her will all the way, torn between the only two emotional ties in her bleak and empty life, but she'd done it. Poor invisible Millie. If she lived, there was no way she could be spared the rest of the nightmare. And she'd known it.

"She's dead," I heard Parks' voice tell me metallically from my lap. I lifted the phone to my ear. "She died a half hour ago. Now what was that about Western Union?"

I clamped my teeth and told myself it was probably just as well, but I felt the gorge rising in my throat again. I didn't know him, but I hated him; for a moment I mourned the sister he'd killed." All right, chief," I said, "put out a pickup order on Millie's brother, Robert Whelan. Charge extortion and murder. You can get his address from the University of California Medical School at Berkeley. And tell the arresting officers to search his place for a tape recorder with a strip in it that sounds like the background noise you might expect in a Western Union office. Maybe he's erased it by now, but probably not. Probably he's—"

"What are you talking about, Train? Damn it, I'm so beat I can hardly find my face with my hands. What the hell is this about the brother and a tape? I thought—"

"Parks, did you hear what I said?"

"Yeah, I heard."

"Do you want me to call Berkeley police myself, or do you want to be the hero?"

"Cool off, Train. I'll do it. Was it him, really?"

"Yes, it was him, and Millie, but ninety percent him. Get him, Parks."

"Yeah, but who'd he murder?"

I hung up. I shouldn't have, I suppose, but since there was only one body in the affair, I knew it would come to him. And besides, I didn't want to talk to anybody any more. I wanted to brood about Millie's brother. He was a medical student and needed money—that's all I knew about him. Maybe he had only a little while to go and could smell the big payoff at the end of the course and was running out of money and couldn't stand the thought of dropping out. Or maybe he was failing, and hating himself, or maybe he'd just gone sour, or maybe he was bad to begin with. Maybe he'd asked Millie to ask Taylor for help, but Millie, the invisible woman in Taylor's eyes, wouldn't even try and the idea of kidnapping Lance developed in his mind. He'd borrowed her car, for a weekened maybe, and fixed the box in the floor.

And maybe, I thought, she didn't even know it was there until she got his call at the booth on Main Street. And maybe—my mind ran on—she didn't know anything about it at all until he arrived on the scene the night before at a quarter to twelve or so with his club and his capsules and his poisoned meat and his hypodermic. Then, when she understood what he was up to, she insisted that Lance at least be kept in the house—and that had sealed her doom. "When you get back from delivering the money, sister dear, take these capsules in this little brown bottle and you'll feel like a million—trust me." Or maybe he'd known he'd have to kill her in any event and had given her just one lethal dose. And then a few days after the funeral, he'd drop by the house, tears in his eyes, and collect her car. Who would know?

I was asleep in my chair when the phone wakened me. It was Parks. They'd caught Whelan, he told me, found the Western Union tape and hypodermic needle and other paraphernalia in his room. He'd confessed to everything and was being held without bail.

Did I want to see him? Parks asked.

"No. Why should I?"

"Well, in a manner of speaking it was your collar, Sam." It was Sam now. "I even told 'em at Berkeley. I couldn't of done it without you—and that's what I told Taylor, too."

"You talked to Taylor?"

"Yeah, he said he tried to call you but got no answer. Then he called me and we had a nice long talk. Damn nice fella." He was preening himself; he sounded fresh, renewed. "Hey, Sam, how much are you gonna bill him for your night's work?" Taylor had touched his heart, buccaneer and bouncer soulmates now. He really wanted to know.

"I don't know," I said, "But whatever it is, it won't be enough."

Talmage Powell
Drawer 14

No cracks about my job, please. I've already taken more than enough ribbing from campus cutups. I don't relish being night attendant at the city morgue, but there are compensations. For one thing, the job gave me a chance to complete my college work in daytime and do considerable studying at night between catnaps and the light, routine duties.

In their tagged and numbered drawers, the occupants weren't going to disturb me while I was cracking a brain cell on a problem in calculus. Or so I thought.

This particular night I relieved Olaf Daly, like always. Olaf was a man stuck with a job because of his age and a game leg. He lived each day only for the moment when he could flee his profession, as it were. Like always, he grunted a hello and a goodbye in the same breath, the game leg assisting him out of the morgue with surprising alacrity.

Alone in the deep silence of the anteroom, I dropped my thermos, transistor radio, and a couple of textbooks on the desk. I pulled the heavy record book toward me to give it a rundown.

Olaf had made his daily entries in his neat, spidery handwriting. Male victim of drowning. Man and woman dead in auto crash. Wino who didn't wake up when his bed caught fire. Male loser of a knife fight. Woman found dead in river.

Olaf's day had been routine. Nothing had come in like the dilly of last week.

She had been a pitiful, dirty, lonely old woman who had lived in a hovel. Crazy as a scorched moth, she had slipped into a dream world where she wasn't dirty, ir old, or forsaken at all. Instead, she had believed she was the Fourth Witch of Endor, with power over the forces of darkness.

The slum section being a breeding ground for ignorance and superstition, some of her neighbors had taken the Fourth Witch of Endor seriously. She had looked the part, with a skull-like face, a beaked nose with a wart on the end, a toothless mouth accenting a long and pointed chin, and strings of dirty hair hanging lank about her sunken cheeks. She had eked out a half-starved living by telling fortunes, performing incantations, predicting winning numbers, and selling love potions and spells. To her credit, she never had gone in for the evil eye, her neighbors reported. If she couldn't put a good hex on a person, she had refused to hex him at all.

On a very hot and humid night, the Fourth Witch of Endor had mounted the roof of her tenement. Nobody knew for sure whether she had slipped or maybe taken a crack at flying to the full moon. Anyhow, she had been scraped off the asphalt six stories below, brought here, and deposited in Drawer 14. She had lain in the refrigerated cubicle for four days before an immaculate son had flown in from a distant state to claim the body.

She hadn't departed a moment too soon for Olaf Daly. "I swear," the old man had said, "there's a hint of a smell at Drawer 14, like you'd figure sulphur and brimstone to smell."

I hadn't noticed. The only smells assailing my nostrils were those in a chem lab where I was trying hard to keep up with the class.

I turned from the record book for a routine tour of the building.

Lighted brightly, the adjoining room was large, chill, and barren. The floor was spotless gray tile with a faint, antiseptic aroma. Across the room was the double doorway to the outside ramp where the customers were brought in. Near the door was the long, narrow, marble-topped table mounted on casters. Happily, it was empty at the moment, scrubbed clean, waiting for inevitable use. The refrigeration made a low, whispering sound, more felt than heard.

To my right, like an outsized honeycomb, was the bank of drawers where the dead were kept for the claiming, or eventual burial at city expense.

Each occupied drawer was tagged, like with a shipping ticket or baggage check, the tab being attached with thin wire to the proper drawer handle when the body was checked in.

I whistled softly between my teeth, just for the sake of having some sound, as I started checking the tabs against my mental tally from the record book.

As I neared Drawer 14, I caught myself on the point of sniffing. Instead of sniffing, I snorted. "That Olaf Daly," I muttered. "He and his smell of sulphur and brimstone!"

A couple of steps past Drawer 14 I rocked up on my toes, turned my head, then my whole body around.

Olaf had not listed an occupant for Drawer 14, but the handle was tagged. I bent forward slightly, reached. The whistle sort of dripped to nothing off my lips.

I turned the tag over casually the first time; then a second and third time, considerably faster.

I straightened and gave my scalp a scratch. Both sides of the tag were blank. Olaf was old but far fron senile. This wasn't like him at all, forgetting to fill in a drawer tag.

Then I half grinned to myself. The old coot was playing a joke on me. I didn't know he had it in him.

The whistle returned to my lips with a wise note, but not exactly appreciative. I took hold of the handle and gave it a yank. The drawer slid open on its rollers. The whistle keened to a thin wail and broke.

The girl in the drawer was young. She was blonde. She was beautiful, even in death.

I stood looking at her with my toes curling away from the soles of my shoes. The features of her face were lovely, the skin like pale tan satin. Her eyes were closed as if she were merely sleeping, her long lashes like dark shadows. She was clothed in a white nylon uniform with a nurse's pin on the collar. The only personal adornment was an I.D. bracelet of delicate golden chain and plaque. The plaque was engraved with initials: Z. L.

I broke my gaze away from the blonde girl and hurried back to the anteroom. At the desk, I jerked the record book toward me. I didn't want to misjudge old man Daly.

I moved my finger down the day's entries. Hesitated. Repeated the process. Went to the previous day by turning a page. Then to the day before that. Nobody, definitely, had been registered in Drawer 14.

I puckered, but couldn't find a whistle as I turned again to the door of the morgue room. There was a glass section in the upper portion of the door. I looked through the glass. I didn't have to open the door. I'd left Drawer 14 extended, and blonde Z. L. was still there, bigger than life, as big as death.

Carefully, I sat down at the desk, took out my handkerchief, wiped my forehead.

I took a long, deliberate breath, picked up the phone, and dialed Olaf Daly's number. While his phone rang, I sneaked a glance in the direction of the morgue room.

Olaf's wife answered sleepily, along about the sixth or seventh ring. No. I couldn't speak to Olaf because he hadn't come home yet.

Then she added suddenly, in a kindlier tone, "Just a minute. I think I hear him coming now."

Olaf got on the line with a clearing of his throat. "Yeah, what is it?"

"This is Tully Branson, Mr. Daly."

"I ain't available for stand-in duty if some of your college pals have cracked a keg someplace."

"No, sir," I said. "I understand, Mr. Daly. It's just that I need the information on the girl in Drawer 14."

"Ain't nobody in Drawer 14, Tully."

"Yes, sir. There's a girl in Drawer 14. A blonde girl, Mr. Daly, far too young and nice looking to have to die. I'm sure you remember. Only you forgot the record book when she was brought in."

I heard Mrs. Daly asking Olaf what it was. The timbre of his voice changed as he spoke in the direction of his wife, "I think young Branson brought straight whisky in his thermos tonight."

"No, sir," I barked at Olaf. "I need it, but I haven't got any whisky. All I've got is a dead blonde girl in Drawer 14 that you forgot to make a record of."

"How could I do a thing like that?" Olaf demanded.

"I don't know," I said, "but you did. She's right here. If you don't believe me, come down and have a look."

"I think I'll do just that, son! You're accusing me of a mighty serious thing!"

He slammed the phone down so hard it stabbed me in the eardrum. I hung up with a studied gentleness, lighted a cigarette, poured some coffee from the thermos, lighted a cigarette, took a sip of coffee, and lighted a cigarette.

I had another swallow of coffee, reached for the package, and discovered I already had three cigarettes spiraling smoke from the ashtray. I gave myself a sickly grin and butted out two of the cigarettes to save for later.

With his game leg, Olaf arrived with the motion of a schooner mast on a stormy sea. I returned his glare with a smile that held what smug assurance I was able to muster. Then I bowed him into the morgue room.

He went through the swinging door, with me following closely. Drawer 14 was still extended. He didn't bother to cross all the way to it. Instead, after one look, he whirled on me.

"Branson," he snarled in rage," If I was twenty years younger I'd bust your nose! You got a nerve, dragging a tired old man back to this stinking place. And just when I'd decided you was one of the nicer members of the younger generation, too!"

"But, Mr. Daly . . ."

"Don't 'but' me, you young pup! I'll put you on report for this!"

I took another frantic look at Drawer 14. She was there, plain as anything. Blonde, and beautiful, and dead.

Olaf started past me, shoving me aside. I caught told of his arm. I was chicken—and just about ready to molt. "Old man," I yelled, "you see her. I know you do!"

"Get your mitts offa me," he yelled back. "I see exactly what's there. I see an empty drawer. About as empty as your head."

I clutched his arm, not wanting to let go. "I don't know what kind of joke this is . . ."

"And neither do I," he said, shouting me down. "But it's a mighty poor one!"

"Then look at that drawer, old man, and quit horsing around."

"I've looked all I need to. Nothing but an overgrown juvenile delinquent would think up such a shoddy trick to oust a poor old man out of his house!"

He jerked his arm free of my grip and stormed through the door, past the anteroom. At the front door of the building, which was down a short corridor, he stopped, turned, and shook his finger at me.

"You cruel young crumb," he said, "you better start looking for another job tomorrow, if I have anything to do with it!" With that, he was gone.

I'd followed him as far as the anteroom. I turned slowly, looked through the glass pane into the morgue room. A dismal groan came from me. Z. L. still occupied Drawer 14.

"Be a good girl," I heard myself mumbling, "and go away. I'll close my eyes, and you just go away."

I closed my eyes, opned them. But she hadn't gone away.

I groped to the desk chair and collapsed. I didn't sit long, on account of a sudden flurry of business which was announced by the buzzer at the service door.

The skirling sound, coming suddenly, lifted me a couple feet off the desk chair. When I came down, I was legging it across the morgue room.

Smith and Macklin, two guys who worked on the meat wagon, were sliding an old guy in tattered clothing from a stretcher to the marble-topped table.

"He walked in front of a truck," Smith said.

"No I.D.," Macklin said. "Ice him as a John Doe."

"Kinda messy, ain't he, Branson?" Smith grinned at me as he pulled the sheet over the John Doe. Smith was always egging me because he knew my stomach wasn't the strongest.

"Yeah," I said. "Kinda." I blew some sweat off my upper lip. "Not like the girl. No marks on her."

"Girl?"

"Sure," a note of eagerness slipped into my voice. "The beautiful blonde. The one in Drawer 14."

Smith and Macklin both looked at the open, extended drawer. Then they looked at each other.

"Tully, old boy," Macklin said, "how you feeling these days?"

"Fine," I said, a strip of ice forming where my forehead was wrinkling.

"No trouble sleeping? No recurrent nightmares?"

"Nope," I said. "But the blonde in 14 ... if you didn't bring her in, then maybe Collins and Snavely can give me the rundown on her."

Smith and Macklin sort of edged from me. Then Smith's guffaw broke the morgue stillness. "Beautiful blonde, Drawer 14, where the poor old demented woman was ... Sure, Branson, I get it."

Macklin looked at his partner uncertainly. "You do?"

"Simple," Smith said, sounding relieved. "Old Tully here gets bored. Just thought up a little gag to rib us, huh, Tully?"

It was obvious they didn't see the girl and weren't going to see her. If I insisted, I knew suddenly, I was just asking for trouble. So I let out a laugh about as strong as skimmed milk. "Sure," I said. "Got to while away the tedium, you know."

Smith punched me in the ribs with his elbow. "Don't let your corpses get warm, Tully old pal." He departed with another belly laught. But Macklin was still throwing worried looks over his shoulder at me as he followed Smith out.

I hated to see the outside door close behind them. I sure needed some company. For the first time, being the only living thing in the morgue caused my stomach to shrink to the size of a cold, wrinkled prune.

I skirted Drawer 14 like I was crossing a deep gorge on a bridge made of brittle glass.

"Go away," I muttered to Z. L. "You're not real. Not even a dead body. Just a—an *image* that nobody can see but me. So go away!"

My words had no effect whatever on the image. They merely frightened me a little when I caught the tone in which I was conversing with a nonexistent dead body.

Back at the anteroom desk, I sat and shivered for several seconds. Then an idea glimmered encouragingly in my mind. Maybe Olaf Daly, Smith, and Macklin were all in on the gag. Maybe Z. L. had been brought in by Collins and Snavely, who tooled the meat wagon on the day shift, and everybody had thought it would be a good joke to scare the pants off the bright young college man.

Feeling slightly better, I reached for the phone and called Judd Lawrence. A golfing pal of my father's, Judd was a plainclothes detective attached to Homicide. He'd always seemed to think well of me; had, in fact, recommended me for the job here.

Judd wasn't home. He was pulling a three-to-eleven P.M. tour of duty. I placed a second call to police headquarters. Judd had signed out, but they caught him in the locker room.

"Tully Branson, Mr. Lawrence."

"How goes it, Tully?"

"I got a problem."

"Shoot," There was no hesitation in his big, hearty voice.

"Well, uh . . . seems like the record is messed up on one of our transients. A girl. Blonde girl. A nurse. Her initials are Z. L."

"You ought to call Olaf Daly, Tully."

"Yes, sir. But you know how Olaf is when he gets away from here. Anyhow, he's in dreamland by this time and I sure hate to get him riled up. He gets real nasty."

Judd boomed a laugh. "Can't say that I blame you. That all you've got on the girl?"

"Just what I've given you. She's certainly no derelict, furthest thing in the world from that. Girl like her, dead from natural causes, would be in a private funeral home, not here."

"So the fact that she's in the morgue means she died violently," Judd said.

"I guess it has to mean that."

"Murder?"

"Can't think of anything else," I said. "It has to be a death under suspicious circumstances."

"Okay, Tully. I'll see what I can turn up for you."

"Sure hate to put you to the trouble."

"Trouble?" he said. "No trouble. Couple of phone calls is all it should take."

"I sure appreciate it, Mr. Lawrence."

I hung up. While I was waiting for Judd Lawrence to call me back, I sneaked to the door of the morgue room and let my gaze creep to the glass pane to make sure the image was still in Drawer 14.

It was. I shuffled back to the desk, feeling like I was a tired old man.

When the phone range finally, I snatched it up. "City morgue. Tully Branson speaking."

"Judd here, Tully."

"Did you ..."

"Negative from homicide, Tully. No blondes with initials Z. L., female, have been murdered in the last twenty-four hour period."

"Oh," I said, sagging, giving vent to a moan of real anguish.

"Checked with nurses' registry," Judd was saying. "There is a nurse answering your description. Young, blonde, just finished training. Her name is Zella Langtry. Lives at 711 Eastland Avenue. She recently went to work at City Hospital. But if any violence occurred to her, it's been in the past half hour. She just checked off duty when the graveyard shift reported on."

His words, coupled with the image in Drawer 14, left one crazy, wild possibility. The inspiration was so weird it turned the hair on my scalp to needles.

"Mr. Lawrence, I have the most terrible feeling Zella Langtry will never reach home alive."

"What is that? What are you saying, Tully?"

"The Fourth Witch of Endor ..." I gabbled . "She was a kindly soul at heart. Never put a bad hex on anybody. Just good ones."

"What in the blathering world are you carrying on about?" Judd asked sharply. "Tully, you been drinking?"

"No, sir."

"Feel all right?"

"I—uh ... Yes. sir, and thanks a lot, Mr. Lawrence."

Twenty minutes later, my jalopy rolled to a stop on Eastland Avenue. I go out, started walking along looking for numbers. I knew I was in the right block, and I located number 711 easily enough. It was a small, white cottage with a skimpy yard that attempted to look more wholesome than its lower-class surroundings.

The place was dark, quiet, peaceful.

I was standing there feeling like seventy kinds of fool when the whir of a diesel engine at the street intersection caught my attention. I looked toward the sound, saw a municipal bus lumbering away.

From the shadows of a straggly maple tree, I watched the shadowy figure of a girl coming along Eastland in my direction. But she wasn't the only passenger who had got off the bus. Behind her was a taller, heavier shadow, that of a man. My breathing thinned as I took in the scene.

She realized he was behind her. She started walking faster. So did the man. She looked over her shoulder. She stepped up the pace even more, almost running now.

The man's shoes slapped quick and hard against the sidewalk. The girl's scream was choked off as the man slammed against her.

They were struggling on the sidewalk, the man locking her throat in the crook of his elbow, the girl writhing and kiching.

I went from under the maple tree like invisible trumpets were urging me on with a blood-rousing fanfare. The man heard me coming, released the girl. I piled into him with a shoulder in his midsection.

He brought a knee up hard. It caught me on the point of the chin. I sat down on the sidewalk, and the man turned and ran away.

Firm but gentle hands helped me to my feet. I looked into the eyes of Zella Langtry for the first time. They were very nice, smoky and grateful in the shadowy night.

"You all right?" I asked, getting my breath back.

"I am now, thanks to you. And you?"

"Fine," I said. "Just fine now."

She was regaining her composure. "Lucky thing for me you were around at the right moment!"

"I—uh—just happened to be passing," I said. "Maybe I'd better walk you to your destination. Won't do any good to report that guy now. Didn't get a look at him. Never would catch him."

"I was going home," she said. "I live just down the street."

We walked along, and she told me her name was Zella, and I told her mine was Tully. When we got to her front door, we looked at each other, and I asked if I could call her some time, and she said any time a phone was handy.

I watched her go inside. I was whistling as I returned to the jalopy.

Inside the morgue, I headed straight for Drawer 14. If my theory was correct, the image of Zella Langtry wouldn't be in the drawer, now that she had been rescued from the jaws of death, as it were.

I stood at Drawer 14, taking a good, long look. My theory was right as far as it went.

The image of Zella Langtry was no longer in the drawer. The new one was quite a lovely redhead.

George Grover Kipp
The Unstained Code

The thing I hated most about Perk Madden was his insufferable arrogance. Between his haughtiness and his big mouth, there were times when I thought I would become physically ill. It didn't help that Perk was blond and handsome and built like Hercules, his two hundred pounds riding neatly on his six foot frame.

In stir, which was where I first met Perk, he was always regaling the other cons with tales of his prowess as a safecracker. A lot of them believed him, too, hanging wide-eyed on every word as he extolled his abilities, á la Jimmy Valentine.

It was downright laughable in a way. If Perk was so damned good, what was he doing in stir? Not that I ever broached the question, mind you. I'm a spindly one hundred and thirty pounder built on a five seven frame and Perk could have gobbled me up with one meshing of his massive jaws.

Why was *I* in stir? Would you believe my dislike of walking got me there? That's how it was, though. I'd been hitchhiking at the time (considerably more hiking than hitching), with the sun bearing down and not a trace of a breeze, when I saw the car standing beside a garage, keys and all. Since it was only fifty miles to Sanger, the home town, I figured I'd reach there and ditch the car on the outskirts before it was even missed. Anything seemed preferable to another eight hours of standing along the highway and watching the cars whiz past. I hadn't made quite twenty miles when the state patrolman pulled me over and waved his revolver under my nose. He was reasonably sympathetic, having done some hitchhiking himself; the judge was another story.

I got three years for my "criminal depredations."

Perk was holding sway over his court when I arrived at Stony Lonesome, and he immediately tried to include me as one of his worshipers. I wasn't buying, though. None of us were behind the walls for exhibiting intelligence, and I wasn't about to subscribe to the notion that Perk was smart or glamorous. Instead, I invested my meager earnings in a correspondence course and began studying to be a locksmith. Actually it was the best place in the world to embark on such a venture. The place abounded with men who knew locks. Probably the best of the bunch was Charlie Judson, the tired old con with whom I shared a cell.

Charlie was tall and cadaverous, and on his sixth and last jolt in prison. He'd run afoul of the Habitual Criminal Act, and was in for the rest of his days. When he left it would be in a wooden overcoat. Still he kept himself busy with reading, studying chess, and helping me with my diagrams of locks and tumblers.

"That creep is bad news no matter how you read him," Charlie said one day when Perk pranced past our cell on his way to the yard for the exercise period.

I should have paid more attention to Charlie's intuition. I mean, after six hitches in stir he qualified as an expert on men like Perk. Instead, I held up the diagram of a German padlock and asked his expert opinion on its merits.

Perk began stopping at our cell on a daily basis, trying to exude good fellowship and establish a certain camaraderie, but it didn't work. I was busy with my lessons and Charlie wouldn't have given him the right time unless Perk was sweating out the hangman. Then I discovered the reasons for Perk's buddy-buddy routine: Gloria.

I had a picture of her on the cardboard box I used for a desk, and every time Perk paused at the cell door he'd practically devour her with his serpentine eyes. Not that Perk could be held entirely to blame. Gloria is one of those women—black hair, snowy skin, and a gamin smile—that appeals to most men.

"Don't be surprised when Madden shows up in Sanger," Charlie said after one of Perk's visits. When I tried to scoff away the idea, Charlie shook his head doggedly. "He's poisoned with self-puff, Butch. He thinks he's the greatest guy who ever lived. And the very thought of you having a woman like that is more than his bloated ego can stand. I've known cons and I've known cons and that creep is about as subtle as a television commercial. As sure as God made little green apples he'll show up in Sanger and make a play for Gloria."

"He sticks his nose across the city limits and the cops will be there to greet him," I snapped. I wasn't afraid Perk might take Gloria away from me; I just didn't want him in the same county with her for reasons best described as Contamination, with a capital C.

"No good, Butch," Charlie said paternally. "When you put the finger on a cluck like Perk, you have to take into consideration his coterie of bootlicking worshipers. Some of them actually believe in that counterfeit maxim: Thou shalt not squeal; and it is counterfeit, believe me. Ninety-five percent of the cons in this joint would sell their own mothers down the river if the price was right. Still, there are those who believe in it, and if just one of Perk's cronies is a believer, you could end up with quite a problem if it became known that you'd put the finger on him."

I hadn't even considered the angle, but it made sense. "So what do I do, Charlie?" I said. "Simply sit still if Perk shows up in Sanger and let him have the run of the town?"

Plucking one of my padlock diagrams off the cardboard box, Charlie held it under my nose. "Anybody smart enough to figure out these things shouldn't let a creep like Perk Madden bother him. You can outthink him in a minute, Butch. But do it real sly-like, and hit him where it hurts!"

I wasn't sure I understood Charlie's reasoning, but I didn't press the matter. I had a lesson to get out, and I still didn't think Perk would show up in Sanger.

Then the long-awaited day finally arrived. My time was served and freedom beckoned. I shook hands with Charlie, doing my best to be blase and not let the lump in my throat show. An hour later, in an ill-fitting suit and with my books and papers in a beer case, I was on the bus headed for Sanger. It was a perfect spring day with fleecy clouds, a soft breeze, and meadowlarks yodeling from the tops of fence posts. It would have been a beautiful day with five feet of snow and a sixty mile an hour gale.

I hadn't told anybody I was getting out. The only person in Sanger I'd kept in touch with was Gloria and I wanted to surprise her. Still, when the bus groaned up to the cafe in Sanger, Arnie Humboldt was leaning indolently against the wall. Arnie is maybe eight years older than me, and a graduate of the same orphanage. He crossed the tarmac, the sun ricocheting from the badge on his shirt pocket, and held out a firm hand.

"Welcome home, Butch," he said around a smile that came all the way from his toes.

I knew without being told that Arnie wasn't at the bus depot by chance. He'd made it a point to find out when I was getting released and had delegated himself to be my welcoming committee—not that his appearance at the depot had interfered with his work. Sanger's six-man police force simply doesn't have that much work to do. What I mean is, they almost always prevent crimes *before* they are committed, which makes for a much better town. Any strangers in town without a plausible reason are invariably the recipients of constant but casual contact with the authorities. Those with larcenous notions find this tactic unnerving in the extreme and usually depart without prolonged delay. The legitimate citizens, salesmen, tourists, and such aren't bothered and everything works out nicely.

"You got any job prospects?" Arnie asked as we walked along the street. Then he hastened to add, "I'm not snooping, Butch. It's just that old man Danvers at the hardware store has been looking for a man and if you're in need of a job it might pay to check it out."

I was certainly in need of a job. The twenty-five dollars the warden had handed me wasn't going to last very long, not with clothes to buy, a room to rent, and dinner with Gloria. "I need the job," I said, "but Danvers may be squeamish about hiring an ex-con. Some people are funny that way."

Arnie gazed innocently into space. "Not Danvers. I've already talked to him about you. He'll be expecting you at nine o'clock in the morning." Giving me a wink, Arnie moved along the street and around the corner."

Actually my readjustment to civilian life came off with surprising ease. With people like Arnie and Gloria and old man Danvers going out of their way to help me, it could hardly have gone otherwise. I went to work in the stock room of the hardware store, which was a break for me. I got to study all the locks and padlocks for free, and figure out how they worked. Spring blended into summer, summer into autumn, and things couldn't have looked better.

Then Perk Madden showed up in Sanger. . . .

I was in the rear of the store, stocking the nail bins, when he came through the door, and Charlie Judson's warning flashed into my mind. I kept on working like everything was just fine, but a knot the size and temperature of the polar icecap was forming in my gut.

Perk gave me his friendliest smile, all teeth and frost. "Hiya, Butch." He was decked out in real swinger style, wearing bell-bottom slacks, alpaca sweater, and suede jacket.

I shook hands without enthusiasm, noting that Perk didn't have the faintest suggestion of a callus. Somebody else had done the work that had paid for his threads. Perk hung around, making small talk, while I finished stocking the nail bins, then crossed the street with me when I took my lunch break.

When I inquired what he'd been doing for a living, he was expansively vague. "I was in aluminum siding for a few weeks, but some character made me a beautiful offer for my territory so I took his money and headed down the road. Right now, I'm looking around for some sort of investment." He was lying in his teeth. Don't ask me how I knew it; I just did.

His remark was the opening wedge. From there, he inquired about the various businesses that might be in need of capital and a partner, but he was more interested in the ones that were outstandingly successful and didn't need either one. After lunch he said he'd see me around, and moved down the street.

"A friend of yours, Butch?" Arnie Humboldt asked from behind me.

It was a perfect chance to rid myself of Perk Madden but Charlie Judson's other words flashed into my mind: "Thou shalt not squeal."

I shook my head. "Not really a friend, Arnie. Just a guy I met in my travels."

That afternoon seemed to drag out for a week, and with my mind on Perk I couldn't attend to the business like I should have. I mixed up two orders of silverware, misplaced a crate of chandeliers, and put two dozen gallons of shellac in with the enamel display. Old man Danvers came by as I was straightening out the cans of shellac and enamel, and he grinned understandingly.

"Well all slip up once in a while, Butch. Just don't make the same mistake twice."

A dozen thoughts fought to get control of my mind at the same time. Did he know who Perk was? Or did he figure Perk and I were real buddies, ready to do things together? I didn't know what I was going to do, but I knew I had to do something.

Two days later, when Perk stopped in at the hardware store again, I still didn't have any answers. "You had lunch with the fuzz," he said conversationally. Then his cold blue eyes got a touch colder. "You wouldn't have mentioned me by any chance? I mean, we've been through the mill, Butch, and we know things other people would never guess—but we shouldn't be telling tales to the wrong people."

"You should drop dead for even thinking it," I said. "First, if I *had* told Arnie about you, he'd have escorted you out of town twenty minutes later. He doesn't know a thing and I'm not going to tell him what he doesn't have to know."

"You're a real cool cat," Perk purred silkily. "I had you figured for a real square, Butch." He looked around like he was considering buying the place. "Uh, whatever happened to your girlfriend, Butch? What was her name?"

What was her name! Perk knew her name as well as he knew his own. "Gloria," I said, frowning. "Gloria Masters. She changed a lot while I was in stir, Perk. When I got home she wouldn't even go out with me until I got a job. Then she refused to marry me unless I had five thousand dollars saved. She's away visiting her grandmother now, but she'll be home next week and, boy, am I gonna surprise her!" I leaned close to Perk and lowered my voice confidentially. I've got the whole five thousand salted down."

Perk's eyes widened greedily, then disbelief spread over his face. "*You* got five grand put away? By working in this crummy store?" A trace of anger flashed in his eyes. "Don't try to con me, Butch. It takes a long time to put that much bread together; a lot longer than you've been working here."

I kept my voice low. "Guess again. An eastern conglomerate bought up a whole bunch of small ranches a while back and I came up with a real brainstorm. I went up the valley to see the head man, and darned if I didn't end up selling him two carloads of steel posts and two more of barbed wire. Of course Mr. Danvers couldn't pay me the standard commission, which is seven percent, without his regular salesmen getting wise, so he put the money in the safe for me. I mean, I sort of infringed on somebody else's territory, another reason the deal has to be kept hush-hush; but as soon as Gloria gets back I'm being promoted to the sales department and Danvers is going to slip me the money a little at a time so nobody gets wise."

Perk licked his lips and studied my face critically, like maybe if I was lying it would show in my eyes. "Five grand is a *lot* of commission," he said skeptically.

"One of the chief reasons it has to be kept quiet," I hissed. I looked around furtively but nobody was close enough to overhear us. "Steel posts and barbed wire go at fifteen thousand dollars a carload, which brought the order to sixty thousand dollars. Seven percent of that is forty-two hundred dollars, no matter how you figure it. The rest of the five thousand I saved out of my salary." I winked slyly at Perk. "You were a salesman in the aluminum siding business so you should know how such things work."

For a few seconds my words didn't register, than Perk came to life with a start. "Huh? Oh, yeah! I see what you mean." He turned toward the door. "I gotta be going, Butch. I've got people to see and things to do. You know how it is, I'll be in touch."

I was in the diner across the street from the hardward store the following night when the explosion reverberated the length of the main street. Opposite me in the booth, facing the street, Arnie Humboldt had just reached for his double cheeseburger. His hand froze in mid-air, his jaw sagged ludicrously as the ruptured windows of the hardware store crashed onto the sidewalk and skittered into the street. Then he was out of the booth and sprinting for the door.

A patrol car careened around the corner seconds later and two more cops hit the street before it was fully stopped. They found Perk in a corner, all tangled up in a jumble of wheelbarrows, hoes, rakes, and shovels. He was cut in a dozen places and bruised from stem to stern, but had suffered no serious injuries. In his pocket were the tools of his trade: nitro, soap, blasting caps, and fuse.

Perk was returned to stir two weeks later ... for fifteen years. His left leg hadn't fully recovered from his entanglement with the tools in the hardware store and he walked with a pronounced limp, but it was the damage to his bloated ego that really pained him.

I was having a piece of hot apple pie and a glass of milk later that day when Arnie entered the diner and slid into the booth across from me. He ordered the inevitable cheeseburger and coffee, then lit a cigarette and leaned back in his seat.

"Funny thing about Perk Madden," he said out of the clear blue.

"Funny?" Nothing about Perk had ever struck me as being funny.

Arnie expelled a cloud of smoke. "Not really funny, actually. More like odd. I mean the way he blew an empty safe that hadn't been used in years, it just doesn't fit the picture. According to his rap sheet he's cracked quite a few boxes. Not that he ever got much money; he just did a good job of blowing them. So why would a man with his experience make the mistake of using four times as much nitro as the job called for?"

I savored a bite of pie. "Who knows? I suppose, working in the dark like that, it would be fairly easy to make a mistake."

Arnie shook his head. "Highly improbable. My own theory is that there were *two* men involved in that fiasco."

A bit of pie skidded to a halt in my throat. "*Two* men?"

Arnie nodded. "The average safecracker will run a bar of soap *or* a chunk of wax around the edges of a safe door, sealing the crack so the soup he pours in at the top doesn't run out the sides or bottom. Soap or wax ... *never both*. Madden had a bar of soap in his pocket, along with his other goodies, but no wax. Yet there were *both* wax and soap on the safe and the door.

"The presence of the wax and the overload of nitro bring up one outstanding possibility," Arnie continued. "There was *another* safe-cracker in the store ahead of Madden. He had the safe waxed and souped, but before he could finish the job Madden came crawling through the rear window, scaring him off. Not suspecting anything, Madden soaped the safe, poured nitro onto the overload of nitro that was already there, and lit the fuse."

"But that leaves a very obvious loose end," I said. "How did this mysterious *first* safecracker get inside the store? The only sign of forced entry was the window Madden admitted jimmying to get inside, and old man Danvers has the only keys to the building."

"Oh, it had to be a man who knew his locks real well, a man who really didn't need a key," Arnie said, stubbing out his cigarette. "Also he had to have access to dynamite and some knowledge of—well, you know, the sort of things a man would learn in stir. ..." Arnie fell silent as the waitress served his order, then resumed when she was out of earshot. "Not much dynamite in this area. Two construction compan-ies have permits for limited amounts, but the big supply here is in the Danvers magazine out at the old gravel pit. The place is double padlocked but there we come to the locksmith bit again. The right man could have gotten through those two locks with no trouble at all."

"You do have a fantastic imagination," I said. "But *two* safecrackers in Sanger? Going after the same safe on the same night? It's a bit hard to swallow, Arnie."

Arnie bit thoughtfully into his cheeseburger. "Okay, so let's assume the first man—and there were two men involved—wasn't a safe-cracker. In which event he had something other than money as a motive—and the only thing that's left is getting rid of Madden. This mysterious first man had a reason to suspect Perk was going to blow the safe in the hardware store, so he slipped in ahead of him, souped it to the brim, and cut out."

I shook my head. "I can't swallow that theory either, Arnie. If somebody wanted Perk out of Sanger, all he had to do was call the police and have a tail put on him. A bit of close surveillance by the authorities would have stampeded him real quick."

"You're overlooking the code," Arnie pointed out. "You know: Thou shalt not squeal. ... Whoever rigged the booby trap for Perk didn't want to chance the stigma of being labeled a fink, so he used cunning and guile and let Perk blow the whistle on himself. As bobby traps go, it was a real beaut!"

"He went to a lot of trouble just to honor a code," I said. "Not that it doesn't make for a helluva story, but you'll never get anybody to believe it."

Arnie downed his last swallow of coffee and stood up. "So what's wrong with honoring a code? I've lived by one for years and I wouldn't dream of violating it. Namely: Never look a gift horse in the mouth." Giving me a somber wink, he moved out the door and into the peace and quiet of the night.

Jack Ritchie

Next in Line

Four of my cigarettes were missing.

Ordinarily I would not have noticed the loss at all. However, I had been attempting to give up smoking and, as a starter, had rationed myself to one pack a day.

This morning I had broken open a new pack and placed the twenty cigarettes inside my silver case. I had then gone downstairs and breakfasted.

I then retired to the library, lighted my first cigarette of the day, and read my daily two pages of *The Mill on the Floss*. As a test of determination, I am determined to finish that damn book if it kills me. At present I have reached page 171.

I had finished the cigarette and the two pages, and then crossed the hall to the drawing room where I worked the crossword puzzle in yesterday's newspaper and kept one eye on the grandfather clock, waiting for nine thirty and time for my second cigarette.

At the half-hour chime, I reached for my cigarette case and realized that I must have left it back in the library. I found the cigarette case on the table beside the easy chair I'd occupied earlier. When I opened the case, I discovered that instead of nineteen cigarettes waiting to be smoked, there were now only fifteen.

My first thought had been of Edwards. Had he taken the cigarettes? But then I remembered that Edwards did not smoke.

What about Henrietta and Cyrus? No, immediately after breakfast, they had driven off together in Cyrus's car to see that attorney in Chicago again about breaking the will.

Except for Edwards, I was the only other person in his huge house at the moment.

I rubbed my jaw.

While I had been seated in the drawing room occupied with the crossword puzzle, I had been facing the open doorway. I had had a clear view of the closed library door across the hall. I was positive that if anyone had entered the library, the movement would have caught my eye. But there had been no one.

Was it possible that someone had entered the library through one of the windows and stolen my cigarettes?

Absurd as the sole motive for breaking and entering, of course; however, taking the cigarettes might simply have been a reflex action on the part of the burglar who had larger things on his mind.

I examined the high windows bordering the north and west sides of the room. Every one of them was securely bolted from the inside.

On the other hand, had one of them been open, and had the burglar bolted it *after* him when he entered the room?

In that case, he must still be in this very room, since I would surely have noticed if he had left the library.

I experienced a sense of proprietary outrage, even though I had been a resident of O'Reilly Oaks no more than two weeks.

I armed myself with one of the fireplace pokers and proceeded to search the large room.

I found no one.

I lit my nine thirty cigarette.

The thief had to be Edwards. He was the only other person in this house. A true burglar would have pocketed the entire case. But only four cigarettes were missing, very likely because Edwards did not believe that I would notice their disappearance.

Was Edwards one of those souls who convince themselves that they are not really smokers if they do not actually buy their cigarettes? Begging or stealing was another matter.

The loss of the cigarettes in themselves was trivial. What intrigued me was how Edwards got into the library without my seeing him and how he managed to leave.

I could think of only one possibility. Ridiculously gothic, and yet in these old houses . . .

I went about the room pressing knobs, protuberances, and carved wooden grapes in search of the device which activated the secret passageway that must be the answer to the mystery.

I had no success.

I pulled the bell rope vigorously.

When Edwards entered the library—by legitimate means—I said, "Edwards, I understand that you do not smoke."

"That's true, sir."

Edwards was tall, in his fifties, and he had served in this house all his life, as had his father and his grandfather.

"Edwards," I said, "has this house ever had any ghosts wandering about the corridors at night? Or possibly even during the day?"

His eyes flickered. "What kind of ghosts, sir?"

"The usual kind," I said. "Headless ghosts, wailing ghosts, ghosts rattling chains, ghosts who smoke cigarettes?"

He thought about that. "In a hosue this size and age, sir, every creak of a floorboard can rouse the imagination. But I assure you that there are no ghosts in this house." He cleared his throat. "Have you heard . . . or seen . . . anything, sir?"

I smiled enigmatically. "How old is this house?"

"General Horatio Bolivar O'Reilly declared it complete in 1842, sir."

"When General Horatio Bolivar O'Reilly built this place, did he whimsically include a few secret passages? I understand such things were popular at the time."

Edwards shifted slightly. "I wouldn't know, sir."

It appeared that further questioning on the existence of the secret passageway—at this time, at least—would be futile. And in the matter of the disappearing cigarettes, I decided that a warning—of sorts— might be sufficient.

I elaborately studied the contents of my cigarette case. "Hm. I could have sworn that I smoked only two cigarettes so far today. And yet now I have only fourteen left. From now on I intend to keep an exact count of my cigarettes, Edwards. I am trying to give up smoking, you know, and I'm rationing myself to exactly twenty cigarettes a day."

"Yes, sir," Edwards said. "I believe I did hear you mention something to that effect several days ago."

O'Reilly Oaks consists of some forty-five rooms, give or take a few. The present acreage of the estate is one hundred and eighty, most of which is either wooded or rented to neighboring farmers. Only the four or five acres immediately about the house are landscaped.

General Horatio Bolivar O'Reilly, tavern keeper and victualer to the army, attained his rank when he raised a battalion of militia during the Black Hawk War. In the course of the campaign, his unit lost over three hundred men—two hundred of them through desertion, one hundred by way of various fevers, and eight through acute alcoholism. No Indian was ever sighted.

Returning from the war a somewhat richer man, General O'Reilly selected this site some fifteen miles from the town of Green River Falls, which in those days had a population of some three thousand souls. Today the population is still under four thousand.

In the days when servants were plentiful and cheap, a veritable army of them attended O'Reilly Oaks. But time, the rising cost of labor, and attrition on the O'Reilly capital took its toll, so that at the death, earlier this year, of Terrence O'Reilly—General O'Reilly's great-great-grand-son, the only occupants of the house were Terrence himself and his man of all parts, Edwards.

When Terrence expired, only three direct, though remote, descendants of General O'Reilly still remained in this world—Cyrus O'Reilly, a certified public accountant in Chicago; Henrietta O'Reilly, who presided over a pool of typists at a mail-order firm in Boston; and myself, Wilbur O'Reilly, who am employed by the Gailliard Steamship Lines, which is based in San Francisco.

None of the three of us had ever met before and we were only vaguely aware of each other's existence. We gathered in the library at O'Reilly Oaks where Amos Keller, attorney and executor of Terrence O'Reilly's estate, read us the will.

It provided that O'Reilly Oaks remain in a trust under Keller's supervision. Any direct descendant of General O'Reilly was welcome to use the house and grounds for his home as long as he wished. The trust also established a fund to cover the real estate taxes and minimal maintenance of the building and grounds.

It further provided that Edwards has the right to remain at O'Reilly Oaks for as long as he chose and that he be paid his regular monthly salary for as long as he lived there.

At the death of the last O'Reilly, the entire estate was to be liquidated and the money realized be distributed to a number of charities.

When Keller finished reading, there was a long minute of silence.

Henrietta, a robust grim-visaged woman, spoke up first. "Let me get this straight. You mean to say that none of us gets a piece of the estate?"

"I'm afraid not," Keller said. "Though, as mentioned, any or all of you may regard O'Reilly Oaks as your home for as long as you live. I am authorized to provide each of you with a monthly allotment to cover food, clothing, and incidentals."

Cyrus O'Reilly was a small man, balding, and wore rimless glasses. "In terms of cash, how much is the estate worth?"

Keller shrugged. "That is difficult to say. There are so many variables. It all depends upon the buyer, the market, the time, and so forth."

"Has it ever been put up for sale?" Cyrus asked.

"No."

"No offer was ever made?"

"Well, yes," Keller admitted. "A group of businessmen did approach Terrence some years ago. They made him a rather handsome offer, but he turned them down."

Cyrus pursued the point. "Why would a group of businessmen want O'Reilly Oaks? I'd think that in this day and age, a house this size would be a drug on the market."

"Possibly," Heller said. "But they intended to turn the estate into a golf course. They seemed to believe that the main building would make an ideal clubhouse."

"How much did they offer?" Henrietta asked.

"I don't know exactly," Keller said. "But I understand it was in the neighborhood of a million." He looked over his glasses. "Do any of you intend making O'Reilly Oaks your home?"

Cyrus studied his fingernails. "I think I'll give it a try."

I smiled. "Frankly, it sounds ideal to me."

The three of us—Henrietta, Cyrus, and I—spent the next few days wandering independently about the house and grounds, assessing the situation.

I found the building quite to my taste. The furniture was a bit dated, but in excellent condition, though a bit dusty on the second and third floors. I selected a second floor suite which caught the morning sun, did a bit of tidying, and moved in.

At breakfast at the end of the week, Henrietta surveyed the old fashioned room without approval. "I'd prefer a smaller, newer place. Especially one that I could call my own."

Cyrus crunched into his toast. "I have an office and a clientele in

Chicago. I don't see how I can seriously consider giving that up for subsistence living."

Edwards had done the cooking and now served.

"Edwards," I said, "the scrambled eggs were delicious. Did I detect paprika?"

"Yes, sir. Mild paprika for interesting color and vitamin C."

"What about you, Wilbur?" Cyrus demanded. "I understand that you have a responsible position for some steamship line. Do you intend to give that up for free room and board?"

I sipped coffee. "I have enough time in with my company to qualify for a half-pay pension. I believe the time has come for me to retire."

After my graduation from college some twenty years ago, I went to sea. Not out of a spirit of adventure, but for the solid economic reason that it was the only job I could find at the time.

I signed on as an assistant to the purser of the *Polylandia* of the Gailliard Line. The *Polylandia*, a new luxury liner based at San Francisco, made most of the ports of the Far East. As of my present leave, I had spent all of my working life on the *Polylandia* in the purser's department.

Henrietta put down her knife and fork. "I'm positive we can break the will."

"Oh?" I said. "On what grounds?"

"I found out that Terrence lived here for the last fifteen years as a recluse, and everybody knows that recluses aren't normal. He couldn't have been in his right mind when he made out that will. We three are the only blood relatives he had in the world, and by all rights we should inherit what he left and split it three ways."

Cyrus concurred emphatically. "We simply can't waste our lives sitting here in this monstrous house. There's a lawyer I know in Chicago who specializes in this type of thing. Will-breaking, you know. He's expensive, but we'll split his fee among the three of us and still have plenty left."

I declined to join them. "Personally, I prefer the situation just as it is. I am by nature sedentary. In my entire service on the *Polylandia*, I went ashore less than a dozen times and then only for souvenir shopping. I even had my appendix removed while aboard the *Polylandia*."

Cyrus crumpled his napkin. "Well, I'm driving to Chicago to see that lawyer. If either of you wants to come along, I've got room in my car."

When Cyrus left, Henrietta rode beside him.

I spent the morning evaluating the kitchen-garden area and the greenhouse. The latter had a few broken panes but otherwise seemed in serviceable condition.

I returned to the house and found Edwards in the kitchen preparing lunch. "Edwards," I said, "do we have anything like a Rototiller on the premises?"

"Yes, sir. All of the gardening machinery and implements are in the shed next to the greenhouse. Do you intend to garden?"

"Yes. For twenty years I have been priming myself with garden magazines. It is now time to give it all a practical try."

Edwards trimmed some scallions. "The late Terrence O'Reilly was quite a gardener himself. He leaned towards vegetables on the premise that if you couldn't eat it, it wasn't worth growing, though he did have a soft spot for iris, moss rose, and heart's ease."

"I am rather inclined that way myself," I said. "I understand that Uncle Terrence was a recluse."

"Not precisely, sir. He did prefer his own company, but he left the grounds now and then, principally for the monthly meeting of the Green River Falls Garden Club. Local gardeners get together on the second Wedenesday of every month at the public library, and I understand that new members are welcome."

"I never met Uncle Terrence in the flesh," I said, "though I do vaguely remember sending him some duty Christmas cards as a boy. He never married, did he?"

"He did, sir. Mrs. O'Reilly died thirty years ago."

"They had no children?"

"They had a son, sir. Robert."

"Dead, I suppose—or else Terrence would probably have left him the estate."

"Yes, sir. Dead. These last fifteen years."

"Then he died fairly young? An accident?"

"Yes, sir. I suppose you could call it that."

"Edwards," I said, "I have the distinct suspicion that there is a family skeleton involved here. What about Robert?"

"He was killed when his automobile plunged through a bridge railing and into the Mississippi River."

"Speeding? A few drinks under his belt?"

"No liquor was involved, sir. But he was speeding."

"Edwards," I said, "I am still pulling teeth. Why was he speeding?"

"Well, sir, he was speeding because the police were pursuing him. He had just escaped from the state prison."

"Why was he in prison?"

Edwards sighed. "Robert was a quiet sort of person, but with a strong sense of justice. A straight A student at the university. Or nearly so. In the final semester of his senior year, he received a B in ethics instead of the A he felt he honestly deserved. He lost his head and shot his professor."

I felt a twinge of sympathy. The only blot on my own academic career had been a C in physical education, a subject which has no place in a true university.

Edwards sliced tomatoes. "Robert was sentenced to life imprisonment, but he tired of life in confinement and managed to escape. For a short while, anyway."

"And now he is dead and buried?"

"Not exactly, sir. Dead, yes. But his body was never recovered from the river."

Henrietta and Cyrus returned in time for dinner that evening.

Cyrus rubbed his hands. "Well, Wilbur, we've seen McCardle. He's the lawyer I told you about. He's positive that we can break the will. He suggests that we do a bit of research and gather evidence about Uncle Terrence. When a man is a recluse for fifteen years, he's bound to develop a few idiosyncrasies—items which, with the proper handling, we can build into a strong case showing that Uncle Terrence's mind wasn't exactly what it should have been."

He turned to Edwards, who was serving dessert. "Edwards, you were with Uncle Terrence all your life, weren't you?"

"Yes, sir."

"Then you must remember certain incidents, certain circumstances, when you might have called his behavior a little peculiar?"

"No, sir. I do not."

Cyrus smiled thinly. "You have a bad memory—is that it?"

"No, sir," Edwards said. "I have a very good memory." He left the room with the empty tray.

"That was clumsy of you, Cyrus," Henrietta said. "After all, Edwards stands to lose something when we break the will. If we want his cooperation, we will probably have to make some kind of a deal with him."

Cyrus nodded. "Well, Wilbur, are you with us?"

"How much does McCardle expect for his legal services?" I asked.

"Twenty-five percent of the estate," Cyrus said.

I smiled. "So each of us, including our attorney, would get one-fourth of what might or might not amount to a million dollars? Minus, of course, whatever it takes to get Edwards to cooperate and minus the inheritance taxes, which I understand are horrendous these days?" I shook my head. "No, I don't consider it at all worth contesting the will. Suppose I did manage to clear one hundred and fifty thousand? If I chose to spend it gloriously, it would be gone before very long and I would be left with nothing. Or even if I invested it wisely, how much could I expect as a return? Twelve thousand a year?" I helped myself to another slice of cottage cheese torte. "No, at this moment I am living in greater comfort and security than I could possibly expect with one hundred and fifty thousand. I am well fed, live in ease, get to pull the bell rope when so inclined, and how could I possibly afford a servant and superb cook such as Edwards on twelve thousand dollars a year?"

"I'd prefer one hundred and fifty thousand in cold hard cash," Henrietta said firmly.

Cyrus nodded. "The hell with security."

During the next week—interspersed with unsuccessful efforts to get Edwards to cooperate with them—Henrietta and Cyrus traveled to

Chicago twice more for conferences with the lawyer.

On the evening of the day Edwards had filched my cigarettes, I sought him out. "Does that station wagon in the garage belong to you or was it Uncle Terrence's?"

"It was your uncle's, sir."

"I don't suppose there would be any objection if I borrow the wagon tonight. This is the second Wednesday of the month, isn't it? I thought I'd drop in at the garden club meeting."

"I'm certain you will enjoy it, sir. Your uncle did." He found the keys to the station wagon and handed them to me.

When I returned from Green River Falls that night after ten o'clock, I found flashing red lights and several state patrol cars parked in the driveway in front of O'Reilly Oaks.

When I entered the house, a solid, uniformed man appeared in the hallway. "Mr. Wilbur O'Reilly?"

"Yes. What is this all about?"

"I am Lieutenant Stafford," he said. "State patrol. I would like to ask you a few questions."

We joined Henrietta and Edwards in the drawing room.

Stafford studied me. "Your cousin Cyrus O'Reilly was found shot to death beside the road to Green River Falls about a half mile from here. Can you account for your time this evening?"

"Of course," I said. "I attended a meeting of the Green River Falls Garden Club. The subject was roses. Now what is this again about Cyrus?"

"His body was discovered in front of his automobile parked on the shoulder of the road at approximately eight thirty this evening. We are fairly certain that he must have been killed within minutes of that time because the road is well traveled and his body lay in the beam of his headlights."

I rubbed my chin. "Cyrus probably made the mistake of picking up a hitchhiker."

"Possibly," Stafford said. "However, in cases like this hitchhikers almost invariably take the car along with them. Also Cyrus O'Reilly's wallet was intact in his pocket and contained several hundred dollars. I doubt that any hitchhiker-murderer would have overlooked something like that."

"Undoubtedly the hitchhiker panicked and fled after the murder," I said. "What was Cyrus doing out this evening anyway?"

"No one seems to know," Stafford said. "He left without telling anyone and no one saw him leave. What time did you leave here this evening?"

"About seven thirty."

"How many people were at this garden club meeting?"

"About twenty-five, possibly thirty. The meeting broke up at about a quarter to ten."

"These people would be able to verify that you were there the entire evening?"

"I was a stranger there. It was my first meeting. Probably no one even noticed me except the secretary when I signed up as a new member at the end of the meeting."

Stafford shook his head. "When you are a stranger in a small town, everbody notices you. So you were there from the time the meeting started until nearly ten?"

I coughed. "Well ... actually I arrived at the meeting a bit late."

"How late?"

I smiled quickly. "There seems to be a fork in the road to Green River Falls and I took the wrong turn. I traveled some distance before I realized that I was on the wrong road and turned back. I arrived at the Green River Falls library at about nine."

Henrietta smiled.

I glared at her. "And where were you at the time Cyrus met his death?"

"In my bedroom reading a book."

"Ha," I said. "And is there anyone who can verify that?"

"Of course not," she said coldly.

"And you, Edwards," I said. "Where were you at eight thirty?"

He seemed surprised at the question. "I was in the kitchen preparing marinade for sauerbraten."

Stafford's eyes went to Henrietta and me. "I understand that the two of you and Cyrus O'Reilly inherited Terrence O'Reilly's estate. Is the probate complete? What I mean is, will the estate now be divided between the two of you instead of three?"

"I'm afraid your information about the estate is wrong," I said. "We did not inherit Terrence O'Reilly's estate. According to the terms of the will, we are merely allowed to remain here as guests for as long as we choose. We do not ourselves own one inch of the property."

Henrietta hastily backed me up. "Not one inch. So you see, officer, there isn't any possible reason in the world why either one of us might have wanted Cyrus dead. We have absolutely nothing to gain by his death."

"Lieutenant," I said, "I believe that there is a nitrate test or something of that nature for detecting gun powder grains on the hands of persons who have recently fired guns? That ought to settle this matter once and for all."

Stafford nodded. "Our technician is waiting in the next room. But murderers are getting more sophisticated these days. Especially where premeditation might be involved. They usually take precautions like wearing gloves or some type of wrapper around their hands and arms when they fire a gun. I won't be surprised if I don't find a thing."

He didn't.

Stafford continued to question Henrietta, Edwards, and me until eleven thirty before giving up for the evening.

The next morning I met Henrietta at breakfast. "Well, Wilbur, now that Cyrus isn't with us any more, we stand to get larger shares of the estate, don't we?" she asked, pouring coffee.

"Henrietta, I still haven't the slightest intention of contesting the will."

She smiled thinly. "Of course not. Wilbur. And neither have I. At least not right now. We'll wait a while, won't we? Six months? A year? After all, even though the police apparently can't prove a thing about Cyrus's death, it isn't wise to appear so greedy." The smile disappeared. "It's got to be either you or me, and it certainly isn't me."

"What isn't you?"

"You understand perfectly well what I mean, Wilbur. One of us murdered Cyrus and I know it isn't me. You're a lot deeper and cleverer than I thought. That innocent expression doesn't fool me for a moment. I intend to keep an eye on you and I shall take precautions."

"Precautions? What precautions?"

"I shall send a sealed letter to a friend of mine with instructions that it is not to be opened unless I meet death under mysterious circumstances."

"Henrietta, I simply don't follow you."

She smiled grimly. "In my letter, I shall accuse you of murdering Cyrus."

I stared at her coldly. "You have absolutely no proof."

"Of course I haven't. If I had, I would most certainly have turned it over to the police. However, in my letter I shall say that both you and I conspired to murder Cyrus for bigger shares in the estate, and that now I suspect that you have plans to kill me too and take over everything. I think that would make the police sit up and take notice if something should happen to me, don't you, Wilbur? The confession of one of two conspirators would make quite a bit of trouble for you."

"Henrietta," I said, "has it ever occurred to you that there is a third person in this house who might want to see Cyrus dead?"

"Edwards?"

"Of course. After all, if you and Cyrus had broken the will, he would stand to lose his home and job."

"But we offered to cut him in."

"Yes, but your offer may not have been enough. Or he may prefer that status quo. He might regard O'Reilly Oaks as his home as much as Terrence O'Reilly did—certainly more than you or I do."

I finished my coffee. "I am now going to send a sealed letter to a friend in which I state flatly that the three of us—Edwards, you, and I—conspired to murder Cyrus for fun and profit and that I now strongly suspect that the two of you are about to murder me, too." I smiled. "I will also state that you and Edwards have been having an outrageously erotic love affair."

She flushed. "Me? With a servant?"

"My dear Henrietta," I said. "It's been done before."

As it turned out, neither of us ever sent those letters.

I went to the library, lit my first cigarette of the day, and picked up *The Mill on the Floss*.

When I dispatched the obligatory two pages, I searched for yesterday's newspaper and the crossword puzzle.

Where had I left the paper? Oh, yes—in the sunny alcove at the first floor landing.

I left the room, found the newspaper, and paused there to read an article I'd missed yesterday. When I finished, I went back down the stairs to the library.

I had finished approximately half the crossword puzzle when the grandfather clock across the hall chimed the half hour.

Time for my second cigarette. I reached for my case on the table beside me and opened it.

Five of my cigarettes were missing. When I had left the room I had not taken the case with me and evidently while I was gone ...

I went to the bell rope and pulled vigorously.

Edwards appeared. "Yes, sir?"

"Edwards," I said, "I am missing five cigarettes."

He frowned thoughtfully.

"Edwards," I said. "Do you agree that there are only three people in this house?"

"Absolutely, sir."

"Good. I know positively that I did not smoke those five cigarettes, and I also know that the very odor of tobacco makes Henrietta ill. What does that leave us with, Edwards?"

He evaded my eyes. "I don't know, sir."

"It leaves us with the inescapable conclusion that the person who stole those cigarettes is you, Edwards."

Edwards rubbed his neck. "Yes, sir. I confess. I took the cigarettes."

I regarded him sternly. "Edwards, aren't you ashamed of yourself? After all, your salary is quite generous. I should think that you would be able to buy your cigarettes, it shouldn't be necessary to steal them. Do you have an explanation?"

He hung his head. "Sir, when I stopped smoking, I swore never to buy another cigarette, However ..."

"Ah," I said. "You left yourself a loophole. You did not forswear to beg or steal cigarettes, did you?"

He looked away. "I think steal is too harsh a word, sir. Filch, perhaps ..."

"Edwards," I said, "above and beyond the filching, there is one other thing about the incident which bothers me. How the devil did you get into the library? There must be some secret passage. When I left this room, I walked up to the alcove at the first landing to retrieve the paper. I was up there for perhaps two or three minutes, reading, but I faced the open library door down below me. While I did not actually stare at it, it was within the periphery of my attention. I am certain that I would have caught the movement of anyone entering the library."

Edwards chewed his lips for a moment. "As you went up the stairs to the landing, sir, your back was toward the library door. I took that moment to slip into the library."

"Very well," I said. "Then how did you get out of the library? You surely wouldn't have had enough time to enter it, steal the cigarettes, and leave during the relatively short time my back was turned."

Edwards rubbed his jaw. "I hid behind the door, sir. As you reentered the library and walked toward your chair, your back was again turned. I darted out of the door."

I sighed. "Then there is no secret passage?"

"No, sir. No secret passage."

"Edwards," I said, "I admire your timing, but this filching of cigarettes had got to stop."

"Yes, sir," Edwards said firmly. "I'll see that it doesn't happen again."

The weeks passed rather quietly and the second Wednesday of another month appeared.

I borrowed the keys to the station wagon from Edwards.

"The garden club again, sir?" he asked.

"Yes." I said. "This month we have a vegetable gardener as guest speaker. Hungarian wax peppers are his specialty."

"I'm certain it will be interesting, sir. I do hope you don't take the wrong fork in the road again, sir."

"Not very likely. I know my way around by now."

At slightly after nine o'clock that evening, as I sat in the audience in the lecture room of the Green River Falls library, I felt a tap on my shoulder.

It was Lieutenant Stafford of the state patrol accompanied by another uniformed officer. Stafford backoned and I followed him outside, acutely aware that I was the cynosure of all eyes.

On the steps outside the building, he said, "Were you in there all this evening?"

"Since eight o'clock. Why?"

"Would the people in there be willing to swear that you were?"

"You'll have to ask them. But I assure you that I did not leave the room. As a matter of fact. I occupied the seat next to the mayor. His field is geraniums. Frankly, I've never cared about geraniums. All the ones I've seen appear to be perpetually dusty. What is this all about?"

"Your cousin Henrietta was found shot to death beside her car on the road to Green River Falls by a passing motorist at eight thirty."

I frowned. "Henrietta shot beside the road? The same as Cyrus?"

He nodded. "Same road, same place, same time. Probably the same gun. We'll establish that later. Now let's go back inside."

I balked. "You mean you're going back in there and break up the meeting just to ask if anybody remembers me?"

"Exactly."

We marched back inside where Lieutenant Stafford mounted the podium and took command of the meeting.

It was most embarrassing, but he found a number of people, including the mayor, who were willing to swear that I had been in my seat in the audience when the meeting began at eight and had not left it until called outside by Stafford. I had the feeling that my new notoriety would either get me expelled from the club or nominated for its presidency at the next election.

Stafford took me to state patrol headquarters where I was given another nitrate test, which, of course, proved to be negative.

Nevertheless, I was then taken into a small interrogation room for further questioning.

"Frankly," I said, "outside of some psycho lurking beside the roadway and killing without reason, I think your only bet as the killer is Edwards."

"Edwards? That butler, or whatever?"

"Why not?" I said. "Where was he at the time Henrietta was murdered?"

"In the kitchen grinding dry bread for wiener schnitzel."

Wiener schnitzel? I considered that tenderly. Usually it also meant cucumber slices in thick cream.

"What possible reason would Edwards have to kill your cousins?" Stafford asked.

"They were planning to break Uncle Terrence's will and convert the estate into cash. Without my cooperation. I assure you. Nevertheless, if they had succeeded, it would have meant that Edwards would lose his job and domicile."

"You think he'd kill two people just to keep his job?"

"If one also considers room and board, I would say that we are talking about a package deal which exceeds fifteen thousand dollars a year. Giving Edwards a conservative additional twenty years of life, that could amount to something over three hundred thousand dollars. Surely something worth killing for."

Stafford did not seem impressed with a motive stretching over twenty years. He regarded me thoughtfully. "Now that your cousins are dead, that leaves only you. The last of the O'Reillys. Is that the way you planned it all along? Eliminate them first and then step up and break the will? There's no point in dividing the spoils three ways if you can hog it all."

I shed the accusation with dignity. "I have a perfect alibi."

He grunted. "I always distrust perfect alibis and I always break them. Do you have a twin brother by any chance?"

I smiled. "I am one of a kind. I would not have it any other way."

It was after midnight before Stafford released me and had me driven back to my car.

In the station wagon, I hesitated.

I most certainly did not murder either Cyrus or Henrietta, though, frankly, I did not mourn their passing.

But that left only Edwards. He had to be the murderer. After all, who else was there? I did not really put much stock in the roadside-psychotic theory.

But if Edwards was the murderer, was it safe for me to return to O'Reilly Oaks?

I pondered that.

Edwards had killed Henrietta and Dyrus because they were intent on breaking the will. But I had no such intention. Besides, I was, after all, the last of the O'Reillys. If anything happened to me, the estate would be liquidated, leaving Edwards homeless and without a job.

No, it might be a bit sticky living in the same house with a murderer, but my life was his life. If he harmed me, he would be cutting his own throat, so to speak. I should be perfectly safe at O'Reilly Oaks.

In time Stafford would undoubtedly gather enough evidence to arrest Edwards, but until then there was no point in my moving to some wretched motel. I drove back to O'Reilly Oaks and had a good night's sleep.

In the morning, after showering and dressing, I went to the bureau drawer where I kept my cigaretes.

I frowned as I looked down at the opened carton. I had purchased it yesterday and removed one pack. There should now be nine packs left. But there were only six.

Damn Edwards. First four cigarettes. Then five. And now three whole packs. And after he had firmly promised that he would stop . . .

I stared down at the cigarettes for perhaps a full minute.

Of course, I thought. Of course. That would explain everthing. I filled my case and went downstairs.

I waited in the breakfast room until Edwards appeared.

"Edwards," I said, "I have been putting two and two together. Rationally it would appear that we two are the only people in the world who have motives for the deaths of both Henrietta and Cyrus."

"It appears so, sir."

"However, Edwards, I know that I did not kill either Henrietta or Cyrus. And I have the strange suspicion that neither did you. And neither, Edwards, do I now believe that you stole those cigarettes. Any of them."

Edwards coughed slightly.

I smiled. "I put this to you, Edwards. When Robert O'Reilly's automobile plunged over that Mississippi River bridge, he did not

NEXT IN LINE   67

drown, but managed to crawl out of the water and make his way back home. And once here, he concealed himself somewhere in this house and has been hiding here ever since."

Edwards avoided my eyes.

"Edwards," I said, "he must have needed the assistance and connivance of another party or parties to survive here. After all, he had to be provided with food, drink, and whatever." I smiled again. "Edwards, why don't you just supply him with cigarettes, too? Why does he find it necessary to steal them?"

Edwards sighed heavily. "Actually Robert was a nonsmoker until recently. But he has begun to acquire the habit."

I helped myself to the platter of browned sausages and delicately fried potatoes. "I assume that Robert killed Cyrus and Henrietta because if they had managed to break the will, he would have lost his sanctuary?"

"Yes, sir. The house would have been sold and the new owner would in time have become aware of Robert's existence. So Robert forced both of your cousins to drive to the spot where their bodies were found, shot them, and then walked back across the fields to the house."

Edwards poured coffee into my cup. "what do you intend to do now, sir?"

"I will have to inform the police, of course, and have them root out Robert."

"Sir, do you enjoy living in this house?"

"Certainly."

"Sir, Robert O'Reilly is the son of Terrence O'Reilly. As such, he has a perfectly legitimate and primary claim to his father's estate. He could go to court and easily break the will and its provisions for your occupancy here."

"But Robert is a murderer and a murderer cannot legally profit from his murders."

"True, sir. But Robert did not murder his father, and the date of his father's natural death is the point from which he would lay claim to the estate. As for your cousins, they did not own any part of the estate nor have a natural claim to greater than Robert's. In other words, he may have murdered them, but it was not to gain control of the estate. He felt he already had that legally, whenever he chose to make himself known."

Edwards returned the coffeepot to its trivet. "Besides, sir, are you quite positive that the police could successfully prove that Robert murdered your cousins?"

"Well . . . no. But still, Robert is an acknowledged murderer. There is that matter of the ethics porfessor. Shouldn't he be returned to prison for that?"

"Possibly, sir. However, if you were responsible for sending him back, he might be inclined to a bit of vindictiveness and pursue his claim to the estate. He might be a felon, sir, but he would become a rich felon and your landlord. Undoubtedly he would evict you and perhaps even charge you room and board for the time you have spent here."

I sipped my coffee slowly while Edwards waited.

"Edward," I said, "suppose Robert takes it into his head to murder me, too?"

"Sir," Edwards said earnestly, "when the last O'Reilly dies—which for all practical purposes means you—the estate will be liquidated. Robert might forestall that by emerging from his hiding place and laying claim to the estate, but that would mean he would be sent back to prison. That is the very last thing in the world he wants. He would not dream of harming you, sir. I'm sure he wishes you a long life."

I sighed. "Edwards, there is a secret passage into the library, isn't there?"

"Yes, sir. From inside the library it is revealed by pressing the posterior of the cherub blowing the trumpet on the wainscoting to the right of the fireplace."

"And the passage leads to where?"

"A bedroom on the third floor."

"Is that where Robert keeps himself?"

"No, sir. His quarters are behind false walls."

I quickly held up a hand. "Never mind. The less I know about his exact whereabouts, the better. And, Edwards, perhaps it might also be wiser if Robert did not know that I am aware of his existence."

"I understand, sir."

After breakfast, I retired to the library. I lit a cigarette and picked up *The Mill on the Floss*.

Was Robert watching me at this very moment? There obviously had to be some type of peephole. Was he waiting for me to leave my cigarette case behind again? But why should be? After all, he had those three packs he'd taken from my bureau drawer. At this moment he was more than likely in his hiding place contentedly puffing tobacco.

I put down the book, rose, and examined the wainscoting. I found the cherub with the worn posterior.

Gingerly I pressed it.

The wainscoting slid noiselessly back, revealing an opening somewhat narrower and shorter than a normal doorway.

I hesitated at the darkness within, but then pulled out my cigarette lighter. Using its flickering light, I stepped cautiously into the opening.

I noticed a small knob just inside. Evidently it opened and closed the passage from the inside.

I left the passage door open and slowly made my way up the narrow stone stairs. There was the smell of dampness and mold, but there were no cobwebs. After all, they couldn't exist long if Robert kept tramping up and down all the time.

I ascended past what I estimated to be the second floor and continued upward until I faced a blank wooden wall.

I found a small knob similar to the one downstairs and turned it until the panel in front of me slid to one side. Whatever one could say about Robert, he certainly kept the mechanism of these doors well oiled.

I entered a small bedroom stale with the smell of disuse. Very likely long ago it had been occupied by one of the maids.

Footmarks, grimed from the passageway, faded to the hallway door.

In the hall they seemed to disappear entirely—however, when I got down on my hands and knees I could just barely make them out again. I trailed them to a doorway down the hall.

Was this Robert's hiding place? Not exactly, I supposed. Edwards had mentioned that Robert's haven was concealed behind a false wall, though probably this door was one way of getting to that false wall.

I hesitated between caution and curiosity and then edged the door open slightly. The medium-sized room appeared to be well lighted and it was empty of human life.

I stepped quietly inside and glanced about.

Where might this walled-off compartment be? Not that I had any intention of disturbing Robert. I simply wanted to know where it could be found.

Certainly not on the east and north sides of the room. They were thoroughly windowed. And not the south, either. That bordered the corridor.

I studied the plastered west wall. There had to be some indication of the secret entrance, but there seemed to be none. Not even a hairline crack.

I opened the doors of a free-standing wardrobe and found neatly hung clothes.

But of course! This must be Edwards' room. I had never been inside it before, but now I recognized some of his clothes.

I should have realized at once that this room was lived in. Not a mote of dust anywhere. A clean-smelling comfortable room that I myself might occupy, except that I would add ashtrays.

My eyes went to the wastebasket. It contained a discarded magazine and ...

I peered closer and lifted the periodical.

There—amid various debris—lay three unopened packs of cigarettes. My brand.

I thoughtfully returned to the wardrobe and examined the soles of Edwards' shoes. Yes, one pair of them bore traces of the unmistakable grime of the secret passageway.

Discarded cigarettes? Grime on the bottoms of Edwards' shoes? A smooth plastered wall that showed absolutely no signs of any entrance to a hideaway. A *supposed* hideaway?

My mouth dropped.

I had been flimflammed. Yes, that was the only word for it. Flimflammed.

Robert was unequivocally dead. He died when his automobile went off that bridge—body recovered or not. He was not lurking in the walls of this house nor had he stolen a single one of my cigarettes.

Edwards had cleverly reanimated him solely for my benefit.

Why?

I saw it all now.

With the deaths of Henrietta and Cyrus, I became the sole surviving O'Reilly and, as such, had to be preserved.

I had declared that I had no intention of challenging Uncle Terrence's will, yet there ever remained the danger to Edwards that someday in the future I might change my mind. After all, a million dollar estate could be a constant temptation, especially now that I would have to share it with no one.

No, Edwards had to meet that hanging threat by creating, or recreating, Robert.

If Robert existed—or at least if I believed that he did—it was pointless for me to ever consider contesting the will. Robert had a prior claim and would step forward if I tried.

Yes, Edwards had been clever, but the charade was over with now and I would tell him so. It would undoubtedly destroy his sense of security, but the truth must out.

I stalked downstairs and found Edwards in the kitchen doing the breakfast dishes.

He wiped his hands and turned. "Yes, sir?"

Edwards had been born in this house, as had his father, and his grandfather. He belonged here as much as any O'Reilly. He loved it, he served it, he killed to protect it.

I rubbed my jaw. He had also been so considerate as to commit the murders at a time when he thought I would have a perfect alibi—though, of course, he could not have anticipated that I would take the wrong turn in the road on the night Cyrus met his death.

Edwards waited.

I cleared my throat. "Edwards, about this business of Robert filching my cigarettes. Perhaps you'd better see to it that he is regularly supplied. At least a pack a day."

He nodded eagerly. "Yes, sir. I'll put Robert's cigarettes on the master shopping list immediately."

The wiener schnitzel that evening was absolutely delicious.

Stephen Wasylyk
A Little Time Off

The explosion came at mid-morning, booming off the surrounding hills. Malone lifted his head, listening until the echo died, shrugged and went back to fishing, casting his line upstream with skilled precision and letting it drift toward him. He was a big man with broad shoulders and a craggy face too white to have spent much time outdoors, and beneath the broad-brimmed hat, his pale blue eyes shifted and probed the waters of the creek, looking for the best places to drop the feathered fly.

It was mid-afternoon when Sheriff Tom Fulton, throwing a lanky shadow across one of Malone's favorite pools, called to him. Malone pretended he didn't hear. He knew instinctively that Fulton was there because of the explosion, and he didn't want to get involved. He was here to fish, and that was all.

Fulton was a hard man to ignore. "Ten minutes, Dave. That's all I want. You owe me that much!"

Malone sighed and reeled in his line. Trust Fulton to bring that up. Fulton was the one who had found the stream for him and got him permission to camp here on private property.

"Ten minutes," he said as he waded ashore. "You have nine minutes and thirty seconds left."

"I need advice and an opinion. You hear the explosion this morning?"

Malone put his rod down and reached for a cigarette. He nodded.

"Fellow named Hardy over on the lake," said Fulton. "His boat blew up. At first I thought it was a simple accident, his outboard motor, or gasoline can. Trouble is, an explosion like that couldn't really cause much damage, so George Kasky volunteered to do some diving. You know George. Used to be an underwater demolitions expert with the navy. Runs the hardware store now. George put on his gear and brought some stuff up from the bottom that looks very interesing."

"How interesting?"

"George says if that was a gasoline explosion, he never set a charge in his life."

Malone stripped his cigarette down and rolled the paper into a tight ball in his thick fingers. "Sounds like a lot of fun for you. Why do you need me?"

Fulton squatted on the grassy bank and fumbled for his pipe. "Because I'm a hick sheriff and you're a high-powered detective from the city. If someone killed Hardy, it's more your line than mine. Will you give me a hand?"

"I thought you could call the state police in a case like this."

"Sure I can, but I'm up for re-election this fall. I'd like to handle this on my own. Means a lot of votes if I pull it off."

"What do you expect me to do that you can't do for youself?"

Fulton lit his pipe with slow, measured puffs. "Just come along and keep me from making a fool of myself."

Malone chuckled. "That's a big assignment."

"Laugh. At least I know when I'm in over my head. You coming?"

Malone began stripping off his waders. "Always liked a man who admits his deficiencies. Where do you want to start?"

"At the lake. Kasky is waiting for us."

"This is going to be one of the most ridiculous investigations on record. I'm at a big disadvantage up here."

"A ridiculous investigation is better than none," said Fulton. "You know all the rules, what to look for, how to handle the questioning. I don't."

"Forget it," said Malone. "It all comes down to common sense, hard work, and luck. Mostly luck."

Kasky pushed up his mask and let his mouthpiece drop when he saw Malone. "You going to help, Dave?"

"Certainly not with the diving, George. Fulton's upset because you say someone blew up the boat."

"Take a look for yourself." He held out the remains of a gasoline can. "It took more than gasoline to tear this apart."

Malone agreed. "I'm no expert, but you're probably right. Couple of sticks of dynamite?"

"Or the equivalent. Furthermore, this Hardy had an open rowboat with an outboard motor. No place for fumes to accumulate. The boat didn't have a chance to burn because it was smashed to bits. Even the motor mount was bent."

"The only thing I can see is that someone planted dynamite on Hardy's boat," said Fulton.

"If Hardy wasn't carrying it himself," said Malone dryly. "You find any pieces of a timer, or something else that could set it off?"

"Not a thing. That bottom is sand, and I was looking real good."

"Where was the boat located?"

"Almost in the center of the cove. No way for anyone to throw something into it."

"Okay," sighed Malone, "I agree it looks like someone killed this Hardy. Who had a reason?"

"Practically everyone on the lake," answered Fulton. "He was a greatly disliked man. Treated his wife mean and the other people about the same."

"Need something a lot more specific than that."

Kasky's eyes shifted. "There's a candidate, if you want to listen to rumors," he said. "Man named Price. Lives next door to Hardy and was supposed to be too friendly with Hardy's wife."

"Anyone else?"

Kasky shook his head. "Not that I know of."

"How about Hardy's wife."

"Now you know why I need you," said Fulton. "I never thought of dynamite as a woman's weapon."

"Who would have a better opportunity to get explosives into Hardy's boat?"

"I guess you're right. What now?"

Malone looked out over the lake. Prevented by the tree-covered steep hillsides from approaching by land, curiosity seekers cruised or sat motionless in a half-dozen boats around the mouth of the cove.

"Let's see if any of these people actually saw the explosion," Malone suggested.

The second boat they hailed, a sleek speedboat, held a teenaged couple.

"Sure we saw it," said the boy, adolescent-thin, with long blond curls over his ears. The girl was tanned and bikinied.

"Jack was checking the engine. We happened to stop almost here when the explosion came. There was a *crack*, then *vroom!*" The girl looked at Malone with eyes that suggested she preferred mature men.

Malone was amused. "*Crack vroom?*"

"Crack vroom", she repeated firmly.

"Anyone else around?"

"No," said Jack. "The boat was by itself."

"That was all?"

"That was all. We went over to help, but there was nothing we could do. Someone called the sheriff and he came out."

Fulton made a note of their names. "Where now?"

Back to my fishing if I had any sense, reflected Malone, but Fulton would never forgive me. He sighed, wondering where he could go just once to get away from people and their problems. It seemed like they were always conspiring to keep him from enjoying a little time off. He scratched his chin. "Have you talked to the widow?"

"Only to tell her Hardy was dead and to have her make the identification."

"What was left to identify?"

"His face and head weren't too bad. The blast caught him lower down. He was wearing a life jacket, which kept him afloat. We didn't have to dive for him."

The slight blonde who opened the door to Fulton's knock didn't look mature enough to be called a woman, in spite of the wedding ring on her finger, until Malone looked into the violet eyes and realized she had been a woman for a long time.

"You don't mind if I ask you a couple of questions, Mrs. Hardy?" Fulton's voice was apologetic.

Her answer was to sob and collapse on Fulton's chest, while he stared helplessly at Malone over her head.

Malone felt like laughing. This was a situation Fulton would have to handle alone.

"It's Quentin Price," she sobbed. "He said if I didn't marry him he'd kill me."

"I don't understand," said Fulton, his face perplexed. "Why should he say that?"

The sobs grew louder. "I don't know why he would threaten me."

Fulton patted her back encouragingly. "You stay here. I'll talk to him."

Outside, he looked at Malone. "How can I question her when she's like that?"

"You can't. Just try to get back to her later."

Malone followed him next door. Hardy's cabin was buried in the woods, with a footpath leading to a small dock at the lake. Price's cabin sat in splendor above a long sloping lawn that ran to the lake's edge, all the trees before it removed.

"When did he clear this out?"

"Last spring . Blasting out the stumps sounded like a small war."

"He might have had a few sticks of dynamite left over."

"Something else that never occurred to me," Fulton admitted.

Fulton knocked, and the man who let them in had a disdainful expression on his round, bulbous-nosed face. His eyes were small and close together, iron gray hair cut short, the corners of his mouth turned down.

"What do you want?" asked Price.

"We just came from Mrs. Hardy," Fulton told him. "Threatening a woman any time is bad enough. You must be sick to threaten her just hours after her husband died."

Price snorted. "Sick, hell! She's the one that's sick. She's glad to get rid of him. That grieving widow business is just an act."

Malone said quietly, "You expected her to welcome your proposal?"

Price jerked a thumb at Malone. "Who is he?"

Fulton explained that Malone was a friend.

"I don't have to answer his questions."

"You don't have to answer any questions," said Fulton, "but when people don't answer, they usually have something to hide. Do you have something to hide, Mr. Price?"

"Not a thing. As far as Mrs. Hardy is concerned, I had plenty of reason to think she'd welcome my proposal. We'd talked about it often enough. I wanted her to file for divorce, but she was afraid of Hardy. Now that he's gone, I thought she'd be happy about it. Instead, she turned on me and told me to get lost, so I lost my temper."

Malone decided the story was so ridiculous it had to be true. "When did you see Hardy last?" he asked.

"This morning. He couldn't get the outboard started. I went over to help him."

"He act any differently this morning than usual?"

"Not that you could notice. He thought kicking the outboard and cursing it would make it work. It took him less than a minute after I got there to blame me for the motor not starting. I finally got it going for him, he stowed his gear and took off."

"You like to hunt, Mr. Price?" The heads mounted on the wall and the well-polished rifles in the gun cabinet made the question unnecessary.

"In my younger days," said Price. "Now I just stalk them. I gave up killing a long time ago."

"Were you in your cabin when the explosion took place?"

"No. I went for a walk after breakfast. I was on the trail that circles the lake."

"Anyone with you?"

"Alone." He hesitated. "I hoped to meet Noreen Hardy, but she didn't show up."

"This thing between you and Mrs. Hardy. There have been rumors . . ."

"The rumors are true," said Price dryly. "Why do you think I got so mad when she told me to take off?"

"And she's had a change of heart?"

"Evidently. Don't ask me to explain it."

"Someone will have to," said Fulton. "I'll probably be back."

Fulton led the way to the trail above the cabins, a footpath through the trees that wandered from shore to halfway up the surrounding hills, following the outline of the lake.

Fulton waved. "This is where he says he was. What do you think so far?"

"Nothing," said Malone. "You don't need me. You need an expert with a crystal ball. If I ran into something like this in the city, I think I'd ask for a transfer to the traffic division."

Fulton grinned wryly. "Don't ever say we don't do things different up here in the woods."

"Look at what you have: a man dead in an explosion out in the middle of a lake, no one near him; no solid evidence of what caused the explosion other than the expert opinion of one man, who says nothing normally on the boat could have exploded so violently; no clue as to what set the explosion off; nothing yet as to who put the explosive in the boat and how; your chief suspect not only with the opportunity but with no alibi.

"To top the whole thing off, your suspect, if he did do it, wasted his time because the woman he did it for has evidently thrown him over now, and he threatens to kill her, too. Will you please tell me why you couldn't leave me alone to fish in peace?"

"Because misery loves company," said Fulton. "Why should I go crazy by myself?"

"Take me back," said Malone wearily. "I'm just a hard-working cop on vacation, not a miracle man. If you get any more to go on, let me know and we'll talk about it."

The sun was gone when Malone, his dinner in his creel, decided to try one more cast and call it a day. He sighted along the rod, drew his arm up, and dropped the fly exactly where he wanted it—and suddenly realized how Price could have killed Hardy and left no evidence behind.

He reeled in his line and headed for his trailer. The evening had turned cool and dark clouds were rolling in from the west. Rain tonight, maybe all day tomorrow; another day wasted, even though the bone-dry forest could use a good soaking.

Malone shook his head. Next year he'd spend his vacation, if he could manage one, deep sea fishing at the shore.

He finished his brook trout and was relaxing with a cigarette when headlights and the purr of an engine told him he had a visitor. Malone moved to the shadow of the trailer.

The car stopped and Fulton moved into the firelight.

Malone stepped out.

"Why are you hiding?" Fulton was puzzled.

"Not hiding. Just being careful. You're supposed to have a killer running loose."

"I never thought of that. Maybe you'd better stay clear of things from now on. I certainly don't want you getting hurt."

"You get anything?"

Fulton shook his head. "Don't know any more than I did this afternoon. I wanted to ask what you thought I ought to do. Call in the state police? Hold the inquest and let it go as death at the hands of someone unknown?"

"That won't close your investigation, will it?"

"No, but remember, these are summer people. They'll scatter, principals and witnesses both, in a couple of weeks, and that will be the end of it."

"Questioned Mrs. Hardy yet?"

Fulton grinned wryly. "Every time I come near her, she breaks into tears."

"Take a guess. Is she just emotional, or evading questioning?"

"I'm no psychologist. All I can do is try to talk to her."

"If Price is your man, I have an idea how he could have done it," Malone said slowly.

"That's more than I could come up with. How?"

"He could have planted some dynamite left over from clearing those trees almost any time. Could have substituted a gasoline can with a false bottom holding the explosive, for instance. Later, sitting on the hillside above the cover, he could have put a bullet into the dynamite whenever he pleased. That could account for no traces of a timer, and for the girl's hearing a crack before the sound of the explosion."

Fulton fingered his jaw. "He could do it, too. He has the rifles and he's good enough with them. But suppose someone saw him carrying a rifle through the woods?"

"No one did, or you haven't turned anyone up yet."

"Still not enough to pick him up," Fulton said sadly.

"You might get a break," Malone encouraged him. "If he killed Hardy, he did it to get Hardy's wife, but she doesn't want him now. What's his next step?"

Fulton whistled softly. "Since he's already threatened her, I can see him going after Noreen Hardy."

"You have someone watching Price?"

"I don't have a fifty-man force. What I want something done, I do it myself."

"Then I wish you luck, and you'd better have a raincoat handy."

Listening to the rain beating on the trailer, Malone found himself feeling sorry for Fulton. If Price was his man, waiting in the rain would be worth it. And if it wasn't Price, then who?

Everything pointed to Price. There was no getting away from it, and maybe that was what was wrong with the whole thing.

Malone's fingers began imitating the drumming of the rain on the roof. Something was wrong somewhere and he couldn't quite pin it down. He felt as if he and Fulton had been led by the nose down a road someone meant them to travel. No matter how you looked at it, evidence or no evidence, it always came down to the people involved.

Take Noreen Hardy. If she was fooling around with Price, and then threw him over when her husband was dead and she was free, she obviously wasn't interested in him except for one of two things: either she wanted him to do the job, or she was setting him up to look as if he'd done it.

Or take Price himself. If he had done it, would he be egotistical enough to set it up so that everything pointed to him, then defy Fulton to prove it? Or would he behave like anyone else, knowing he'd be the chief suspect, and cover his tracks as much as possible?

Malone leaned back and stared at the ceiling before reaching for his rain gear.

The Hardy house was dimly lit. Malone's flashlight beam found the path through the trees as rain rustled through the leaves and touched tree trunks with dark, shining wetness. A thoroughly miserable night, thought Malone, hoping he'd flush out Fulton before reaching the cabin.

Halfway down the path, a dark figure stepped out in front of him.

"Put out that damned light," said Fulton. "It's a good thing I recognized you when you got out of the car."

"Who is in the cabin?"

"I put Kasky on as deputy. He's keeping Mrs. Hardy company."

"While you stand out here in the rain?"

"I want to be able to move around, not stay cooped up. I've been wet before."

"Price in his cabin?"

"He sure is. As far as I know, he hasn't left it go get at her. Hasn't even talked to her since this morning."

"Those cabins have phones?"

"Some do, some don't. Both of these do."

A bobbing light left Price's house and headed for the Hardy's.

"Then he goes," whispered Fulton. "Let him go in. I told Kasky to hide if someone came to the door, so he'll cover her from inside while we cover from out here."

The light approached the house, hesitated, went out as the door opened.

Malone and Fulton moved quietly through the rain to the door.

"This is no good," complained Malone. "You won't hear or see anything from out here. If it were an ordinary summer night, the windows would be open. In this rain, the house is closed tighter than a drum.

"I really don't expect anything to happen," said Fulton. "I wouldn't be that lucky. Price will probably talk to her, and that's it."

Malone thought of the unpleasant look on Price's face and was sure Price wouldn't settle for just talking.

The shot came with dull suddenness. Fulton beat Malone through the door, taking the wind and the rain with them, to see Price sprawled awkwardly on the floor, a knife near his outstretched hand. Noreen Hardy crouched against the wall, and Kasky, gun in hand, stood staring at the body.

"I had no choice," said Kasky. "He came at her with the knife."

Fulton called for the ambulance, which took Price away, dead, and Noreen Hardy on a stretcher because she needed a sedative. Fulton locked up the cabin.

In Fulton's little office in town, the three men sat, drying out and drinking coffee.

"That settles it, I suppose," said Fulton. "It was Price all the way."

Kasky was nursing his cup of coffee. "I'm sorry I had to kill him."

Malone looked at him. For a man who had just killed another, he looked very calm.

"Maybe that was what we were supposed to think," he said slowly. "Price was the fall guy all along."

They stared at him.

'Someone else set Price up, with the help of Mrs. Hardy, and only one man could have done it."

"You're crazy," said Kasky.

"Not me." He turned to Fulton. "Who first said dynamite had been used?"

Fulton thought. "Kasky."

"Exactly. Just think of all the answers he gave you, free of charge. Dynamite. No timing device. If there had been one, only he could have brought it up from the bottom of the lake or left it there. Who told us about the rumors concerning Price and Mrs. Hardy? Kasky.

"Suppose the explosive wasn't planted on the boat at all? Who could swim around underwater in that cove without being seen? Kasky. Who is the underwater demolitions expert? Kasky. He could have fastened it without Hardy's knowing it. You want to prove it? Get another diver to go over that lake bottom. I'm sure you'll find something Kasky conveniently overlooked. Start asking around to see who noticed Kasky and Mrs. Hardy together. I'll bet she spent a great deal of time in his hardware store and, when you come right down to it, whose idea was it for him to be in Noreen Hardy's cabin?"

"His idea," said Fulton grimly. "He volunteered, just like he volunteered to do the diving."

"There's a phone in the cabin. Want to bet Noreen Hardy didn't call Price to come over? Want to bet Price never brought that knife with him?"

"That's where you're wrong," said Kasky softly. "He had the knife all right, and he would have used it. I killed him to save Noreen's life, and I did it as a legally sworn deputy. You won't hang that on me."

"Maybe not," said Malone. "But I'm sure Fulton will hang Hardy's killing on you, especially if Mrs. Hardy decides talking is a good idea, which just might be the case. I don't think she expected you to kill Price."

Fulton beckoned to Kasky. "Maybe you'd better wait in a cell, George, until we can go through the formalities. I don't feel like chasing you, if you decide to run."

"You'll never make this stick. Malone's out of his mind."

Fulton shrugged. "Then you'll go back to your hardware store with my apologies."

When Fulton came back, Malone pushed to his feet and slipped into his raincoat. "You wanted advice and an opinion. You have them. Can you handle it from here on in?"

"If I can't, I don't deserve to win that election this fall. You going back to fishing?"

"In this weather? You'll find me in my trailer, reading."

Fulton grinned. "Good book?"

"Supposed to be," said Malone. "About a detective who really moves. Three beautiful women fall in love with him, he shoots six gang members between the eyes, gets beat up ten times, and finally corners the murderer on the roof of the tallest building in town."

Fulton held the door open for him. "Just like you."

"Not exactly," said Malone wearily. "I understand he gets a real vacation at the end."

John Lutz
Understanding Electricity

Glistening with chrome and tinted glass, the headquarters of the Powacky Valley Light and Power Company soared needlelike fifty stories heavenward, as if taunting the lightning. In the building's top floor were the spacious, ultramodern offices of the company's top executives, and in a tasteful outer office sat the moderately attractive, though impeccably groomed, Miss Knickelsworth. She smiled with her impeccably white teeth, lighting up her whole mouth if not her face and unchanging wide brown eyes, and said, "Mr. Appleton from out of town is already in the conference room, Mr. Bolt."

B. Bainbridge Bolt, president of Powacky Valley Light and Power, revealed his own capped dentures, nodded, and strode briskly past her and through a tall doorway. He was the "human dynamo"-type executive in image and action, and was proud to think of himself as such.

Behind Bolt, Elleson of Public Relations entered the office with a PR smile for Miss Knickelsworth as he strode through the tall doorway.

Five minutes later young Ivers, regional vice-president and re-nowned hard charger, went into the conference room. The smile he flashed on Miss Knickelsworth was his bachelor's best, but she responded with the blank expression that had earned her the company title of "Miss Resistor" two years running.

Grossner of Advertising followed Ivers in, then old Stabler of Customer Relations, who was something of a fixture with the company. The tall doors were silently closed on the outer office wherein sat Miss Knickelsworth, and after orderly hellos and introductions the immaculately attired, somehow similar men all sat down at a long, tinted-glass conference table with gleaming chrome legs and trim. The table matched the glass and metallic decor of the large room. Everyone had his accustomed place at the long table but for Appleton from out of town, who remained where he'd been sitting at ease in his chrome-armed chair at the opposite end of the table from B. Bainbridge Bolt, who cleared his throat and drew a slip of paper from his attaché case.

With a nod to Appleton from out of town, Bolt said, "There is some business to be discussed before we get on to Mr. Appleton's investiga-tion of yesterday's five o'clock power failure ... if Mr. Appleton agrees."

"Surely," Appleton said, nodding ever so slightly his handsome head of flawlessly combed graying hair.

"We have something of a public relations problem," Bolt went on, "concerning our last raise in the rates for electricity. Let me read you this note that arrived in the morning mail."

He placed gold-rimmed reading glasses on the narrow bridge of his nose and glanced commandingly at each man. The note read:

Gentlemen:

I was shocked by your letter stating that my monthly bill was ten days past due. At your current rates, I'm afraid that you find me a little short. However, I do believe ten days is rather a brief period of neglect and that it does not behoove a company of your stature to conduct yourself in such a negative manner. In farewell, I regretfully must fuse and refuse to send your requested remittance, and as another futile outlet for my frustration I have wired my congressman direct.

Tired of plugging away,

A. C. McCord

Bolt lowered the slip of paper, sat back and sipped on a glass of juice from the silver tray Miss Knickelsworth had left on the table.

After a pause, Stabler of Customer Relations said, "The work of a madman in its phrasing, but other than that it seems the usual sort of letter we receive."

"There's one other difference," Bolt said dramatically. "This is a suicide note."

"That should solve part of our problem right there," young Ivers said. "Especially since this McCord was obviously unbalanced when he wrote such a letter."

"How did he commit suicide?" Stabler asked.

"He wrote and mailed this note yesterday," Bolt said, resting his large clean palms on the metal table trim. "He left a carbon copy in his home; then, during our Karl and Karla Killowatt commercial before the five o'clock news yesterday afternoon, he pulled his radio into the water in his bathtub with him."

Grossner of Advertising looked concerned.

Bolt sat unnaturally still, as if waiting for something.

"Wait a minute!" young Ivers said. "Is this McCord—"

"Still alive." Bolt finished the sentence without a question mark.

"Of course!" Elleson said. "The power failure at five yesterday! It must have coincided with his pulling the radio into the tub with him."

"Almost," Bolt said. "McCord was found stunned, in a state of shock, but still alive. He'd also left a message for a reporter friend, explaining what he was going to do, and his story was written up in the papers for tonight's late edition."

"But the man's obviously a maniac," Ivers said.

"Remember," Grossner cautioned, "our last rate increase was legal, but not what an uneducated public would call ethical."

"They were notified of the public hearings," Ivers said, referring to the public notices in the newspapers that Elleson and Grossner had cleverly worded for maximum confusion.

"There were the necessary three people at the meeting," Elleson said. "The vote constituted a majority."

"No one is arguing the legality of the last increase," Bolt said sharply, to stop that area of discussion. "That and the subject of this meeting are poles apart. What we have here is a problem in maintaining some rapport with the public, and I've taken some steps to insulate us from any critical comment."

"If the story will be printed showing us in an unfavorable light," Ivers said, "it seems that the cat is already out of the bag."

"What I have done," B. Bainbridge Bolt said, "is to change the nature of the cat."

Elleson, the PR man, nodded approvingly, though he resented not being consulted on the matter. Appleton from out of town chuckled softly.

"We have taken space in both daily newspapers to remark on the silver-lining-in-every-cloud aspect of a power failure saving a life." Bolt paused.

"There's a switch," Ivers said brightly.

"Excellent," Elleson said admiringly, but he wondered if it was.

"Agreed," Grossner said, "but won't it also draw further attention to the incident?"

"To continue," Bolt cut them off reprovingly, having successfully sprung one of his little conversational traps, "we will then explain how Powacky Valley Light and Power is generously paying for the would-be suicide victim's complete recovery."

"Great!" Grossner said. "Really socket to 'em!"

"I believe we will have gone full circuit," Bolt said smugly. "Transformed a lemon into lemonade."

Everyone laughed as always at the familiar lemon analogy.

"But how do we know he *will* recover?" Ivers asked. "People who unsuccessfully attempt suicide usually try again."

Bolt shrugged. "Doesn't matter. The whole thing will be out of the public's collective mind in a week or so. This McCord ought to stay alive that long. Right now he's confined in the psychiatric ward at State Hospital at our expense, undergoing electrotherapy treatment."

"Can you be sure of that?" Appleton from out of town said.

"Of course," B. Bainbridge Bolt said.

Appleton smiled indulgently. "I mean, what if he escaped? What if he somehow made his way here, to Powacky Valley Headquarters?"

"I get it," Grossner said. "He could do something drastic—generate some tremendous adverse publicity."

"Not only drastic," Appleton said, "but fantastically daring and grand."

Bolt squinted at Appleton. Several throats were cleared.

"Security isn't very tight here," Appleton said. "An imaginative man could find out things, make his way to the top."

Bolt leaned forward in his chair and cocked his head. "You're not—"

"Correct," Appleton from out of town said. "A. C. McCord, at your service."

Ivers' eyes widened. "But ... where's Appleton?"

"Tangled up in some high-voltage lines, actually," McCord said, placing a small black box on the table. He smiled. "I took the liberty of attaching some wires to the table and chairs," he said, "so together you can all experience with me, one of your many customers, the unpleasant sensation of being overcharged," and he pressed a button on the box.

"Watt now?" Miss Knickelsworth asked herself in the outer office as her electric typewriter suddenly went dead.

Anne Morice
False Alarm

At seven twenty-three P.M. on Wednesday, June eighth, a warm and cloudless evening, the Swains Lodge burglar alarm rang in the Maresfield police station eight miles away. A call was put out to the patrol cars and was answered by Police Constables Fiske and Gillespie, then four miles northwest of Swains village, who were instructed to proceed to the Lodge. They turned into the driveway exactly thirteen minutes later, which broke all previous records. They were nevertheless at least ten minutes too late.

The Lodge was separated from its nearest neighbors by a large flower garden and paddock on one side and several acres of woodland on the other, but a number of private citizens still heard the alarm.

Air Marshal Stevenson and his wife, Pamela, were sitting on their terrace, sipping pre-dinner sherries and not finding much to say to each other. This was a new and disagreeable experience for them both. Their marriage, which had endured for thirty-five years, had been exceptionally harmonious, and occasions of this kind were normally animated by the cosy exchange of news and gossip.

However, a month had gone by since Dick Stevenson's retirement from the air ministry—a month in which they had been required to spend more time in each other's company than they really liked. To Pamela's increasing dismay, instead of using his new-found leisure to improve his golf game, chop and store firewood for the winter, or take the dogs for long walks in the Harmans' woods, Dick was beset by a craving for constant reassurance that he was still the human being about whom her life revolved, and not a castoff, expendable has-been.

Unhappier still, his sense of disorientation and insecurity had led him to take on a number of unnecessary household chores for which he was totally unfit. Only that morning Pamela had exhausted herself finding tactful ways to fend off his proposal to rearrange the entire kitchen to make it more efficient for her.

And so the burglar alarm, piercing faintly through the peaceful evening, came as a welcome diversion.

"Not the Lodge again surely?" Pamela asked, looking quite animated.

"It sounds distinctly like it, I must say," Dick admitted. "Allowing for wind direction and one thing and another, I'd be inclined to say that's where it's coming from."

"Wind direction, my foot!" Pamela said, forgetting herself. "You know as well as I do that the Harmans are the only people around here with a contraption like that."

"It doesn't seem to do them much good, though."

"Apart from advertising to all and sundry that they've got plenty worth stealing," Pamela said. "Maisie Harman thinks it's a crazy idea, but she told me the insurance company insisted on their installing this very sophisticated alarm system after their second burglary. This one makes how many? Four?"

"Must be three or four," Dick agreed.

"Including the time their London place was burgled while they were down here. They'd no sooner gone back to tidy things up there than the Lodge was broken into."

"Yes—some people seem to have all the bad luck, don't they? Bad show too, in this case, seeing what a goodhearted, generous couple they are. Do you think I should wander down and see what's going on?"

"No, Dick. I do not! The alarm rings in the police station. It's their job to cope with it."

"Yes, but remember how long it took them to get up here last time? I might at least prevent those swine getting away scot free. I could probably manage to block the drive with our car."

"And get the car smashed up for your pains? Have you forgotten how they knocked the gate down that time, in their stampede to get away, when some well-meaning person tried to shut them in? Besides, they'll have grabbed whatever they came for and be miles away by the time you could get there," Pamela added, with the inconsistency which, lately, Dick was beginning to find profoundly irritating.

The alarm was also heard a hundred yards up the lane in the saloon bar of the White Hart, this Wednesday evening being, as so often, a quiet one. Two old men were playing a slow game of dominoes, a youth and his girlfriend nursed their crash helmets and sipped shandy in stony silence on a bench near the door, and Peter Logan was standing at the bar chatting to Molly Taglett, the landlord's wife.

He had arrived about five minutes earlier and had been greeted by a shout from Molly. "Evening, Pete! Message for you. Your wife's been on the blower."

"Oh, really? When was that?"

"Oh, 'bout ten minutes ago—no more. She said to tell you one's your limit tonight. You're needed at home—seems you've got company. Nice thing, isn't it, for me to tell the customers to push off the minute they stick their noses round the door?"

"Better make it a short one then, Molly. Scotch on the rocks, if you'd be so good."

"Coming up! And she wants you to take a bottle of the claret with you," Molly said, holding a glass against the mouth of a bottle she held upside down above her head. "I've just been to fetch one up from the cellar. It's over on the side there. How's that for service?"

"Terrific as usual. What's up, then?" Logan asked. "Jack taking the evening off?"

"Not exactly. He had to go to the dentist, poor old Jack."

"Bit late for that, isn't it?" Peter asked, leaning on the counter.

"Didn't have any choice, did he? Woke up during the night, see, screaming in agony. He thought it must be an abscess or something, but the dentist didn't have a single appointment to give him right through the day. He told Jack as it was an emergency he'd see him after surgery hours, at half past six, it was the best he could do. And won't Jack be in a find old state when he gets home? Expecting me to trot up and down with hot milk and brandy half the night, I shouldn't wonder. No peace for the wicked, eh? Still, it could be worse—it's always pretty dead in here Wednesday evenings."

It was then that they both heard the faint, far-off, unmistakable whine of the burglar alarm. The pair on the bench remained as impassive as ever, and although one of the domino players briefly raised his head and sucked hard on his pipe, this could have indicated that he was merely working out his next diabolical move.

"Oh, not again!" Molly said.

"Not what again?"

"Another break-in at the Lodge. You must have heard about them. It must be the third time they've copped it in a year. Wait a bit though. That's funny!"

"Funny for whom?"

"I didn't mean like that. I was thinking it doesn't happen as a rule when they're staying down here. The thieves generally wait till they're back in London, to give themselves a clear field."

"And what makes you think they haven't gone back to London? Don't they only use the place for weekends?"

"Well, no, not always. Sometimes they stay down during the week this time of year, when we've got the fête and the cricket matches and all the rest of it. The funny thing is that I happened to notice a car by their front door when I went by this morning. The gate was wide open, too."

"Probably just a delivery van or something."

"Could be. It looked like a private car, though. Oh, well, damn all we can do about it," said Molly.

"I don't know," Peter said, finishing off his drink and reaching over to pick up the bottle of claret. "It's a bit out of my way, but I suppose it wouldn't do any harm to go round by the Lodge and take a look. I mean, if by some chance these chaps have miscalculated and Mrs. Harman should be there on her own, things could be a bit dodgy."

"I wouldn't if I was you. You can bet they checked the place was empty before they went in, and you could be in real trouble if there happened to be three or four of them on the job. Besides, it rings down at the station and the police will be on their way by now. I daresay they wouldn't thank you for interfering."

"That's true—and I admit I'm not really cut out for heroics. Apart from which, I'll probably be in for all the trouble I can cope with if I don't push off home pretty soon. Good night, Molly. Give Jack my commiserations and don't go stinting him on the hot milk and brandy."

"No—and you drive carefully, mind. We don't want this place getting a bad name and there'll be coppers about this evening."

"Too right," he agreed, pausing by the door. "'Night, then. Be seeing you."

The White Hart was set a few yards back from the lane and had a gravel front yard large enough to accommodate half a dozen cars. Peter Logan's was the only car there, and there was a motorcycle parked in the center of the remaining space. As he came out of the pub he heard the growl of a motor engine approaching in low gear. Two seconds later a black Cortina came swinging sharply toward him, causing him to jump to one side. The driver noticed the bike just in time but, in swerving to avoid it, slightly grazed the rear offside of his car against the telephone kiosk at the corner of the lane.

"Jack seems to be in a bit of a hurry," Peter remarked, climbing into his own car, where his passenger was already waiting. "And how are you, by the way? Everything okay?"

"Everything's just fine."

"Well done! I got the plonk, incidentally," he added, switching on the ignition, and they both laughed.

At seven forty-five P.C. Fiske telephoned the station from Swains Lodge to report and to ask for instructions and assistance. Three police cars set out from Maresfield approximately ten minutes later. These contained Inspector Watson, accompanied by a sergeant, closely followed by a team of photographers and fingerprint experts and a second sergeant and the police surgeon bringing up the rear. P.C. Fiske, having now positioned himself by the front door of the Lodge, saluted as the inspector stepped out. "This way, sir," he said.

"Just a minute, Fiske. Before we get started, how did they get in?"

"Downstairs cloakroom, sir, round the back. Leaded window and just the one pane broken—enough to get a hand in and release the catch. It was the only one in the whole house that wasn't double glazed so far as we've been able to ascertain."

"And Mrs. Harman?"

"In the lounge, sir."

"Right. Be with you in a moment."

The inspector walked over to the second car, which had just drawn up, put his head in the window, issued some instructions to the occupants, and then returned to the front door.

"All right, Fiske. Lead the way."

There seemed to be very little out of place in the room Fiske had described as the lounge but which its owners called the drawing room. Some books had been removed from a glass-fronted cabinet and thrown on the floor, two or three bureau drawers were opened and their contents disturbed, and a Dufy painting of sailing boats and parasols on an expanse of green water was on the floor , exposing a small built-in safe it had concealed on the wall. But to the naked eye, at least, no attempt had been made to open the safe.

The inspector's principal concern was with Mrs. Harman, who was lying face down on a Persian rug beside the fireplace. The back of her skull had been smashed in. After a cursory examination, Dr. Elliott, the police surgeon, gave it as his opinion that she had been struck from behind with a blunt instrument, and that death had occurred within the previous thirty to fifty minutes. P. C. Fiske was privately of the opinion that this was one verdict that could have been arrived at without benefit of an expensive medical training.

By twenty minutes to ten the ambulance and technicians had departed and Inspector Watson had performed the disagreeable task of locating Mr. Harman at his London club and breaking the news to him. He delegated P. C. Gillespie to remain on duty at the Lodge until relieved, then turned to Fiske and issued a more complicated set of instructions.

In pursuance of these, as he himself was later to put it, Constable Fiske drew up outside the White Hart five minutes before closing time.

The public bar was dark and empty and there was no one left in the saloon except Molly, who was listening to a Big Band program on the radio as she sloshed dirty glasses through a trough of water beneath the counter.

"What's this, then?" she asked, switching off the radio as he entered. "Jumping the gun a bit, aren't we? Still five minutes to go, I'd like you to know."

"In that case," Fiske replied, seating himself at the bar, "what's it to be?"

"Oh, well, that's very nice of you. Thanks, I'll have a bitter lemon, if you don't mind. I don't want to be unsociable, but I've got a long night ahead by the look of things. What can I get you?" she asked.

"I'll have the same, please. Seeing as I'm on duty."

"You are? Oh, of course, I get it now. You mean the Harmans? There really has been another break-in at the Lodge?"

"That's right," said P. C. Fiske. "Didn't you hear the alarm?"

"Oh, sure—but those things go off by mistake as often as not, don't they? Somebody forgets they're switched on and opens a window or something."

"Not this time."

"That right? They take much?"

"I can't say for sure till the owner gets here. It doesn't look like it, though."

"So why all the panic?"

"No panic, Mrs. Taglett. Just a few routine inquiries, if you'll be so good."

"I know. Like whether we've had any strangers in lately—men with stockings over their heads, that kind of thing."

"And have you?"

"Sorry to disappoint you, but the answer's no. We get our usual share of ships that pass in the night. Had a couple in this evening, as it happens, but nothing in your line."

"How do you know?"

"Well, I just know, that's all. It was a young fellow and his girl. Come on a motor bike. Never seen them before and shan't worry if I never do again. They were here about forty minutes and a couple of shandys was the sum total. Besides, they were sitting over there good as gold when the alarm went off, so that's no interest to you, is it?"

"Who else was in tonight?"

"Well, let's see now. Apart from the three or four regulars in the public, who come at five thirty and bang on the door if we're two minutes late opening, and Brothers Charlie and Bert with their domino set, as per, I don't think there's been a bleeding soul. No, hang on a bit, I'm a liar! Pete Logan dropped in for a few minutes. But he's a regular, too, in a manner of speaking. Often stops off here on his way home of an evening."

"Logan? I can't call that name to mind. Is he a local, too?"

"He is now—him and his wife. They're a nice young couple and real country types, for all he works in London. Very busy with the gardens committee, secretary of the village cricket club, you name it. They moved into Campion Cottage when old Goodchild went to live with his daughter. Know who I mean?"

"Roughly. How long ago was that? Eighteen months? Two years?"

"Yes. Doesn't time fly? But they're all right, the Logans are. When we heard that alarm go off, Pete would have been all set to go down to the Lodge and investigate if I hadn't stopped him. He was afraid it could have been rough on Mrs. Harman if she happened to be there on her own."

"So why did you stop him?" Fiske asked.

"Are you joking? I pointed out that these chaps can turn nasty—but they're usually pretty well behaved so long as no one tries to get in their way. Or so I've heard."

"That's not always true, unfortunately."

"No? Somebody got hurt, then? Oh, I know, I know—you're here to ask questions, not answer them. But Pete was in here propping up the bar when the alarm sounded, so that's a washout, too, isn't it? I'm sorry I can't be more help."

"Oh, I wouldn't say that. We can't afford to overlook anything. You say he was on his way home from London—so he must have gone past the Lodge before he got here. There's just a chance he'd have noticed something out of the way. Anyway, I'd better clear it, I suppose, before I report back. You don't happen to know the Logans' telephone number? It might be more tactful to give them a ring before I go barging in."

"Not offhand, but not to worry. They've got company tonight, so they'll still be up. Anyway, you can't ring them, come to think of it. Their number's out of order."

"Oh, is it? How do you know that?" he asked.

She set her glass down on the counter with a thump and stared at him, her mouth open. "Since you mention it, I don't know, do I? And it's not true anyway. She rang me up only this evening to ask me to tell him to take a bottle of wine home. Now there's a funny thing! I must be dreaming or going bonkers or something. All the excitement, I suppose."

"I expect so."

"I'm afraid I can't tell you their number, but they'll be in the book by now. The phone's out in the passage. The brewers don't allow us to let customers use it—they have to make do with the public one out-side—but I expect there'd be an exception for you, seeing as it's official business."

"I don't think I'll bother," said Fiske, "since you think they'll still be up. I'll just get along there right away. What about the other lot," he added, collecting his hat and gloves from a bar stool, "the people just up the road? Any chance of finding them at home, watching the ten o'clock news?"

"No good asking me, we're not on those terms. Air Marshal Toffee Nose looks in occasionally on a Sunday morning to patronize the peasantry or when he's run out of cigarettes, but we never see her, so your guess is as good as mine."

"I'll have to chance it, then. Good night, Mrs. Taglett, and thanks for all your help."

When he had gone, Molly swilled out their two glasses in the trough, left them upside down to drain, and went over to lock and bolt the door. After a final look around, she switched off the lights and went upstairs to relate the whole saga to Jack, who was not in a receptive mood.

"Something fishy about it, if you ask me," she announced at the end of her recital.

"What way, fishy?" Jack inquired, drawing the sheet and blankets up to his neck as though to protect himself.

"Oh, you know—'just routine,' he says, in that cheesy voice they put on—but you know as well as I do, Jack, this isn't the first time the Harmans have had this trouble, poor things, and when have we ever had the coppers round before, just answer me that?"

But Jack either could not or would not. He rolled his head sideways, placed the hot water bottle against his jaw, and closed his eyes. Molly sighed, picked up the empty tumbler, and plodded downstairs to make him another hot drink.

It was not part of his assignment, but training and sheer force of habit caused Fiske to make a brief inspection of the yard before leaving. There were several tire marks in the gravel, some of which he identified as belonging to a motorcycle, which had evidently tipped over at one point. The driver's door of the black Cortina was locked, as was the one behind it, and there were some unidentifiable lumpy objects on the back seat, covered by a piece of sacking. It was while running his torch over the two nearside doors, which were also locked, that he noticed some traces of red paint on the otherwise clean bodywork. From them, he glanced automatically at the telephone kiosk a few yards away. It had a new looking scratch on it at about the right level, and he found himself staring at it in an abstracted fashion for almost a minute. However, it was scratched and dented in a good many other places as well and badly in need of a coat of paint, and he recognized that, even in conjunction with some other information that had come his way during the past ten minutes, he was still a long way from proving anything.

There being nothing more to delay him at the White Hart, he climbed into his car, still deep in thought, and proceeded to his next two ports of call. However, his luck ran out, for there were no lights showing in the Stevensons' house and, as he discovered a few minutes later, the occupants of Campion Cottage had also apparently retired.

All right for some, he thought, then opened his notebook and jotted down some of the facts he had gleaned before driving back to the station to incorporate them into his report.

Three weeks later Fiske tapped on the door of the chief superintendent's office and was told to enter.

The chief was going through a stack of folders on his desk. After glancing up briefly, he turned over a page with one hand and with the other gestured to Fiske to be seated.

"Be with you in a minute, Fiske," he said.

"Thank you, sir."

Two or three minutes went by before the chief superintendent closed the file.

"I've just been going through Inspector Watson's report on the Harman case. There are some interesting features."

"Yes, sir."

"And you appear to have distinguished yourself, constable," the superintendent said, thinking to himself, I'm beginning to sound like a bloody schoolmaster.

"Thank you very much, sir," Fiske replied, sounding modest and eager, like a bloody head prefect.

"Yes, and Inspector Watson has given you quite a writeup. I'm not inclined to think it will cause any serious delay in your promotion either."

"Thank you, sir," Fiske said again after a slight hesitation.

"Well, Fiske, you understand, of course, that this is off the record and principally, I should add, to satisfy my own curiosity, but this report naturally confines itself to bare facts—I'd be interested to learn what first put you on to this pair of beauties?"

"It was really Mrs. Taglett who gave the game away, sir. She's rather a chatty sort of person," said Fiske.

"That was lucky for you."

"Yes, sir. Very lucky indeed."

"Still, all credit to you for taking advantage of the fact. Precisely which beans did this garrulous lady spill into your lap?"

"There were really three things," the constable said. "The first was her telling me how the Logans had dug themselves in up here, even though they were newcomers, in a sense. Like him being secretary of the cricket club and all that sort of thing."

"That doesn't sound particularly heinous."

"No, sir, perhaps not—but then, you see, I already knew—that is, everyone knew—than Mr. and Mrs. Harman were dead keen on these village affairs and were always coughing up contributions for one thing or another, so it gave me a possible connection between them and Logan."

"Tenuous, but worth pursuing, as you've proved. What was the second thing?"

"That also was a bit—what was that word, sir?"

"Tenuous?"

"That's right. It was Mrs. Taglett telling me that after the alarm had gone off Logan was all for going down to investigate, only she put him off the idea. But it's the reason he gave that was interesting. He said it would be rough on Mrs. Harman if she were up at the house on her own, and that struck me as funny. What I mean is—we happened to know that she actually had been there on her own and he might have known it, too, if he hadn't been in London all day, or if he'd been home first and seen his wife. But Mrs. Harman didn't normally come down without her husband, and I wondered why he thought she might have done this time. It made me wonder whether it could possibly be that she'd had an appointment with Logan—something about the cricket club, for instance. Quite a jump in the dark, you might say, but what really made me feel it was worth following up was the bit about the telephone."

"The telephone?"

"Mrs. Taglett mentioned that the Logans' phone was out of order, but when I asked her how she knew she couldn't tell me. She'd just spoken without thinking. But a few minutes afterwards I saw that kiosk they've got there on the corner and it struck me the reason Mrs. Taglett might have said what she said what she did was because Mrs. Logan had rung her up about the wine from a public call box. Mrs. Taglett was singlehanded that evening and probably not paying much attention, so it hadn't properly sunk in."

"Yes. I see. Go on, Fiske."

"None of it meant very much on its own, sir, but when I got up to the Logans' house there wasn't a light on anywhere, so either they were out or they were having an early night. Whichever it was, they had been lying about having company.

"Well, how I worked that out was like this, sir. If it had been a bottle of gin or scotch, say, that Mr. Logan was to take home with him, that might have been because they were expecting company in the early part of the evening—but wine usually means dinner, doesn't it? Anyway, with people like them it does, and I couldn't somehow swallow the idea that they'd had friends in to dinner, seen them off, done a bit of tidying up, and gone to bed with the lights switched off, all by half past ten."

"Yes, one might be forgiven for finding that unusual, and so I suppose at that point you suspected that telephone call about the wine must have been bogus. Mrs. Logan hadn't needed it at all—it was simply a prearranged code they'd fixed up between them."

"Something like that did occur to me, yes, sir," Fiske admitted, looking so crestfallen at this usurpation of his role that the superintendent felt constrained to toss the ball gently back into his court.

"Well, don't keep me in suspense!" he said. "Where did you go from there?"

"Well, sir, after I'd put it all together as you might say, I decided to try a bit of reconstruction. Supposing Logan calls at the Lodge on his way home? Mrs. Harman is expecting him and lets him in herself, but he has a pretty good idea what she wants to talk to him about and he's already made up his mind to kill her."

"Not a bad guess. He'd been forging checks, hers among them. She was always doling out checks for a new cricket pavilion and so forth—so he'd had plenty of opportunity to study her handwriting. It looks like Mrs. Harman had begun to suspect him, but being a decent soul, she wouldn't tell her husband about it until Logan had had a chance to clear himelf. How about his car, though? He could hardly have risked being seen driving away in it?"

"He parked it off the road, a bit higher up on the edge of the wood, more likely, Plenty of picnickers and so on do that on such a fine evening, so it wouldn't have been remarked on."

"Yes, that'll do, I should think. And then?"

"Then he makes some excuse to get Mrs. Harman to turn her back on him and he clubs her. When he's sure she's dead, he turns the room over a bit to make it look like the thieves had lost their nerve and scarpered. Then he goes out by the back door, heaves a brick through the cloakroom window, comes back in again, leaving the door open for himself, and switches on the burglar alarm. Then all he has to do is walk out again and shut the back door behind him. The whole thing needn't have taken more than four or five minutes. It was the next part that was more dodgy.

"He'd have been able to tell, almost to the minute, what time he'd get to the White Hart, but it wouldn't have been all that straightforward for his wife. Someone could have dropped in, or rung up and gone on talking just when it was time for her to leave. That would have been awkward. He had to be in the pub when the alarm goes, so he'd want to know how long he'd got to wait for it, what to order and how fast to drink it, and that. So that would be why they rigged up their signal. The telephone call about the wine was to let him know her position and that she was all set to go into action."

"Well done, Fiske—I'm impressed! And what part of the action had you reserved for Mrs. Logan?"

"Once I'd got that far, sir, it began to seem obvious. All she had to do was cut through that corner of the wood, approach the house from the back, stick her hand through the broken window pane to release the catch, and set off the alarm. She didn't even need to go inside—just nip back the same way she'd come."

"I congratulate you, though I'm not certain you're right in every particular. That business of tumbling the room about, for instance, may not have been just artistic trimmings—we think it more likely that he was looking for a forged check or some evidence of that kind—but you weren't far off the mark. What you couldn't have known, because none of us did till later, was that Logan had already spent two years inside on a fraud and forgery charge. He changed his name when he came out, moved to a new locality, and set about becoming a pillar of village society."

"But the old habits proved too strong," Fiske said.

"That's the truth of it, I daresay. Well, thank you, Fiske. This has been illuminating and I shouldn't entirely blame you if you were feeling a trifle pleased with yourself."

"Oh, no, not all that much, sir," Fiske replied, displaying a return of the boyish modesty as he stood up to leave. "It was Mrs. Taglett who did most of the work. Besides, like you've always said yourself, sir, it's what seems like the unimportant details that really count—and once you've got enough of them you can't easily go wrong."

The superintendent, not noted for his sense of humor, watched him go with a gleam of wry amusement. He couldn't recall having uttered such words, but he no longer had any doubt at all that P. C. Fiske was destined for early promotion.

Gerald Tomlinson
Flight of the Sparrow

He examined the face critically, his appraising eyes taking in every metallic feature. The verdict was damning.

The scratch started a millimeter below Liberty's eye, cut straight down her cheek, sliced across her neck and through her dress, and nicked the top of the seven in 1799.

No scratch had been mentioned two years earlier in the auction catalogue's description of the U.S. Large Cent—no imperfection of any kind. "Red uncirculated," the catalogue had said. "Well-struck 1799–over–98 rarity. A superb specimen from the Brasyer Collection."

It was red, a deep uncirculated copper red, evenly colored and perfectly struck. There was no question about that. The aloof Miss Liberty, her bust chastely draped, had never looked better—except for that scratch. The restruck nine over eight in the date showed clearly even without the magnifier.

But the coin was spoiled by its flaw: a fatal flaw, an infuriating flaw. It was no bargain-basement coin, no throwaway even in its marred state, but it was not a connoisseur's item either, not a superb specimen. The scratch was deep, narrow, soul-lacerating.

Jago Strand, precise as an assayer in his movements, placed the coin on the top of his portable tabletop desk. His hands moved slowly in soft plastic gloves, surgeon's gloves, as he rubbed a speck of dust off the desk's polished ebony surface. Setting an attached magnifier aside, he snapped off the high-intensity lamp beside it, removed his gloves, and took a long sip of scotch.

He still had work to do, but it looked as if the work would be anticlimactic. He had hoped for a better night. The 1799–over–98 was the only coin of the seven that really made a difference. A key coin, a true rarity in uncirculated condition, it had been tonight's single target. It was intended to upgrade his U.S. Large Cent collection, to replace his Extremely Fine 9–over–8, a dark brown cent that had once belonged to a retired army colonel in East Tennessee. For two years Strand had wanted an uncirculated 9–over–8. Now he had it. But there was no way at all for this damaged Miss Liberty, gorgeous as she once must have been, to replace the colonel's lady—the scratch took care of that.

And because of the scratch, she would be dangerous to sell to a dealer. She was rare enough to be watched for. She was unique, in fact, in her present condition. A marked woman.

Strand knew he could dispose of the coin, but not across the counter. Not in person. He could sell it by mail to H. M. Luker, the discreet shadowy figure with an unlisted phone number and an unadvertised post office box in Cincinnati. But the value of the coin would be heavily discounted.

He could mail it to Luker, no questions asked, no explanations given, and receive a money order for maybe a thousand dollars. He would get his payment by return mail, care of General Delivery—where?—well, Pittsburgh would be convenient. He gave the idea some thought.

Leaning back in his desk chair at the Lord Hewitt Hotel, Jago Strand stretched his legs and studied the reflection of his face in the mirror. It was an ordinary face, a man-in-the-crowd face, the kind no one remembered. An ideal face for anonymity, it had served him well for most of his life. He was forty-eight, and he had been on the road, solitary and single-minded, for twenty-five years.

"The Sparrow," they called him in police circles, perhaps because he flitted in through windows opened with the aid of a glass-cutter and a suction cup, or more likely because once inside a house or apartment he never took more than ten coins, and seldom that many, no matter how large or dazzling the collection. It was his self-imposed limit. The numismatic journals, also struck by his tiny appetite, picked up the nickname "The Sparrow."

He stared hard at his reflected image. His face was round and unsparrowlike. Moon-shaped, with rimless glasses over wide brown eyes, it was a face without distinction—but also without post office notoriety. It was a face without a printed number, or a distinguishing-marks notation, or a list of federal offenses, or a string of known aliases. It was a face that could and did stay out of trouble.

But it was a face alive with purpose, if anyone had stopped to notice, which fortunately for the success of his enterprises no one did—at least no one who mattered.

Jago Strand, endowed with intelligence but little formal schooling, had always liked charitable gestures and a certain kind of drama. Tonight was a time for both. He took a small Jiffy shipping bag from one of the many compartments in his suitcase and, copying from his notebook, wrote out a name and address on it in a large childish script. The name was Reuben Armitage, and the address was a local one, a few miles from the hotel.

Until two hours ago Reuben Armitage had been the owner of the scratched Large Cent. Armitage had bought it for twenty thousand dollars at the New York auction disposing of the Brasyer estate. Strand pasted a fifty-cent stamp on the shipping bag and printed FIRST CLASS—SURPRISE! underneath it. He laid the bag on the hotel's TV set, to be mailed in the morning.

Next he opened a miniature leather wallet holding six other coins he had taken from the Armitage display case. Pulling on his gloves, moving the magnifier back in place, and snapping on the lamp, he started through his lesser gains.

The first three, all 1794 Large Cents, were in Very Good to Fine condition, desirable coins but fairly common and easy to sell to a legitimate dealer.

The fourth coin surprised him. A 1795 Large Cent, Lettered Edge, it had looked ordinary in the dim light of the Reuben Armitage library, but now it appeared to be an uncirculated specimen, almost as choice as the 9–over–8—and minus the scratch. Strand examined it minutely, skeptically at first, then appreciatively. Armitage had never displayed or acknowledged ownership of this coin, and Strand wondered why. He whistled softly. No minor item, this.

The last two Large Cents were not worth much: a 1796 "Liberty" Error in Fair condition and a counterfeit Chain Type 1793. He wondered if Armitage had known the 1793 was a phony. He supposed so. The distinguished old judge, a contributor to the *Red Book*, was regarded as an authority on early Large Cents.

Some collectors, Strand knew, would hold onto a counterfeit coin almost protectively rather than admit their error in buying it. Strand had never understood that attitude and found it strange that a collector of Armitage's stature would display a fake. To him a counterfeit coin was no better than a harlot masquerading as a great lady. A sham and a disgrace, such a coin deserved nothing but the garbage heap. He put it in the hotel's ashtray. Strand never knowingly sold a counterfeit.

Tossing his gloves on the bed, Strand poured himself another shot of scotch. He was proud of his U.S. Large Cent collection. With three more coins, it would be complete.

He had already finsihed every set of every higher-denomination coin through the gold Double Eagles.

Only Half Cents remained.

For twenty-five years he had concentrated on assembling these sets, one set at a time. He had never stolen coins outside his current field of focus, no matter how valuable they might be. Barber Dimes, his finest collection, had required nineteen months to complete and had taken him from Seattle to Sarasota.

After twenty-five years he could map out a three- or four-month itinerary with ease. He had crisscrossed the United States dozens of times. He loved the land, loved the open road, loved the shifting scenery. But he knew in his heart that his deepest response to the varied and striking geography would always be. "Kankakee is an 1866 Proof Nickel"; "Butte is an 1854–S Quarter Eagle"; "Santa Barbara is an 1878–CC Trade Dollar"; "Natchez is an 1883–O Eagle."

Of course, the unexpected sometimes occurred, like last week's out-of-the-blue report in *Coin World* of this 9–over–8 Large Cent owned by a collector in Short Hills. Then Strand would change his plans to accommodate the opportunity.

It was a lonely existence, about as lonely as life can get. Jago Strand had forgone a home, a wife, a family, and a social life. He had passed up friends and lovers and quarrels and confidences. He was a lone wolf—or, as the police would have it, a lone sparrow. Coins were a mania with him, and obsession. He was a man with a dream, and his dream had nothing to do with traveling, stealing, or selling. It had to do with collecting, with assembling so brilliant an array of United States coins that it would deserve, and would have, its own museum. The Jago Strand Coin Museum, now only a vision, would one day be a reality, a white marble shrine located outside Waco, Texas. It was not so mad a dream either, because he had already bought the land for it, more than forty acres, and had talked to a Texas architect about the best design for a small coin museum.

A pretty fair achievement for anybody, Strand told himself, but a stunning achievement for a seventh-grade dropout whose stepmother had considered him a mental case and whose father, during one of his week-long binges, had broken Jago's jaw with a kick, and followed it up by breaking his heart with a torrent of abuse for Jago's dead mother.

At eighteen Strand left their home in Waco, swearing revenge, vowing to return in triumph. He would show them. He would show everyone, show the whole world.

He took up auto theft in Oklahoma with predictable results. Arrest and conviction. His two years at El Reno Reformatory were brutally unpleasant, but they provided him with all the practical education he needed. He became an avid student of crime. At El Reno he met a chubby young man, Will Holford, whose business was selling illegal handguns and whose hobby was stealing coins. Through Holford's enthusiasm, Strand became interested in coins, studied numismatics in the prison library. He also became interested in avoiding further time behind bars.

He was never arrested again. And he succeeded from the outset in his chosen career. The Strand Collection, every coin of it stolen, was by this time one of the three or four finest in the nation. His only regret was that no one else knew of his hard-won triumph. Recognition would have to come later. It might come posthumously, given the nature of fame and the statute of limitations, but that was all right. Famous artists and writers had struggled, penniless and unknown, through lives different in detail but not really different in kind from his.

Few men built monuments to themselves in their brief lifetimes. Strand, in his own eyes, had already done so. All he needed now were three more Large Cents, eighty-two Half Cents, and a Waco contractor.

He closed and locked his pullman-sized suitcase, one half of which contained coins and equipment. The other half held clothes. He combed his thinning grey hair, washed his hands, and took the elevator downstairs.

At a coffee shop off the lobby he ordered a hamburger and coffee.

His evening meal never varied. Business seemed slow in the coffee shop. It was half past eleven at night, and two young women, the only other customers, sat a few stools away from Strand, smoking and talking. They paid no attention to him.

A few minutes later a pair of men in cheap business suits sauntered in and sat down across the double counter. Strand studied them without appearing to. He disliked what he saw. One of them, slender and angular, had pointed ears, a closed-lip smirk, and eyes that opened and shut in slow motion. His companion, slightly taller and vastly heavier, wore a black brush mustache and a grey gabardine suit that matched his partner's in bagginess.

Laurel and Hardy, without their bowler hats.

Or maybe Keystone Kops. They had that curious, starchy look of law about them. Which could mean nothing, or everything. Plainclothesmen, like uniformed police officers, do more than their share of sitting around coffee shops, often with nothing on their minds except cheesecake of one kind of another. Whoever they were, Strand would have preferred to see truck drivers or college kids in their place.

If the men in fact carried badges, they acted yawningly indifferent to him, no more excited by his presence than they were by that of the languid waitress or the sugared doughnuts.

When Strand finished his hamburger and coffee, he slipped a clad, worthless quarter under the plate, paid the check at the cashier's counter, and strolled out the door.

Laurel and Hardy followed him with their eyes, one vacuously, the other cheerily.

Back in his room on the fifth floor, it hit him, the jolt sudden and terrifying—hit him like his drunken father's kick on the jaw.

Three coins!

A 1799–over–98 Large Cent that had been a perfect specimen when Reuben Armitage bought it at auction. Now, inexplicably, it was scratched and unmistakable.

A counterfeit 1793 Chain Type Large Cent. A counterfeit that Armitage would have been unlikely to keep, much less display in his library.

An uncirculated 1795 Lettered Edge Cent, a coin that, according to Strand's best information, Armitage had never owned.

No wonder two plainclothesmen were in the coffee shop of the Lord Hewitt Hotel.

For the third time in his twenty-five-year career, Jago Strand had been set up. He was sure of it.

Never mind how it had happened. Never mind that he was still free and unshackled a couple of hours after the theft. The law's delay could be explained in any number of ways—and there was no time now to count the ways. Strand's work called for big gambles. It called for contingency plans, steady nerves, and fast incisive thought.

What use did the pursuers intend to make of the three coins?

The 1793 counterfeit. Was it really no coin at all, but a disguised bug or beeper?

The 1795 Lettered Edge. Was it a unique specimen, planted at high cost, to trap and prosecute him?

And the oddest coin of the seven, the 9–over–8 with a scratch. Why that one? A damaged classic, irreplaceable. The thief would try to sell it, of course, even in its dire state. But to whom? Ah, to H. M. Luker—nobody else. Jago Strand knew that. Did his pursuers know it, too? Had the law finally caught up with Jago's shadowy Cincinnati fence?

Strand crossed to the phone on the Formica-walnut desk and dialed O. "This is a credit-card call," he said, and gave a false but acceptable ten-digit number followed by a letter. Then he said, "I'm calling area code 513," and recited the rest of Luker's unlisted number. To the hotel operator's request for his name and room number he said. "Lloyd Penner, Room 519."

After two rings on the long distance wire, a low pleasant voice answered. "Yes?"

"Mr. Luker, please."

"This is Mr. Luker speaking."

Strand hung up.

It was not Mr. Luker speaking. Strand knew H. M. Luker's high-pitched tenor as well as he knew the inflated prices in this year's *Red Book.*

He poured another shot of scotch and gave the situation some thought. A man needs a certain amount of paranoia to put together a string of six hundred successful coin thefts over a period of twenty-five years. Strand had his share of paranoia, usually under careful control. He knew he might be wrong to expect trickery, there might he no one on his tail, but in his line of work the vaguest hint of trouble had to be considered a sure thing. That was what kept him out of jail. He had to act as if a host of avenging angels from the American Numismatic Society were about to descend on his room. He had to act.

He studied road maps of New Jersey and Pennsylvania, memorizing his route. He pored over airline schedules, laying his plans.

Unlocking his suitcase, he pulled out ten small Jiffy bags and a sheet of postage stamps. He snapped open the compartment of a precious blue box labeled "Large Cents—Strand Collection" and, taking out the one worthy Armitage coin, the 1795 Lettered Edge, he dropped it in the ashtray beside the 1793 counterfeit. No coin, however desirable, was worth his loss of freedom and the possible jeopardy of his dream.

He put fifteen or sixteen Large Cents into each of the Jiffy bags. With a black felt pen he scrawled "Mr. Hugh Garth, c/o Nicobar Motel, Parkersburg, West Virginia" on each of them and with a red felt pen he wrote FIRST CLASS MALL at the left of each address. After carefully removing the perforated edges from the postage stamps, one of his minor obsessions, he pasted two one-dollar stamps on each Jiffy bag.

A package drop a few doors down from Strand's room sent the nation's second best collection of U.S. Large Cents on its way out of New Jersey. This meant trusting delivery of the coins to the U.S. mails, but in Strand's enterprise it was essential to weigh risks. They might be slow and chancy, but they were, in their own way, inviolable.

Back in his room again he opened the shipping bag he had addressed to Reuben Armitage, the first-class surprise containing the 9–over–8. He dumped the other six Armitage coins into the bag with the damaged lady. This bag, holding all seven of the suspicious Armitage coins, he put into a side pocket of his sports jacket.

Under less pressing circumstances, he might have gambled that the counterfeit 1793 was the only plausible carrier of the electronic tracking device he was sure had put Laurel and Hardy on his trail. He was certain no one had seen him in Short Hills and that no one had followed him from the scene of the theft to Morristown.

But there was always the chance of being wrong, and it was too big a chance to take. All seven coins would have to go.

His few clothes shoved hastily into his suitcase, Strand left the hotel by the fire stairs and walked rapidly to his grey Dodge van. He checked the taillights. Sure enough, one of them was broken. The famous comedy team had learned his room number from the beeper, he supposed, checked out his auto license number at the registration desk, and then smashed the taillight to make it easier to tail him if necessary. They had probably also clamped a second beeper on the chassis.

The hotel parking lot was night-misted and silent as Jago Strand pulled out onto the city street and headed for Interstate 287.

Nobody followed him onto the Interstate. Accelerating smoothly, he fixed the speedometer needle on fifty-five. He never risked a speeding ticket unless he had to.

He slanted off at the Route 10 exit, heading west. Traffic was light, and so was the rain, no more than a drizzle. Every mile or so he flicked the windshield wipers on and off to clear the mist.

About fifteen miles down the road he picked up a pair of headlights in his rear view mirror. Persistent headlights. He slowed gradually to forty, then to thirty-five, hoping they would pass. He pulled into a department store parking lot, drove around it randomly, and pulled back on the road. The headlights stayed with him.

At one of the half dozen traffic circles on Route 10 he made his move. He veered sharply right onto an eastbound road, turned quickly into a McDonald's parking area, circled the building in a counterclockwise sweep, and turned back toward the circle, where he angled onto Route 46, heading farther west.

The trailing headlights missed the unexpected left, wheeled past the golden arches, and had to make a screaming U-turn to get back to the circle, falling far behind.

Strand stomped the accelerator to the floor, trying to lose them for good at an intersection two miles ahead, where the map showed four main highways coming together. The road curved and twisted its way west, and beyond the intersection the trailing lights were gone. He breathed a sigh of relief.

The headlights did not reappear. If a beeper was on the car and the comedians had taken a wrong turn, the signals would soon start to become fainter to the pursuers. His escape plan was to stay on 46, but Laurel and Hardy had no way of knowing that. They had to be lucky or they had to correct their mistake quickly.

Four miles west of Hackettstown, two headlights rocketed into view behind him. Seeing them loom up at that speed, Strand knew whose they were. The road was an empty two-laner, the drizzling rain had stopped, and the trailing car came up closer, rode the bumper of Strand's van for half a mile, then backed off a little. There was nothing subtle about the pursuit now.

Strand ignored the speed limit and pushed the Dodge to full throttle. Eighty miles an hour. Eighty-five. The rusted but dependable van would never qualify at Daytona, but it gave the driver everything it had. Strand expected the trailing car to try to jam him off the road, or worse, that one of the pair might start shooting.

Nothing happened. Just pursuit. The two vehicles roared through a number of small towns, raced along the Pequest River, and blazed through two traffic lights in a place called Buttzville. One of the lights was green, the other red. Strand's accelerator pedal mashed the floor, but the two headlights hung in, gleaming in his rear view mirror like a pair of satanic yellow eyes.

One good thing: he was sure the pursuers had no local police help. Despite their appearance, they were not ordinary lawmen. They could not summon help. They were either private eyes or thieves themselves. No matter. Like Strand, they were on their own. Otherwise the chase would have been over at Hackettstown, maybe sooner.

Strand allowed himself a tinge of optimism.

The road widened to four lanes as the road map had shown it would. With the speedometer needle hovering between eighty-five and ninety, he fleetingly saw BELVIDERE and a left-turn arrow. It came too late to make the turn safely, but there was no choice. He jerked the wheel left at the last urgent moment. The van, never noted for its stability, swayed around a concrete island on two wheels, screeching, skidding. It straightened out and barreled toward the Delaware River.

Laurel and Hardy careened wildly after him.

No other traffic was in sight on the narrow concrete road.

Four years ago, during a lazy week on the Outer Banks of North Carolina, Strand had prepared for an emergency like this. He had bought a box of eight-penny finishing nails, filed down their heads, and welded them together by threes into huge spiked jacks. Three dozen lay in a long bottom-hinged wooden box behind the rear axle. A cable ran to a lever near the driver's seat.

Strand yanked the lever and the jacks dropped.

First he heard a sprinkling sound like the patter of rain on a tin roof, then a chilling squeal of brakes. He saw the headlights in back of him lurch crazily, fall away, and flicker into the woods at the right side of the road.

He did not hear a crash but knew there must have been one. The comics had earned two flat tires at least, maybe three. Maybe four.

Nobody followed him through the old town of Belvidere, whose prim frame houses hugged the road, their occupants long since asleep. No one trailed him across the narrow bridge to Pennsylvania.

On the other side of the river, in the shadow of a darkened hotel, he stopped and reconnoitered, a task that took him less than thirty seconds. He made a sharp right turn onto an asphalt drive sloping down toward the river. The driveway led to a house trailer parked about two hundred yards away. There was no sign of life in or around the trailer.

He braked the van near the water and got out. Crickets chirped in the night air. The rolling waters of the Delaware slapped softly against the bridge's concrete supports. A thin new moon hung in the sky and the surface of the river shone as black as rat snake.

He walked to the river's edge, took the Jiffy bag from the pocket of his jacket, and, with no more hesitation than a foot soldier hurling a grenade, tossed the seven Armitage coins into the inky waters of the Delaware. Then, alert and watchful, he climbed back into the driver's seat and drove for three miles before he found the spot he wanted.

First he saw just a broad, overgrown driveway. Next, against the night sky, he saw where the driveway led. It led through a copse of trees to the hulking cinder block shell of a burned-out building.

This was the place. He pulled into the rutted driveway, bounced a few hundred feet to a concealed parking spot behind the cinder block ruin. He doused the lights and killed the engine.

He stuffed his now useless Lloyd Penner wallet, containing a driver's license, car registration, and credit cards, into the glove compartment. Lloyd Penner was about to disappear. The van would have to stay behind, but its owner and driver would dissolve without a trace.

Jago Strand, ready for almost any disaster, carried a back-up identity in his suitcase, complete in all details. This new set of licenses, papers, and credit cards was made out in the name of Hugh Garth of Alexandria, Virginia. Mr. Garth was a new creation, an imaginary architect who was fortunate enough to own a current and legal set of Virginia license plates for his red Kawasaki motorcycle. Strand kept the motorcycle covered with canvas and mounted upright in the back of the van.

Like any less well-to-do transient, Strand carried his personal belongings in one suitcase. His forty-nine sets of U.S. coins were stored more than a thousand miles away in a safe-deposit box in Houston under his own name. The incomplete Large Cent collection was on its way by first-class mail to a motel in Parkersburg. The rest—his custom numismatic apparatus, his safe-deposit key, his coins for sale, his modest wardrobe—were in the suitcase.

Leaving the driver's seat of the Dodge for the last time, he closed the door quietly and walked to the rear of the vehicle. To his puzzlement, the rear door was unlocked. Could he have forgotten? No use speculating now. On the floor of the van, as far to the left as it would go, he had installed a motorcycle carrier. Tie-downs held the Kawasaki securely in place.

He hauled his makeshift loading ramp, a two by ten pine board, into place. He pulled the canvas off the Kawasaki, unhooked the tiedowns and wheeled the cycle to the ground. Carrying the weathered board to an inside wall of the cinder block shell, he dropped it beside a rusted, doorless white refrigerator.

He used the tie-downs to fasten his suitcase to the seat of the cycle. It was a tight fit for driver and luggage, but the trip was less than thirty miles.

About five minutes after the Dodge van had disappeared behind the abandoned building, Strand's red Kawasaki street bike emerged. Jago Strand, suitcase, and motorcycle bore left onto the asphalt and leaned resolutely into the darkness, pointing toward Easton and escape.

After half an hour of A-B-E Airport—serving Allentown, Bethlehem, and Easton—came into view. It was a bright modern facility with a two-level roadway system for arrivals and departures that skirted Airport Road, just off truck-clogged Route 22.

Jago Strand, chilled from his wind-whipped jaunt, aimed down Airport Road, plucked a parking check from the automatic ticket dispenser, parked the Kawasaki near a flight of concrete steps leading to the departure level, unhooked his suitcase, and carried it to the Allegheny ticket counter.

It was three A.M. Except for a sleeping businessman sprawled in a molded plastic chair, the waiting room was deserted. Even the Allegheny agent, a frail young man with horn-rimmed glasses, seemed somnolent.

"A ticket on the seven o'clock flight to Parkersburg," Strand said, pushing his suitcase onto the baggage scale.

"Certainly, sir," the agent said, frowning and beginning to press buttons. "You realize, of course, that Flight 281 leaves at seven tomorrow evening, not this morning."

"A night flight?" Strand asked incredulously. "That's sixteen hours from now!"

"That's right."

"Well," he said, feigning annoyance. "I may as well buy the ticket.

Can you check my bag?"

"Certainly. A one-way ticket?"

"One way." Strand shoved an Air Travel card across the counter. It was made out to Hugh Garth of Alexandria, Virginia. Garth's address was that of a telephone-answering company that also provided a mail-forwarding service. Mr. Garth, like Lloyd Penner before him, intended to pay his bills.

With the ticket and baggage claim check in his pocket, he phoned for a single-room reservation at the Nicobar Motel in Parkersburg; then he took the escalator down to the arrival level.

As a matter of policy he would not risk flying. He knew that it was statistically safe, but he also knew that the aircraft was out of his personal control. He wanted to be in command of every aspect of his life.

The airport's choice of rental cars proved to be Hertz, Avis, National, and Dollar-Rent-a-Car. Opting for Number Two, he rented a station wagon. He gave his destination, falsely, as Cleveland—a further precaution. He could always claim that a sudden press of business had diverted him from Cleveland to Parkersburg.

He drove to the parking lot, intending to stow the Kawasaki in the back of the rented car. Only temporarily, though. The motorcycle would soon be rusting at the bottom of a nearby river in case it had been spotted by someone.

His headlights picked up the gleaming red cycle and he pulled up beside it. The lot was well lighted but desolate. No loitering here, he thought. In about twelve hours he would be in Parkersburg, a new man.

As he stepped out of the station wagon, he heard the scraping movement behind him of shoe leather on asphalt. Whirling around, he found himself face to face with the narrow-eyed fat man of the comedy team who had emerged from behind a black sedan, aiming a 9mm Beretta at him, a silencer decorating its barrel.

"Freeze," Hardy said, his double chin quivering.

Strand froze.

"Easy now. Toss your wallet on the ground in front of you."

Strand obeyed.

"Your plane ticket in the same place."

Strand tossed down the envelope. "Where's Laurel?" he asked grimly, without thinking.

"Where's who?"

"Your partner."

"Hospital in Hackettstown. His tires hit some carpet tacks outside Belvidere."

"*His* tires? Where were you?"

Hardy scowled. "Two guys, two cars, Strand. That's simple arithmetic. When you skipped the Lord Hewitt before we hit your room, my partner tailed you. I stayed behind for a while to search the room. I found the edges of some postage stamps in your wastebasket and checked the mail drops at the hotel, with a little high-priced help from the night clerk. We uncovered some packages headed for the Nicobar Motel in Parkersburg. I'm letting them travel. I don't rob the U.S. mails."

Tears of anger began forming in Jago Strand's eyes. It had all been so carefully planned.

Hardy went on. "My guess is that your airline ticket says Parkersburg, too. And your I.D. stuff must say Hugh Garth." He leaned over and, puffing from the exertion, picked up Strand's wallet and the Allegheny envelope. "How'm I doing?"

Strand said nothing.

"We've been after you for about two years now. I guess when we pick up your baggage in Parkersburg we'll put our hands on a very big coin collection. Warm?"

Strand cursed himself for not carrying a weapon. He hated guns on principle and had never supposed he would need one, but a man can have too much caution. There was no way he could argue with that quiet-talking Beretta. Frustration clogged his speech. "How—?" he choked.

"How did I find you?" the fat man asked cheerfully. "CB radio contact with my partner. A little horse sense. A little luck. A beeper on the Kawasaki. No big deal."

"You're—federal?"

The big man chuckled. "Hey, you're not much on faces, are you, Strand? I mean, sure, I've put on a few pounds, but—"

"*Will Holford!*"

"You got it, Jago. Your old coin-collecting pal from reformatory days. I figured you for the Sparrow way back in the sixties when I was doing time at Lewisburg. I mean, you were always crazy as a hoot owl. But it took a while to catch you. You're pretty tricky. I needed to find myself a partner who knew a few things I didn't know."

"Laurel," Strand said in a tired whisper.

"Who's this Laurel you're talking about? The guy whose car you busted up back there is a crony of yours. H. M. Luker from Cincy—who's also a friend of the famous Reuben Armitage. Why, Hal Luker and me's got a collection of coins that'll put the Smithsonian's to shame. Just wait'll we add your junk to it!"

So this was the way it was going to end: Jago Strand, after twenty-five years on the road, a connoisseur with a coin collection that rivaled the greatest, standing helpless and bereft at the edge of a rain-glazed parking lot, his coin museum no more than a mirage, his life a nomadic waste, his possessions reduced to a bugged Kawasaki and a shiny blue business suit. He started to sob.

"Shut up," Holford said.

But Strand was not listening. All this life he had avoided risks, played it safe. It had always worked. But now—It was too much. Luker and Holford were not collectors, they were parasites. Thieves. Opportunists. *Comedians*. His self-control taking flight, he lunged blindly for the gun.

He never reached it.

There was a muffled slam, a gasp, and Jago Strand, a stricken sparrow, collapsed in a little heap beside the red motorcycle.

Raymond Mason
Martha Myers, Movie Star

Mabel was very unhappy about her life. She was also unhappy with Henry. She was in her middle thirties, had mousy brown hair, most of her own teeth, and considered herself in appearance not unlike Martha Myers, the movie star, although she didn't really resemble anybody who was in the movies.

Henry, on the other hand, was short, middle-aged, bald-headed, and had a little mustache. He was very attached to his home and to his wife and to his garden in the basement. He only deserted them on Thursday night when his lodge held its weekly meeting.

Mabel didn't like Henry. She knew it wasn't the right thing to do when she had married him three years before, but she had been so short of choices at that time. She had come to the small town they lived in only a short time before that and she hadn't had any money and the only place she had been able to find work was in a boarding house where she had to wait tables and do domestic work. When Henry proposed, it had been an out. She left the boarding house.

Try as she might she couldn't get Henry to join another lodge, so he could be gone *two* nights a week. He would shake his head in a resolved fashion and say he wasn't the kind of man who deserted his wife and home to indulge in recreation. One lodge was his civic duty, but two would be giving in to selfishness on his part.

Everything about Henry griped Mabel, even down to the little bow tie he snapped on every morning. But his damned garden in the basement probably bothered her the most. This was complete foolishness and a waste of time. The only good part of it was that she didn't have to look at him in the house while he worked on it; but he was always calling for her to come down and see what he was doing. This griped Mabel too.

Nothing ever grew in the garden. There wasn't any sunlight to help the growth so nothing ever stayed alive that managed to come through the ground in the beginning. The basement was damp and dark.

Mabel was trying to solve her problem. It probably wouldn't do her too much good to divorce Henry; not in this town anyway. Henry had lived here all his life and the judge would probably be inclined to see things his way and there probably wouldn't be a chance for alimony. Besides, what grounds did she have? Outside of the fact that Henry was a jerk and she was still a young and attractive woman. Whenever she thought this way she always looked in the mirror, but the cheap mirrors Henry had bought really didn't do her justice. They didn't bring out the find contours of her face.

Henry was in the basement working in his garden after dinner. Mabel was reading a movie magazine and for the millionth time in her life was saying to herself how much she resembled Martha Myers, the movie star, and it was a mystery to her why people weren't mistaking her on the street for Martha.

"Mabel," Henry called, "I'd like for you to see something."

"I'm not coming down to that mangy basement," she screamed. "Not in a trillion years." She yanked at the corners of her movie magazine and stared harder at the pages.

"Ah, Mabel, come on down. I want to show you something."

She didn't answer.

"Please, Mabel. Come down and look."

"Fiddle with your garden, you jerk, and leave me alone."

"But it's about the garden, Mabel. Come on. You'll like it. Honest you will, honey."

Mabel sat in her chair doing a slow boil. She knew he would keep this up until he either drove her out of her mind or she went down and looked at some stupid worm or a part of a broken bottle he had turned over.

She slammed her movie magazine on the floor and went to the basement steps. She moved down them slowly, shivering from the dampness coming up to her.

The light was on in the basement and Henry was standing in his overalls next to a huge pile of earth. He was perspiring but there was a big smile pasted across his face.

"What do you think of it?" he cried excitedly.

"Of what?"

"Of the work."

She walked closer. Then she realized he had dug a large hole nearly six feet deep in the soft earth. "Now why the hell have you done that?"

His smile became even larger. "You know you joke with me all the time about nothing ever growing in the garden."

"Nothing ever does."

"Well, it will now." He picked up a bucket filled with grey dust and held it up to her.

She jumped away.

"This is a new fertilizer and it has to be put several feet underneath the things being planted. It will take the place of sunshine and warmth."

"You jerk, calling me down here to see a hole in the ground." Mabel turned away and was about to start up the stairs. Then she turned around and looked back at Henry and then at the huge hole in the ground.

It was certainly big enough.

Her eyes moved around the basement and they fell on a hammer just a few feet away from Henry. She stepped lightly towards it.

Henry was pouring the grey dust into the large hole. "You should take a greater interest in the garden down here," he said. "Someday they'll run a whole series about it in a magazine—how we're able to grow things in a damp, dark basement."

She was looking at the back of his head. Well, why not plant Henry in the damp, dark basement? Nothing else would grow here, anyway.

Splat! The hammer hit him in the back of the head and Henry's round little body dropped into the big hole, making the grey dust rise.

Mabel looked down into the hole and Henry was almost completely covered by the grey dust. He looked like he had been dead for a long time; maybe five or six thousand years like some of the mummies she had read about in the magazines. She was a little sad, looking down at him, exactly as Martha Myers would look sad if Martha was trapped by a Henry and had hit him on the back of his head with a hammer.

Mabel took up the shovel and began throwing the dirt back into the hole. It was back-breaking work but it had to be done. No one must ever find him. It was against the law to kill people, even jerks like Henry, and she had to work quickly. She had read about true crimes like this before. A magazine had had a story almost exactly like this once, with pictures and everything, only it was a man who had done it to his wife. Well, turnabout was fair play, wasn't it?

It was a hell of a job and the dirt wouldn't fit back into the hole from where it came. This made her angry and she was certain that Henry was probably taking up too much room in the hole. That was what made the dirt come out long. He was still being a jerk. She threw the extra dirt around on the rest of the garden, not covering anything up because nothing was growing anyway.

But looking at it bothered her. It seemed like somebody could be buried here. If the police or anyone came here they would probably think somebody was buried in the garden. It was all bare and it was covered with loose dirt. It didn't really look like a garden.

She ran upstairs and brought back two potted philodendrons. She dug a hole in the loose dirt and planted the flowers, pots and all. Then she covered them well, so that nothing showed except the plants.

Mabel made several trips upstairs until she had found every potted plant—and there were quite a few since Henry liked them—and returned to the basement and set them up as though they were growing there.

After two hours of this she looked at the indoor garden and laughed. Nothing had ever grown this well before. In fact, nothing had ever grown before and now there were ten or eleven full-grown plants coming out of the ground. They were strung out all over so as to cover the space.

Mabel went upstairs and took a long hot shower.

Later, she was sitting up in bed reading her movie magazine when it occurred to her that someone might wonder what happened to Henry.

After nobody saw him for a couple of weeks somebody might begin to get nosy. Although he really wasn't important to anybody and he didn't have any family, somebody might wonder. There were always a lot of busybodies who were anxious to make trouble, even if it was only over some little jerk like Henry.

She shook her head. This was an awful lot of red tape to go through. If Henry had only agreed to join a second lodge and be gone two nights a week instead of one, all of this probably could have been avoided. But having him around pestering her six nights a week had just been to much. She'd really had the patience of Job to have endured it this long.

But somebody would wounder where he was and that would have to be taken care of.

Mabel went to the typewriter and put a sheet of paper into it. With the first finger on each hand she typed:

> Dear Mabel,
> I have never been worthy of you dearest love and I know it.
> So I am talking a coward's way out of everything. I am running away with another woman who I am worthy of. She is not as beautiful or as charming as you and she doesn't look like any movie star but since I am unworthy of you I want to let you be free to lead your own life. I am sorry about being a coward and running away with another woman.
> I'll always love you,
> Henry

She signed Henry's name at the bottom of the letter. But she had been signing his name so many times over the three years they had been married that she could forge his signature perfectly. He had always had the habit of forgetting to sign his paychecks on the back and she had had to learn to sign his name so she could cash them.

Then she reread the letter. It was the kind of a letter a jerk would write.

The next morning when she woke up at ten o'clock she went into the kitchen and began preparing her own coffee in the electric coffee pot. This was something new because Henry had always made the coffee in the morning and it had always been warm and steaming when she got up. That had been one thing Henry had been good for.

Then she went to the telephone and called the company Henry had worked for for twenty-eight years and asked for Mr. Abernathy, who owned the place.

By the time he got to the telephone she had begun to cry, just the way Martha Myers, the movie star, would have cried if her husband had run away with a woman.

"Mr. Abernathy . . . This is Mabel." She bawled some more. "Henry ran away and left me. He ran away with a girl of the streets. He ran away with some tramp."

"What? Henry ran off with a woman?"

"Yeah." She had stifled her tears now and decided to read the letter to Abernathy.

After she had finished reading the letter, the other end of the telephone line was silent. Abernathy said nothing. Mabel wondered desperately if he had believed her. Of course, she knew it would be a shock to anybody because who in hell would run off with a little jerk like Henry unless it was some sophisticated young woman who was forced, through circumstances, to do work that was unbecoming to her and who felt sorry for Henry?

The silence continued and it began to scare her. What the devil was wrong with Abernathy, anyway?

"Mr. Abernathy, are you still there?"

"Yes . . . yes, I'm still here." He paused. "I want to extend to you my deepest sympathies, Mabel. But you must look at it as God's will."

"Yeah. Sure. God's will." She hung up and looked at herself in the cheap mirror on the wall that really didn't tell the whole story. "What did he mean by that?" she asked the ordinary-looking person in the mirror.

She shrugged and let it go at that. She was happy the old geezer had swallowed the idea of Henry running away with somebody. She laughed out loud. Honest, they had to be pretty dumb to believe that story. Dumb-looking little jerk, Henry, finding anybody who would want to run off with him.

Well, it was a big world.

For the next week, half the people in town came to call on Mabel and express their sympathies over what that little jerk Henry had done to her. She served tea to everybody who came, which were mostly old women, and let each and every one read her badge of disgrace— Henry's letter to her.

People invited her everywhere so it would help her forget her terrible ordeal and she practically didn't have to cook any more because everyone in the nieghborhood was bringing her hot food all the time.

This was more like it. People were paying attention to her. Still, nobody came out outright and said she looked like Martha Myers, the movie star, though when she would casually mention it they would agree with her right away. Some of them even said that she had been awfully sharp to have caught the resemblance.

Mabel had now become very popular. There was a time or two when she thought about Henry planted down in the garden but she tried not to let this worry her. He was happy down there. He had always loved the garden and to putter in the dirt. Now he was part of the earth itself. Besides, he didn't have any fun living anyway. He probably didn't even have much fun at the lodge, Mabel thought. If he had, then why hadn't he joined another one. Heaven knows, she'd asked him enough times.

She took a trip to the basement one afternoon and noticed that the philodendrons were growing really well—much better than they ever had just being in their pots. Maybe Henry had been right about his new fertilizer. And then again, maybe Henry was helping quite a bit himself. It was about time Henry was doing somebody some good, Mabel thought, even if it had to be himself. It was true that he never did any bad but that was exactly the trouble with him, the jerk. If he'd have roughed her up a little now and then or cursed her when she was giving him the silent treatment or gone out and got drunk once in a while or anything like that it would have been different. But no, he was always so quiet about everything. A woman like herself, with the same fire and warm blood and everything that Martha Myers showed she had whenever Mabel saw her on the screen couldn't be expected to tolerate a mousy jerk like Henry forever now honestly, could she?

All during the week the people continued inviting her and were nicer to her than ever before, and noticed things about her which she was glad they noticed because what was the sense of all of it anyway unless people noticed things, like the two new dresses she bought, black ones of course because it wouldn't be wise or delicate to wear anything else.

The tenth day the doorbell rang and Mabel hurried to answer it. She was wearing her best dress and she already had the cookies and tea prepared for an afternoon session. The only bad thing was that Henry's farewell letter was beginning to wear out from too much handling. She thought that it might be an idea to type up a new one, but discarded that since sombody might notice, and she certainly didn't want any busybody noticing anything strange now. No, she would just have to be more careful about handling Henry's letter, make it last.

Mabel opened the door and Officer Merkin was standing there. He was the policeman who lived a block away from them.

"Good afternoon, ma'am," he said.

"Why, hello, Officer Merkin, won't you come in?" Mabel said. "I'm so glad to see you."

He followed her into the house.

"I suppose you've heard about Henry?"

"Yes, ma'am, I have. And the missus and I want to say that we're all for you, ma'am. No decent man runs away with some other woman when he's already married."

"Thank you, Officer Merkin. You're very understanding. Do you like sugar and cream in your tea?"

"I'm sorry, I'm no duty. I never drink on duty."

"On duty?"

"Yes, ma'am. You see we have a missing persons section here at the police department. It's not a very important section because practically nobody ever comes up missing in a little town like this. But I'm in charge of this department and somebody is missing now. Henry's missing."

"Why yes, Henry is a missing person if you look at it that way." She thought about it. "Of course, he really isn't missing. He ran away with some hussy, some girl out of the gutter."

Officer Merkin nodded.

"But if there's anything I could do for you I'd be more than happy to."

Officer Merkin nodded again. "Yes, ma'am. I wonder if you could come down to the station and fill out some forms. It will make it official that way. The next of kin is supposed to do that, you know. It won't take you very long if you'd care to come along now."

"Of course; I'd be glad to. Let me get my hat."

Mabel found her and went out the front door with the policeman. She turned to him and said, "Do you ever see Martha Myers, the movie star, in the movies?"

"Sure. See her all the time. Why'd you ask?"

"No reason. I just wondered."

At the police station Officer Merkin was very kind to her and showed her which spaces to fill out on the form and which ones not to pay any attention to. Government forms were always like that. The politicians didn't have anything better to do than to dream up forms for people to fill out and they always put too many spaces on them.

All the policemen there were very nice. But there was one old drunk they had arrested who wasn't nice at all. He kept screaming that he had been buried alive or something and she thought this was a perfectly horrible thing to even be discussing, let alone yelling it at the top of his lungs. Nobody was ever buried alive, anyway. They were always hit in the head with something first.

The other person she didn't like was a cheap blonde who sat on a bench with her legs crossed. She looked like a woman of the street, somebody who would probably run off with a happily married man. Her type was always in the movies. But no movie star like Martha Myers, the movie star, ever played a part like that. Somebody who was not a star always played those parts.

She brought the form over to Officer Merkin's desk. Most of the blanks were filled out. He motioned for her to sit down and she did.

The telephone rang and he picked it up.

"Yeah?" he said. "Really?"

There was the sound of someone speaking in the earpiece but Mabel couldn't hear what was being said.

"I declare. I wouldn't believe it."

Noises.

"Well, you never know."

Then he hung up the telephone and he was looking at Mabel. His face was very serious now and he seemed to be touching his holster with one hand as though he were about to arrest a dangerous criminal. "They found Henry, ma'am."

"What?"

"Yes, ma'am. Some of the boys went out to your place while we were here. They found him under the philodendrons."

"No. That's impossible. They couldn't have found anybody. Henry ran off with some girl of the streets. The little jerk ran away from his wife and his responsibilities."

"He didn't run anywhere, ma'am. He was planted in the garden."

Mabel jumped up, carried away by the moment. What would Martha Myers, the movie star, do in a situation like this? "Why? Why? Why did you even look for Henry in the garden? Why would you think anything could happen to Henry in his own house? The house with a wife that loved him!" Mabel was so carried away she was almost ready to faint.

"Why couldn't he have run away with some other woman?" she shrieked.

The blonde had come across the room to get a closer view of the performance, and was standing next to her as she gestured. She poked Mabel in the ribs. "I told them he didn't run away with anybody. He couldn't have run away with anybody 'cause I'm the other woman, hon," and she motioned toward herself. "Every Thursday night. Just me and old goodtime Henry. And he wouldn't have run off anywhere without taking little me along."

Mabel passed out, falling flat on her face. Martha Myers, the movie star, might have fainted that way, but probably not.

Pauline C. Smith

Happy as a Harp Song

The three sisters, Amabelle, Amanda, and Amalia, looking like slightly withered flowers, clustered in a drooping bouquet on their front porch. They separated as I wheeled my Volks into the dirt yard, as if each were plucked individually and placed against the porch railing, and when I stepped from the car to stand in the dust the required distance from "the girls," as they were always called, they turned up their vaguely smiling flower faces in welcome.

"I am Jane Flagg," I announced unnecessarily. They nodded in unison.

There is a rule, in this isolated hill country, that visitors bide their time, keep their distance, and wait to be asked to enter, so I leaned against the car and went through the formalities of asking about the health of each, agreeing that the weather was fine indeed and discussing the condition of the crops before ever revealing the nature of my visit.

The three wore dotted swiss dresses, ruffled and ribboned—probably hand-sewn by Amanda from material stolen by their father thirty years ago out of a boxcar that had been shunted to a siding. At least, the story went that way. It was said then that the old man carted away enough bolts of cloth to cover those girls for the rest of their lives, and I guess that was true because you certainly don't see dotted swiss any more.

Their hands, resting on the porch railing, looked like two dead brown birds and four dead pale birds and I knew the time was ripe to state my mission. I took a step toward the porch and said, "I guess you know that I've opened up a shop in my folks' old home place down in Mountain Hollow." Three heads inclined.

"I hope you might permit me to display some of your fine handiwork."

The door was then opened and I was allowed to enter the house and observe Miss Amalia's exquisite china painting and the fine needlework of Miss Amanda. It was all there in the big square room where these three sisters had lived together for more than sixty years.

A huge stone fireplace, with an iron-doored kiln built at the side, took up most of one wall. Wide-planked, boxed-in stairs led to the second story "sleep rooms." It was this big downstairs room that held the sisters' lives, all of their dreams, and the fruit of their talents.

I walked over Miss Amanda's beautifully stitched hooked rugs and touched the heavy splendor of her crewel work that curtained the crude tiny-paned windows. Miss Amalia's china painting art made the big, dark, heavy-beamed room a bright garden spot with violets and roses climbing the plates, pitchers, cups, and teapots shelved along the walls.

My customers would go mad!

The two sisters, Amanda and Amalia, unfolded with pride when I exclaimed my delight, and closed in again as soon as I asked for some of their treasures for my shop. "But you have so many," I said, overwhelmed by stacks of crocheted bedspreads, yards of embroidery and all the floral china, "so many things you don't use and that people would love to buy. Wouldn't you rather have the money?"

Two prim mouths pursed at mention of such an indelicate subject as money, and four tan eyes boycotted me . . . but Amabelle, not so proper as her sisters nor so impractical, briskly ordered Amalia to the shed for a bolt of "Daddy's flannelette to cut in squares and protect that nice rose-pattern tea set," and Amanda to get busy and "roll up a bedspread so the fringe won't tangle."

"Remember," Miss Amabelle said sternly, "it's time you began to bring in a little money, too."

That was how I was able to stock the Jane Flagg Old Time Store with china as beautiful as old Havilland and needlework as handsome as that of the Victorians, and how Amalia and Amanda finally became so money-hungry that they not only forgot their manners, but they hid the truth behind sweet-sounding words.

I remember the sisters from back when I was a little girl, and they seemed as old then as they do now—delicately breakable, fragile with age. My father used to say of the family that it had been weakened by cousin marrying cousin on down through so many years that the last three girls had come out a little half-baked. To that, my mother always answered with a reprimanding click of her tongue, which didn't stop my father for an instant. If he was in a story-telling mood, he'd go on with the one about Amanda. It seems Amanda, the seamstress, was given a box of needless (presumably heisted along with the bolts of cloth from the boxcar). Then it seems that Amanda, when selecting a needle for her work, was apt to toss several aside before finding the one she wished to use, which interested Amalia so that she asked, "Why are you throwing all those other needles on the floor?" and Amanda replied that it was because all the points were on the wrong ends, to which Amalia advised, "Don't throw them away. Keep them and use them on the other side of the goods."

Such apocryphal anecdotes are a form of humor in these parts, and the sisters, particularly Amalia and Amanda, came in for their full share. Not so much Amabelle, however. Amabelle was the smart one, normal enough to be restless in these isolated hills and normal enough to want money in a moneyless community. So Amabelle took off for the city, and there she got herself a factory job and worked long enough to come back to the place of her birth and draw Social Security.

One day each month she sprints down those mountain roads, picks up her Social Security check from Mrs. Milton Kearney at the post office, gets it cashed at the general store, buys some supplies that she puts in an old flour sack, and trudges back up the mountain.

That's the way it was, that is, until I moved back from the city and set up my store in the old family home and Amabelle came in to see what was the "mighty miration goin' on," and poked around the shop that features old-time quilts and embroideries, featherwork, waxwork, woodwork. She said the things were mighty pretty, but she had two sisters who could put it all to shame, and I asked who they were. When she mentioned Amanda and Amalia, I remembered my father's old tales and knew who she was.

It was some months before I got up that way and was allowed to bring down the tea set and the bedspread, but from the first day Amabelle set foot in the shop and I got a load of the filled-up flour sack over her shoulder, I'd made sure Tommy was on hand to drive her home in his jeep.

They became good friends, Tommy and Miss Amabelle—that is, as good friends as Tommy ever makes and as good friends as Miss Amabelle would ever make, or anybody else in this mountain community. It's not that these people are unfriendly, but rather that they are shy and very private. They have taken Tommy to their hearts in their oblique and sometimes taciturn way, probably because they expect of Tommy only that which he can give. Which is good. It is, indeed, why I brought Tommy back here to where my roots are.

Brian, my ex-husband, Tommy's ex-father, wanted me to put him away, wall him up, cage him in. Well, I didn't. I brought him home to Mountain Hollow where he is appreciated for all the qualities he does have and not looked down upon for those he lacks.

So Tommy, who is dependable within his sphere of ability, knew which day of the month Miss Amabelle could be expected and at what time on that day she would be ready to have him pack her and her supplies into his jeep and drive her up the mountain to her home.

Amanda's and Amalia's reluctance to part with their art for indelicate payment vanished the moment I sold the tea set and bedspead and sent them their money less the twenty percent commission I always charged. I'll bet it was the first cash they'd ever had in their lily-white hands, and it was surely the first they'd ever made by dint of their own efforts and they turned money-greedy. Each month after that, on the day Tommy drove Miss Amabelle and her supplies home, Misses Amalia and Amanda were ready for him with carefully rolled bedspread, folded and wrapped embroidery, flannelette-separated chinaware, and outstreted hands in case something already on con-signment might have been sold.

"Well, how are the girls?" I'd ask Tommy once he'd carefully brought in the new merchandise.

"Fine, Mom," he'd say.

"What were they doing?" I'd ask as I laid out the beautiful painted china and unfolded the lovely stitchery.

"Golly, Mom, just waiting for me," he'd say as he turned, flat and squeaking on his rubber soles, eager to get out to his jeep so that he could shine the engine.

If Miss Amabelle had pressed him into a chore or two once the jeep was packed with china and embroidery, our dialogue became more extensive because, of course, there was more to tell. He would explain how he climbed to the roof to patch a shingle or leaned on the shovel to dig up a garden plot of ornery clay (in between the times that Tommy did these chores, Miss Amabelle crawled along the roof and patched her own shingles and leaned on the shovel and dug her own garden plots) ... "And what was Miss Amanda doing then?" I asked. "Golly, Mom, she went right back to her sewing," which offered me a brief and involuntary wonder if she had trouble finding needles with points all on the same ends. "And Miss Amalia?" I requested patiently ... "Golly, Mom, she went right back to her painting." I then asked about Miss Amabelle. "She was showing me what to do, Mom, and telling me how to do it," said Tommy. And I bet she was doing just that. Miss Amabelle was a real pusher, and I had the feeling the outside work might be getting to be a little too much for her. She'd tell him what it was she needed done, and then she'd tell him to do it because she was going to give him a piece of gingerbread afterwards... the gingerbread to pay for his work; a rather backward approach, but logical. Miss Amabelle not only did all the outside work, she also did the cooking. I didn't know what those two fluttery sisters of hers would ever do if Amabelle went first. Well, I was to find out.

It was spring and muddy, and Miss Amabelle's day. When she did not arrive, Tommy fretted all over the place at this break in his routine. Tommy in a fret is more mobile than oral—he gets his jeep engine shined to mirror-brightness and then he paces. Well, he was beside himself because this was Miss Amabelle's day and she had not appeared.

I raised my head from my books and said, "What's your problem?"

"It's Miss Amabelle, Mom," he said, his face a tangle of worry. "This is her day, Mom, and she isn't here. Where could she be?"

"Well," I said, "maybe she's late."

He shook his head vigorously.

"It's muddy out," I said. "Maybe she decided to put it off for today, the mud is probably ankle-deep up on the mountain road ..." I looked into Tommy's empty face with nothing to do, and suggested, "Why don't you drive up there, Tommy, bring her down and take her back again after she picks up her check and gets her supplies?"

Inspiration! His face broke into a beatific smile and he splayfooted it
out of the shop on the instant.

I went back to my books, only lifting my head again when the jeep
streaked past the shop and clattered over planking to rise the
mountain road. Tommy was on his way.

There were no customers that afternoon. Since they are all city
people, they rarely show in the middle of the week—even my weekend
customers, with the energy crisis, were greatly minimized. So it was a
quiet day and I got my bookwork all finished (I am no bookkeeper)
when I realized the shop was getting dark and looked at the wigwag
clock on the wall to discover that Tommy had been gone for five hours!

No Amabelle. No Tommy!

I sprang to my feet, raced to the front door, opened it and leaned out
to see Mrs. Milton Kearney just as she locked the door of the post office.
She nodded sedately and observed, in her precisely cool voice, that
Miss Amabelle had not arrived to pick up her mail.

"I know," I said as Ellie Evans and Mr. Purvis emerged from the
general store across the street and called out, together, that Miss
Amabelle had not been in to get her supplies.

"I know," I said.

The main street of Mountain Hollow was settling down to rest, but
what had happened to Tommy during all those hours, and where was
Miss Amabelle? The setting sun had faintly tinted the sky, leaving the
caked dried mud of the road a glassy gray.

I panic the moment Tommy is not where he is supposed to be. It's not
that I consciously think he might be in trouble, it's that I unconsciously
think of all the trouble he could get into... and he never does—never,
never, I told myself as I hurried through the living quarters behind the
shop and flew out the back door to my Volks.

I wished I had chains—I shuddered at the thought of mud-slick
mountain roads under bald tires. I jumped in, drove from the back
yard and around to the street. I braked and listened—that was when I
heard the roar of the jeep as it clattered over the corrugation of planks
from the mountain road to main Mountain Hollow. I leaned forward,
watching as Tommy drove the jeep straight down the middle of the
road as usual, swerving to the left as he parked in a fluid swish of mud
before the shop.

I backed up behind the house, breathed a sigh of Tommy-relief, and
went inside, through the house and to the shop. He was still out in
front, of course, hood up, shining the engine in frantic haste to beat the
gathering twilight.

He was mud to his knees! Why was he so all-over muddy?

I turned on the lights of the shop, prepared to wait, knowing it
would be fruitless to ask questions before the jeep engine was sparkling
bright. He folded his polishing cloths, stowed them away in the jeep
and it was then that I realized he had brought no china or needlework

down from the mountain just as he had brought no Miss Amabelle.

"Stop!" I cried as he opened the shop door and was about to step inside.

He looked up, shook his head in bewilderment, and said, "Stop what, Mom?"

"Look at your shoes," I cried. "Stiff with mud! Take them off at the sill."

He leaned down, laboriously untied the tennis shoes, and stepped out of them. I picked them up, led him through the house to the back porch, met a little resistance when I ordered him to take off his pants right out there before the world, but since the world was not out there after all, but in their homes preparing for supper, I convinced him it was a proper procedure under the circumstances.

While he took a bath, I banged the dirt-caked pants against the porch railing and left them there for washing day, then I hosed off the tennis shoes and brought them in to set before the oven.

"Now," I said to Tommy after his bath and while we were at supper, "how did you get so muddy? Did you have tire trouble on your way up?"

"Up to where, Mom?" he asked.

"Up to Miss Amabelle's house."

"She wasn't there, Mom."

"She wasn't where?" Our interlocution was beginning to sound like the zany conversational gambits in one of my father's folktales. "You mean she wasn't home?"

"She wasn't there when I did the digging."

"Digging?" I cried. "Why in the world were you digging? In all this mud!"

"Miss Amalia and Miss Amanda *told* me to. They said Miss Amabelle wanted me to dig a garden."

"Oh," I said, and started to eat. Then I put my fork down. "A *garden*?" I cried. "Now? In all the *mud*? Why, no one could grow anything in mud like this. It'll be a week or more before the ground's fit to dig and plant after all the rain."

I pushed back my plate while Tommy continued to shovel in the food, totally unconcerned, of course, as to the state of the ground for planting... being only the digger, who followed directions, and not a planter who must gauge weather conditions, seasonal changes, the dark of the moon... *And I bet that was it!* Or, anyway, some folklore rule that determined Miss Amabelle to get her potatoes-or-whatever planted by the dark of the moon or the light of the moon or however the moon on high might be, regardless of the ground below.

"Well, for heaven's sake," I exclaimed under my breath, a little resentful that poor Tommy had been pushed into a muddy, back-breaking job for no reason except, perhaps, to follow a harebrained folk tradition. "I would have thought Miss Amabelle could have waited a week or so to have you dig up that garden ..."

Tommy looked up. "It wasn't Miss Amabelle, Mom. It was Miss Amanda and Miss Amalia who told me Miss Amabelle wanted me to do it. They said Miss Amabelle was plumb wore out and went to sleep."

"Oh, for heaven's sake," I exclaimed again. Miss Amabelle had probably scurried her old bones out there in the mud thinking to get her digging done and then scurry down the mountainside for her Social Security check, but "plumb wore out" with the digging, gave up and went to bed.

"Well," I said, "I hope she's all right."

"Miss Amalia and Miss Amanda said Miss Amabelle was sleeping right peaceful and they thanked me for digging the garden. They even sang songs to me, Mom."

"That was nice," I said.

"I sang with them..." Of course, my big, happy, singing sheep! "I didn't sing much, though. I was too tired and the ground was heavy and hard to dig."

"So that's how you got all muddy," I said. "You didn't have tire trouble after all."

"I had tired trouble," said Tommy, putting down his fork and smiling broadly at his own cleverness.

Now that I am becoming accustomed again to the strange doings of these mountain folk of mine, and able to interpret their reasons—sometimes—I thought no more about the muddy garden plot until a couple of days later, after the sun had come out hot and dried the mud to thick crust. Then I began to question Miss Amanda who came into the shop in a dotted swiss dress, her dotted swiss house slippers covered by a vintage pair of galoshes.

"Miss Amanda!" I exclaimed. "What are you doing in town?"

"I came for this," she said quaveringly as she dropped to the Shaker rocker and held up the brown window envelope that held Miss Amabelle's Social Security check, "and Mr. Purvis at the general store wouldn't give me any money for it so I could get our supplies ..."

"Well, no," I explained. "Miss Amabelle must endorse it first, and to endorse it she has to write her name on the back of the check." Then I asked why Miss Amabelle hadn't come into town for her own check as always. "Is she sick?"

"Oh, she's fine," said Miss Amanda. "Miss Amabelle is as fine as angels' wings and as happy as a harp song. But I come down to get the check and nobody will let me have any money so I can buy the supplies for Amalia to cook." She held up the forlornly drooping flour sack to show how empty it was and started to cry.

Well, I thought, Miss Amabelle is finally delegating responsibility and not any too soon, either. Those sisters have been lounging over their art and stitches all the years she's been trudging down that mountain road and trudging back again to cook the food her money buys, and I leaned over to pat the heaving shoulders. "Well, now," I said, "I believe I have one of your hooked rugs here in the shop and I'm quite sure my hooked-rug customer will be in this weekend to buy it. How about if I give you the money now, and you can get your supplies?"

She was startled by a suggestion that offered new and uncharted paths for her sluggish brain to follow. "Then you can take the check back to Miss Amabelle and have her endorse it and Mr. Purvis will give you the money later," I explained. "By the time you have finished shopping, Tommy will be here and can drive you back up the mountain," which solved all her immediate problems and made her happy as a harp song (that was a strange aphorism—but then, these hill folk come up with strange ones, most of which I have forgotten). She clutched her money in a pale fist, tucked the brown window envelope down in the bodice of her dotted swiss dress, and tripped off.

Just as expected, Tommy drove up in front of the shop at the same moment Miss Amanda emerged from the general store, the half-filled flour sack over her shoulder. He helped her into the jeep, stowed the flour sack in back, and took off in a splatter of half-dried mud, with Miss Amanda clutching the edge of the jeep door for dear life. It was probably the first time she'd ever ridden in anything faster than a rocking chair.

I didn't think about it . . . I simply did not think. That's the way it is here in Mountain Hollow—finally, the strange things these people do are not strange at all, but ordinary. So I didn't think about it until the very next day, when Miss Amalia popped into the shop.

First Miss Amanda, then Miss Amalia! These two, who had probably not been in town since the death of their father or Miss Amabelle's time in the city, whichever came last . . . "Miss Amalia!" I exclaimed. "What are you doing in town?" which seemed to be my daily question. She, too, wore a dotted swiss dress and galoshes over her dotted swiss house slippers.

"I came into town," she said, dropping into the Shaker rocker, "and got the money for Amabelle's check."

"Well, of course," I said. "How is Miss Amabelle?"

"She is fine as angels' wings and happy as a harp song," and there was that expression again.

Miss Amalia looked fragilely flowerlike as always, but I got the impression that day that she was far stronger than she appeared. My impression could have arisen when she said in her prim yet pert way, "Since you paid Amanda for the hooked rug not yet sold, could you please pay me for the hand-painted fruit bowl not yet sold?" ending the request with a smile.

Well, I paid her without argument and she rocked in the Shaker chair, the money from Miss Amabelle's check in one hand and the money from her bowl in the other, until Tommy arrived from Old Man Hardwicke's place to take her home.

It was a strange situation and I knew it, but here in Mountain Hollow we do not pry into other folks' strange situations, at least not until they become so strange we simply have to—or, at least, until *I* simply had to, which time occurred a month later.

Spring had advanced dryly, mud ruts turning to dust that seeped in through the window cracks to coat the spool cabinets, baby cradles, carved figurines, and aridly mist the sheets of plastic covering afghans, rugs, and bedspreads.

Tommy, shining his jeep engine out in front of the shop, was waiting for Miss Amabelle. This was her day to come into town and pick up her check. I discovered that I, too, was waiting—waiting uneasily, hoping that it would indeed be Miss Amabelle and not one of her sisters—not wishing to reach back into the dark section of my mind to bring forth the suspicion that lay there.

So Tommy shined away happily, and being busy inside the shop, I did not look up until the tinkling sound of the bell on the front door roused me to turn and face Amanda in dusty dotted swiss from neck to toe, carrying the brown window envelope in one hand and the folded flour sack in the other.

Good grief! This was a replay!

She lowered herself decorously into the Shaker rocker and I plumped myself down on a counter and waited for what I knew was sure to come.

Come it did. In a voice as tinkling as the doorbell, Amanda told me how she had picked up the check from Mrs. Milton Kearney, how Mr. Purvis again explained the need for Miss Amabelle's personal endorsement ... how, therefore, she lacked today's money to pay for this month's supplies, and expected, passively, the amount that would eventually be due her for a consigned bedspread, crewel embroidery tapestry, or whatever...

The whole thing was weird!

I thought again of my father's tale of Amanda and the needles and decided right then and there that here was a woman who, while confused, certainly knew the sharp end from the blunt end and which one to use.

"Now, Miss Amanda," I said in head-on confrontation, "why doesn't your sister come in and pick up her check?"

"Because *I* picked it up," she explained. "*She* will put the name on it and bring it back tomorrow."

To indicate the state I was in—also, perhaps my reluctance to think anything was wrong with this very wrong situation—I paid her for an unsold bedspread, sent her on her way for her supplies and a jeep ride up the mountain without analyzing her obliquely frank answer to my obscurely direct question until that evening when I lifted the plates from flannelette circles, put them up on plate stands for display and draped the exquisitely embroidered luncheon cloth over the counter .... *Then* I remembered the words of my question and her reply, and knew, with trembling prognostication, that I would see Miss Amalia the next day, the sister to whom Miss Amanda referred, and not Miss Amabelle, the sister about whom I was asking.

I paced the floor, and when Tommy came in at dark after polishing his engine to eye-stunning brightness, I said, "Sit down, Tommy, I want to have a serious talk with you."

He dropped immediately to the floor and crossed his legs. He becomes a floor-sitter as soon as I say I want to talk to him.

I took the shaker chair and leaned forward. "Now, Tommy," I said, and wondered where to go from there. "Now, Tommy, do you remember the day you drove your jeep up to the girls' house in order to bring Miss Amabelle to town so she could get her check?"

"Sure, Mom. Golly yes, Mom," his face as placidly empty as a dry stream bed.

"And you got all muddy?"

His forehead wrinkled in an effort to remember.

"You came home late and shined the jeep engine, then I made you take off your shoes at the front doorsill, and your pants out on the back porch..."

A glimmer of insulted recall shone in his eyes. "I shouldn't take my pants off outdoors, Mom," he said. "You know that."

"Yes, I know that, Tommy, but it was almost dark and there was no one around and you were very muddy. You were muddy because you had been digging up at Miss Amabelle's. You were digging a garden, you said."

"I was?" he asked.

"You were what?"

"I was digging a garden up at Miss Amabelle's?"

"The ground was wet that day and you came home all muddy. I thought you'd had tire trouble, but you said—"

"I said I had tired trouble." Tommy smiled broadly, remembering his joke—and that was the key! If I could only turn it just right to unlock a misunderstood memory that I might be able to understand ...

"Well, you certainly were tired," I said. "You must have done a lot of digging that day."

"Golly, Mom," he said, "the ground was heavy and hard to dig."

"It was Miss Amalia and Miss Amanda who asked you to dig the garden. That's what you said."

"Golly yes, Mom. Miss Amabelle never asked me to dig a garden like that..."

I held my breath.

"... so deep! Miss Amabelle always said to dig a shovelful deep and that would be just right, but Miss Amalia and Miss Amanda kept saying deeper, go deeper, deep enough to plant the box under the flower garden.

I let out my breath.

Tommy, surprised by what he had suddenly remembered, and rather baffled by the memory, was trying to sort it out. "They had to put the box in first," he said wonderingly, and clapped a hand over his mouth in sudden regretful and total recall.

I said, "They told you not to tell about the box, didn't they, Tommy?"

He parted his fingers in order to say, "I didn't mean to, Mom. They said the box was a secret. The flowers are growing now. Just like Miss Amalia and Miss Amanda said they would."

"I am sure they are, Tommy. But about the box under the flowers. How big was the box? Can you remember?"

He looked around for an associative size and did not find it. He rocked on the floor, his arms would around his knees; then, suddenly, he stretched out and, looking with surprise at his length, said, "Golly, Mom, about as big as me."

I sighed.

"And heavy." He blew out his breath, remembering the heaviness.

"You dug a deep garden—a hole—a trench really," I said carefully, "and then, after that, you put the box in the trench—but before that, where was the box?"

I had lost him. Too many befores and after—and it had all happened too long ago. "You sang ..." I tried to recapture him.

"Miss Amalia and Miss Amanda sang a lot," he said. "I only sang some because I was tired."

"Where was Miss Amabelle?" I asked, but now I knew for sure where she was.

"Miss Amabelle was plumb wore out. She was asleep." he said.

I smiled in agreement. "Feeling fine as angels' wings and happy as a harp song."

Tommy's face brightened. "Golly yes, Mom. That's what they said. They said Miss Amabelle was flyin' makin' music, and I said how could she when she was asleep, and they said she could, and I covered the box with dirt and Miss Amalia and Miss Amanda each took a handful of it and dropped it over the place I'd dug and covered up, and then they sang some more and I sang with them except I didn't know the words."

"That's all right, Tommy." I leaned close and patted his shoulder. "A lot of us don't know the words to other people's songs."

There was only one thing left to do and I did it. First, I ordered Tommy into the kitchen. "I have a roast in the oven," I told him, "for supper. What I want you to do is go in there and watch it. Pull a chair up before the oven and keep an eye on the little glass window and watch the roast cook. I'll be in soon and take it out and then we'll eat. Do you understand?"

He nodded, unfolded himself from the floor, and splayfooted to the kitchen where I knew he would watch that roast through the glass window with undivided attention until I told him he could desist.

Then I phoned the sheriff.

He answered immediately. I think he lives there in his county office on his swivel chair, killing flies and hoping, with each ring of the phone, that it will be a simple call, one that won't keep him away from his swivel chair too long.

He remembered me from when I managed to get him off his duff long enough to watch Tommy solve a patchwork-quilt case he didn't even know he had. "Mrs. Flagg," he said, alerted from his slow drawl, "Tommy's mother," and I could visualize him picking up a pencil stub to take notes. "Well, Mrs. Flagg ..." after I explained that Miss Amabelle was dead; and "Mrs. Flagg!" when I said I knew she was dead because she had been buried—and I certainly knew she had been buried because Tommy buried her. "Mrs. Flagg!" he yelped through the phone just before I informed him, with dignity, that of course Tommy didn't know he had buried Miss Amabelle; he thought he had buried a heavy box.

However, it was Miss Amabelle all right, I continued, because they'd had a funeral service, including the singing of hymns.

"Mrs. Flagg!" yelled the sheriff who, being a sheriff, was sure that this was a case of murder, and was scared to death of it.

"Murder?" I exclaimed. "Miss Amabelle probably fell off the roof and broke her neck normally, or her heart gave out while she was gardening—"

"But, Mrs. Flagg ..." interrupted the sheriff, and I explained that the reason for the secret burial was undoubtedly Miss Amabelle's Social Security checks, which the sheriff understood with relief. Then I had to inform him that forgery being a criminal offense, and using a deceased sister's Social Security checks being a federal offense, he'd better get out of that swivel chair bright and early in the morning so he could catch Miss Amalia before she got that check cashed, and dig up the grave to find out for sure that Miss Amabelle had died of a broken neck or a heart attack.

"Yes, Mrs. Flagg," he answered, and I went into the kitchen to take the roast from the oven.

My father may have been right when he said that Miss Amalia and Miss Amanda were both half-baked—but they were still smart enough to know they'd better keep Miss Amabelle alive when they found her broken and dead under the eaves of the roof.

They must have talked it over and weepingly made their plans, having an awful time getting that big old feedbox out of the rickety hayloft—two fragile flowers like that must have had a struggle!

They must have rejoiced when Tommy came roaring up in his jeep. Here was a digger to move mud they couldn't budge in order to bury an accidentally dead sister that they must keep alive in order to use her Social Security checks.

Also, they must have labored long over Amabelle's signature when they discovered they had to write it on the check—not to make the signature authentic (that wouldn't enter their minds)—but only to write the letters in correct sequence, which is probably all that Mr. Purvis of the general store would require, too.

If those sisters were half-baked, they were still cooking with all they had!

They couldn't understand why dear Amabelle had to be dug up and carted off to the county coroner for autopsy when they had buried her so respectfully with hymn-singing and all. Nor could they understand why it was that the Social Security money was so rudely whisked away from them after all their arduous plodding of the mountain roads and all their careful writing of a name.

Those two! They had no idea what the sheriff and I went through to keep them law-abiding citizens—by reimbursing the government for an "incorrectly endorsed" Social Security check and notifying the social Security Office of Miss Amabelle's demise so there wouldn't be any more checks to be "incorrectly endorsed."

Those two, so innocently guilty, understood only that I was the one to upset their applecart—I and my prying ways! From that time on, they dealt not with me but through Tommy. Tommy takes their supplies to them. Tommy brings in their beautiful china and lovely Victorian stitchery, and Tommy takes their money to them when I sell what they produce, and I sell it all.

Tommy still thinks Miss Amabelle is sleeping. "As fine as angels' wings," he tells me, "happy as a harp song . . ." And maybe that's the way it is.

Donald Martin
Meditations Upon a Murder

I had been contemplating the murder of my roommate for some time. This was not from any particular dislike of Charles, merely that the whole idea began as a thought in an odd, and I presume unguarded, moment, and that it intrigued me from the very first and continued to intrigue me.

Charles was not an especially offensive person (our victims seldom are), but he was something of a fool and undeniably a person of little consequence, destined from the first to be a failure. He was certainly a consistent failure in his studies. (One of his favorite sayings was, "My marks are so low they're threatening to sprout roots.") But he could afford to be indifferent to his academic inertia because his father was a Midwesterner of some wealth who had accepted Charles as the innate failure that he was and planned eventually to have him absorbed into the family business.

After rooming with him for a semester, I gradually developed a feeling of contempt for Charles.

Seeing the same person day in and day out cannot help but grate upon the nerves. The very fact that I could sit with him for hours in the evenings and think about murdering him was, I think, indicative of the esteem in which I held him. He would sit in his chair across the room reading a sports magazine, utterly oblivious of the world which had passed him by but which, he seemed to know, would be back to retrieve him. I conceived of Charles as finally succeeding, attaining his apogee as a corpse. I saw him as making a fine corpse, taking that admirable, mediocre, lackadaisical, and completely unfettered spirit to the grave with him.

I had been working extremely hard at my studies at that time. Perhaps Charles's jejune presence was unnerving. The study of medicine is, I think, exceeded in its arduousness, puzzlements, and abstruse problems only by the study for the ministry. In fact one of my professors suggested that I go away for a semester and take a rest, the strain was that apparent, but I refused. I had worked too hard, dreamed too long about being able to practice medicine, so that delay in attaining my goal by even a few months was unbearable to me. Of course I was working hard, but I believed that a man's capacities for work had no limitations, that any alleged limitations were imagined, and that a man could go on for infinite cerebral distances. That was my precise conception of the mind: infinite.

I soon found, however, that thinking of Charles as a corpse was a most relaxing and stimulating diversion. After closing my books for the evening, I would lean back in my chair and stare at him. It is amazing how when you are close to a person, that is living with him for some appreciable length of time, his importance as a human being shrinks and you are not at all averse to thinking about murdering him. At least that is the way it was with me. I could never have thought of murdering a perfect stranger because I had never had anything to do with that stranger, and to even think of harming such a person would be inconceivable. But with someone that I knew it was different. When I was younger, and living at home, I often thought of murdering my brothers or my father or my mother. Often I had it planned down to the finest detail. Once I took my youngest brother ice skating on the pond near where I knew there was a break in the ice, just to see how close I could actually come to the break. With a bit more urging he would have skated there, but I desisted because the very closeness of death (and the knowledge that I could have achieved it) was sufficiently exhilarating. So the more familiar I became with Charles, the more I could see him as a corpse, alive one moment, dead the next . . . as simple, as complete, as irrevocable as that.

He was a light-hearted and at times likable chap. He had no financial cares; I had many. Once when I was stuck for the rent he got it up for me and never said a word.

"I'll pay it back," I said.

"Forget it," he told me, standing in the middle of the room and taking imaginary pitching windups and strides and deliveries. (He had been an excellent pitcher in high school, so he said.) "Just give me a free aspirin sometime when you're a big shot surgeon."

I did not plot it to be the great classic perfect crime of our time. It was none of that. I had read too many stories about would-be perfect crimes. The criminal had made clinical studies of every detail and still had been caught. My stand was, to a point, fatalistic. I believed that you were going to make certain unpreventable mistakes, leave several unclipped threads no matter how meticulous you were, and that it was simply a matter of how astute the investigating policemen were. No crime could be perfect, perfection being of course an unattainable entity, a brew as yet without a recipe. So, gambling against the perceptive faculties of the law, I planned Charles's murder in a general way, not concerning myself with masses of detail.

One evening Charles was in a rather glum mood, something quite uncommon for him. I was at the typewriter typing some papers for class, a tedious work because, in order to pick up some extra money, I often made a half dozen carbon copies and sold them to my classmates. I noted that Charles was unusually quiet this evening. That, too, can be annoying when it is unharmonious. I stopped typing and turned to him.

"What seems to be your trouble?"

"It's nothing organic," he said.

"Is the trouble in your father's leter?" I asked. He had received a long letter that morning.

"Yes," Charles said glumly. "That's a pretty good diagnosis. He's unhappy with my work and wants me to come home."

"To put you to work?"

He nodded. Poor fellow, he had a streak of laziness in him that was a veritable groove.

"What are you going to do?"

I asked, not without some concern, for I was not anxious to see my prime victim fly off.

"I don't know. I've been stalling him for months. I've used up just about every dodge."

"I suppose he's threatening you with financial extinction?"

He nodded. I had never seen him so unhappy, poor chap. It depressed me. Suddenly it came upon me, all at once. It was as startling as a revelation. I even had the thought at the moment that Charles wouldn't mind what I was going to do—not that this was going to be any act of mercy, no murder is ever that; these so-called acts of mercy are merely the subtle releases of certain stormy inhibitions. I got up and—I remember everything distinctly, it is all clear and sharply defined in my memory—walked to the other side of the room, and picked up a rather gothic-looking candlestick which we kept on the bookcase merely for decorative purposes, turned it upside down in my hand, and approached Charles from the back, my eyes fixed upon his unsuspecting head. I raised the candlestick and brought it down on his head with all my strength. Much to my surprise, and consternation, instead of crumpling, he leaped up, staggering forward on drunken legs, holding his head, reeling around the room, his eyes wide and glazed, filled with dying. He rammed into a table, upsetting it, sending a glass shattering upon the floor. Then he stopped, his body drawing magnificently to its full height, arched backward, and then broke, collapsing, striking the floor with a rush.

I stood transfixed for a moment, staring at him. Then I saw the blood. It was leaking from a gash just above the wrist that had been made by his falling on the broken glass. For some unaccountable reason the blood terrified me, unnerved me. I dropped the candlestick and rushed to him. His eyes were still wide open but were vacant; all semblance of life had passed out of them, but still the blood ran from his wrist. I reached up and grabbed some sheets of paper and pressed one of them down on the wound. Then I reached up and flicked off the light. Crouching there in the dim light of the room, I pulled away the paper and I could make out that the bleeding had stopped. I took the bloodied paper, tore it into bits and flushed it down the toilet. I washed a few spots of blood from my hands and went back into the room. The stillness was positively tingling. I remember standing there for a long time, listening to the awesome stillness.

Then I set about to complete the last phase of my task. I picked up my late roommate and carried him to the back door. Ours was a basement apartment and the back door opened onto a yard that was adjacent to an alleyway, across the street from which was the park. It was quite late now and I had few qualms about carrying Charles. I moved with him through the yard, squeezed through the shaggy hedges into the alley, and came out to the street. The street was empty. I would have to gamble that no one was watching from a window. Carrying him in my arms now, he'd been slung over my shoulder before, I crossed the street and went into the park and in a secluded place put him down where, I was certain, he would be found and considered the victim of a mugging. I cleaned the money from his pockets, removed his watch (which I disposed of down a sewer) and came back to the apartment. Trembling with excitement, I righted the fallen table, swept up the glass, washed the blood from the linoleum, and went to bed, waiting for the police to come in the morning, waiting to defy them.

They came earlier than I expected. It was about seven o'clock and I had just gotten up. Looking at Charles's empty bed made me sad for a moment, but only for a moment. The doorbell rang then and, straightening myself and not without a bit of rebellious pride and anticipation, I went and opened the door. I found myself staring into the face of a detective, a plainclothesman. It was not an unpleasant face, but a trifle cynical. He was bored by crime. He identified himself, opening a wallet and snapping it shut with a tired and practiced gesture, and he and I sat down and talked. Almost immediately his eye fell upon the candlestick which had resumed its place on the bookcase and kept returning to it as we spoke. He told me that my roommate had been found in the park bludgeoned to death. I expressed great horror, naturally, but I did not indulge in any false theatrics, for Charles was, after all, merely a roommate.

"When was the last time you saw him?" I was asked.

"Yesterday morning," I said. "He left early and that was the last I saw of him."

"Weren't you concerned?"

"No, he often stayed out an entire evening. He was bit of a playboy. In fact I thought you were he when the bell rang."

"You say you didn't see him at all yesterday?"

"Only in the morning."

"Where were you last night?"

"I spent the evening here," I said. "Working. Typing these papers."

"These very papers?" he asked indicating what I had typed.

"Yes. These very papers."

"Last night?"

"Yes."

Now that it is all over I am amused. They were rather clever after all. First, they knew that Charles had been carried into the park because there had been no dirt on his shoes. But the most damaging thing, indeed the fatal thing, was the words that I had impressed upon Charles's forearm with my carbon copy page when trying to stifle his bleeding arm. There were only a few words there and barely legible, but it was enough. What I am amused about is that the incriminating words were from a passage I had written declaring the pristine responsibility of the physician to humanity because of the sacredness and the importance of every life.

I was adjudged criminally insane, but I think they misunderstood and exaggerated the whole business.

Robert Arthur

You Can Die Laughing

I suppose I really should be having hysterics and screaming. But my goodness if I had hysterics at every crisis in my life, I'd have precious little time for anything else. A lady's life is full of unexpected difficulties—the cook leaves, the cleaner sends back the wrong dress, the souffle falls—a thousand things can go wrong. She gets used to coping with problems. And I shall cope with this one.

When I am upset, my method of calming myself is to sit down and write out the situation in full. By the time I have finished, I always find I can think straight again. So that's what I am doing now. In three hours, Jack Holden is calling for me to escort me to the Rexleys' for drinks. I'm sure that by the time he gets here, I'll know what to do about this.

I'll begin with my husband, Bert Willoughby. Fat, red-faced, and considered jolly. The life of the party. The kind of man who loves jokes. Imitation spiders in the bed. Buzzers that shock you. Things like that, the more outrageous and unexpected the better. I suppose that a hundred times I was on the point of screaming at Bert's jokes, from sheer irritation. But I simply smiled and pretended to be amused. A lady does not show her feelings. She may even want to kill someone, but she never reveals that she does. She just smiles.

That's how dear Mother brought me up, and I can flatter myself that Mother would have been proud of the way I've lived up to her training. Even when I decided to kill Bert—

But I'm getting ahead of myself, a simply dreadful habit.

I married Bert after Mother died. I was twenty and quite penniless, though beautifully trained in such arts as flower arrangement, making lobster bisque, organizing a charity ball or a dinner for twenty, things like that. (Father died, most inconsiderately, when I was twelve, and his insurance barely tided us over until my coming-out party.)

When I met Bert, he was a plump young man with a jolly laugh. He had money, of course, a business of his own—export-import. Mother always said it was every bit as easy to love a rich man as a poor man, and I believed her. But dear Mother never did meet Bert. I'm sure even she would've agreed it is impossible to love a man who is happiest when giving guests highballs in dribble glasses.

I dare say that in the fifteen years of our marriage I daydreamed a dozen times about killing Bert. But naturally I didn't do anything about it. One simply doesn't go around killing someone without a proper reason.

Then Bert gave me a reason.

He came padding in from the television one night, a grim look on his face. I was at my desk writing up my calendar for the week. Tea with Mrs. Aylesworth and her Garden Committee. A Red Cross meeting. An afternoon at the hospital as a Gray Lady.

"Betty," Bert said in a querulous voice, scowling at me, "you know what I learned today? Jack Holden's been stealing from the firm. In the morning I'm turning him right over to the police."

I confess my heart skipped a beat and I went cold all over. Jack, dear Jack, stealing from the firm? Jack was Bert's confidential secretary and he received a good salary. But he did love luxury and so I really couldn't blame him for what he'd done. It was Bert's fault, actually, because if Bert hadn't kept me on such a stingy allowance I could have given Jack the money he wanted.

For a moment I could only stare at Bert, wondering if he knew about Jack and me. But obviously he didn't, so I pretended indignation.

"He certainly should be in jail!" I exclaimed. "But, dear, you're leaving for Mexico City on Sunday night. If you have Jack arrested now, think what that'll do to office morale during the two weeks you're gone. There will be nothing but gossip and speculation the whole time. Nobody'll do any work. So wouldn't it be wiser to pretend you don't know, and wait until you're back to have him arrested?"

"By God, Betty, you're right," Bert said. "You're right as usual." He put his hand over his stomach and grimaced. "Ahhh, stewing over Holden has made my indigestion worse. No use ruining my stomach and my trip worrying about the office all the time I'm gone. I'll do like you say. I'll wait until I get back."

"That sounds very wise to me, Bert," I said. Dear Mother told me that men always love approval, and I can vouch that it is true. "In fact, I suppose, you'll be extra friendly with him, so he won't suspect anything."

"Right." Bert yawned and scratched himself. "I'm off for bed. Got a big banquet tomorrow night. Jolly George Gordon, the TV star, is going to be there."

"Really?" That was why Bert had indigestion—because of all the banquets he loved to attend.

"That card!" Laughter creased Bert's round face. "I'd sure love to be on his show. Think I'll ask him, maybe suggest a stunt. All he can do is say no."

With that he went upstairs to bed. Jolly George Gordon is the master of ceremonies for Bert's favorite television program, *Answer or Else*. On it contestants do ridiculous stunts for large prizes. You know the kind of thing I mean. Bert, of course, would be right in his element throwing a pie in someone's face.

As soon as I heard Bert's door close I made up my mind—about his dying, that is.

I couldn't bear the thought of Jack Holden in jail. Dear Jack, darling Jack, so tall, so handsome! Oh, he could make a woman's pulse beat faster, make her feel admired and appreciated! After Bert hired him, and Jack and I met, life at last took on meaning for me. Bert was away on long business trips quite often, and it was then Jack made up to me for all the years I had endured Bert. We were meant for each other. I could no more live without Jack than without my little Georgian house in the country, my rose garden, my lily pool, my Empire drawing room.

And if Bert had Jack jailed, I'd not only lose Jack, I'd lose everything else as well. For Jack would be certain to let slip our relationship, hoping to win mercy from Bert. But Bert, like so many jolly-seeming men, is cold and ugly underneath. As soon as he knew Jack was my lover, he would throw me out of the house without a penny. Then what would happen to me?

The thought was not to be tolerated. I simply refused to let my whole way of life be destroyed in that manner. And the only way to prevent it was for Bert to pass on. After all, we all must. And certainly nothing could be more logical than that, could it? I often wonder why men like to consider women illogical.

I picked up the phone and dialed Jack's apartment.

"Darling," I whispered, in the soft, low voice dear Mother taught me, "come over tomorrow night. Bert will be at a banquet. No, don't ask why, but it's very important to both of us. I'll tell you everything when I see you."

I hung up before he could ask quetions. I didn't want to worry him. Men do worry so. By the time I saw him I would have a plan all worked out, just as I worked out plans for my committees. I knew I might have a little trouble persuading Jack, but when he realized the alternative was years in jail, he would surely agree to my scheme.

I turned to my writing desk and began to make notes, for putting a thing down on paper does help me to clarify my thinking. In an hour I had it all worked out. Simple and foolproof. It would happen on Sunday night, the night Bert was supposed to fly to Mexico. That way his absence wouldn't be missed for several days. By then—well, he'd be where he would never be found.

I tore my notes into shreds and dropped them into the wastebasket. Then I made out my annual check to the Society for the Prevention of Cruelty to Animals and went to bed.

And then it was Sunday evening. Time for Bert to catch the train for the city, to get his plane for Mexico. Time for Bert to pass away.

But of course he didn't know that, so he was in quite a good humor. I fixed a special going-away dinner, and at my urging Bert invited Jack so Jack would have no suspicions. The three of us had quite a gay time, even though Bert's indigestion was bothering him. Bert told jokes and we laughed at them. He also told us of meeting Jolly George Gordon, the TV star.

"Wonderful fellow," he chuckled. "We got along like a house afire. I'm going to be on his show in the fall. We kicked around some ideas for stunts. I gave him a couple that appealed to him."

Jack was perspiring a little. I noticed his hand tremble and so I poured him another drink. As I'd expected, it had been difficult at first to persuade Jack. But I'd shown him what it meant to both of us, and he had agreed.

Bert looked at his watch.

"I'll go get the car, bring it around front," he said. "If it's not going to start, I want to know it in time."

He went out chuckling. Jack wiped his face and his fine brown eyes looked worried.

"Betty," he said, "can't we handle this some other way? I mean, even if I do go to jail it might not be for more than a year. And if I throw myself on his mercy—he's not such a bad fellow, carries some of his accounts who can't pay for years—"

"Darling," I told him soothingly, "I know how you feel. But Bert is really vindictive. He'll fight to get you the maximum sentence. And he'll blacklist you—even years from now, after you'd got out, you'd have trouble getting another job. It has to be done my way. I couldn't bear it with you in jail, I simply couldn't."

I put my arm around him and pulled him to me to kiss me. When we separated he said hoarsely, "Betty, Betty darling. You're what I live for. We'll go through with it. We have to."

"Nothing will go wrong," I assured him. "And I have Bert's power of attorney. After he's gone we'll run the business together. Think of the wonderful times we'll have with no Bert to worry about."

"Okay, Betty." He smiled now, "You've convinced me. But I wish it was over with."

Bert came in with his hand at his stomach, as though he had a pain. I was rather glad he couldn't read my thoughts just then. A lady should keep her thoughts to herself, and I do. Writing them down, like this, then tearing up the paper, is the only safe and genteel way.

"All set," Bert said. "Betty, did you pack my indigestion pills?"

"In your traveling kit," I told him. Then I saw the spot on my dress. When he kissed me, Jack's brandy must have spilled on it. "I'm afraid I have to change my dress," I told Bert. "It won't take five minutes. I'll meet you in the car."

I went up to change; I couldn't very well go out wearing a soiled dress. When I came down, Bert and Jack were in the car and Bert was telling about a dishonest employee he once sent to prison for a term of years. It was his sly way, I knew, of making Jack worry. But I was glad, for it confirmed what I'd been telling Jack about Bert's vindictiveness.

I drove, as I'm a much better driver than Bert. Women are really better drivers than men because they take things more calmly. Bert sat beside me and Jack in back. I had persuaded Bert to take the express at Ellenville, instead of the local at Bartlett. At Ellenville a lot of people always got on the Sunday express back to the city. On such a crowded train no one later would be able to remember whether Bert had been aboard or not. One must think of such details.

I drove to a small hill overlooking the station. Then I stopped and turned out the lights.

"Hey, Betty!" Bert protested. "What's the idea?"

"Oh, it's such a wonderful night," I said. "Let's sit and enjoy it. We can see the train coming and be there in plenty of time. And you don't need to buy a ticket. Your commutation ticket is good on this line too."

"Anyway," Jack put in, "you always say these trains are late half the time, Bert."

"That's right," Bert chuckled. "Say, did I tell you the one Jolly George Gordon told me, about the engineer whose train was always late and when he was asked why he said—"

I didn't listen. I was watching the darkness intently. The train often *was* late. Sometimes it didn't even run; our commuter service is by no means dependable. I wasn't going to be caught by some silly mixup in the service. Dear Mother trained me always to think of everything that could go wrong in any situation.

Bert rambled on. Then I saw the yellow glow of the train headlight. The long diesel rounded the curve and Bert stirred.

"Time to get going," he said.

"Yes, Bert," I said. "Jack!"

It was Jack's cue. He acted with commendable coolness, lifting the length of iron pipe I had slipped into the back of the car and bringing it down on Bert's head.

Bert let out a yell and jerked around. But Jack swung again and it was all over. I was glad it had been so quick. I hate to see anyone suffer.

For a moment neither Jack nor I moved. The train below us came in, stopped; the people surged on; then it pulled away again. After that the silence of the night pressed in on us. But it was not a true silence. The trees rustled as if a thousand tiny tongues were whispering. A hoot-owl gave forth several scream-like hootings. And a strange gurgle came from Bert's throat—his last breath coming out as his muscles relaxed. In a fantastic way, it sounded like a chuckle.

"He isn't dead!" Jack exclaimed.

"Of course he is, sweetheart," I told him. "Everything has gone perfectly and in no time at all it'll be over."

Bert had slumped down against the seat and was threatening to get blood on the seat cover. He always was untidy. But I was prepared. From under the seat, I pulled out an old towel and quickly wrapped it around Bert's head. Then I eased him down, so he couldn't be seen from the outside.

"I'll feel better when he's out of sight," Jack said. Already his voice was stronger because of my practical gesture. Three-fourths of life, Mother always said, is made up of attending to small deatils. "Let's get going to that damned haunted house. Bert's mentioned the place so often, it's only fitting he should be buried there."

I started the car. After a few minutes I turned into swampy woods, worthless for anything—the timber poor, the ground wet, the whole place unhealthy. Bert had owned it all. He'd taken over a defaulted mortgage on it years ago because he was in love with the fact that a ramshackle old house in the middle of it was supposed to be haunted. He'd even started to fix it up until I persuaded him to abandon the whole thing.

Half a mile in the woods, in utter isolation, we came into a clearing. Our headlights illuminated a sagging Colonial with broken windows. A small tree had fallen against it.

"If that place isn't haunted," Jack said, "it'll do until a real haunted house comes along." He had brought along a flask and was feeling himself again. "Maybe Bert'll give it an authentic ghost. Now what do we do, Betty?"

"Dig a grave for Bert in the cellar. I've tools in the trunk of the car, two electric lanterns, a tamper—"

"Even a tamper!" Jack said. "You're wonderful, really wonderful. What other woman would have thought of bringing along a tamper!"

I appreciated the praise, but my goodness, it was elementary to think of a tamper. I really do believe that any woman who can plan a dinner for twenty-four important guests and have it go off without a hitch can plan most anything at all.

Jack got the tools out. Then he and I lifted Bert out and sat him up at the base of a tree, where he couldn't leave any marks on the car upholstery. As Jack turned away, he gave an exclamation of alarm.

"Betty! Look here."

He was pointing at a crumpled cigarette package lying in the road. His finger, his whole arm, shook violently.

"Someone's been here!" he told me with anguish.

Certainly someone had been there. The question was, when. I picked up the empty pack. It was very damp.

"It was dropped here days ago," I said. "It rained night before last. You know sometimes hikers or hunters come this way. It's really nothing to worry about, Jack. In a few days I'll have this road barricaded and the house nailed up. Then no one will come near here until the place rots away."

With that I led the way into the gloomy, evil-smelling old house. Down in the basement, we dug a grave for Bert near one wall. It was not deep, but deep enough. We were both rather anxious to be finished.

Then we went back outside to get Bert.

And Bert was gone!

Beneath the tree where we had left him was the towel which had been around his head. And that was all. I was simply astounded.

"Someone's been here!" Jack said hoarsely. "Someone's taken him away."

But he was just being irrational. No one could have come up that road in a car without our having heard him. I don't deny I was a bit perturbed, but I refused to show it. A lady maintains her poise at all times and thereby sets an example to others, dear Mother used to say.

I flashed the electric lantern around in the darkness. Somewhere an owl hooted raucously. Around us the darkness and silence pressed in. There was no sign of Bert.

He had vanished like one of those silly magic tricks he was so fond of.

I was becoming annoyed. I remember thinking with a feeling of outrage that Bert never could be trusted not to upset my plans at the last minute. Then I saw something move in the bushes some yards away.

"Jack! Over here!" I ran to the spot. It was Bert, dragging himself along the ground. He stopped as I ran up, and tried to sit erect, parting his teeth in a grimace, a mockery of a smile.

"Betty, my dear," he said with difficulty, "a joke—on you. One of my best. I wasn't quite dead. Now you'll have to kill me all over again."

He started to laugh. Abruptly he stopped; his eyes closed; he slumped back to the ground. I watched him suspiciously, in case it was just another of his jokes, but he did not move. I felt his pulse. Bert was quite dead.

Jack was a little shaken—dear Jack, he is really very sensitive—but soon all was over. We tamped the earth down hard in the cellar, effaced any signs we had been there, and let ourselves out. It really had gone very smoothly, all things considered. One must be prepared for minor hitches in any undertaking.

We drove directly home. And after Jack had a drink, he drove back to the city. With him he took Bert's bag, briefcase, and one of his hats. The briefcase and bag he was going to put into one of those ten-cent lockers at the station where, after a few days, they would be found and taken to the general office. Bert's hat, Jack was going to hang in the crowded, busy bar in the terminal, where it too would be found in a few days.

The picture would be clear. Bert had reached the city, and having an hour to wait for the limousine to the airfield, had checked his bag and stepped in for a drink or two.

After that—what? Bert had vanished. Maybe he had gotten drunk and been robbed and killed. Who knew?

Men have vanished before.

And will again, goodness knows.

That was last Sunday, three days ago. Three serene days—except that sometimes I heard the echo of Bert's last, dying laughter in my ears. Three days while Jack and I waited, to allow time enough for us to get worried at not hearing from Bert in Mexico City.

So far, everything has gone exactly as I planned it.

But now, if I were an ordinary woman, I really think I would scream.

Today I received a letter from Bert!

It came special delivery. Postmarked in the city last night. Addressed in Bert's handwriting. But the return address!

X. Bert Willoughby, Basement Apt., The Haunted House.

I just caught myself from giving a shriek when I saw it; it was such a shocking thing to read. *Ex* Bert Willoughby. Meaning he was dead. And buried in the cellar of the haunted house. And knew it!

Although dear Mother taught me that it is always best to face up to a different situation without delay, it took me an hour to bring myself to open the letter. Even then I was jittery.

This is what the letter said:

Dear Betty:

Farewell and hail! We who are dead salute you. Congratulations on your first murder. How did it feel from your end of the proceedings? From my end it was interesting, but damned uncomfortable. The waiting was the worst.

You do have a good mind, Betty. I daresay you'll make a great success of the business. Perhaps I should have let you help me long ago. Well, now it's too late for regrets. I'm dead and buried and glad of it. Because at last the pain is over—and it was getting pretty bad toward the end.

What pain? Why, my indigestion, of course. Only it was cancer. I didn't tell you because I didn't see any point in it. These last few months I've been getting the business ready to turn over to you in good shape. My trip to Mexico was to be the last item of business. On my return, the hospital, a few lingering months, then finish. You would have been free of me. Thank you for sparing me those months, Betty my love, my own true murderess.

I stopped reading at that point with a feeling of outrage. Bert had known he was going to die and hadn't told me! It was typical of his lack of consideration for me. Then the letter went on:

Then I learned about Jack—I mean about you and Jack. That made me rather angry. First I planned to throw you out. Then it occurred to me it might be amusing to watch your maneuvers if you felt your guilty little secret threatened. And you know I've never been able to resist a joke.

I didn't expect to be murdered, I confess. But that night I broke the news about Jack being a crook, and went noisily to bed. I then picked up the extension phone and heard you make a date with Jack. Later I peeked down and saw you scribbling away, saw you carefully tear up what you had written. When you were asleep, I came down and rescued the scraps, tore up some old shopping lists of yours to put back in the basket, and took the scraps to the office next day.

It took me an entire day to assemble them. I was fascinated by the little murder plan they revealed. And—I decided to let you carry it out. Why not? I was going to die anyway. Why should I linger and suffer for months? You were doing me a favor. And what a chuckle it gave me to think of you and Jack going to all the trouble and risk of committing a murder you didn't need to commit.

What are you thinking now, Betty? Whatever it is, believe me, I'm laughing. Drive by the old haunted house and perhaps you can hear the laughter coming from the cellar where you buried me.

You're wondering what I've done about it, aren't you? The answer is—nothing. I left no message and I left no clue. As of this moment only you and Jack and I know that I have been murdered. I won't tell. Will you? Will Jack?

If your plans work out, congratulations. But honestly, will you ever know another moment's peace of mind? When your dear, virile Jack touches you, will you enjoy his caress—or will you suddenly feel his hands to be my cold, clammy ones and will you shudder? Just a little? Or scream? When the doorbell rings, will you jump, wondering if it's the police at last?

With that thought, I remain,

Yours ghoulishly, Bert

That was the letter. I read it over and over. It had been written the week before, of course, and left with some mailing service to post. That was plain enough. Writing it as if from the grave was part of Bert's twisted sense of humor.

And now that I have written this all out, I understand Bert's actions perfectly. I can see that Bert is telling the truth when he says he left behind no clues to his death, no accusation of me. Because he expected my conscience to punish me, once I knew he had known all along that I was going to kill him. He expected my fears to destroy everything that exists between me and Jack. He expected me to be reduced to a nervous wreck, by constant fear that someday some message he had left behind would bring the police to my door.

But the arrival of the police would spoil the joke! So I know the police will never come. As for my conscience—dear, naive Bert never learned that a lady doesn't have a conscience, she has good manners instead.

Tomorrow Jack and I will go to the old house and dig Bert up, bury him someplace else. We can't go tonight, because Jack is picking me up to escort me to the Rexleys'.

Harry Rexley is an old friend of Bert's. He phoned me yesterday and said I simply must come over this evening. He wouldn't take no for an answer. I didn't want to go, but as I explained to Jack, it will be a perfect opportunity to act worried about not hearing from Bert. And then in another day or two I'll call the police, who will be baffled by the mystery.

But tomorrow Bert moves to a new address. Dear Mother used to say, a careful woman is one who is careful.

There's the bell now. It's Jack; I heard his car. Poor Bert, the final joke and the last laugh are on you! What a wonderful time Jack and I are going to have together.

Statement by Harry Rexley:

Mrs. Bert Willoughby and Mr. Holden arrived at my home at five to ten in the evening. At ten o'clock, I switched on the television to *Answer or Else.* Before Bert—that's Mr. Willoughby—left for Mexico, he made me promise to watch the program on this particular evening, for he had thought up an interesting stunt they were planning to use. I was to get Mrs. Willoughby to come over to the house and turn on the program without telling her why. A surprise, you see. Everything was normal until Jolly George Gordon, the M.C., said ...

Excerpt from transcription of Answer or Else, *Production No. 115:*

"...Well, folks, you've all seen what we just did. We gave those three young couples pickaxes, shovels, lanterns, and maps. Now if they follow those maps correctly, they'll be led to some genuine buried treasure—a small metal box with with five hundred silver dollars in it, and folding money for five thousand more. Yes sir, five thousand of Uncle Sam's fattest and greenest pieces of legal tender. The first couple to dig in the right place gets the loot—but this is what they don't know and you do!

"The treasure is buried in the cellar of a house way out in the woods. My crew went out a week ago and buried the chest in the cellar and smoothed it all down so no one could guess. But along about midnight those three young couples are going to meet in that cellar and they're all going to start digging like mad. Before they're finished, they'll probably dig up that entire cellar because it's only a small chest and it's buried pretty deep—you have to earn buried treasure, you know.

"And while they're digging, my sound effects crew is going to broadcast into that house a few little sound effects. For, you see, it isn't just an ordinary house. It's an old Colonial mansion that has a genuine ghost. Yes sir, Mr. Bert Willoughby, the owner, has vouched for it. It's a genuine haunted house, folks, but we're going to broadcast into it the sound of rattling chains, moans, groans, and squeals, just in case the ghost is scared away by all this activity and doesn't get around to making any weird noises.

"Those young folks are certainly in for a surprise tonight. Aren't we just *awful?*"

Statement by Harry Rexley, continued:

... and that's when Mrs. Willoughby started to scream as if she would never stop ...

C. B. Gilford
Beware: Dangerous Man

Elaine Karnes heard her husband drive the car into the garage, and became uneasy when he didn't come into the house. It was past six, almost dusk, and he should have been starving after his day at the office and then the long drive home, at the remotest edge of the suburbs. She didn't want the steak to get overdone, and besides she was puzzled. So she went outside to find him.

The first thing she noticed was that he had switched on the light in the garage. She hesitated a moment in the driveway, expecting him to emerge. But he didn't. And then she heard the sound of the running water and saw the hose leading into the garage. He was washing the car—before dinner, and doing it inside the garage.

She went only as far as the doors, and called to him. He must have been crouching down in front of the car because she didn't see him at first, and then, finally, he straightened up. He turned off the water at the hose nozzle before he looked at her. She couldn't see his face too clearly, but she sensed trouble. So she went to him, squeezing between the side of the car and the garage wall.

"David, what on earth are you doing?"

She could see his face now. He had pushed his hat back off his forehead. His lean, tanned face was oddly pale, and his brown eyes had a strange, bright look in them. Water had splashed liberally over his once-neat gray tweed suit but he was unaware of it.

"Elaine, maybe I've done a foolish thing." His voice was strained, a bit unnatural. "Maybe dishonest, too, I don't know."

She went the rest of the way to him, and into his arms. But his embrace was stiff, formal, almost unfriendly.

"What's all this about, darling?" she said.

"You remember Pharaoh, Vandrak's dog? That Great Dane next door?"

Remember Pharaoh? What a question. She thought of the uneasy, half-frightened feeling she had every time she saw him. The huge thing went out on a leash mostly, but every once in a while he escaped, and roamed the woods separating their house from the Vandraks'. And sometimes he wandered into the yard, loping around like a scavenging beast of prey, sniffing, pawing into the ground if he found something worth investigation. At such times she stayed inside the house. She'd never had the nerve to approach the dog, or to try to run him away from their property.

"Well, I hit it with the car, Elaine. I killed it."

She couldn't help feeling relief that this was all that was troubling her husband. Why this was the end of a nuisance.

"It was just after I passed Vandrak's house," David went on hastily, as if he thought he had to justify himself to her. "You know how the trees shadow the road, and anyway it was beginning to get dark. The dog just suddenly dashed out of the woods in front of me. I didn't have time to stop. I tried to swerve, but hit it anyway. Hit it real hard. Must have knocked it about ten feet off the road. Well, I stopped and got out and looked at it. It was just lying there. Couldn't see any sign of life ..."

He hesitated, and his hands clutched her shoulders hard. His eyes seemed to search her face, for approval, or sympathy, or something.

"Well don't you see, Elaine?" he went on. "I had a sort of choice to make. The dog was already dead. There was no point in getting help for it, or anything like that. But even though it wouldn't help the dog, I knew it was Vandrak's dog, and that I ought to call Vandrak right away. It was the least I could do, you might say. But then there was the fact that the dog had annoyed us, and you were scared of it even. Plus the fact that Vandrak is such an unpleasant guy. I just knew what he'd say, that I'd killed the dog deliberately. He'd raise a real row, sue me or something. Lord, I wouldn't mind paying him the value of the dog, but I knew he wouldn't be satisfied with that. He's vindictive. You could never be sure just what Vandrak would do or how he ..."

He stopped, out of breath, his eyes begging her to understand what he was saying.

"So you didn't tell Vandrak," she finished for him. "You got back in the car and drove home before he saw you."

"Well, it isn't quite the same," he argued, defensively, "as leaving a human being in the road."

"I'm not blaming you, David," she told him. But she was oddly, intangibly disturbed. "I'm sure I'd have done the same thing that you did."

"I'll send Vandrak some money anonymously. I just want to avoid the man, that's all."

"Yes, I do think you should pay him."

"I had to wash the car off. There was some blood and dog hair on the fender, but I think I took care of it ..."

He pointed to show her. What he hadn't been able to eliminate was the considerable dent in the right front fender. Still, it wouldn't be too noticeable, if one weren't looking for it. The headlight was still intact.

"I'll take it to some garage in some other town," he said, "and get that staightened out as soon as I can."

She nodded her agreement. "Now let's go in the house," she said. "There's a steak on the fire, but we'll have a drunk first."

"All right. But let me hose out the garage first; then I'll be in."

She left him there, heard the water as it was turned on again. Back in her kitchen she took a couple of highball glasses off the shelf and mixed drinks for both of them—a bit stronger than usual. By the time she had them ready, he came in.

"Got to change these wet clothes," he said.

She waited for him in the living room where she'd built a fire in the fireplace. The evening was just chilly enough to justify a fire, and it was positively wasteful not to have one with so much wood around the place. David came in finally and she handed him his glass. They sat together on the sofa, very close.

"Do you really think I did the right thing?" he asked after a long moment.

"Darling, I've already told you I approved."

"I was a coward."

"But you're going to pay him. That's the most you could do anyway. After all, it was an accident. You couldn't help it."

"Vandark might suspect me anyway. There aren't many cars on our road."

"Darling, please don't figure out ..."

"I won't be able to get the car fixed till Saturday. I just hope Vandrak doesn't get a chance to notice it before then."

"Darling, let's forget about Vandrak."

He had stopped talking and was sipping from his glass when the doorbell rang. She felt the sudden tensing of his body at the sound, and she jumped ahead of him to answer it.

When she opened the door, there were two men standing there, one a man in ordinary clothes and the other a policeman in uniform. The one not in uniform showed her his wallet, however, with a brightly gleaming badge inside it.

"Detective Sergeant Riconda," he announced himself. "This the David Karnes residence?"

She nodded.

"Is Mr. Karnes at home now?" he asked.

She nodded again, trying to be nonchalant, trying to fight back that unnameable dread she had felt before. Why were police coming about this matter of a dog? What had Vandrak told them?

"Could we speak to Mr. Karnes?"

She stood aside, inviting them to come in. Both the officers took off their hats as they entered. David rose to meet them in the center of the living room. Sergeant Riconda got right to the point.

"Mr. Karnes," he said, "were you involved in an accident a few minutes ago?"

She saw that David was pale, but his voice was steady enough when he answered. "Yes ... yes, I was."

"And you left the scene of the accident?"

"Yes ..."

"After first getting out of your car, and discovering that the victim was dead, that is?"

"Yes, I got out and looked at the dog ..."

"Dog?"

There was a momentary silence. David looked puzzled. "Yes," he said finally. "My neighbor's Great Dane. That's the accident you're talking about, isn't it?"

Detective Sergeant Riconda was an oldtimer, in his forties, beginning to incline to both stoutness and baldness. He didn't become at all excited. "I'm afraid not, Mr. Karnes," he said. "I don't know anything about a dead dog. I'm talking about an accident in which a woman was killed."

David opened his mouth to speak, didn't succeed on the first try.

Riconda elaborated. "Your neighbor, Mrs. Paula Vandrak." He consulted his watch. "I guess this happened about—about twenty minutes ago. Mr. Vandrak said he heard his wife's scream from the direction of the road. He couldn't see what was happening because his house is competely cut of from the road by trees. But he ran in the direction of the scream. And he got there just in time to see the car drive away. He was pretty sure it was your car, but he got the license number anyway. It checked. And then Vandrak found his wife lying by the road, dead . . ."

"But I hit a dog!" David had found his voice now. "I ought to know. I saw what I hit, and I got out of the car afterwards. Sure, I ran away, and I should't have done that. But I didn't hit a woman! I hit a dog!"

Riconda looked genuinely puzzled. He exchanged glances with the uniformed officer, who shrugged his shoulders.

"Look," David said suddenly, "maybe a woman was killed. But there's a dead dog down there on the road too, isn't there? A Great Dane?"

In the silence that followed, Detective Sergeant Riconda shook his head slowly in answer to David's question.

But he didn't seem a rash man. David's sincerity apparently impressed him. His brow was furrowed.

"I have two stories," he said finally, "yours and Vandrak's, and they contradict each other. But the evidence is on Vandrak's side because we've got the corpse of a woman and not of a dog. There's another piece of evidence, however—your car. If there's blood or hair or anything like that on the front of your car, Mr. Karnes, it would tell us what you hit. So, if it was a dog you have absolutely nothing to worry about."

That was when Elaine saw her husband wilt, and she ran across the room to him.

He took her into his arms and held onto her so tightly and savagely that she could scarcely breathe. "What have I done, Elaine? What have I done?"

"Are you talking about your car?" Riconda asked.

David nodded. "I washed it off," he said. The words came out choked, broken. "I scrubbed it clean. There's still a dent in the fender, but that's all you'll find. The evidence was there, but it's all gone now."

Riconda didn't didn't speak for a while; when he did, his tone had changed. It was harder now, harsher.

"Mr. Karnes, we'll have the lab boys go over your car anyway. Even if you did wash it, you might have missed something. In the meantime, I think you'd better come with us."

David let go of his wife, quickly, without looking at her. And he continued to avoid her eyes while he got his hat and coat. But she caught him at the door as he preceded the officers out. She held onto his arm and stopped him.

"David!"

"What are you thinking, Elaine?" he asked, still not looking at her. "Do you think I killed Mrs. Vandrak and ran away?"

She had no difficulty answering him. "You said you killed the dog, David. I believe you."

David put his hand on hers and squeezed it. Then he went out the door. The two officers followed him, and she was left alone.

As soon as they took David away, she contacted George Newell, the only lawyer they knew, and a friend, and George accepted the case. He called back later, reported he'd talked to David. But bail hadn't been set yet; so David couldn't come home. Things didn't look too bad, though. There were lots of things still to be checked through.

She couldn't help worrying, even though Newell had told her not to. And it was difficult for her to sleep that night in a house that seemed suddenly empty. In the morning there were dark circles under her eyes.

The lab men arrived shortly after dawn. She watched them work, gave them as much information as she could. They left without telling her what, if anything, they had found.

George Newell came just before noon. Like David, George was a young man just getting started in a career. He was confident and energetic, and Elaine was sure that he was smart, too.

"When will David come home?" was the first question she asked him.

"Not for a while yet," Newell told her. His lean face looked serious. "Felling runs quite high against hit and run drivers, you know."

"But he killed a dog."

"That's what we'll try to prove, but we haven't yet."

"What about the lab tests on the car?"

"Negative. Your husband did a good job of washing it. Later we might get them to tow the whole car in so that they can give it a more thorough going-over. But the car angle doesn't look promising, Elaine."

She tried not to despair. She hadn't put much hope in the car anyway. "Did you talk to Mr. Vandrak?" she asked.

"I met your Mr. Vandrak. I heard him re-telling his version of what happened." Newell offered her a cigarette, which she refused, then lit one himself. "Strange sort of a guy, isn't he? I don't think I like him very well."

"David and I never got along with him. That's why David ran away in the first place. He didn't want to stir up trouble with Vandrak."

"Yes, I know."

"I've been thinking, Geroge. I couldn't sleep much last night, so I had plenty of time. Can I tell you what I've been thinking?"

He smiled. "Of course, Elaine. What is it?"

"Well, I've been thinking about Vandrak mainly. Supposing David is telling the absolute truth—and I'm sure he is—that makes Vandrak a deliberate liar, doesn't it?"

Newell shrugged, ground out his cigarette. "It would seem so," he said. "Unless a real strange coincidence of some kind happened, involving two cars. But I think we can rather safely assume that if David's story is true, Vandrak is very probably lying. But why should he lie, Elaine? Can you tell me that?"

"I've thought of one reason," she said, frowning and biting her lip in the customary way she had when something was puzzling her.

"What's that?"

"Maybe he murdered his wife."

Newell stood up suddenly. He paced the rug a few times, finally stopped in front of Elaine's chair, his face grim. "That's interesting," he said. "What gave you such an idea?"

"Two things."

"What things?"

"For one, I happen to know the Vandraks didn't get along. I don't know all the reasons, but one at least was the dog. Paula hated Pharaoh. She told me that a dozen times. And her husband loved the dog, worshipped it. He tried to keep it in the house or on a leash as much as he could for the dog's sake. He didn't want the dog running loose. He was afriad something might happen to it ..."

"Wait a minute," Newell interrupted, pacing to the fireplace. "It's conceivable then, isn't it, that if Vandrak was so fond of the dog, and saw David hit the dog, he might want revenge, might frame David for a more serious crime—homicide."

Elaine followed the lawyer to the fireplace. "I think Vandrak would be just the kind," she said, "to do something as abominable as that."

"But do you think he'd go so far as to sacrifice his wife in order to ...?"

"Why not, if he hated her? Supposing, for instance, she'd been responsible for Pharaoh's getting loose, so he could run into he road and get killed. Then Vandrak would have been furious with her at the same time he was mad at David."

Newell smiled. "Elaine, this all sounds vaguely plausible, but it is guesswork."

"Vaguely plausible? You'd think it was more than that if you knew

Vandrak." Suddenly somehow she felt certain. And no masculine logic or incredulity would ever change her mind. This was the way it had happened.

"You mentioned two things that made you think of murder," Newell said. "What was the other?"

"Arnold Vandrak couldn't have been too fond of his wife because several times he tried to make love to me."

"What?"

"Oh, I don't mean he'd want to kill his wife because ... because of me." Elaine walked away. She couldn't help feeling embarrassed. "It just proves that he wasn't terribly in love with his wife, that's all."

"Did David know about these ... passes?"

"No, I never told him. I didn't think it was serious enough. And David's the kind who might take that sort of thing very seriously. You see, I was always quite sure I could handle Vandrak, but I wasn't so sure I could handle David if he knew about it."

"I see ..." Newell said, but both his face and voice registered a certain amount of doubt.

"It was really so silly," she went on, "so kind of amateur. It always started when the dog would get loose and Vandrak would come looking for him. Sometimes he'd find the beast lolling about our yard. He knew I was afraid of him; so he'd ring the doorbell and start apologizing. Rather than invite him in, I'd step out on the porch. That's when he'd try something. But he wasn't very insistent, so I wasn't really worried. Just the same, after a while I began listening to his apologies through the screen door."

Newell lit another cigarette thoughtfully. "Okay," he said. "Let's suppose David's story is the correct one, and also that Vandrak murdered his wife. You seem to be the detective, Elaine. How did he manage it?"

"I've thought of an answer to that, too."

"You've a fertile imagination, I must say."

"George, I'm trying to help David ..."

"Of course. Of course you are."

She sat down again before she spoke, and she spoke calmly and slowly. It was all so terribly clear and certain in her mind. "All right," she said, "it starts when David's car hits the dog. Vandrak either sees it happen, or is close enough to hear the squeal of brakes and tires. At any rate he's there on the scene when David drives away, and he recognizes the car. He's angry at David, and very likely he's also angry at his wife. Let's say she was responsible for the dog's getting loose. But, at the moment, he's angrier at David. He runs down the road after the car. It's about three hundred yards to our house. By the time he arrives, David is in the garage, with the light on, washing the dog's blood off the fender. That gives Vandrak his idea—David won't be able to prove he hit a dig instead of a woman. So Vandrak goes back to where the accident occurred. There's the dead dog. And, let's say, Paula Vandrak is there, too. So he kills her ..."

"How, Elaine? Does he ask her to wait while he gets his car and runs her down?"

"George, you're ridiculing me."

"No, I'm not. But all this conjecture, Elaine, has to be able to stand up. The police doctor is quite sure Mrs. Vandrak's fatal injuries were the result of her having been hit by a car."

"Well, maybe Vandrak did it that way. But I don't think so. I think he killed her on the spot, right there in the road, by a blow of some kind, with something big—something that would make it appear Paula *had* been hit by a car. That's a minor detail ..."

"A minor detail? Elaine, it isn't!"

"Just let me finish, George. He killed Paula and he left her there, and he took the dog away. The dog hasn't been found since the accident, has it?"

"No, Vandrak claims the dog seems to have run away."

She stood up, the certainty burning in her now. "That's ridiculous," she said triumphantly. "That dog was as devoted to Vandrak as he was to it. It would never run away."

"We can't prove that, Elaine."

She walked to him. "George," she began very slowly, "if I could discover where Vandrak buried that dog, it would save David, wouldn't it?"

The lawyer nodded, but grudgingly. "I suggest we convince the police," he said, "that they look for the dog."

She smiled because now she actually felt like smiling. "George, dear, most of this neighborhood is woods. The police aren't going to dig up all of it, are they? No, I'm the one for this. I've got to get Vandrak to lead me to the dog's grave."

Newell took her shoulders, and he really looked concerned. "Elaine, if Vandrak is a murderer, that could be dangerous."

"Don't you remember," she said, "Mr. Vandrak is very fond of me."

She stood in front of her full-length mirror, studying the reflection objectively. What she saw was good. Her blue eyes were bright, shining, showed no traces of sorrow or tears. Her black hair was tired back neatly with the blue scarf. Her skin had a healthful, outdoor glow. And her face was pretty besides. But it's that outdoor look about me that Vandrak must like, she decided. Paula had been definitely the hothouse variety, not the type to have any affection at all for Great Danes.

She buttoned the jacket of the corduroy suit. Her figure was right, too. All the necessary curves, but at the same time lithe, athletic. Her legs looked just fine in the knee-length wool stockings, and even the walking shoes were feminine enough.

Forgive me, David, she told him silently, over the miles of their separation. I'm dressing to please another man. A beast of a man at that. A murderer. But he's got to like me. It would even be convenient if he'd sort of fall in love with me.

She left the house, locking the front door behind her, and walked down the road. When she came to Vandrak's driveway, she turned in. The house itself, a small ranch type, appeared in a moment from behind the trees. A funeral wreath was hanging on the front door. She walked to the door and rang the bell.

No answer came. So she walked around the yard, making a full circuit of the house. She tried to make it appear casual, on the chance that Vandrak was lurking inside and was watching her. She didn't notice any sign of a fresh excavation. But she'd been almost certain there wouldn't be. He wouldn't have been foolish enough to bury the dog too close. When she finished her tour, she sat down on the front steps and waited.

It was half an hour later that Vandrak's car ascended the driveway. She stood up, smoothed out the wrinkles in her corduroy suit, watched him get out of the car and come toward the door, laden with what seemed to be a sack of groceries.

He stopped short of the door because she was blocking his entrance. He stood there for a moment, and then he said, "What do you want, Mrs. Karnes?"

He was a big man, but lean. His bigness was in his height, in the width of his shoulders, the length of his arms, the size of his hands. He was inclined toward hairiness, so that his jaws, even when freshly shaved, gave a dark look to his face. His heavy brows so overshadowed his pale, deep-set eyes that the eyes seldom gave any clue to what the man was thinking. She had never been afraid of him before, but now, in the certainty that he was a murderer, she was. It was her first job to keep from revealing her fear.

"I haven't seen you since the accident," she told him. "I wanted to talk to you. To tell you ... how sorry I am ..."

His eyes remained enigmatic. "That's very kind of you." Then he waited, staring fixedly at her till she had to look away. "Is that all, Mrs. Karnes?"

"Is there anything ... anything at all ... I can do?"

"I'm a very self-sufficient man, Mrs. Karnes."

She argued desperately. "But I want to help ... somehow. I feel so guilty ..."

"For what your husband did? Paula's dead, and there's nothing anybody can do about that."

There was sorrow in his face and in his voice, but she knew it was all hypocrisy. Like every good murderer, the man was a clever actor. Her acting would have to be better. And when it came to acting, a woman had a trick a man could never match. She could cry.

"Oh, Mr. Vandrak, I'm so sorry," she began, and she let the tears flow.

"Please, Mrs. Karnes ..."

She sensed a sudden unsureness in him. Perhaps he felt something of the same attraction toward her that had prompted him to make advances on previous occasions. Or perhaps he was too businesslike a murderer to let himself be distracted from his problem of self-preservation by a woman, and so was trying to get rid of her without knowing quite how to manage it.

But she mustn't let him manage it. If he was to lead her to the dog's grave, she had to stay close to him. She lifted her face so that he could see her tears. And she could actually see the unsureness in the man now.

"Please, Mrs. Karnes," he said again. "You'd better go home now."

"I can't bear to go home," she sobbed.

"I realize you must miss your husband ..."

She acted on the inspiration the instant that it came. "I'm not concerned about him," she said savagely. "He's a beast, a murderer. I don't ever want to see him again ... never, never!"

The outburst took Vandrak by surprise. The tiniest of sparks lighted in his pale eyes. Vandrak wasn't a man who'd sacrifice or even risk much to possess any woman. Nor would he jeopardize his own scheme of murder for a woman's sake. But if a woman like Elaine practically threw herself at him ...

"It's you I'm sorry for," she said, pressing her advantage. "I want to do something to make it up to you. Isn't there anything ...?"

He was interested, tempted, but he was still cautious. "Mrs. Karnes, I appreciate your sympathy. But you'd better stay away from me. I don't think people would understand ..."

"I don't care about people!" she said obstinately.

The tears were flowing freely down her cheeks. She knew her own power of femininity, and she exerted it. She stood there, knowing she looked helpless, appealing, and wanted to look that way. The ripe plum ready to fall into his lap.

Why shouldn't he accept her? She saw the temptation working inside him. He was visibly torn by his uncertainty. The wild thought entered her mind that perhaps she'd been part of his motive for murdering his wife after all. The thought frightened her. She wanted to draw back.

But it was too late. One of his hands still held the sack of groceries, but the other one reached for her. She knew the man's tremendous strength from the instant of his first touch. With that one hand he drew her toward him. She fought the fear and loathing inside her, kept her face raised to him, steeling herself for what might have been his kiss.

But it never came to that. He must have tried to shift the sack of groceries so he could draw her close, and the sack slipped out of his grasp. It ripped, fell, and all of its contents scattered on the ground.

The occurrence startled both of them, and they drew apart instinctively. She looked down. The sack had contained groceries. A loaf of bread. Coffee. A few cans of vegetables. But the rest—most of it—was meat. Neatly wrapped white paper packages of meat.

Vandrak's voice interrupted her before she could weigh the significance of what she saw. "You'd better go home, Mrs. Karnes," he said.

She looked up at him. His manner had changed completely. That temporary weakness in him that had made him try to embrace her had disappeared. His face was darker than ever, and his eyes were cold. Hatred emanated from him. Implacable, single-minded hatred.

"Let me help you with these ..." She said it automatically, thoughtlessly.

"I don't need your help. I just want you to go."

She backed away from him. He followed her with his eyes, and the menace in his eyes was immediate, personal. She turned away, wanting to escape his gaze. But she felt it on her as she ran down the driveway, until the screen of trees separated them finally, and she was back on the road again out of his sight.

She stopped there, out of breath. She wanted to cry real tears now, tears of frustration and defeat. She had tried to make friends with Vandrak and had failed. And all because when he'd tried to kiss her, he'd dropped a sack of groceries.

A sack of groceries which was mostly packages of meat ...

That was when it came to her. A woman might shop that way, but a man never would. And certainly not a man who was so new at the job of taking care of such things himself. Vandrak hadn't shopped wisely, hadn't bought a big supply of meat at a sale or something, or to stock a freezer. That meat was needed for something ... now.

The dog wasn't dead. There was no grave. The dog was alive. Hidden somewhere. And it had to be fed.

She hadn't gone home, as Vandrak had told her to do. She'd started walking down the road, but then she had detoured into the woods, and was headed slowly back to Vandrak's house.

It was fairly clear to her now. Pharaoh was alive, and Vandrak loved the dog enough to try to keep it alive—even, perhaps, with some risk to himself. If he could keep the dog alive, heal its injuries, he could bring it home some time in the future and simply tell everyone that the prodigal had returned.

But meanwhile he had to keep it hidden. Not in his house. At least not yet. That would be too dangerous. What if the dog should make a noise when a policeman happened to be around? Nowhere on the immediate premises, probably. Somewhere in the woods then. There were plenty of places in the woods.

So she'd had a choice to make. She could have notified either Detective Riconda or George Newell. That would have been the safest thing to do. But George couldn't search for the dog and better than she could. And Riconda, even if he were interested, could so easily bungle things with his direct policeman's approach. Then Vandrak would be alerted, would either move the dog farther away, or maybe even, in desperation, kill the dog himself and bury it.

So the best way and the quickest way was to watch Vandrak, and follow him to wherever the dog was hidden. Vandrak might be suspicious. All those packages of meat spilling on the ground had unnerved him. But Vandrak was by no means certain that she knew what the meat signified. And he'd have to go to the dog. Because if he didn't, the dog would starve. So she had a chance of finding out where the dog was hidden. A fairly good chance.

And David's freedom depended on her.

She made her way through the wooded area carefully. Though it was still early spring, most of the trees and bushes were in leaf. Stealth and concealment were not too difficult. She worked her way slowly, finally came to within sight of Vandrak's house.

She only hoped he hadn't already gone after the dog. She could see that he'd picked up the groceries. And his car was still there. Possibly he was inside. So she found a spot where she could sit and watch the house and not be seen if Vandrak should suddenly come out. Then she waited.

Time passed. The thought occurred to her that Vandrak in all likelihood would wait till dark before starting out on his errand. She hoped not. She didn't want to try tracking him through the woods in darkness. She was afraid of him enough in daylight. But two hours went by without sight of him. The sun drooped low in the west. Within the woods dusk came early.

Then Vandrak appeared at the back door. He carried a small package, and he plunged swiftly into the woods toward the rear of the house. Fortunately, he'd worn a light tan jacket. It made him a bit easier to follow in the growing darkness.

She pursued him as fast as she dared. She made noise, but she was lighter and smaller than he was, and therefore made less than he did. She could only hope that the noise he was making would render him oblivious to all other sounds.

The tan jacket moved rapidly. Vandrak was an athlete, and these woods were familiar to him. Elaine had to run to keep up. Branches and thorns grabbed at her hair and her clothes, scratched, tore. She knew if she had to confront Vandrak again, she couldn't rely on attractiveness to assist her. Once she tripped and fell, and when she got up, she felt there must be blood on her face.

It seemed to go on forever, that chase. She had known these woods were extensive. She'd told George Newell they were big enough to discourage anyone from searching haphazardly for a grave. But she hadn't realized how big they were. It seemed she'd been running through them for hours. She had no idea if there were any houses near, or where a road might be.

But just when she thought she'd reached the point of exhaustion, the tan object up ahead stopped moving. She halted her own headlong pace quickly, knowing that noise was dangerous now that Vandrak wasn't making any.

Vandrak was with his beloved Pharaoh. And he'd be there for a little while, tending the dog's wounds, feeding him, comforting him probably. So she had time to move slowly, watching every step. The light in the woods was gray and misty now, though up in the tops of the trees there was the reddish glow of the setting sun.

It took her as much as five minutes to creep near enough to sight the tan jacket again. Vandrak was very close to her, actually, perhaps less than a hundred feet away. She hadn't seen him sooner because he was crouched down on the ground. She edged still closer till she could see the dog, too, just to make absolutely sure.

Her first thought was that she would never have found this place had she been searching alone. And a dozen policemen, for that matter, could have easily missed it. Vandrak had made the dog a shelter of branches and leaves that looked just like the rest of the underbrush. Pharaoh lay under this crude roof, motionless. She caught just the barest glimpse of his tawny coat. Most of him was swathed in bandages. But Vandrak had been clever enough not to use white cloth for bandages. They were of some dark color, dark green, she thought.

Vandrak was kneeling over the dog. She wasn't exactly sure what he was doing. But his voice came clearly enough. "Hurts, doesn't it, Pharaoh? Poor old king of Egypt. Hurts real bad. I know it does. But it's going to be all right. I told you that, Pharaoh. It's going to be all right."

And every once in a while, punctuating the man's words, the dog answered with a soft whine, complaining, yet patient, affectionate. He was a hurt dog, a badly hurt dog.

What she had figured out for George Newell had been right or mighty close to right. Now they could prove that David's story had been the truth. He had hit a dog. And Vandrak would have to explain why he had lied and would have to account for what happened to his wife.

All she, Elaine, had to do now was wait there till Vandrak went home, try to identify this spot in the woods somehow, and then get to a telephone.

She was crouching there, comfortable in this thought, when Pharaoh began to growl. She didn't understand at first what the growling meant. And neither apparently did Vandrak. He talked soothingly to the dog. Only after a minute or two did he stop trying to placate the dog and begin looking for the source of the disturbance.

Elaine also knew that the dog had growled because he had sensed an alien presence. She stayed where she was, holding herself perfectly still. She couldn't outrun Vandrak. She would have to outwait him. She was concealed behind a screen of underbrush, her clothes were dark, and the sun was almost gone. So perhaps he wouldn't see her.

But Vandrak also must have been aware of the near approach of darkness, and that if he were being spied upon, he'd have to find the spy quickly. Spurred by Pharaoh's ever more insistent growls, he started to search. The direction in which the dog was looking was the direction he took, and it was leading him almost straight to Elaine.

Halfway to her, he hesitated. She held her breath, hoping that he was giving up. But Pharaoh barked. It was a low, weak sound, not the full-throated roar of which the dog was capable. Vandrak was urged on by it. He halved the distance again that was between him and Elaine, and then he stopped a second time. He was looking right at her.

"Well, Mrs. Karnes, what do you think you've found?"

She was certain from his tone that he wasn't bluffing. If she stayed where she was, it might anger him. If she tried to run, he'd pursue her. She did the only thing that was left. She stood up and walked toward him.

"I've found the missing dog," she said, and her voice was surprisingly clear, confident. "My husband's car did hit a dig after all, didn't it, Mr. Vandrak?"

"That's right, Mrs. Karnes," Vandrak said. He was standing in shadow, and she couldn't see his eyes.

"Which means he didn't hit your wife, Mr. Vandrak." She was only a few steps from him now, and she stopped.

"That's right again, Mrs. Karnes. I killed Paula."

"You confess then?"

"Sure. Sure I do. Out here where nobody but you can hear me."

His body was tense, and she knew her danger. But she had to brazen it out. "When the police find the dog," she reminded him, "they'll know the truth, too."

"*If* the police find him, Mrs. Karnes. But they're neither as clever nor as interested as you." He grinned, wide enough for her to see. And then he sprang.

She tried to avoid him, but he was too quick. He bore her to the ground under the weight of his body. She had no chance to kick, only to claw with her nails. She did this as his hands found her throat. Her breathing was cut off, and a blackness not of the night descended on her.

Then she heard Pharaoh barking.

And it was as if the dog was speaking to his master. As if commanded to, Vandrak loosened his grip on her throat. But he stayed where he was, and she awoke again to the sight of his face inches above her own, and the hot wind of his labored breathing falling on her face.

"Thanks, Pharaoh," she heard him say. "You're right, old king. This would have been a mistake."

Then he looked down at her. In the semi-darkness, his pale eyes gleamed like an animal's. "That's one smart dog," he said. "If I choked you to death, I'd have to bury you somewhere around here. And they'd search for a missing woman, though they wouldn't for a dog."

She didn't ask him what his alternate scheme was.

But he told her. "I guess you're going to have to be killed by a hit and run driver like my wife was."

She felt the weight of his body leave her suddenly, and then she herself was rudely jerked to a standing position. Instinctively, she opened her mouth to scream. Vandrak struck her across the face with his open hand, jarring her scream into silence before it could be completely uttered. Pharaoh barked enthusiatically, ecstatically, Elaine thought.

"Hush, Pharaoh," the man said. He turned to her. "Don't try screaming any more, or I'll hurt you real bad. Now we're going to the road."

She was too weak to walk. He dragged her. He was strong, for he could manage her weight even though deliberately she gave him no help. With her body useless, her mind raced. How was he going to make it appear that she'd been killed by a car? Certainly she wouldn't stand conveniently in the road until a car came by. But he'd managed it with Paula, she thought suddenly.

Behind them, and receding, Pharaoh was still barking. Vandrak stopped once and, looking back, called out, "Shut up! You hear me? Shut up!" But the dog's barking continued to pursue them from an ever-increasing distance.

In the woods it was almost completely dark now. But up ahead Elaine saw dusky light where the woods ended. That was the road. She didn't recognize it. Vandrak must have chosen to come out at a place that was unfamiliar to her, perhaps a place farthest from any human habitation. Fifty feet or so short of the road he stopped and looked around.

She'd saved her breath, having let him drag her as dead weight. Now she would fight him, she decided, to the last. If she could break loose for just one second, she might elude him, now that the woods were dark.

Vandrak held her by both her arms, cruelly hard, his heavy, enormous hands crushing into her soft flesh. But he made no move. Instead, he seemed to be listening. While he listened a car went by, a dim blur on the road, a quick surge of sound fading quickly again into silence.

One of Vandrak's hands shifted, went to Elaine's throat. But he didn't try to choke her. He exerted only enough pressure to remind her that he could choke her. He laughed softly, and there was a hint of madness in his laugh.

"It worked with Paula," he whispered savagely. "The police doctors were fooled completely. I hit her, you see, right on the jaw. No marks of choking on the throat. Just a solid blow on the jaw, enough to stun her, you see. And then I took her legs and swung her around and smashed her against a tree trunk. One big blow, you see. Just one blow like a car hitting her ..."

The horror of what he had revealed galvanized all her energy. She kicked and fought furiously until she was free, falling over backward onto the ground. He leaped for her, found the cloth of her jacket. But she rolled to one side, leaving him with cloth in his hand. She was halfway to her feet when he found her again. They wrestled together. An immense pain grabbed at her shoulder. She had only one thought now. If he kills me, I want them to know he did it with his own hands ... I don't want him to go free ... and then they'll know too that David isn't a killer ...

She didn't hear the voices or see the beams of the flashlights—and probably Vandrak didn't either—until the men had almost converged upon them. Then she managed one scream before Vandrak struck her.

Lying in the hospital bed, she was told everything.

She was bruised, terribly so, but nothing more serious. George Newell had gotten worried after their talk together, phoned her in the afternoon, received no answer. Finally, he went to Vandrak's house, found the car there and the man gone. He phoned the police. But nobody knew where to look until the dog started barking. Even then, they'd been just in time.

It was David who told her all this. Very concerned about her. Very grateful. Very happy to be free.

Arthur Porges

The Fanatical Ford

"Fords is the worst," the old man quavered, fixing the reporter with an indignant eye of watery blue. "They stick together like—like them hillbillies that are all relatives, even though they're scattered to hell and gone over Kentucky. You be sure to put that down, young man: the others is bad, but them Fords is the worst. Family pride, by God!"

The reporter nodded, scribbling expert shorthand in his notebook. Quite a character, this old boy. A brand new approach to insanity. Too bad this wasn't a TV assignment; it would be nice to get a salty tape of that voice. Reminded him of Walter Brennan.

He wrote: "Fred Marer, a leather-faced, gimlet-eyed veteran, is being persecuted—" No. Better: "—claims to be a victim of the oddest persecution—"

Marer broke into this train of thought. "I know just how it started. Back in 1913, it was. Before you were born, likely. I made my Pa's Model T real mad. I was only a kid then, but I had a nasty mouth—You getting all this?"

"You bet I am, Mr. Marer. It's a remarkable story."

"And a whole pack of lies, you're thinking," the old man said shrewdly.

"It's not my business to decide that," the reporter replied in a bland voice. "I just report the facts. There may be good reason for your belief. Now, about this Model T you—ah—antagonized. I didn't know"—he smiled—"that they were so touchy. My grandfather called his names any decent mule wouldn't have tolerated. Once I remember he even gave it a good boot in the radiator. About a quart of bolts and things flew off, but that didn't seem to matter; the car still ran—when it had a mind to." He paused, flushing. He was talking too much, and personalizing the old car as foolishly as Marer.

"That's right," the hermit agreed ruefully. "They wasn't easy to insult. Not a whole lot of pride when you're turned out on an assembly line. Not like a Rolls. But you see, Mr.—ah—"

"Nelson."

"—Nelson—most people abused their Fords in a kinda half affectionate way. Oh, the owners got mad enough—stuck in mud, or engine dead on a cold morning, or gears wouldn't mesh—but it was like quarreling between husband and wife. When they really love each other, it doesn't go deep and fester. But I had a lippy mouth, and maybe too it was one of those here natural enemy things. I'd had my heart set on a bigger, better car, and took it out on this one.

"Don't ask me what I said because it's too far back. Wasn't one thing, anyhow—more the last straw in a heap of insults. Know when it happened, though. I was cranking her one cold morning—real winters there; not like California—and she just wouldn't start."

"Why 'she'?"

"Dunno. But it was a 'she' all right. Nobody can hold a grudge like a female. You know about a woman scorned; you ain't that young, I reckon. Anyhow, like I'm saying, you remember—guess you wouldn't, a kid like you—how a Model T'd go 'er-rah! er-rah! er-er-er!" when she was cranked. A sort of sneer it seemed that morning, with me late for work and colder'n Eskimo's nose in Alaska." He paused to spit reflectively. Overhead two ravens flapped, calling harshly; and high above the clouds there was hissing scream of a jet cargo plane, Los Angeless bound.

"It was something in her tone that riled me up, and I cussed her out good. And that wasn't all. I hauled off and hit her a terrible clout with the jack handle. Made a big dent in the hood, and just ruined a headlight. Knocked it out of kilter." He nodded knowingly. "That Model T never looked right again. She was like a purty gal with a cast in one eye. When you spoil a woman's looks, watch out—that's all! After all our other fighting, this was the finish. She really hated me. And it wasn't just her; she passed the word along. Them Fords was like a family, and stuck together. You hurt one, you hurt 'em all. It was as if I'd belted the whole cussed tribe, instead of just one female. And that wasn't all; the other cars—different makes—joined in soon enough. Maybe an Olds didn't like a Ford, but I was a common enemy to 'em all."

"When was the first—ah—attack?"

"Why, that there very Model T tried to kill me a dozen times before we got rid of her. Once I started to crank her up and, mind you, I *know* she was in neutral. But the minute she turned over, she got into gear somehow. I jumped aside just in time. Damned if she didn't chase me over a field, turning when I did. And the proof is that when I jumped a gully, instead of her going on, like a car would if it was really out of control, she stopped and went back to neutral. *She* wasn't a-going to smash herself up! Doesn't that prove it?" he demanded belligerently. "No car that ain't chuck full of spite behaves that way."

"Sounds reasonable," Nelson agreed, wooden-faced.

"Well, I finally persuaded my dad to sell the car. Then we bought an Olds. And it was just as bad. Nothing merry about that durned heap. Twice it backed up on me sudden-like when Pa was driving. He swore he didn't touch the reverse and I believe him. Pa was a good driver. Naturally, I wouldn't ride in the thing at all after that, but it was always trying to get me anyhow by backing, swerving, or speeding up without no warning. Pa used to say I was a jinx—'cause that there Olds didn't act normal when I was around. You just bet it didn't! I tried to tell him about how I was in bad with Fords, and how they was pizening the other cars against me, but Pa just laughed. Ma kinda believed me—she was afraid of most machinery and hated to see horses disappear—but Pa never paid no mind to her.

"It got so I wasn't safe on the street. You saw them clippings. Does it seem natural to you that one man could of been in so many auto accidents? Looky here." He thumbed a fistful of yellow papers. "In 1920 I was almost killed three times by cars that just went wild, running up on sidewalks and things. Usually the driver had a clean record, too. I've had both legs broken eight times, my collar bone five, and ribs moren'n you can count. Here! In 1932 a dump truck that was parked by the curb—no driver, even—suddenly let go with five tons of gravel. Cut my legs up something fierce. You should see the scars. Now if that don't show—"

"It's certainly a remark—" No; he'd said that once. "Extremely interesting. What happened after that?"

"What d'you expect? Nothing but more of the same, and oftener, as cars increased. Busses, trucks, taxis—even a tractor, but it was too slow. They were all after me. And how about this, young feller? Twice the house I lived in was pretty near wrecked by big interstate trucks running wild off the highway. Bruises—the bed saved me the first time. And then a broken ankle. After that I stayed on the little back roads. Think that solved the problem? Not on your life! First thing you know there was motorcycles and jeeps." He rubbed a thin, white scar on his stubbled chin. "Fellow with a motorcycle did that in forty-five. Claimed the machine went wild. *I* was a good fifty yards off the dirt road, hunting mushrooms. If it'd hit me square, I wouldn't be here. When that kid looked at his steering gear, wasn't a blamed thing wrong."

"You must have collected a fortune in damages or insurance."

"What if I did!" the old man flared. "I had it coming, didn't I? Even if the drivers wasn't to blame, somebody had to pay my doctor bills. Why should I tell 'em it was the autos—them cussed Fords mostly—and not me. Who'd believe me? It's only my lawsuit money that lets me live in a safe place like this." He waved one gnarled hand. From their bench outside the mountain cabin, they could see for miles over the rolling California hills, already seared by the dry summer. Nowhere another human to be seen—only a few sleek brown and white steers.

"Couldn't even get no insurance after a while," the old man said querulously. "So I'd just collect my damages. They tried to prove I was causing accidents deliberately, but most of the drivers was honest about it, and there was witnesses, anyhow. They always said how the cars went out of control.

"Then after they got to building them cars with the hoods like big mouths. They—what're you snickering at? Young whipper-snapper—you don't—"

"Sorry," Nelson said, gravely contrite. "It wasn't at anything you said. Just reminded me of a cartoon. Please go on. Mr. Marer; this is quite a story. I mean, quite fascinating. Valuable, too," he added hastily.

The old man gave him a suspicious glance. "I'm telling the gospel truth, exactly like it happened. Ain't nothing wrong with my memory. Right now I could tell you the serial number of the Model T that started the whole thing. And that there car musta been junked before you were born." He paused triumphantly. "Twelve thousand and twleve, it was—easy to remember."

"One of the early ones, all right. But about those new hoods. You were saying—"

"Yeah, lemme tell you about that. You'd think I'd have the sense to keep away, but those cars looked so different. They didn't seem like the same tribe. No reason for *them* to carry on the grudge. That Model T had been rust for thirty years or more. After all that hiding out in the back country, I figured maybe them Fords had forgotten me." He glowered into space, savoring his grievance. "Damn hood snapped down just like big jaws. All I wanted was a little peek at the motor; hadn't seen one close up since twenty-nine." His shoulders fleted reminiscently. "Lucky I had on a padded jacket. But my back ain't been right since."

"What about foreign cars? You could have lived abroad."

"That's what you think! Teach your grandmother to suck eggs. I tried that, just once. Took my five thousand dollar damages when a motor scooter knocked me into a gully, and went to Europe for a year. In the first place, there's a lot of American cars there. They was made here, and got tipped off in the factory. The ones made in Europe, like the British Fords, soon caught on. It's a system like that there Mafia. They all hung together. I was chased by M. G.'s, Jaguars, Dauphines, and Volkswagens. Sure, I could live in Ethiopia or Libya where there ain't but a few cars in the whole country, but I'd sooner take my chances." He shook his head in disgust. "They don't even pay good damages in Europe."

"Well," the reporter said, pocketing his notebook, "you've finally licked the problem, I see. No car can get up here, that's for sure. But what do you do about supplies?"

"Mule pack up the trail. It's not too bad a walk, but nothing on wheels can make it."

"And you've lived here—how long?"

"Eight years. I'm almost seventy. Down there I couldn't move fast enough for them new models. The 1953 bunch was bad enough! I ain't hankering to tangle with no 1960 Ford."

"You're safe. Not even the new army scout-cars could get up here. Seems to me you've won in the end."

"I ain't so sure. Them Fords don't give up easy. They'll never rest till I'm dead. It was a Ford I insulted, and it's a Ford that'll kill me. But by God, at least it won't be a Model T—they ain't many of them around these days. You'll send me a copy of the paper—make it a couple?"

"Sure thing," Nelson promised, knowing that he wouldn't. Better to forget than offend the old guy; and the old guy was certain to resent any objective treatment of his story. A typical paranoiac, but what an imagination!

"Now, if you'll let me take those pictures ..." Nelson went to the gadget bag, and took out the press camera. "On the bench first. That's it."

The old man sat there stiffly erect, his wrinkled, tanned face sternly dignified. The reporter snapped the shutter with the easy confidence of a man who never doubts the quality of his negatives.

"Now let's do one with you shaking your fist as if—ah—cursing that Model T of yours."

Marer looked doubtful. "It'll make a silly picture," he objected. "You ain't got the right idea. This is a serious business."

"Come on," Nelson urged. "You want people to hear your side of the thing, don't you? They seem to think you're either a clever insurance swindler or a bit—see what I mean? Look, if the photo's a little unfair, what of it? That makes people read your story, and that's what you're after."

"All right," Marer said reluctantly. "Where'll I stand?"

"Right here in the clearing. Good. Now shake your fist. No, harder—up at the sky, like an angry prophet. That's the idea—hold it."

He was just visualizing the caption: "CURSES MODEL NEMESIS," when there was a whistling scream and an earth-jarring impact that flung him dazed to the hard ground. When he recovered his senses, some moments later, and shoved a heavy plank from his bruised body, he saw that where the old man had stood there lay a jumble of wood and metal fragments, many of them bloody.

It took him some time, shaken as he was, to identify their origin. The wood must have come from a large packing case; and the crumpled wheels, battered radiator, and assorted engine parts placed the contents. Above all, there was the famous old black, shiny finish on the metal.

He learned later that the reconditioned Model T was on its way by air cargo to Los Angeles, when it had fallen, in mysterious circumstances, through the hatch.

But what bothered him most was its serial number: twelve thousand and twelve.

Alvin S. Fick

A Grave on the Indragiri

"Why bother after all this time? 1909, you say? Three years ago. I should think you'd be satisfied to let it lie."

The man behind the dark oak desk seemed hesitant to answer. He passed a meaty red hand over his shaven skull.

Alex Pine looked at him through half-closed eyes, assessing the muscle beneath the middle-aged fat. Colter's huge hands with scarred knuckles and wedge-shaped fingers protruded from a conservative business suit. Here was a man of great strength, perhaps a product of the docks. Maybe those shoulders came from tossing forkfuls of hay and manure on a Sussex farm, or from early years in a peat bog.

With this toe Pine hooked a chair close to his own in front of the desk, crossed his ankles, and placed his feet on its red cushion. In other offices in other parts of London he would not have done that. The gesture was a simple one, not calculated insolence but intended to move the business at hand out of the drawing room into the alley, or at least into the carriage house.

Colter seemed unwilling to make the concession. He stared at Pine's feet on the chair, a barely perceptible shrug of his massive shoulders rippling the dark material of his coat.

"Because I want to know, that's all." He aimed a forefinger at Pine. "Twenty pounds a day and expenses. Take it or leave it."

Through the open window Alex Pine could hear the clop of hooves in the street below, the creak of wheels on ungreased axles a counterpoint to the rumble of lorries with hard rubber tires carrying freight to the docks down by the river. Now and then a freshet of breeze brought in the mingled odors of the shipping district.

"A thousand pounds at the finish if you bring me conclusive evidence that my brother was murdered."

"Not for five thousand unless I'm satisfied with your answers to my questions," Pine said. "I agree it seems a little odd that your brother Kevin would drop dead at thirty-eight when he seemed to be in prime health. But you being in the rubber business yourself know conditions in Sumatra are not conducive to long life.

"So what if his wife says it was a heart attack brought on by heat and overwork? What difference does it make if she is wrong and he was shoved into his grave by some little-known tropical disease? There aren't any medical examiners a hundred miles up the Indragiri River. Why does it matter to you now? What's over is over, and you say yourself neither his wife nor the company he worked for stood to gain anything by his death. Why push it?"

"If your brother—" Colter began.

"I haven't a brother, and I still don't understand why you delayed, but I acknowledge the point. Tell me more about your brother's wife."

"She's a Dutch girl Kevin met while she was attending school here in England. At first I thought he was a bloody fool. He hadn't a quid in his trousers when he met her, all his money having gone for the clothes of a dandy. He borrowed a great deal of money from me. He spent most of it on a diamond ring and wining and dining her.

"Not long after they were married, he stopped by to tell me he was going to be made overseer of a rubber plantation in Sumatra. Marie, his wife, has a father who is a member of the firm, Benskoten Rubber Company, which owns several plantations there. That's the last time I saw him. He died at Benskoten's Plantation Number Three."

"Did you hear from him after he went there? Any letters?"

"Not a one, although his wife wrote to my wife a couple of times."

"Then he never repaid the money he owed you?"

There was disgust in Colter's negative grunt. "The closest I got was a wink on his wedding day—like a man who just had a long-odds winner at Ascot."

"This would be expensive, Mr. Colter. There's time involved in the travel as well as the investigation. And what if I find evidence that your brother died of natural causes?"

"In that case I will pay you two hundred pounds."

Pine whistled softly. "You're that anxious to prove it was murder? What makes you think I won't fake some evidence for eight hundred pounds?"

"Because I checked thoroughly into yoru background before I asked you to come here, Mr. Pine. Your little investigations business comes highly recommended. Compared to such a reputation, the money is a paltry sum. Besides, I would not take kindly to being fleeced."

He picked up a pencil from his desk and snapped it between thumb, forefinger, and middle finger, then turned in his chair and threw the pieces out the window.

"Thirty pounds a day," Alex said. "Mogging about in the jungle is unhealthy—fever, tigers, and all that."

Colter nodded reluctantly, then extended his hand across the desk. Surprise was evident in his lifted eyebrows when he felt the strength in the detective's grip.

He summoned an ascetic-looking clerk in striped pants from the outer office and issued instructions in a low voice.

He turned to Pine. "I would like you to leave by the end of the week. Humes here will give you a draft on my bank for three hundred pounds, also an address in Singapore where you will be able to draw more money as needed. But I will expect reports regularly."

"No." Pine's voice was flat, unarguable. "No reports until my work is finished. I'm going to be too busy to write letters home like a boy away at boarding school."

Jason Colter came out from behind his desk. "I urge you to be discreet."

Pine ran a hand through a thatch of hair the color of a rusty bucket.

"It has been my experience," he said, "that blabbering about one's business does little to further it."

Papers, packing, and transportation arrangements took little time for Pine, since the packing was all he did himself. The rest was handled with her usual quiet efficiency by Jennifer Hemming in his Chelsea office beneath his living quarters.

"Oh, dear, Mr. Pine," she said when he told her of the trip, "you'll be gone so long." She bent her grey head quickly over a desk drawer so he would not see the moisture glistening behind the silver-framed glasses, but the mothering in her voice was inescapable.

"Maybe not so long, Miss Hemming. I think this Colter fellow is angling in a pond that has no fish. And I'm hanged if I know why."

She smiled up at him. "Oh, but you will find out."

What could be better than having Jennifer Hemming as office factotum, proxy mother for the one he never knew? Nothing, aside from a wife.

Before he left on Friday, he rode many vehicles and stretched his long legs over what seemed to be half the streets of London. He spent some of the three hundred pounds' advance money in pubs whose clientele preferred its darker recesses to the sunshine outside. He bought uncounted rounds of ale and stuffed pound notes into pockets of scruffy jackets, all the while adding information to his leatherbound pocket notebook. Some facts he learned in better restaurants from business acquaintances whose Regent Street clothes and distinguished looks were scarcely in keeping with the type of information they disclosed.

Now he knew why Jason Colter wanted proof that Marie Colter had murdered her husband. With that information, he would be able to blackmail her to extract vital favors from her father, favors that could ultimately lead to a virtual monopoly of England's rubber-importing business. What had burned in those hungry little eyes was not a zeal for justice, but greed.

Pine was not surprised. Sometimes he did not like the flavor of his work, and this was one of the times. But if he backed off it would leave a void that Colter more than likely would fill with someone who might not share Pine's scruples about manufactured evidence. And besides, the pay was good.

On the morning of his departure he stopped at a bookstall near Fleet Street where he bought a thick packet of old boy's papers. He stood at the rail clutching the package beneath his arm as the *Sutton Victor* edged away from its berth below High Bridge and slipped into the stream for the crossing to LeHavre and on to Singapore. He could think of nothing more pleasant or diverting on the long hours of the voyage than to revisit the pages that had put so much ginger into his youth. He looked forward to a reunion with *Pluck, Chums, The Boy's Own Paper,* and *The Bull's-Eye.* Indeed, it was reading the exploits of Sexton Blake that had lured him into a career in detection.

During the nearly two-day passage of the Suez, Pine sat on deck in the shade of an awning, alternately reading and watching the passing ships slide by, steel fish cleaving the desert that stretched away on both sides. He mixed little with the other passengers, spending some time rereading his notes. Folded into the notebook were two letters, both obtained from Mrs. Jason Colter. That had been a coup, but it would remain so only as long as she kept silent about it.

"Oh, I hope I am doing the right thing," she had said when he visited her in London the day before he left. "If you don't mention these letters to Jason, he won't know. He knows I received them, but he never expressed the slightest interest in their contents. And in view of his intense feelings about his brother, I never said much other than to pass along the gossip Marie wrote."

"Did you know your brother-in-law's wife well?"

"Not terribly. I saw her several times just before the wedding, but almost immediately she and Kevin went to Holland to visit Nikolaas and Beatrice Berchem—her parents. But I like her. She is a lovely girl."

She hesitated before going on, apparently satisfied that as long as she was surrendering the letters, and inasmuch as the conversation was to remain confidential, expression of her own intuitions could do no harm.

"I never liked Kevin, Mr. Pine. He had a charm and attractiveness that I can see would have overwhelmed poor Marie. But it seemed to me a veneer over something hard and cruel."

Again she paused. "I don't know why I'm saying this to a stranger, but I think hardness is the strongest bond Kevin and my husband had. Jason is the same way."

"And I gather it was on that visit to the Berchems that Kevin Colter was appointed plantation manager."

"Yes, the two of them left for Singapore without coming back here."

"Thank you, Mrs. Colter, for letting me take these letters and for speaking freely. I'm sure you see it's best that neither of us mention any of this to your husband."

Mrs. Colter touched his sleeve.

"You couldn't possibly think that Marie—" Her face was pale. "If I thought you would think such a thing I never—" Pine could see the trembling in her throat.

"Please, don't torture yourself. It's far from my mind, especially since I suspect it's the one thought your husband cherishes."

Singapore hadn't changed much since Alex's last time there four years before when an admiralty case had taken him through the city on his way to the naval base at Seletar near Johore Bahru. It came to

him as he was paying the ricksha driver in front of the King's Arms
Hotel that that was in 1908, at about the same time Kevin and Marie
Colter were on their way to Sumatra. Perhaps they had stopped here in
this very hotel.

The manager of the Singapore office of Benskoten Rubber, Anders
Van der Neer, was cool at first, then deferential, then confiding and
friendly. Pine thought that if he stayed another ten minutes the man
would become positively obsequious.

"That's the story, Mr. Van der Neer. I've been seeing these ads in the
Times for months offering investment opportunities for private individuals in this remarkably fast-growing rubber industry. I thought I
would stop off on my way home from Hong Kong to check into the
possibilities."

The slowly revolving ceiling fan stirred Van der Neer's thinning
straw-colored hair. He dabbed with a handkerchief at the perspiration
on his shiny round face.

"We're so pleased you have selected Benskoten Rubber for consideration." Van der Neer started to rub his hands together, then quickly
changed the motion and pressed his fingertips together.

"But you understand that I will not make a heavy commitment until
after I see the nature of your planation operation."

"Of course. You are an astute businessman, after all."

"Then it's settled? You will arrange a trip upriver to a plantation? I
would prefer to visit one that has been operating three or four years,
not less, and preferably not much more. That's the perspective I want
to see."

"Certainly, Mr. Pine. Tomorrow at ten o'clock I will send over one
of my most trusted associates to accompany you on the coastal steamer
to Tambilahan. From there a company boat will take you up the
Indragiri to Benskoten Three. I can't think of a more representative
plantation for you to see."

Pine was reviewing his good fortune the next morning in his hotel
room while packing a small bag when there was a knock on the door.

Kiri Sembawa, the Benskoten representative, was young, probably
in his mid-twenties. His English was impeccable, with a hint of Oxford.

"I grew up in an English home here in Singapore," he explained. "I
was a combination houseboy and gardener for the people who raised
me. They sent me to England to be educated. Both of them died of fever
five years ago." The smile which had lighted his nutbrown face flickered
out.

"A moment ago I was congratulating myself on my good luck in
getting to see a Benskoten rubber plantation with no delay. Now I see
this has been enhanced by having the best guide possible. I am most
fortunate." Pine shook Sembawa's hand with warmth.

Later they sat together on packing cases as the company boat nudged inland against the current of the Indragiri. Pine smoked a disreputable-looking pipe, with helped some against the mosquitoes. Kiri Sembawa sat close enough to indicate the pipe fumes were preferable to the insects.

"Who is plantation manager at Benskoten Three?" Pine asked.

"A man named Keeling. He's Dutch. He speaks a little English, but I can translate for you if you like."

"I have a smattering of Dutch and German, but I will be grateful for any help you can give." Pine tamped the pipe with the head of an iron spike that had been cut off an inch and a half down the shank.

"Who preceded him?" Pine watched the handsome brown face for any change in expression. There was none.

"A man named Kevin Colter, and Englishman."

"Colter." Pine stared off at the jungle crowding the water's edge. "I know a family named Colter in London. Different family, probably. Still, the man I know is in some aspect of the rubber business, I think."

"Mr. Colter was married to a Dutch woman."

Pine turned slowly and his ice-blue eyes locked with Kiri Sembawa's dark ones. "Surely not a woman named Marie?"

Surprise flickered across Sembawa's face but it was gone in an instant.

"Yes, Marie," he said. "It must be the same Colter."

Pine's pipe clattered to the deck and he leaned over to retrieve it. "What did you mean when you said he *was* married to a Dutch woman?"

"Mr. Colter is dead. He died nearly three years ago. His wife went back to Holland. Her father is one of the owners of Benskoten Rubber."

"Well, I wouldn't have believed it possible. That must be the brother of the Jason Colter I know. I seem to recall he mentioned a younger brother. He died, eh? He couldn't have been over—what would you say?"

"I would guess mid- to late thirties. No more."

"Was it an accident?"

"Heart attack." Sembawa paused. "They say heart attack brought on by overwork, fever, the heat, all the things that kill men in a tropical climate."

"I suppose it wasn't easy to get a doctor to such a remote place to confirm the cause."

It was a long time before Sembawa answered.

"No, there was no doctor." Then after an even longer pause: "I don't think he died from a heart attack."

Alex Pine dropped his pipe again, only this time it was not a piece of stage business.

It crossed his mind that he was at a decision point in his investigation. By Anders Van der Neer's assertion, this was a "most trusted employee." Would a revelation of Pine's true purpose result in a closing of channels to him? Was someone in Benskoten covering a murder? Or was Sembawa's suspicion groundless? If he was right, weren't chances good that this would lead where every instinct told him he did not want to go to find a killer, to Marie Colter?

He remembered the anguish in the letters back in the hotel safe in Singapore. Damn! He did not like where he was headed.

"I'm not an investor, Kiri." It was the first time he had spoken Sembawa's first name. "I'm a private detective. I have been misleading Benskoten Rubber and you. I don't care that much about my duplicity where the company is concened, but I apologize for doing it to you. Now, we can go back downriver on the next available boat if that's what you want, if that's wat your loyalty to Benskoten tells you to do. Or we can work togther to unravel this thing. I don't know where it will lead. Helping me may cost you your job, although I promise to do everything I can to protect your interests. It's up to you."

The only sound above the hum of mosquitoes was the gurgle of water against the side of the boat and the chuffing of the small engine that powered it.

"I will help." Kiri Sembawa spoke firmly. "I think we should try to find out what happened." He hung his head. "What happened beyond what Mrs. Colter told me."

"Good!" Pine thrust out his hand. "I'm relieved to be able to tell you what I know. I have been retained by Kevin Colter's brother to investigate the circumstances of his death. Back in the safe at the hotel are two letters written by Marie Colter to her sister-in-law. From them it is quite clear that her life at Benskoten Three with Colter was pure hell. It's not all spelled out, but obviously her husband was drinking heavily, and apparently he was consorting with women from the native quarters. He was beating the workers, and it seems to me that this, combined with the abominable conditions suffered by the laborers, was of even greater concern to her than her own health and safety."

"Yes," said Sembawa. "Some of this she told me during our one meeting before she left Singapore. How bad it really was I learned during my trips to the plantation in the months that followed."

"Then there's every chance he might have been killed by a native, or one of the imported laborers—a Javanese, a Chinese, anyone. There would have been many with a motive."

"They were the only white people on the plantation. All of the *mandoers*—foremen—are Sumatrans of Javanese. Oh, yes, and a couple of Batak foremen."

"Batak?" Pine knocked the ash from his pipe into the river. "I read somewhere that they are the mountain people—cannibals, perhaps. Is that so?"

"No doubt they used to be. I know they will only work for a Batak foreman. Independent, you might say."

When they arrived at Benskoten Three it was still daylight. From the dock Pine could see the *kampong*, a huddle of huts and shacklike buildings on stilts. In the filth beneath them children played in the shade. He wrinkled his nose over a stench he did not care to analyze.

"Some of what you smell comes from the drying sheds in the clearing behind those trees. Some of it comes from the bullock pens. And of course a lot of it is human. It helps keep the mosquitoes at a bearable level."

Pine's impression was one of unremitting squalor and he said so.

"Yes, it is bad. But it was much worse before Mrs. Colter. She did much while she was here. Once Mr. Van der Neer told me Mr. Colter returned some supplies—extra food and medicine, I think—that Mrs. Colter had ordered. He said Mr. Colter was trying to hold down expenses to show a good profit margin."

Sembawa led the way upriver to a slight rise where the jungle had been cleared. There in a small fenced enclosure was a log cross. They stood a few moments in silence at Colter's gravesite.

They were walking back downriver toward the plantation manager's cottage where they were to stay when Sembawa spoke again.

"Mrs. Colter gave me a rather large sum of money to be spent on screening, food, and medicine for the *kampong* before she returned to Holland. Over the past three years she has sent smaller sums, always with instructions not to reveal the source."

Before they mounted the steps to the manager's cottage Pine touched Sembawa's arm.

"We are agreed that I am an investor?"

"An investor." The response was soft, reflective in tone.

The manager, Keeling, was only as cordial as he had to be. He was short, thick set, and his hair was cropped close. He used little English. His Dutch was laden with low German derivatives. Pine was increasingly grateful for Sembawa's presence, since Keeling's conversation was limited to an occasional grunt or belch between vast draughts of beer during supper. A bachelor, who arose before sunrise and lived only for the plantation work, he retired early after pointing out two cots on the screened porch.

Alex Pine sat on his cot and watched the most spectacular sunset he had ever seen.

During the following day it was not difficult to maintain the subterfuge of being a potential investor in Benskoten Rubber Company. Keeling ignored him. Pine was fascinated by his tour of the plantation, during which Sembawa pointed out a large stand of trees ruined by bark cancer—brown bast—from cutting too much and too deeply into the latex channel.

"That was done while Mr. Colter was in charge," Sembawa said. "He was trying to increase production."

They watched gangs of Chinese laborers clearing brush and trees for new plantings of *hevea*. Much of the planting was done among old growth with little more than token clearing by machete.

In the afternoon Pine asked to see the spot where Colter died.

"It was in one of the small cottages just north of the *kampong*. The native foremen live in them with their families."

Kiri led the way. "Here," he said, "this one. It's empty. Usually one or two are usused. Since Mr. Colter died here, none of the foremen will use it." He opened the door of the screened porch for Pine.

"Everything is quite the same as it was three years ago?"

"Exactly. Nothing has changed. You might think someone would have taken the gin bottle from the table, but people are afraid to come into the building."

"Birds have nested here. "Pine pointed to the droppings on the floor and at the shreds of rusted screen around the porch. "Where was Colter's body found?"

"Here." Sembawa placed a hand on the back of a bamboo armchair, frightening a small rodent which scurried from beneath the half-rotten and moldy cushion.

Pine nodded, then strolled slowly around the room, brushing away cobwebs, seeing as much with the tips of his sensitive fingers as with his eyes. He sniffed at the empty gin bottle without touching it, knowing as he did that he move was futile. His hands slid down the legs of the small round table. He looked at the underside of it, then gave the chair the same careful scrutiny. Always he was touching, touching. He seemed to have fogotten his companion.

On the third circuit of the perimeter of the room his fingers touched something just above head height at the juncture of the screen door frame and the wall. He stopped. He blew away a dusty shred of cobweb. A shaft of the late-afternoon sun shone on his hand as the long sinewy fingers worked at the small protrusion. And then he held out his hand to Sembawa. In his palm lay a small object with a sharp point. "That lump on the end is a pith air stop. It's a dart. Poisoned, I would guess," he said.

He walked to the opposite side of the porch where he looked down to the ground, then turned and sighted along his outstretched arm.

Kiri Sembawa was impassive. The smile Pine expected to see on his face did not materialize.

"I did not think you would find anything. I looked several times, but I missed seeing it." Sembawa walked over to the door and stood looking past the *kampong*, out over the river. He looked shriveled and shrunken, now less than shoulder height to the tall Englishman.

"You don't seem pleased that I did."

"I hoped you would not." He turned. "Now I tell you something I prayed I would not have to tell you. I hoped you would go back to your man in London and say there is nothing, that his brother died like it was said—of a heart thàt failed from too much work, too much drink, too much heat, too much fever." Sembawa paused, reluctant to continue.

"He died from being too much the kind of person he was," Pine said. "That includes the things you said and a couple of others. It should surprise no one that a Batak he had beaten crept up to the cottage one dark night and popped him with a poisoned dart. There's no lamp here, but maybe the one on the table inside was lighted. That means the light would be dim here, accounting for his missing the first time on such short range."

"I don't think that happened."

"Kiri, there's no need to make trouble for any of your people here.Colter's dead. I know of no one who wished him back. Going out without an apparent mark on him from some kind of substance that stopped his heart seems better than he deserved."

"I don't think a Batak killed him, or a Sumatran, or a Javanese or Chinese. I think Mrs. Colter killed him."

"Granted she had reason. I was half trying to find a way to determine if she slipped something into his drink. I think now there's no need to pursue that line of thought." Pine took his notebook from his pocket and inserted the dart between the leaves.

"Are you returning directly to London from here, to report to your Jason Colter?"

"No. I'm going to Holland first to see Mrs. Colter."

"Then I must say what I must say and perhaps it will change your mind. But first I must apologize even as you did on the boat. I did not tell you everything. I saw Mrs. Colter just once, in a room in the same hotel where you are staying. Mr. Van der Neer sent me there to pick up the money I told you she gave me for supplies for the plantation. When she asked me into her suite I could see she had all her belongings in a corner of the room, ready to be taken to the ship for her return to Holland." He seemed to lose his continuity of thought. After a while he said, "She was a lovely lady."

"That's all?" Pine said.

"Among her bags and boxes of things in the corner was a long tube. It was a blowgun."

A lovely lady. Alex Pine agreed. In Mrs. Jason Colter's living room he had seen a photograph of Kevin and Marie Colter. Marie's was the bright-eyed, cream-skinned, blonde beauty of the Nordic. He remembered the firm stance of her figure, the hint of the kind of strength that will do what must be done, that endures.

Now he knew why Jason Colter had sent him here. The man surely had read those anguished letters, in spite of his wife's assuming he had not. And it had taken him three years to get his business affairs to the point where he could take maximum advantage of his suspicions—suspicions that were uncannily correct.

On their way back down to the river both were silent. They stood a while on the dock watching two elderly men fishing. Small clusters of insects danced above the water in the rays of sunlight shafting through the trees. After a while they sat on pilings a little distance from the fishermen. Pine filled his pipe, holding the match a time before addressing it to the tobacco, his attention diverted by a strikingly attractive girl who had come down from the *kampong* and walked out on the dock to talk to one of the fishermen.

She was dark and lissome, and as she leaned over to talk to the old man something on a chain around her neck swung out from between her breasts. If flashed in the sunlight.

"That is Kusu," said Sembawa.

"She's beautiful", murmured Pine, firing another match with his thumbnail. When the girl walked past them, she smiled shyly at Kiri. Although she couldn't have been more than sixteen, the fullbodied grace of womanhood was in her stride.

They watched until she disappeared into one of the huts in the *kampong*. He started to ask Sembawa a question, changed his mind, then turned his attention to the pipe, which he relighted.

They left Benskoten Three just before noon on the following day and returned to Singapore.

It was several days before Pine could find passage to Holland. Singapore, with all its attractions, had begun to pall, and he missed London.

He had no plan for handling his meeting with Marie Colter. During the long sea trip he reread her letters with a growing feeling of intrusion. Referring to his notes did not improve his mood. When he began to dislike himself thoroughly, he put the matter out of his mind.

The brief letter he sent her the morning following his arrival in Rotterdam was carried by a messenger, who brought back an affirmative reply.

On the following morning Pine rented a bicycle and pedaled the six miles from Rotterdam to a pleasant brick home in the outskirts of Schiedam on the road to Vlaardingen. It was sunny and warm, and he enjoyed the exercise.

A maid answered his summons at the door. The bell control intrigued Pine with its brass chain and ring that hung down from a brass tube through the door jamb and activated a chime within. He regretted that the plump young woman in the pink apron chose to lead him around rather than through the house, thus depriving him of an opportunity to see the interior mechanics of the device.

Marie Colter was in a back arbor arranging flowers. She came out to meet him, her hand extended.

"Forgive me for meeting you here. Katje should have taken you into the house and called me."

"No, no. It's too lovely a day to be inside." Pine returned the smile that lighted the woman's face. The white of her even teeth against her tanned face, her blonde hair slightly askew and gently riffled by a breeze, moved Pine in a way he was not prepared for—in spite of having seen her picture.

"Shall we sit here?" She motioned toward a small bench beneath the arbor.

Pine sat. He had had weeks to prepare for this moment but now that it was upon him he felt like a tongue-tied schoolboy. He studied her face intently, in a manner unconsciously developed over eleven years of investigative work. "I don't know why you carry matches for that pipe," his friend Fletcher of Scotland Yard had once said to him. "You could ignite it with a burning glance."

Marie Colter's hazel eye met his without flinching. In them he saw a pain that abided.

She helped him. "I now why you're here," she said.

"You do?" He waited. Then: "Of course, your sister-in-law. Do you mind telling me what she wrote to you?"

"She only said you were coming because Jason wanted you to ask me something about my husband's death. I have told everything." She bit her lip. "I told him in a letter that went with the report sent to him by the Benskoten Rubber Company. But what now, after nearly three years? Helen seemed nervous in her letter."

Pine thrust his hands into his pockets searching for the familiar reassurance of his pipe. He had forgotten it. It was on the bedside table in the hotel in Rotterdam.

"I am frightened, too." Her voice was a whisper.

"Do you know I have been to Sumatra, to Benskoten Three?"

She tried to speak but could not get the words loose from the roof of her mouth. She shook her head no. "I feel that you know much." She pressed her hands into her lap to keep them from trembling.

"I know much, but not all. I can guess at some. I'm here to try to learn what is hidden, not to judge you. I haven't decided what to tell Jason. Before I left London I spent nearly three days learning things about him that would set his sainted mother spinning in her grave—if that's where she is and if sainted is the word."

"Do you think I murdered my husband?"

"I think there are things that might indicate you did—motivation, opportunity, perhaps even a witness."

"I did kill him, but I didn't mean to. It was an accident. Kevin was so hard on those poor people. I could have stood nearly anything except the sadistic way he used the plantation workers."

She clasped and unclasped her green-stained fingers. "We had a terrible argument one evening about my going into the *kampong* where I tried to help care for the sick and aid the women giving birth—that sort of thing. He had been drinking, as he always did, only this time he beat me. He was a big man and it's a wonder he didn't kill me. He left the cottage to meet a girl, he told me. I had begun to have horrifying nightmares, and that night, around eleven, I awoke screaming.

"I remembered the blowpipe and darts given to me by a Batak father whose fever-stricken son I had cared for and given medicine to. He had taught me to use the pipe, just as an amusement. I had become quite adept. I decided to go down to the empty cottage where Kevin met his women. I got the blowgun and some darts from a storage room off the kitchen."

"The darts, Mrs. Colter. Tell me about the darts."

"They had no poison on them—I swear they were harmless. The Batak man told me there was no danger without the poison. I crept up to the cottage. There was a lamp burning inside with enough light shining on the porch for me to see. He—there was a girl there, Kusu, a very young girl I knew from the *kampong*. Mr. Pine, how can I tell you? She was not more than thirteen, a child. I don't know why he didn't take her inside, off the porch. He was in the chair. His back was toward me. I only wanted to frighten him, to make him realize that if he continued in his abuse of all of us his life was in danger."

She held out her forefinger to show how she had enlarged a small hole in the screen and inserted the blowgun. "I don't see how I could have missed, but I blew a second dart at him because I was sure the first missed. Then I ran."

The two of them sat for a while, Pine listening to the birds in the trees at the back of the garden, Marie Colter hunched up and pale beneath her tan.

"I think that's the one thing I miss most when I'm at sea," Pine said, "the sound of birdsong. I didn't realize it until just now."

"I only wanted to frighten him," she whispered.

"The darts and pipe—do you still have them?"

"No. I brought them home as a kind of souvenir, but they haunted me so that I burned them. But before I did I had a chemist in Rotterdam check the darts for poison. He said there wasn't a trace. I think someone may have exchanged poisoned darts for the harmless ones I had."

"And switched them again in the confusion afterward? Did anyone know where you kept them?"

"The houseboy, a gardener—both natives. My husband treated both of them worse than animals. But there were others. Kusu was not the first young girl from that family that he—"

Pine studied her face, now wet with the tears of released tension.

"For three years you have been tormented by the idea that you killed your husband."

"What difference is it really?" She looked up at him. "Nothing changes the fact that I killed him. Even knowing I did not intend to or want to doesn't lessen it for me."

"And what if I tell you that you did not kill him, not even accidentally, that he died precisely the way you told the Benskoten office in Singapore and just the way you wrote to the Colters in London, that he died from drinking and fever and heat and wenching, that he did in fact die from a heart attack? It happens, even at his age."

"Would to God I could believe that."

"You can, Mrs. Colter, you can." He put his hand on her arm. "I searched the porch of that cottage with great care. I found two darts stuck in the wall opposite where your husband was sitting. Both of your shots missed."

Pine got up to leave. "Of course, I could be wrong," he said. "It is possible that someone else came by after you ran back to the cottage and did what you failed to do—hit the target."

"Then I did not kill him? You are certain?"

"Not a chance. Unless you haven't told me the truth about how many darts you used."

"Two!" She half shouted it. "Two only—and you found them! What can I say to thank you for lifting me up from this pit?"

"There is no need to. I am rewarded by the sight of the relief on your face."

He declined to stay for lunch, but was ravenous by the time he had pedaled back to the hotel. While he ate, he wrote a carefully composed letter to Kiri Sembawa.

The ship from Rotterdam to London was well out into the channel chop, pointed toward the mouth of the Thames. Alex Pine stood alone at the lee rail watching the wind feather the tops of the waves into the white spoondrift. He felt inside his jacket for his notebook and took out a slip of paper that had the name and address of a Singapore laboratory printed at the top. He read it again.

The enclosed dart carries traces of a deadly poison used by the Batak people of Sumatra in the hunting of large mammals. It is as yet unnamed, nor has it been determined the plant from which it is extracted. A very small amount of the poison has a paralyzing effect on the heart muscles, and possibly other vital organs, including the brain.

He tore the paper into small pieces that the wind carried away. Then he opened the notebook and let a single innocent-looking dart flutter down to the water. He watched until a wave rolled over and engulfed it.

O. H. Leslie
It Started Most Innocently

When Leon Whitehall had the heart attack which forced him into retirement, the outlook for the future wasn't entirely bleak—especially for Mrs. Whitehall. A handsome matron in her fifties, she put her hands on her still-shapely hips, rolled up her mink sleeves, and pitched into battle. She was going to make Leon's retirement years a time of happiness and peace, if it cost them every nickel of the sizeable pension and trust fund he took away from the United Motor Corporation, of which he had been First Vice President.

"*First* of all," she said, "we're going to tear off that horrid old front porch. Nobody, just nobody has front porches any more; you just look in *Better Homes and Gardens*—"

"But, Louise, I sort of liked that old porch," Leon pouted, making his round face and pink scalp look more like his baby pictures than ever. "It's a nice place to sit and read the paper ..."

"Nonsense," Mrs. Whitehall said briskly. "We'll have much better places to sit. Patios and fieldstone terraces and a sunroom with jalousies. And we'll redo the windows, get new wallpaper. And—oh, Lord, there's so *much* to do, Leon!"

She leaned back in her chair, weary but glowing, as if the tasks had already been accomplished and she was awaiting her husband's praise. But poor Leon only looked glum.

"Don't you *want* a lovely home, Leon? A place to spend your declin—I mean, your retirement years in tranquility? You know that you're a very—sick—man."

"I know," her husband said sadly.

"Peace and quiet," Mrs. Whitehall said sonorously. "Shade trees, a fireplace, stereophonic records. And no upsets. You know what Dr. Middlemark said about upsets."

"Yes, Louise."

"Don't you *want* it, Leon?"

Leon Whitehall, possibly reasoning that he would never attain Dr. Middlemark's goal unless he assented, said:

"Yes, Louise."

"I knew it," she said comfortably. "I knew you wanted it as much as I did, Leon. We'll start first thing next week."

Mrs. Whitehall started, and in the most logical place—the lavender-hued office of an interior decorator named Merwin Dumont. Dumont was a thin, soulful man with Valentino eyes and gray hair that swooped back from his forehead like the wing of a bird. From the moment Mrs. Whitehall explained her ideas, and saw his bright-eyed enthusiasm, she knew she had come to the right doorstep. He visited the Whitehall homestead that weekend, and began to create.

"The mood, the mood," he said, putting a hand over his eyes. "I can see the mood now. Beige subtleties and vivid electrics ... elegance and informality ... I can see it!"

Leon, sitting in the only comfortable chair in the house—a red leather he had owned even as a bachelor—watched the activity but saw nothing.

"I want splashes of color," Dumont said thrillingly. "Absolute splashes, *explosions*. I want stark colonial furniture, simply filthy with brass. And carpets—" He waved his hand, indicating broadloom to the ceiling—"*fields* of carpets!"

"Say," Leon ventured feebly. "How much is all this exploding going to cost us?"

The planners looked at him with pity. Leon said no more.

He said nothing when the reconstruction work began, when the workmen irreverently ripped the nails out of his beloved front porch, when the walls were torn apart to make room for naked planes of glass, when the painting began, and new furniture trickled into the house, when the carpeting was laid. In the hectic days that followed, he complained only once—when he sat gingerly on a fragile early American chair and heard his wife bellow:

"Leon! What are you doing?"

"Sitting down, of course. Why?"

"On *that* chair? I thought you knew better than that. That chair's for *show*!"

It was almost three months later, when all the decorating had been completed, that Mrs. Whitehall first expressed dissatisfaction to Merwin Dumont.

"I don't know what it is," she said, across the luncheon table. "We've done everything, but the house isn't *right*."

Dumont sniffed. "I must confess you're correct."

"What could it be? Is it the wall color?"

"No, the colors are perfect. Exquisite!"

"The carpets, then. Is the beige—*beigy* enough?"

"Couldn't be beigier."

"Then what is it, Merwin?"

The decorator brooded, the Valentino eyes suffering.

"Mrs. Dumont, I don't wish to offend you—"

"Yes?"

"But in the bedroom—those old hunting prints of your husband's. They look simply atrocious with the puce walls. In the den—that monstrous elk's head. In the living room—" He shuddered. "That ghastly red chair ..."

"You're right, of course," Mrs. Whitehall nodded. "But Leon's a fanatic about those things."

The decorator shrugged. "Voilá," he said simply.

Mrs. Whitehall braced herself. "Say no more, Merwin. I'll speak to my husband tonight."

No confrontation scene in Tolstoi was ever more impassioned than the one which took place in the Whitehall home that evening. At first Leon was disbelieving. Then, he raged and fumed and sputtered. Then he began to plead—if not for the hunting prints and the elk's head—for the big red chair he loved so much. But he hadn't reckoned on Mrs. Whitehall's cunning. Instead of rebuttals, she used tears.

"To think how I've *slaved* to give you a home you can be proud of," she said, "To think how I've *sacrificed*—"

"Now, Louise—"

"And this is your gratitude. This is how you thank me!"

"Louise, listen—"

The victory was won by only a few drops of the salty stuff on Mrs. Whitehall's cheek. In the morning, a pickup truck took prints, elk, and the big red chair away.

Yet still Mrs. Whitehall wasn't happy.

"Oh, Merwin!" she cried, poised on the couch in his apartment. "I'm just going out of my *mind* trying to figure it out. It's just not my dream house yet."

"There, there, sweet," Dumont said.

"It's just not fair!" She wiped away a tear (genuine) and put her head on his shoulder. "What's wrong with it, Merwin?"

The decorator frowned. "Well, we did what we could. We replaced everything that didn't belong. Frankly, my darling, there can be only one answer."

Mrs. Whitehall stared at him.

"Leon," she whispered.

Dumont shrugged. "What else is left?"

"Leon!" the woman said, the dawn of realization in her eyes. "Of course! That's been it all along. Not just the chair, or the elk's head. It's Leon. He just doesn't *fit* in that house!"

"As a decorator," Dumont said delicately, "I must agree."

"Why, he's as wrong as he can be. Those funny little legs of his. And the way those *suits* fit him. And that bald little head . . ."

"He's just all wrong," Dumont said gravely.

"*Completely* wrong. He's *ludicrous* in that house, Merwin. He belongs in our *old* house. With the porch—"

"And the hunting prints."

"And the elk's head. And that ratty old chair."

"There you are," Dumont said. "But what can you do about it? You can't send a pickup truck for Mr. Whitehall."

"Can't we?" Louise said thoughtfully.

"What, dear?"

"I mean, can't we, really? After all, Leon isn't a well man, Merwin. That's why he retired. Why, Dr. Middlemark told me himself that any shock—any shock at all—would make Leon's heart go phfft."

"Tut, tut," Dumont said, noncommittally.

"If only there was a shock," Mrs. Whitehall mused. "Something that really frightened him. Can you think of anything like that, Merwin?"

"Oh, well," the decorator yawned.

"Merwin, you're not really *interested*."

"Of course, darling. But it is your house."

A motherly smile crossed the woman's face. "Oh, I know what you're thinking. You're thinking *I'm* not thinking about you. But of course I am, Merwin. After all, I don't want that wonderful house to be *empty*."

The decorator's face changed. It glowed. It shone.

"Have you ever," he said enthusiastically, "considered dropping light bulbs?"

That night, while Leon sat stiff-necked in one of the few chairs permitted him, Mrs. Whitehall tiptoed behind him and went into the asphalt-tiled kitchen. Then she lifted the hundred-watt light bulb to shoulder height, and released it. It exploded like a bomb on the floor, and she gave an involuntary shriek of surprise.

"What was that?" Leon asked casually. "Break a glass, dear?"

She came out to look at him, "No," she said. "Light bulb."

"Oh," Leon said.

"Leon, have you had your ears tested lately?"

"What's that, dear?"

"Nothing," Mrs. Whitehall said, gritting her teeth.

That night, at two in the morning, she leaned across the space between their twin beds and shook him violently.

"Huh? Whuzzit? Wha?" Leon said, blinking in the darkness.

"Leon!" she whispered hoarsely. "I think I hear a burglar downstairs!"

"I didn't hear nothin'," he muttered, face in pillow.

"Leon, I tell you I *heard* him, I heard him!"

He grumbled, threw off the covers, and jammed his small feet into the slippers near his bed. Then he padded to the doorway, stuck out his head, and shouted:

"Hey! Anybody down there?"

When no answer came, he nodded with satisfaction, and returned to bed.

"Leon!"

"I told you nobody was down there!"

Frustrated, but not yet daunted, Mrs. Whitehall got out of bed herself, and went down the stairs into the living room. Of course she knew there was no intruder; it was only part of her imperfect plan. But if Leon thought there was—

She threw back her head and screamed lustily, at the top of her formidable lungs.

A moment later, she saw Leon's head appear in the upper hallway.

"Did you call me, Louise?" he said.

"No," she rasped. "Go back to sleep."

The next morning, weary-eyed from an introspective night, Mrs. Whitehall leaned across the breakfast table and said:

"Leon, do you still have that old gun of yours?"

"Huh? What gun?"

"The hunting gun. The one you shot the elk with."

"Oh, that. I guess it's still in the attic. Why?"

"No reason," Mrs. Whitehall lied.

That afternoon, she rummaged through the attic until she found the gun, a venerable shotgun. Fortunately, she had once learned its mysteries during a skeet-shooting season when she was still a debutante, and was able to load it from the box of ammunition stored beside it. She brought it downstairs, her hand casual around the trigger.

"Oh, Leon," she said. "Look what I found today."

"Louise! For God's sake, be careful with the thing."

"Oh, I don't think it's *loaded*," she said cheerfully and squeezed the trigger, making sure the shot would scatter against the rough fieldstone fireplace where it would do no perceptible damage. The blast was much louder than she expected, and the shot came closer to Leon's pink scalp than she intended. But worst of all, the effect wasn't at all what she'd hoped for.

"Are you all right?" Leon said. "Are you hurt?"

"No, I'm not hurt!" she said angrily.

"That old shotgun has quite a kickback. Sure you didn't get bruised or anything."

"For heaven's *sake*, Leon—I almost blasted your head off. Why are you so worried about me?"

Leon blanched.

"You did almost hit me, didn't you? That was very careless of you, Louise. I ... I think I'd better lie down ..."

He walked off, and his wife watched him hopefully. But by nightfall, he was in good spirits again—and, worst of all, in good health.

"It's just no use," she told Merwin Dumont, with a gesture of surrender. "He's simply shock-resistant, like those watches. Nothing scares him, Merwin."

"Tut, tut," the decorator said.

"The only time he showed the *least* bit of upset was when I fired that stupid shotgun at his head. And most of *that* was because he thought the recoil might have hurt *me*."

"A very devoted man," Dumont said.

"Yes," she said in disgust.

The decorator paddled his fingers together.

"Perhaps your answer is there," he said.

"What?"

"In your husband's devotion. He took these other shocks in stride—but if *you* were endangered—if he thought something had happened to *you*—"

"To me? I don't understand."

"Well, if he thought you had sustained some injury—perhaps even a fatal accident—the shock might accomplish what you're after."

"*We're* after," Mrs. Whitehall said.

Domont coughed. "Of course, we. Now I recall one incident, happened to a friend of mine. He, too, had an unfortunate heart condition. When he came home and discovered his wife dead—she had taken an overdose of sleeping pills, poor child—the shock killed him just as effectively."

"But I can't fake anything like that—"

"Nothing like that, perhaps. But if you could devise something equally dramatic ..."

They fell silent, deep in speculation.

Finally, Mrs. Whitehall said, triumphantly:

"I have it!"

"You do?"

"Yes. I'll *hang* myself!"

Leon Whitehall, even in his retirement days, retained some of his old habits, remnants of his business life. One of these was setting the alarm for seven thirty, and rising promptly when its insistent ring announced another dawn. Mrs. Whitehall watched him set the clock that night, and in the morning, rose half an hour before the clamor started.

She went quietly downstairs, and sat before the early American desk in the hall. Then, on a sheet of her best stationery, she wrote:

Dear Leon—
Forgive me for this. These thirty years with you have been heaven. But now the thought that you might go first and leave me alone is too much to bear. Forgive me, my darling, when you see what is in the basement.
                                                                    Louise

She folded the note carefully, and returned upstairs. Leon was still deep in slumber, snoring lightly. She placed the note on the rounded paunch that protruded under the sheet, and went below again. In the kitchen, from under the countertop, she removed the brown paper parcel she had brought from a shopping tour in town. Then she opened the door that led to the still unfinished basement.

She opened the parcel, revealing a length of heavy brown rope, its end already expertly tied into the ever-popular hangman's noose. Then she looked about the bare basement and realized that she lacked on item to complete her project—something to stand on. There was nothing in the basement, so she sighed and returned to the first floor. A moment later, she was clumping down the basement stairs with a slat-backed early American chair borrowed from the dining room.

She climbed up on the chair and threw the end of the rope around a steampipe. The knot she made to secure it was awkward and lumpy, but it served its purpose. Then, lightly, she fitted the noose around her neck.

Standing on tiptoe, with her head drooping to one side on her chest, her eyes shut, her tongue hanging from her mouth, she rehearsed the pose.

Then she waited, patiently, until she heard the faint sound upstairs. *Tingle-lingle-lingle-click*! The alarm had rung, and Mr. Whitehall had stopped its jangling. Any moment now, he would discover the note.

She waited, still patient.

Then she heard his voice.

"Louise?"

Now! She struck the pose, one hand holding firmly to the loop of tough brown rope to prevent any mishaps. She rolled her head on her shoulder, until it had just the right droop. She stuck out her tongue, and shut her eyes in the resignation of death. She stretched her body as far as it would go, the tips of her shoes barely touching the chair bottom.

She heard the lumbering footstep of her husband, heard him crash and collide with the furniture, and inwardly cursed his clumsiness. Then she heard the basement door open, and his steps on the wooden stairs.

He was in front of her, walking around her, taking in the grisly sight. She thought she could hear his little heart pounding, thundering, getting ready for its last terrible effort, and then—

There was only silence.

"Tut, tut, tut," she heard. "Who would have thought it? . . . of all people."

And then she heard him giggle.

"How do you like that?" she then heard Leon say. "Using one of her best chairs, too. She'd *kill* me if I ever did that."

Then he was chuckling, and she knew that the plan had gone wrong. She couldn't decide what to do next. She wanted to open her eyes and admit the hoax, but she couldn't be sure—

"Her good chair," Leon said.

Then she heard the sounds that she instantaneously interpreted as,

"He's kicked the chair out from under me," for she felt herself dangling.

"Guess she can't yell at me now," he giggled.

"*Leon!*" Mrs. Whitehall cried, no longer caring about her plan. "Leon, let me down!"

He didn't seem to hear her. "Guess I better call the police," he muttered, heading for the stairs.

"Leon!" Mrs. Whitehall gasped, struggling to keep the noose from tightening about her throat, kicking her legs in the air. "Leon, for God's sake—"

"Wonder if that place still has my chair?" she heard him say, as he started up the steps.

"Leon!" Mrs. Whitehall shrieked, her shoes flying off her feet, her whole body writhing with the effort to stay alive. "Leon, Leon, Le—"

Dr. Middlemark pulled the stethoscope from his ears, and said, "Well, it's remarkable, Leon, really remarkable. After that terrible thing happened, I would have expected your condition to be a lot worst. But frankly, you're in pretty good shape."

"It's the peace and quiet," Leon Whitehall said, buttoning his shirt and patting the red leather arms of his chair. "It's the peace and quiet that does it, doctor."

Duffy Carpenter
Last of the Big-Time Spenders

"Are you going to hang someone tonight, Daddy?" Then's T.J., the six-year-old. Of my three children, he is the youngest, and the only member of the clan who is impressed with my being a Small Claims Court referee. Unpaid, of course. I earn my daily bread as a marketing guy for a major corporation.

"Paralegal sounds like you jump out of airplanes to me." That's Meggin, the twelve-year-old-going-on-fifty-four.

"I'm not a judge, T.J. I just settle disputes over small amounts of money below a thousand dollars. As for you, Miss Smarty Pants, 'para' means 'alongside of.' I work *alongside of* the courts to help the judges' case load."

"Well, you're not even a lawyer," Meggin said with some petulance. She hates to be corrected. An inheritance from the maternal side, no doubt.

"I don't have to be a lawyer under the new state law, dear. I have an MBA and lots of business experience, and I took a six-week course and an exam, didn't I?"

"Show her your badge, Dad," T.J. prompted me. He loves the little "Officer of the Court" disk I carry in my wallet. So do I, but I don't admit it.

"Where's David?" I asked my wife, who ignored me. She was still mad at me, and was giving me the silent treatment. The argument is too silly to relate. If you're married, you'll understand; if you're not, you never will, and count your blessings. Meggin, ever aware of her surroundings, filled the void.

"Davey's in a school play and had to leave early for rehearsals," she reported.

I was beginning to think that my nine-year-old didn't exist. I never see him at the breakfast table any more. Since Small Claims is in session at night for the public's convenience, I'm not home for dinner on Tuesdays and Thursdays. I'm not home on Mondays, Wednesdays, or Fridays either, due to business commitments. That should give you a clue to the cause of the frostbite I'm getting from the adult lady at the other end of the table, known to the world as Mrs. Jeff Corbett, nee Sarah (Sally) Barnes.

"Well," I said, getting to my feet, "if I don't see Davey with my own eyes pretty soon, I'm going to report him to the Missing Persons Bureau." I chuckled. No one else did.

I got a kiss from Sally that was in the "for the sake of the children" category and left for work.

It was ironic that my unnoticed jest about Missing Persons was the basis of the third case I heard that evening in Room 407-A at the Municipal Building downtown. The docket read "Acme Investigators *vs.* Crimmer."

Crimmer, Amos, defendant, was a beefy guy around fifty who, I would have guessed, was perpetually rumpled. He certainly was that night. The plaintiff, Calvin Hobbs, looked and dressed casual, like a golf pro. He didn't look like a private detective to me, but he was, and had the credentials to prove it.

I started off. "Gentlemen, before we begin, I want to reiterate some points for the record. You have mutually agreed to waive a hearing before a judge and to submit this to arbitration before a referee. I'm sure the Clerk of the Court explained, Mr. Crimmer, that if you choose arbitration, my decision will be binding and final. With a judge, you have the right to appeal to a higher court. With a referee, you don't. You both understand that?"

They nodded agreement. I don't normally start that way, but this case had over six hundred dollars in contention; $672.50, to be exact. The limit to the amount you can sue for in Small Claims is a thousand dollars, but most cases, at least my cases, involve sums in the fifty to two hundred dollar neighborhood. This case was my biggest so far, and I wanted to make damn sure it went smoothly. Another wrinkle in the pattern was that this was the first time I'd heard a case where a company was suing an individual. All the others were consumers suing retailers over irons that didn't work or shirts lost by a laundry. This was a reverse action, and might even prove interesting.

"Well, Mr. Hobbs, it's customary for the plaintiff to start off, so go right ahead."

"Thank you, Mr. Corbett," the detective said, opening a manila file and resettling himself in the chair across the table from me. Crimmer sat on the opposite side, too, but he put two feet between himself and Hobbs, as if to underscore his disagreement. Hobbs spoke slowly and distinctly. He had obviously spent many hours giving testimony on witness stands.

"The amount in question, $672.50, is money representing fees and expenses incurred in an investigation undertaken by me, Calvin Hobbs, D.B.A., Acme Investigators, operating under state license number 173 ..."

"Excuse me, Mr. Hobbs," I interrupted. "You must know that Small Claims is an informal court, so we can dispense will all the documentation. I don't think Mr. Crimmer is questioning your credentials."

"I'm questioning the expenses he ran up cruising around the damn country, that's what I'm questioning."

"All right, Mr. Crimmer"—I smiled condescendingly as I said it—"you'll get your chance. Now what's the crux of this matter, Mr. Hobbs?"

Hobbs looked a little miffed at having his recitation cut off, but I've had sea-going lawyers start that quasi-legal stuff before, and I was getting expert at stopping it quickly.

"If that's the way you want it, Mr. Corbett." Hobbs said it hesitatingly, as if I had made a grave error, but he was willing to sustain it in spite of his feelings. "On Monday, March 13th, Mr. Crimmer came to my offices in the Grillon Building and hired me to trace his wife, Lillian, who had been missing since Sunday."

"Was a contract signed, Mr. Hobbs?"

"No, Mr. Corbett, but an oral agreement was made, which I believe constitutes a contract."

"I'm aware of that, sir. Go on."

He took a sheet of paper from his folder and laid it on the table in front of me. It was a detailed statement of charges totaling $672.50.

"The charges stated there can be documented with receipts and my expense diary."

I picked up the statement and studied it. "You were on the case for six days for a total of four hundred fifty dollars in fees. And the rest is for expenses, I see. The largest expense was a hundred fifty dollars for a flight to Bridgeport, Connecticut. What does the fifty dollar 'miscellaneous' charge stand for? The rest is highly detailed."

"That's a euphemism for smear money. You know, to buy information. It's all spelled out in my report to Mr. Crimmer."

He went into the file again and came out with several typed sheets held together with a staple.

"Here's a copy for the record."

He put the sheets down on the table, but I left them there.

"We don't keep records. Mr. Hobbs, and unless it is germane, I don't think I'll have to read it. Now, Mr. Crimmer, let's hear from you. Why do you refuse to pay the bill?"

"Because I don't like to be taken for a sleigh ride. Sure, I hired the man, but when he mentioned expenses, I assumed he meant local stuff, you know, gas for his car and things. I didn't plan on him taking a vacation in Connecticut on my money."

"All right, that's a start," I said, going to work. "You dispute the expenses, which we'll put aside for the moment. You do agree to the fee?"

"Not six days' worth, I don't. I run a small garage for a living, and money don't grow on trees. I hired him on a Monday, and on Wednesday I called him to stop looking, and ended up talking to one of those recorder things. The voice, his voice, said was out of the office and to leave a message and I did. I said he's off the case. That's two days' work, as far as I'm concerned."

"Did you get the message, Mr. Hobbs?"

"How could I? I was in Bridgeport. I run a one-man office, sir. When I got back on Saturday night I was shocked to hear what was on the recorder."

"Okay, let's see if we can get some points of agreement here. You agree that at least two days' charges are valid, Mr. Crimmer?"

"Yes, that's one fifty, not $672.50."

"True. Now let's arbitrate. Did you tell Mr. Crimmer that you were going to Bridgeport, Mr. Hobbs?"

"I tried to call him from the airport, but didn't get an answer. The lead was a hot one, so I jumped onto the next plane. Hell, I would have been *saving* him money in the long run. I was hot on her trail and I figured I could have nabbed her. That's the way detective work goes, Mr. Corbett. You tumble onto something and you have to move fast or you end up with a cold trail and weeks of dog work. As for taking a vacation and a joy ride, I can think of a lot nicer places to go than Bridgeport, Connecticut. Hell, he had ten thousand dollars riding on my finding her, so I used my own discretion. That's not out of line with industry practice."

"Ten thousand dollars? Where does that come in?"

"You put the point about the ten thousand dollars in there?" Crimmer looked angrily at the report.

"Certainly I did," Hobbs said to me, not his adversary. "Look, Mr. Corbett, my regular fee is one fifty a day. Mr. Crimmer is quite a haggler, and he offers me a deal. He tells me his wife took off with ten thousand dollars from a strongbox he had in his home. He offered me a bounty of ten percent if I got the money back. I figured it didn't sound like a tough case, so I cut my price in half to seventy-five dollars a day. Okay, so I'm out as far as the bounty is concerned and I'm also out an extra four fifty I would have made if I charged full rate. I'm not complaining on that score. A deal is a deal and I'm stuck with it, but I'm not going to eat the whole loss." He turned to Crimmer. "Didn't you read the report? And why shouldn't I have mentioned the ten thousand dollars?"

"What I own is my business and why should I read the report? It would have been a waste of time."

"I'm the one who wasted the time," Hobbs said. "For all I know, there never was ten thousand dollars, and you were using that as bait to get my price down."

"There *was* ten thousand dollars!" Crimmer said, raising his voice.

I could see this getting heated, so like a good referee I broke the clinch and sent them to neutral corners.

"Gentlemen, suppose we just deal with the facts. How did you proceed with the search, Mr. Hobbs?"

"I dug around locally on Tuesday, talking with neighbors. She didn't seem to have any close friends, and I came up emtpy. Then, on Wednesday, I got lucky out at the airport. A woman of her description had bought a through ticket for Bridgeport, Connecticut, earlier that morning, so I hopped the next plane."

I turned to Crimmer. "What prompted you to call the search off on

Wednesday, sir? Were you dissatisfied with Hobbs in any way?"

"No, but there was no sense in him looking for a dead woman." He said it as if he were commenting on the weather. No change in expression or tone of voice. My mouth must have dropped or something, because he added, "I guess you didn't know that. They found her body over in Mituate in a vacant lot. If I don't look remorseful it's because I'm not. Lillian was a tramp, always was a tramp, only this time her boyfriend, whoever he was, liked ten thousand more than he liked her."

I was still stunned, and said a dumb thing. "She was murdered?"

"Strangled, and the money was gone. It may sound callous, Mr. Corbett, but I've lived with that hussy for twelve years and put up with a lot. This time, it wasn't any ten-day fling with the first pair of trousers to flatter her. She cleaned out the money and was going for good."

"I'm terribly sorry, Mr. Crimmer. When did this happen?"

"The Mituate cops say sometime Tuesday night, and don't waste any pity on me. The cops called me early Wednesday morning after they indentified her from things in her purse. That's when I called Hobbs."

Well, there it was, in my lap. It was as ugly a case as they ever heard over in the Criminal Court, and even stickier. I had a feeling that Hobbs had acted impetuously, but in good faith. It seemed to me that he had used a key phrase, "industry practice"; that is, what is normally done in the course of a private investigation. What were its limits and excesses? I honestly didn't know. A referee is supposed to hand down a decision then and there, but you have a right to reserve judgment, and I did so.

"This is much more complex than I had originally thought, gentlemen, and I am going to defer a finding for one week."

The men looked at each other and then back at me. Both got to their feet. "Shall we come in at the same time?" Hobbs wanted to know, and I said yes. When they had left, I collected the charge statement and Hobbs' report for reference, and called the next case.

Two hours, or, more graphically, two cases (on non-delivery of furniture and an hysterical woman whose hair had turned out the wrong color in a beauty salon) later, I was through for the night. Well, not quite through. I had called the Central Police Headquarters in the far wing of the Municipal Building. Lieutenant Bill Donnagan wasn't in, but he was expected at ten o'clock, so I took my time walking through the deserted halls to his office.

Donnagan is a tough old bird with a growl in his voice and a reputation for gruffness bordering on the rude. A while back, I did him a good turn and gained a friend. A gruff one to be sure, but a friend all the same.

"I hope you're not playing detective again, Jeff," he greeted me as I entered his office. He has two suits, to my knowledge; an old seersucker for summer and a grey nondescript thing for winter. The hat never changed, and had never left his head in anyone's memory. This was early April, and the grey suit looked like it would welcome its coming vacation.

"No, I had enough of that on the cigar case last summer. But I do need some professional advice about how detectives work."

"They don't, didn't you know? We just wait for stoolies to come in."

"Seriously, Bill. You can help me with a touchy one." I went on to explain Hobbs' taking off on a wild goose chase without having cleared it with a client.

When I was through, he sat back and put his feet on the desk. "With a private dick, you never know. Some are square and some are crooked. This guy Hobbs hasn't been around this town long enough to get his nose dirty. Runs a one-man shop, doesn't he?" I nodded. "Well, if he flew to Miami or Vegas, I might say he was boozing up the expense sheet. But not a small city back east, Jeff. It sounds legit to me. In fact, the same thing happened to me years ago. I trailed a bird all the way to New York on a train and caught seven kinds of hell from my senior officer because it wasn't authorized. But then, *I caught* my man. This Hobbs was supposed to be some kind of hotshot, but I guess he's a dope—or maybe just naive."

I got to my feet and started to leave. "I really hate to sock it to a guy who just lost his wife and ten thousand dollars to boot. It was probably his life savings."

"What ten G's?" Donnagan wanted to know. I told him the rest of the story, or rather all of it.

"Crimmer," he muttered. "Sure, Lillian Crimmer. Strangled over in Mituate last month. Mituate TWX'd us and we called the husband." He turned and pulled a clipboard from a row of hooks behind his head and flipped through the pages. "Here it is. There was no mention of her carrying ten thousand dollars."

"She wasn't. It was taken from her by a lover or someone."

Donnagan put the board back on its hook without looking, his feet still on the desk. It must have been a practiced exercise. I would have broken my neck trying it.

"Does something arouse your suspicion, lieutenant?"

"No, my young fellow, and I've got enough problems in this town without borrowing any from Mituate."

On the way home that night and at my regular job all the next day, the germ of something inexplicable was starting to sprout in my brain. Even when I was home that Wednesday night, I had plenty of time to think about it, since Sally was still fighting the cold war.

Question #1: Why didn't Crimmer tell the Mituate cops about the ten thousand?

Question #2: Even if he hadn't cared about his wife, would a man who had just been informed of her murder automatically call to cancel a search for her as his first order of business? Just to save seventy-five dollars?

Nobody is that organized. Or that cheap.

There were other things that bothered me, like if the late Mrs. Crimmer was a bit of a strumpet, what was she doing with access to his safe deposit box? And, for that matter, what was he doing with ten thousand in cash? That's a bad way to keep savings, when it could be earning a dividend in an account.

All this was running around my brain as I sat alone in the den around ten P.M. Sally was ignoring the fact that I had come home early from a planning meeting at the office. On an impulse, I picked up the phone and dialed the Municipal Building. When I got Donnagan on the line, I said, "Could you check and see if Crimmer reported his wife to Missing Persons?"

"Oh-oh," the lieutenant's voice said mockingly, "I could tell something was biting you when you came in here the other night. Why don't you leave it to the police, Jeff? Hell's bells, you wouldn't want some joker from another town messing in your business."

"I'm not 'messing' with Mituate business, Bill. I want to know if he reported her disappearance to the local police here in town."

"Suppose he didn't. Lots of people don't. What do you think they do down in BMP, send out a troop of Boy Scouts every time someone is overdue for dinner? Sure, they check the morgue and hospitals, and that's about it. Jeff."

"Would you check anyway? As a favor?"

He told me to hang on and put me on hold. In seconds, his voice came back on. "Okay, Sherlock, she was reported missing at eleven thirty P.M. on March 14th. Satisfied?"

"No. She was missing on the 12th, a Sunday, maybe earlier. Why did he wait two days to use a free service when he hired a professional tracer just the day before on Monday?"

"How do I know?"

I went on and explained my other suspicions, about the access to cash kept in a safe deposit box, and calling Hobbs the minute he heard she was dead. "Don't you think we ought to make Mituate aware of these facts, lieutenant?"

"This may come as a surprise, Jeff, but Mituate is not a one-dog town and it has a very capable detective division. Don't you think they've checked Crimmer seven ways up and down? The first prime suspect is the spouse in cases like this." From the way my wife had been acting all week, I could see what he meant.

"Now do me, Mituate, and yourself a favor and forget about it. You may not know it, but most police departments are swamped with people who think they have solved crimes. Most of them are little old ladies with nothing else to do, by the way."

On that note, I hung up and took his advice. I also decided to award

Hobbs the entire amount when next Tuesday came around.

The next evening, before my Thursday night hearings started, I vowed to remain uninvolved and aloof and stick to the business of solving small claims hassles. About midway through my last case, there was a knock on my door, and a patrolman in uniform came in quietly, handed me a note, and left.

I excused myself from the weighty problem of whether or not Mrs. Anna Collucci was entitled to a new pair of shoes, even though the shoe store owner now sitting on her right had insisted at the point of sale that she needed size ten and not nine. The note read:

Corbett:
Congratulations. You solved another one.
Drop by after your session for details.

Donnagan

I was so excited and anxious to learn how they had tripped him, I gave Mrs. Collucci the privilege of getting five dollars off on her next pair of shoes. She was still shouting like an Italian version of a banshee as I walked quickly away from Room 407-A toward the police wing.

Donnagan was coming out of his office as I walked up.

"Old lady, huh?" I chided him. "Sherlock, huh? I knew I had a hunch about that guy."

"So did I, although I didn't tell you at the time. Come on, we have him down in the lockup. We're holding him for a Mituate pickup."

We took the elevator down to the cell block and, as we passed through the guard desk, Donnagan was saying, "Damn shame, too. I do the work and Mituate gets a felony murder credit. Well, one hand washes the other."

"We paralegals would call it quid pro quo and all that." I was feeling pretty peppy about my coup and was showing it. "What finally tripped him up, lieutenant?"

"Here's the cell. Ask him yourself."

We came up to Pen 10 and I looked between the bars at the man sitting on the cot. He looked tired and worried and not at all like a natty golf pro, much less a private detective.

"Hobbs? Hobbs did it?"

"That's right, Hawkshaw. We've got a confession out of him. He doesn't look like he wants to talk to you. Come on, I'll buy you a cup of coffee to show the city's appreciation."

All the way to the coffee shop, I was numb with confusion. "This is crazy, lieutenant. I thought Crimmer did it. What did Hobbs have to gain?"

"Ten G's is a big inducement. We didn't know Hobbs was in the picture until you told me about the lawsuit. As I told you, Mituate went after the husband first, but he came up with a solid alibi. They've been concentrating all their time looking for a mythical lover."

"Mythical? But Crimmer said ..."

"One of the first things you learn in police work, Jeff, is that people are always saving face. A guy's wife is missing, so right away she's a tramp. Of course, he didn't bother to tell us that he made life so miserable for her that she just walked out alone. Crimmer runs a crummy little garage, and yet he has accumulated ten G's in cash. What does that suggest to you?"

"Illegal money?"

"No, he's clean. But he is a miser, and that type isn't much fun to live with. If a guy learns that his wife has just been murdered and his first idea is to save some money by canceling a detective, I'd say he was a first-class penny pincher."

"All right, I can buy that. He certainly haggled during the hearing. But why should Hobbs expose himself by suing Crimmer?"

"He was covering himself. If he didn't demand to be paid, Crimmer might have become suspicious once he figured out the fact that only the detective and the mythical lover knew about the money. Eliminate the lover story and who do you have? Hobbs. He got the case on Monday, so he had a hot trail. He catches up with her in Mituate, does her in, and takes the money. Then he goes flying off back east on a supposed wild-goose chase. He also gave himself an alibi until I gave Mituate the lowdown on Hobbs. They went to work and placed him in that town Tuesday night."

"But that's highly circumstantial, isn't it?"

"It was until this morning. The Bridgeport cops canvassed all the banks in Fairfield County and came up with a ten thousand dollar deposit made by a James Morgan on the day Hobbs arrived there. The assistant manager of the bank is flying out for positive identification, but from his description on the phone, it's Hobbs all right."

"Well, I'll be damned," I said, shaking my head. "I guess I'd make a lousy detective, huh? I thought it was the husband, and the real killer was right under my nose."

"Oh, you have the instinct, Jeff. All you need is the direction. Remember, crime takes all types."

"I know," I said woefully. "The only trouble ise, I'm getting to meet every damn type."

Gary Brandner
Parlor Game

Even in bright sunshine Western Avenue is not one of the beauty spots of Los Angeles. In the rain it can be downright ugly. I stood in the rain on the corner of Western and Romaine and squinted up at the window of my new office. The window was dirty and had a crack across one corner and no name on it. The name was down at the foot of the stairs in white plastic letters stuck on a black directory board. D. STONE-BREAKER, PRIVATE INVESTIGATOR.

The new place was not much, but it was no worse than my old office downtown on Fifth. That building was being demolished so they could put up some future slums. It's called urban renewal.

The new neighborhood looked lively enough. Right under my office was the Erotique Massage Parlor. Next door was a movie theater advertising *Hard Core Nudies—Open All Night*. Also in my block were beer bars, pawn shops, a pool room, a Mexican lunch stand, and a Chinese laundry. And a couple of places whose business I couldn't guess.

I was getting wet. I ambled back across the street and started up the stairs. Just before I got to the landing I heard the moist smack of a fist on flesh. I went on up, and there just in front of my office a big-shouldered stud was slapping around a slim girl in cutoff jeans. She had shiny black hair that bounced away from her face every time he hit her. I walked up behind the big guy and grabbed him by the meat of his shoulder.

"You're blocking my door," I said.

He spun around as though he was going to let me have one, too. He had a big-jawed handome face spoiled by a pouty little mouth. When he got a look at my size and my face, which is not cheery at best, he changed his mind about hitting me.

"What's the matter, mister?" he said. "You a hero or something?"

"Beat up your woman someplace else. You're bad for my business."

The girl, who couldn't have weighed more than a hundred pounds, looked from one of us to the other with dark frightened eyes. The left side of her face was red where the guy had smacked her.

Just so she wouldn't think he was chickening out, the tough guy said to her, "Remember, there's more where that came from." He walked away and down the stairs, turning to give me a fierce look when he was out of reach.

The girl was rubbing the side of her face when I turned around. "Damn, I hope I don't get a black eye. Listen, are you the private detective who's moving in here?"

I admitted that I was.

"Can we go into your office?"

"Sure, but we can't sit down. The furniture isn't here yet." I unlocked the door and the girl walked in ahead of me. She was wearing a lightweight shirt with the tails tied in front, exposing a whole lot of skin north and south of the navel. She glanced around the empty room without enthusiasm.

"It'll look better when I get the carpet laid and the stereo in," I said.

She ignored the sarcasm. "I'm Abby Deane. I workd downstairs in the massage parlor." She waited a couple of seconds to let me absorb the information. "Does that make any difference?"

"Why should it?"

"Some people don't want to do business with a girl who works in a massage parlor."

"Some people feel the same way about private detectives. What kind of business did you have in mind?"

"I think I'm getting in some trouble that's bigger than I can handle. I might need your help."

"Tell me about it."

She looked at the big colorful watch strapped to her wrist. "Listen, I have to go now, I've got a ride home waiting for me. I've got to be back here to go to work at seven. I'll come an hour early and talk to you then. If you're going to be here."

"I'll be here."

She started out the door.

"Wait a minute." I eased out past her and walked softly down the stairs. Sure enough, just inside the doorway where the rain wouldn't spoil his hair style was the tough guy with the shoulders.

"Forget something?"

He looked at me and licked his pouty little lips. "What's it to you?"

"I don't like you in my doorway. You scare away clients."

"What are you gonna do about it?"

"You don't really want to know, do you?"

He thought that over, measured me again with his eyes, and decided he had business somewhere else. He sauntered up the street and got into a grubby Volkswagen. From long habit I memorized the license number.

I went back upstairs and told Abby Deane it was all clear below. She hurried out and left me standing in my bare office feeling restless and depressed and listening to the rain rattle against the window.

By six o'clock the movers had all my stuff in place. When I say "all," I mean desk and swivel chair, two straight-backed chairs for clients, a pair of four-drawer file cabinets, and an elderly typewriter with matching stand. For the walls a couple of sincere landscape prints. I was lying before about the carpet and stereo.

An hour later it was dark. The rain still slapped my window and the cars going by on Western Avenue made a melancholy hissing sound. Abby Deane failed to show. I sat there for another hour trying to decide whether I liked my file cabinets on the left or should I move them over to the right. At eight o'clock I decided to leave them where they were. To hell with Abby Deane. It wasn't the first time I'd been stood up. Still, something nagged at me. It was that persistent little nag that has gotten me into more trouble than I like to think about. It couldn't hurt, I decided, to look in downstairs and see if she went to work on schedule.

I let myself out of the office and clumped down the stairs into the wet night. The entrance to the Erotique Massage Parlor was a few steps toward the corner. It is possible, I hear, to get a legitimate massage in one of these joints, but it's the optional extras that pay the rent. This one had a little anteroom with a soft carpet, all rosy lights and strawberry incense. The walls featured unlikely nudes painted on black velvet. A curtain of beads parted and a chesty blonde girl swayed up to me and flapped her eyelashes.

"Hi there," she said. "I'm Bunny."

"You would be."

"How about a nice massage tonight?" Her fingers were already busy with the buttons of my coat.

"Maybe another time," I said. "I just looked in to see if one of the girls showed up for work."

"What's on your mind, fella?" The voice came from across the room where a kid of twenty or so sat behind a small desk. He had oily black hair and an uncertain complexion. One of his hands was out of sight below the desktop where he probably kept something to quiet trouble-some customers.

I went over to the desk and glowered down at him. "There's a girl named Abby Deane says she works here."

"So?"

"Did she come in tonight?"

"You're not a cop."

"My name is Stonebreaker." I jerked my thumb at the ceiling. "I'm your new neighbor."

The kid relaxed a little, but his hand stayed out of sight. "You say you're a friend of Abby's?"

"Just met her today. We had a business appointment a couple of hours ago. She didn't show up."

"No, she didn't come in tonight." The kid brought his other hand back up on the desk. "She didn't call, either."

"Did you try to call her?"

He threw a glance over his shoulder at a door somewhat hidden by a dark red drapery. The door was open a couple of inches. "I couldn't call her because I don't know her number," he said. "I don't know nothing about her. All I do is work out front here."

The door opened inward the rest of the way and a neat little man walked out to join us. He was wearing a dark suit and vest of the type you don't see any more, with a starched white shirt open at the throat. He was bald with a long skinny nose and a little excuse-me mustache.

"What's the trouble, Rick?" he asked the kid.

"No trouble. This guy was just asking about Abby."

"Who are you?"

I told him. He was not impressed.

"My name's Otto Boatman," he said. "I'm the owner. What did you want with Abby?"

"Just curious. She was afraid she was in some kind of trouble."

"It's possible. These girls don't come here straight from the convent, you know. What they do on their own time is none of my business. Yours either, as far as I can see."

"Maybe not," I said. "Would you mind giving me her address?"

"Can't do it. For all I know she's freelancing, and if I steered you that would make me a panderer."

"We wouldn't want to do that," I said. I'd taken it as far as I'd planned to, anyway. I didn't owe Abby Deane a thing. As I started out into the rain something plucked at my sleeve.

"Come back some time," said Bunny. She grabbed my hand and gave it a little squeeze.

I winked at her. "Keep the table warm." I left the massage parlor and stepped into the shelter of the stairwell to read the note she had pressed into my hand. It had Abby's name on it and an address on Willoughby over near the Desilu studios. Inside my head a small, wise voice said, Don't get involved. Sound advice. I got my jalopy out of the parking lot and headed west toward Willoughby.

The apartment was one of those stucco and redwood numbers that went up all over L.A. during the building boom of the fifties. It was a little frayed around the edges now. At one spot rainwater poured in a splattering stream over the clogged roof gutter. The squatty date palms out in front looked wretched. Los Angeles should never be seen in the rain.

I took a look at the six mailboxes. White envelopes showed through the grill of number three, which was Abby Deane's, putting her downstairs at the rear of the building. I walked along the edge of a small swimming pool to a redwood fence with a metal 3 hanging on the gate. Inside the fence was a two-by-four patio with a sliding glass door into the apartment. I pushed the button and listened to the harsh buzzing inside. Nobody came to let me in.

Okay, said my wise little voice, you've done all you can. Let's get out of here.

In a minute, I told the voice. Why, I wondered, if Abby Deane was on her way home when she left me this afternoon, didn't she take in the mail? I popped the door lock with no trouble and stepped into a small, cluttered living room. A quick look in the kitchenette, bath, and bedroom turned up no dead bodies. So much for the good news.

I prowled around a little, getting a feel for the girl who lived here. There was food in the refrigerator and the usual junk in the bathroom, plenty of clothes in the bedroom closet and drawers, and a matched pair of suticases under the bed. If Abby Deane had gone on a trip, it must have come up mighty sudden. On the way out of the bedroom I stopped to admire a mounted Polaroid shot of Abby and oily-haired Rich from the massage parlor. They were standing by the pool outside her patio with their arms around each other, grinning self-consciously.

A card table was set up in one corner of the living room. Among the papers spread across the top was a pocket-sized address book. I thumbed through it and glanced at the clusters of numbers inside that were almost surely names transcribed into a simple number-for-letter code. All the groupings under the *A* section began with the figure *1*, under *B* the figure *2*, and so on. It wouldn't take the CIA to crack Abby's code.

Also on the table was a sheet of lined notebook paper ruled into three columns. Entries in the first cloumn were dates, in the other two were figures in the thousands. For every date the figure in the second column was larger than the third. The dates covered the month just past, but the figures meant nothing to me. I stuck the sheet in my pocket along with the coded address book in case it might mean something later. I went out the way I came in and clicked the lock on the sliding door back into place.

A cold wind was blowing the rain around and Western Avenue was deserted when I strolled back into the Erotique Massage Parlor. Bunny and another girl, both in shorty nightgowns, were sitting on the floor with a deck of cards telling fortunes. Rick slouched behind the desk reading a motorcycle magazine. Bunny saw me first and started to get up. I waved her back down and walked over to the desk.

"It's not nice to lie to people, Rick," I said.

"What do you mean?"

"You told me you didn't know Abby Deane or anything about her. I just came from her place, and there was a nice picture of the two of you groping each other out by her pool."

Bunny came over to join us. "Is Abby all right? How come she didn't show up tonight?"

"I don't know if she's all right or not," I said. "She wasn't home. Why did you hold out on me, Rick?"

He jerked his head back toward the curtained door, closed tight now. "The boss was back in the office, and he don't want me to date any of the girls. He'd fire my butt if he knew."

I pulled out the address book and the sheet with the figures and showed them to Rick. "These were in Abby's apartment. It looked like she'd just been working on them. Do they mean anything to you?"

Rick shook his head.

I said, "If this book is what I think it is, your girlfriend might be in as much trouble as she thinks she is."

Beside me Bunny drew in her breath sharply. "Can we go in the back and talk?"

I nodded and followed her through the curtain of beads. Along one wall were half a dozen stalls with what looked like padded operating tables inside. Curtains could be pulled across the front for privacy. Straight ahead was a washroom with a couple of showers. Bunny and I were the only ones back there. She took me into one of the stalls.

"I didn't want them to hear this up front," she said.

"Something about the address book?"

She nodded. "Abby had a little thing going on the side. When a customer came in and took a shower—everybody has to take a shower first—Abby would go through his wallet. She never took anything, just wrote down the names. The next day she'd check out the names to see if any of the johns were rich or famous or anything. If he was a nobody she'd forget it. If he was some guy with money, she'd call up and see if he, um, wanted to give her a little present or whatever you call it."

"You call it blackmail," I said.

Bunny toyed with a bottle of scented oil from a shelf over the table. "Abby didn't think of it like that. She never asked for a whole lot of money, and I don't think she'd have done anything about it if the john refused to pay."

"Are you telling me the names in this book are the guys on her sucker list?"

"Maybe. She said she kept them in some kind of code."

"Yeah, very clever of her." I left the massage booth and rattled back out through the beads.

Rick looked up quickly from the desk. "Are you going to try to find Abby?" he asked.

"Why should I?"

Bunny came up behind me and said, "Because you're a detective and she came to you for help."

"I do this for a living," I told her. "Helping people buys no bananas."

She looked disappointed in me. "How much do you charge?"

I named my daily rate.

Bunny looked over at Rick. "I'll go half if you will."

"I don't know, that's a lot of money."

"After all, you did have a thing going with her."

After a little more discussion they came up with the money. I pocketed the bills and went home, where I did the first thing a good detective will always do. I called the police.

Sergeant Dave Pike of L.A. Robbery-Homicide used to be my partner before I left the force over a disagreement I had with the Supreme Court. Dave came on the line after a minute or so of clicks and buzzes.

"I've got a missing girl," I told him. "Age twenty-two or twenty-three, five foot five, maybe a hundred pounds, long black hair. Bruise on left side of face. When I last saw her she was wearing short cutoff jeans and a shirt tied in front with a lot of bare skin showing."

"Hang on a minute while I check with DB."

While I waited for Dave to query the detectives on dead body detail, I shook out a Pall Mall and lit up. I was down to one pack a day, but it didn't look like I would get any lower.

Dave came back on the line. "No stiff answering that description. It's a slow night for killings."

"Must be the rain," I said. "Give me a call if she turns up, will you?"

"Sure. Stonebreaker?"

"Yeah?"

"Are you sitting on anything that I ought to know?"

"I hope not, Dave, I sincerely hope not." I hung up and scowled at the phone for a while. I didn't much like the idea of Abby Deane being dead, but little girls who play with blackmail are likely to get that way.

The next day was another dreary wet one. I ate a late breakfast at a Mexican cafe that served *menudo*, and went over to the Department of Motor Vehicles on Hope Street. I paid a small fee to the girl there and she punched out the license number of the tough guy's Volkswagen on a computer keyboard. In a couple of seconds a name and address flashed on the TV-like screen in cool blue letters. The name was Joseph Kady, the address was up in the Silver Lake district east of Hollywood.

The place was one half of a duplex on a street of tired little houses that looked as uncomfortable in the rain as I felt. I picked my way across the muddy front lawn and knocked on the door. A washed-out brunette of about thirty opened up. She had nervous, unhealthy eyes.

"I'm looking for Joseph Kady," I said.

"What do you want with him?"

"I'm a private investigator." I flashed my card, which the woman ignored. "I want to ask him a couple of questions."

"Oh my God, what's he done now?"

"I don't know that he's done anything. Is he there?"

"No, he's at work. You're not from the probation office, are you?"

"No. Where does he work?"

"He's got a job as driver for Lew Harvester."

"The state assemblyman?"

"That's right. Joe says he's going to be governor some day."

"That's nice. Have you got Harvester's address?"

She went away and came back with a number on Roxbury Drive in Beverly Hills. I thanked her and left. While I was driving out Sunset I got to thinking that Lew Harvester—rich, important, ambitious—was a likely candidate for blackmail. I pulled to the curb and got out Abby

Deane's address book. Under *H* I found 12-5-23 8-1-18-22-5-19-20-5-18. It didn't take a computer brain to translate that into *Lew Harvester*. The mix of letters and numbers under the name would be the Beverly Hills address. I put the book away and drove on through the rain. In the mirror I noticed that a black Buick that had stopped half a block behind me started up again when I did.

The lawn in front of Harvester's white colonial house was a little smaller than a football field and green enough to hurt the eyes. I walked up the wet flagstones leading to the front door and thumbed the button. Inside the house a set of chimes played a muted tune. While I waited I glanced over at the three-car garage. The door was raised, and inside a man in a grey uniform was peering under the hood of a Mercedes. I couldn't see his face, but I recognized the shoulders. I could talk to Joe Kady later if I had to.

The front door opened and a man in a tailored leisure suit grinned at me and stuck out his hand. He smelled of expensive cologne.

"Hi, I'm Lew Harvester. I expect you're Frank Endersbee from the citizens' committee. Come on in, Frank, and get out of the rain. Isn't this weather something else?"

"I'm not from the citizens' committee, Mr. Harvester," I said when he was through greeting me. "My name is Stonebreaker. I'm a private investigator."

He dropped my hand as though it had grown fur.

"Can we go inside and talk?" I said.

"Why, uh, yes. Certainly."

Harvester led the way through a living room filled with furniture that looked too good to sit on. We went into a smaller room where there were soft leather chairs, a clean desk, and lots of books in bright new bindings. Harvester perched uncomfortably on the edge of the desk. His politician's smile had come all unstuck. He looked worried.

"I'm looking for a girl named Abby Deane," I told him.

He made a try at looking mystified. "Should that name mean something to me?"

"How about the Erotique Massage Parlor on Western Avenue?"

"I—I don't know what you're talking about."

Harvester's eyes got all shifty and he started to sweat. He couldn't lie worth a damn. He would probably never make governor.

I spelled it out for him. "Abby Deane worked at the massage parlor. She had your name in an address book as one of her customers. Yesterday your chauffeur was down there slapping her around. Today the girl is missing. What can you tell me about it?"

Harvester stood there stammering and blinking, the guiltiest man since Jack the Ripper.

There was a movement behind me, and a cool blonde woman in a tailored pants suit came into the room.

"Let me handle this, Lew," she said to Harvester. He gave her a grateful look and hurried out.

"I'm Christine Harvester," the blonde said when we were alone. "I'm the one you want to deal with."

"I do?"

"Sometimes my husband suffers a lapse in judgment. Like getting drunk at a fund-raising dinner last month and going off to that massage parlor with his so-called buddies. Trying to prove his manhood, I suppose."

I could see where Harvester's manhood might need reinforcing, but I didn't mention it.

Christine Harvester went on, "Then when that little tramp came around asking for money, Lew went to pieces. I had to handle that for him, too."

"So you sent the chauffeur out to beat up the girl."

"Of course not. I sent Joe to pay her off. Getting rough was his own idea. He probably kept the money I gave him for himself."

"It's tough to find good help any more," I said.

"Joe doesn't know it yet, but he just lost his job. Now, what about you, Mr. . . . Stonebreaker, was it? How much do you want? I don't suppose you'll take a check, so I'll have to go to the bank."

"How much do I want for what?" I said.

"For the girl's address book. I heard you tell my husband about it. Just give me your price and let's not waste time."

"The book is not my property," I told her. "And even if it was, it wouldn't be for sale. That's not my line of work."

She gave me a look that could knock a man down. I found my own way out and across the acre of green to my car.

Driving back to Hollywood I added up the score so far, and it depressed me. It was still raining, Abby Deane was still missing, and the Buick was following me again.

At least I could do something about the last of those problems. I waited for a stoplight where the Buick pulled up behind me, then got out of my car and went back to knock on the driver's window. He rolled it down a couple of inches and I looked in at a pair of beefy individuals in expensive suits and tinted glasses.

"Hi, fellas," I said. "If it would make it any easier for you, I can write out a schedule of where I'll be the rest of the day. Just in case we get separated in traffic."

The hood on the far side leaned toward me. "Smartmouth son of a . . ."

"Shut up," the driver cut him off. To me he said, "Mr. Giordano wants to talk to you."

"Mr. Anthony Giordano?"

"That's right."

"What if I don't want to talk to him?"

"Mr. Giordano wouldn't like that."

We could have carried on the tough guy dialogue for a while, but I was tired of standing out in the rain. I parked my own car and got into the Buick. We drove in silence out to the gleaming high-rise island called Century City where Anthony Giordano kept a suite of offices. "Tony John," as he was known to his pals, had a finger in most of the illegal pies in the city, but he worked hard at keeping his name out of the papers.

We found Giordano on the twenty-first floor of one of the steel and glass towers. The layout was more like a plush apartment than an office. There were a couple of furry sofas, a free-form coffee table, built-in audio equipment, and a bar. Giordano was standing in front of a tall, tinted glass window with his hands clasped behind him. He had a beautiful health club tan and shiny black hair that faded to a dramatic white at the temples. He got right to the point.

"I want to know what your interest is in Otto Boatman and his massage parlor."

"Maybe I wanted a massage."

"Or maybe you're doing a job for Boatman."

"What if I am?"

"I'm curious. Let's say I have a certain financial interest in the operation."

"Let's say you own it."

"Not me personally," said Giordano, "but the people I represent."

"Uh-huh. No, I'm not working for Boatman. I'm trying to find one of his girls. Abby Deane. Know here?"

"No. I don't get involved with the merchandise."

"Good for you. You must have been watching Boatman for some reason, to pick me up this fast. Are you worried about him?"

"My people like to keep an eye on their investments, that's all. Thanks for coming in, and good luck in finding the girl."

"Sure."

Giordano walked over and touched a button that was concealed in the arm of a sofa. The door opened immediately and the hood who drove me out stepped into the room.

"Vinnie, take our friend wherever he wants to go," he said, and I was dismissed.

I had Vinnie take me back to my car, which was looking cleaner than it had in months after being rained on for two days. The talk with Giordano gave me something to think about as I drove back to my office. When I got there, I had even more to think about. My answering service had a message for me to call Sergeant Pike. I dialed the police number and got right through to Dave.

"We found your girl," he said.

"Where?"

"Griffith Park, in the brush along the road that goes up to the observatory. A cruiser was checking out a lost child report, and there she was. White female, early twenties, black hair, dressed the way you described."

"Dead, I suppose."

"Sure, dead, what do you think? Strangled with a necktie still knotted around her throat so tight the coroner had to cut it off. No I.D. on the body. Who is she, Stonebreaker?"

I gave him Abby Deane's name and the address on Willoughby.

"Anything else?"

I hesitated. "Not yet, Dave. I'll get back to you."

"Stonebreaker, you're holding out on me."

"Would I do that?"

"You would."

"I'm just looking out for my client's interests, Dave. I guarantee that by tonight you'll know everything I do."

Dave Pike started to chew me out, but before he could really get going I told him goodbye and hung up.

At about seven o'clock I strolled into the strawberry scented anteroom of the Erotique Massage Parlor. A customer sidled out through the beads as I entered. He assumed a preoccupied look, as though he were just gathering material for a book.

I ignored the customer and walked over to the desk where Rick was looking at me worriedly. "I've got bad news," I said.

He shook his head and gestured toward the door behind the red drapery. The door was open a couple of inches.

"This is something your boss ought to hear, too." I said it loud enough to make sure he did.

Otto Boatman came out of his office wearing the same dated three piece suit as the day before. His narrow striped tie was also out of step with the current fashion. At the same time Bunny came through the bead curtain. She was wearing see-through harem pants and some spangles across her chest.

"What is it I ought to hear?" Boatman asked.

"First, Abby Deane is dead."

It took a second for them to absorb the information. Bunny was the first to speak.

"What happened?"

"She was strangled and dumped in the weeds in Griffith Park."

"Do they know who killed her?" Rick asked.

"Not yet, but they will soon."

"What do you mean?" said Boatman.

"Chances are it was somebody from right here at your massage parlor."

Bunny's eyes went wide. "You mean one of us?"

While they all stared at me I went on. "When I talked to her yesterday Abby was in a hurry to meet someone who was supposed to give her a ride home. Who but somebody she knew from here would pick this spot to meet?"

"I hope you're not including me," said Boatman.

"I haven't seen her since night before last," said Rick.

"I don't even own a car," said Bunny.

"Even though she wasn't very good at it," I went on, "Abby was a blackmailer. It figures that she was killed by somebody she was trying to shake down. I wondered what she could have on anybody that was heavy enough to get her killed. Some people might be embarrassed to be caught going into a massage parlor, but you don't commit murder out of embarrassment. On the other hand, if you were stealing money, very dangerous money, you might go all the way to keep that quiet."

"I don't think I like what you're getting at," Otto Boatman said.

"No, I don't suppose you do, Otto. I had a talk with Tony John today, and he let me figure out who really owns this place. I also got the idea he doesn't quite trust you."

Boatman whitened around the nostrils, but he kept his indignant expression in place.

"At Abby's apartment I found a sheet of paper that shows he was right." I let Boatman have a quick look at the page with the columns of figures. "It doesn't take an accountant to figure out that after each date the first figure is the money you took in, the second is what you reported to Giordano. Tony John would be very interested in this."

"That piece of paper doesn't mean anything," Boatman said, but there was no conviction in his voice.

"You probably met Abby here to talk about her price for keeping quiet. The price must have been too high."

Boatman's little eyes glittered. "You're just guessing. You don't have one real piece of evidence."

"Gathering evidence is the D.A.'s job," I said. "Sure, maybe you can beat the rap. If you want to. Then again, maybe you'd rather be safely locked up than out on the street where Tony John can reach you. It's something to think about."

Otto Boatman started to come apart then. "If only she hadn't started snooping around in the office. She shouldn't have tried to hold me up. I didn't mean to ... I would never have ..."

Boatman swayed on his feet. Rick got up fast and let him drop into the chair. The little man sat there staring at the wall. His face was the color of mozzarella cheese. I picked up the phone.

After the police came and took Boatman away, I stood out on Western Avenue with Rick and Bunny in front of the padlocked massage parlor. The rain had quit and people were beginning to show up on the street.

"You know," Rick said, "you really didn't have much to go on." He sounded resentful, as though he had caught me cheating.

Bunny came to my rescue. "Well, I think you were fantastic, the way you figured it all out." Then she added, "But you were guessing a little, weren't you?"

"Not much," I said. "You see, I didn't exactly tell Boatman about the most important piece of evidence."

"What's that?" Rick asked, right on cue.

"The necktie he used to strangle Abby. I had to get a look at him tonight to make sure he usually wore one. That corny suit and vest outfit looks even worse without a tie, but last night he had his collar open."

Bunny said, "But why would he leave the tie behind after he . . . after he . . . ?"

"The knot was too tight for him to pull it off. He couldn't risk parking up there indefinitely, wrestling with a dead body. He probably got nervous and shoved her into the brush when he heard a car coming."

I was losing Rick's attention. He shuffled his feet and looked up at the sky, where the clouds were breaking up and stars were showing through the chinks. He said, "At least it stopped raining. Look, man, I think I'll split."

It was nice to know Abby Deane's death hadn't ruined his whole day.

Bunny was fidgeting, too. "Hey, I ought to go, too, you know."

"Go ahead."

"I mean, I'd stick around, but the night's young and a girl has to make a living. Unless you're interested?"

"Some other time," I told her.

Bunny gave me a farewell smile and strolled up the street in her short, tight skirt and vinyl boots. The storm was over, the people were out, and on Western Avenue it was business as usual.

Len Gray

Albert and the Amateurs

He came in the Commons swaggering and smiling, and he said, "Hey, kid, you look like you could use some money."

I put my book down on the lunchroom table. "No," I said. "No, I don't need any money."

His smile fell into the top pocket of his silk jacket. "You don't need any bread?"

"No. Not really."

"How come?"

I pushed my book away and said, "I have no reason to tell you."

"Oh, come on. I'm dyin' to know."

His face did look a little pale. "Well," I told him, "in that case, I must inform you that I'm a service veteran, I receive my educational benefits which allow me to go to the graduate school on this campus, and when I need more money I earn if from my part-time job. But you already know about that."

He sat back in his chair, putting protesting palms out in front of him. "No, no! I know nothin' about your job!"

"Oh, but you do," I said. "You know that I work evenings over at the plant and you also know it's one of the few remaining places that pays its payroll in cash because we're in a rural area and many of the workers live a long way from here and therefore they couldn't cash an out-of-the-area check very well, so Mr. Morris—he's the manager, and I think you know about him, too—Mr. Morris pays once a week in cash. And now you want to talk to me."

"You got it all wrong." He looked around to see if there were any interested witnesses to our conversation.

"No. No, I have it all right and what you want me to do is let you inside the plant to steal the money in our combination vault and maybe hit me on the head, just a little, and then you'll leave and send me a check later. Am I close?"

"Not so loud." He looked over his shoulder. "Keep it down and we can work this out."

I shook my head. "I'm sorry. I have all the money I need and I am not a crook. I would advise you not to attempt a robbery because you will only fail. Like all the rest."

He licked his lips. "Can't you keep your voice down?"

"No. And I am about to start screaming. I am going to scream for the campus police and they will either catch you or you will go away and I CAN GET BACK TO MY BOOKS!"

People were already starting to look at us.

"You are one big idiot, fella," he told me, sneering.

"POLICE! POLICE! THIEF!!"

For a rather big man, he moved quite fast. He moved so fast, in fact, that I had time for another half of a chapter before the campus police arrived—puffing.

Late that night, my silk-jacketed friend slipped inside the grounds, past the security cars that regularly patrolled the outside fence area.

He came in (I had him in my field glasses nicely while he was still on the grass over there by the fence), and I let him get real close to my well-lit security building before I turned loose the dogs.

We use four Dobermans and I made sure, earlier in the evening, that they had not had dinner. I heard the usual noises and the usual screams, but by that time I was well into another chapter and he just had to wait his turn.

The dogs weren't very nice to his silk jacket.

Three weeks later, out of the corner of my eye, I saw her come in and she came all the way across the Commons floor, past all sorts of empty tables, and came up to me, beaming, and said, "Hi!"

"No," I said, "I'm sorry. It just won't work."

"I beg your pardon?"

"I mean, it won't work. You're very attractive but it's been tried before. Unsuccessfully. I might add."

"Just what are you inferring?" She stood above me, staring down,

Sighing, I moved my tray of food. Several of the fellows nearby were looking over here and they weren't staring at me.

"What I'm inferring," I said, "is that someone has sent you in here. You are very attractive and I hardly think you would come all the way to this table, past football players, baseball players and a few rich kids, the ones with the cashmere sweaters, just so you could sit with me, Albert Stevenson."

She blinked. "You're cute, Albert." She tried very hard.

"No, I'm not cute. I'm a little under five foot six and I'm at least fifteen pounds overweight. I've never really cared for girls. I'd rather eat." I reached for my chocolate pudding.

She sat down across from me. I spooned in my pudding and she watched my spoon, she watched me and then she said, "I heard you were a little weird."

"Oh?"

"Uh-huh. And you want to know something?"

"I already know. They were right, right?"

She blinked. "You're no dummy, either."

"Thank you for that."

"Don't mention it." She was watching me again as I reached for my vanilla ice cream.

Suddenly embarrassed, I said, "Would you like some?"

She stared at me. "Well, well, he's a gentleman, too." She had very short, beautiful red curly hair and I thought her face was just fine.

"Would you like some?" I asked, repeating myself.

"Yeah, you know, I would. Halvsies?"

I nodded and got her a clean dish. We sat at the table eating our ice cream in silence until she said, "I never should have let myself get talked into this in the first place. I belong in the big city. Where it's warm." She looked at me. "You ever come to the city?"

"Once in a while."

She gave me a phone number and her name, which was Pat, and said I should call her sometime. I shrugged but it really didn't sound like too bad an idea.

"I've gotta go," she told me.

"Goodbye."

"Take care of yourself, Albert."

"I will."

"And Albert?"

"Yes?"

"Watch out tonight."

"Your friends?"

She seemed to think about it. "Friends? No. I don't think they really are, at that. So long, Albert."

I said so long and went back to my books. Later, at work, three men hopped down out of a low-flying helicopter and they had guns in their hands and hoods over their heads. I told the dogs to keep quiet while I hit the release mechanism of the tear-gas propellants which shot fifty yards in the air, landing at the intruders' feet.

From all the noise and sobbing they made, I guessed that they couldn't breathe very well under the hoods. They tried to dance around and reach up for the rope ladder to the helicopter, but the pilot had the good sense to fly away. I left them out there a while and then I threw them a few more canisters of gas and after they had gotten down on the grass and were crying considerably, I walked out, gas mask on, and picked up their guns and we waited for the outside security police to make their next round.

As you can probably tell, it goes on like this all the time. You see, we're located, as I mentioned earlier, in a rural community and that makes some of the big-towners figure they can come in here and more or less have their own way. Our jail has held a lot of people who felt this way, people who were waiting to be transferred to the state prison system.

To show you how bad things can get, I had no sooner gassed the three from their helicopter and was back reading, a few days later, in the Commons, about to bite into a tuna sandwich when this fraternity person, a guy I hardly knew, came up to me and said, "Albert, I have got to have some money!"

I put down my sandwich and said, "I think I have a couple of dollars. Here, let me check."

He grabbed my arm, looking anxious. "Albert, Albert! You don't understand the situation."

"I guess I don't." I went back to my sandwich.

"No, you don't, Albert. I need a *lot* of money!"

"Uh-oh."

"What did you say?"

I told him what I had said. "Don't ask me to do anything dishonest," I added.

"Oh, I'm not, I'm not! You don't have to do a thing. That's just it."

"I don't follow you," I said, beginning to follow him.

"You just sit there. Sit there in your little shack and kind of shut your eyes. You know."

"While you walk by. With your eyes and your sack open. Is that it?"

"I think you understand now, Albert."

"No."

"No? You don't understand?"

"No, I won't do it."

He panicked. "Albert, you've *got* to do it!"

"How much money do you owe them?"

"Huh? Why do you ask that?"

"I remember you now. You're the one with the crazy Pogo stick, the one who works out at the costume factory, the one who spends his vacations in Las Vegas losing all his money. How much is it this time?"

He didn't want to but I made him tell me anyway. "Albert, I owe two guys nine thousand dollars."

I considered the figure. I chewed on my sandwich and then I told him, "If I were you, I'd start saving my money."

Believe it or not, he had the audacity to glare at me. I tell him "no soap" on any partnership of crime and *he* gets mad at *me!*

"Albert, you are one big louse."

"I'm busy. Goodbye."

"You're going to regret this, Albert."

I looked up from my sandwich and my book. "I just hope that *you* don't regret it. Stay away from me and my work. Clear?"

Instead of answering, he stormed away out of the Commons. I shook my head and reached for my pudding.

It's always the same. As I sit now in my security shed, thinking about it, it always turns out the same.

People come up to me and pretend to be friends, but it's only the money they're after, not my friendship. They always have to try for the money and, of course, they've all failed.

Mr. Morris, my boss, a man I've known all my life, thinks I have a lot to do with it and I like to think he's right. I'm the one who thought up a lot of the special security, something I learned in the service. When Mr. Morris found out I was majoring in criminology at the college, he just had to have me around at night to supplement the regular staff and it's worked out well for us both.

It's worked out well for me, particularly, because I've been able to protect the cash source until I figure out a way to take it myself. All these other people are showing me the ways not to do it and the books I'm reading are giving me a lot of ideas about how professionals did things and got away with them.

When you add it all up, I can just sit here until I have the right plan and then I'll have maybe two hundred thousand one week. It'll be mine, all mine.

I might even go into the city and call Pat and buy her an ice cream—or something.

But all that must wait. You'll have to excuse me because I think I just saw a pigheaded idiot go past the fence on a Pogo stick.

Bill Pronzini

Thin Air

The man I'd been hired to follow was named Lewis Hornback. He was forty-three, had dark brown hair and average features, drove a four door Dodge Monaco, and lived in a fancy apartment building on Russian Hill. He was also cheating on his wife with an unknown woman and had misappropriated a large sum of money from the interior design firm they co-owned. Or so Mrs. Hornback alleged. My job, if I could manage it, was to dig up evidence to support those allegations.

Mrs. Hornback had not told me what she intended to do with any such evidence. Have poor Lewis drawn and quartered, maybe—or at least locked away for the rest of his natural life. She was that kind of woman—a thin, pinch-faced harridan ten years older than her husband with vindictive eyes and a desiccated look about her, as if all her vital juices had dried up a long time ago. If Hornback really was cheating on her, maybe he had justifiable cause. But that was not for me to say. It wasn't my job to make moral judgments—all I had to do was make an honest living for myself.

So I took Mrs. Hornback's retainer check, promised to make daily reports, and went to work that same afternoon. Hornback, it seemed, was in the habit of leaving their office at five o'clock most weekdays and not showing up at the Russian Hill apartment until well past midnight. At four thirty I found a parking space near the garage where he kept his car, on Clay near Van Ness. It was a cold and windy November day, but the sky was clear, with no sign of fog above Twin Peaks or out near the Golden Gate. Which was a relief—tail jobs are tricky enough, especially at night, without the added difficulty of bad weather.

Hornback showed up promptly at five. Eight minutes later he drove his Dodge Monaco down the ramp and turned left on Clay. I gave him a block lead before I pulled out behind him.

He went straights to North Beach, to a little Italian restaurant not far from Washington Square. Meeting the girlfriend for dinner, I figured, but it turned out I was wrong. After two drinks at the bar, while I nursed a beer, he took a table alone. I sat at an angle across the room from him, treated myself to *pollo al diavolo*, and watched him pack away a three course meal and a half a liter of the house wine. Nobody came to talk to him except the waiter; he was just a man having a quiet dinner alone.

He polished off a brandy and three cigarettes for dessert, lingering the way you do after a heavy meal. When he finally left the restaurant it was almost seven thirty. From there he walked over to Upper Grant, where he gawked at the young counterculture types who frequent the area, did a little window shopping, and stopped at a newsstand and a drugstore. I stayed on the opposite side of the street, fifty yards or so behind him. That's about as close to a subject as you want to get on foot. But the walking tail got me nothing except exercise. Hornback was still alone when he led me back to where he had left his car.

His next stop was a small branch library at the foot of Russian Hill, where he dropped off a couple of books. Then he headed south on Van Ness, north on Market out of the downtown area, and up the winding expanse of Upper Market to the top of Twin Peaks. There was a little shopping area up there, a short distance beyond where Market blends into Portola Drive. He pulled into the parking area in front and went into a neighborhood tavern called Dewey's Place.

I parked down near the end of the lot. Maybe he was meeting the girlfriend here or maybe he had just gone into the tavern for a drink; he seemed to like his liquor pretty well. I put on the grey cloth cap I keep in the car, shrugged out of my coat and turned it inside out—it's one of those reversible models—and put it on again that way, just in case Hornback had happened to notice me at the restaurant earlier. Then I stepped out into the cold wind blowing up from the ocean and crossed to Dewey's Place.

There were maybe a dozen customers inside, most of them at the bar. Hornback was down at the far end with a drink in one hand and a cigarette in the other, but the stools on both sides of him were empty. None of the three women in the place looked to be unescorted.

So maybe there wasn't a girlfriend. Mrs. Hornback could have been wrong about that, even if she was right about the misappropriation of business funds. It was nine forty-five now. If the man had a lady on the side, they would have been together by this time of night. And so far, Hornback had done nothing unusual or incriminating. Hell, he hadn't even done anything interesting.

I sat at the near end of the bar and sipped at a draft beer, watching Hornback in the mirror. He finished his drink, lit a fresh cigarette, and gestured to the bartender for a refill. I thought he looked a little tense, but in the dim lighting I couldn't be sure. He wasn't waiting for anybody, though, I could tell that; no glances at his watch or at the door. Just aimlessly killing time? It could be. For all I knew, this was how he spent each of his evenings out—eating alone, driving alone, drinking alone. And his reason might be the simplest and most innocent of all—he left the office at five and stayed out past midnight because he didn't want to go home to Mrs. Hornback.

When he had downed his second drink he stood up and reached for his wallet. I had already laid a dollar bill on the bar, so I slid off my stool and left ahead of him. I was already in my car when he came out.

Now where? I thought as he fired up the Dodge. Another bar somewhere? A late movie? Home early?

None of those. He surprised me by swinging back east on Portola and then getting into the left-turn lane for Twin Peaks Boulevard. The area up there is residential, at least on the lower part of the hillside. The road itself winds upward at steep angles, makes a figure-eight loop through the empty-wooded expanse of Twin Peaks Park, and curls down on the opposite side of the hill.

Hornback stayed on Twin Peaks Boulevard, climbing toward the park. So he was probably not going to visit anybody in the area; he had bypassed the only intersecting streets on this side, and there were easier ways to get to the residential sections below the park to the north. I wondered if he was just marking more time, if it was his habit to take a long solitary drive around the city before he headed home.

There was almost no traffic and I dropped back several hundred feet to keep my headlights out of his rear-vision mirror on the turns. The view from up there was spectacular; on a night like this you could see for miles in a 360-degree curve—the ocean, the full sweep of the Bay, both bridges, the intricate pattern of lights that was San Francisco and its surrounding communities. Inside the park we passed a couple of cars pulled off on the lookouts that dotted the area: people, maybe lovers, taking in the view.

Hornback went through half the figure-eight from east to west, driving without hurry. Once I saw the brief, faint flare of a match as he lit another cigarette. When he came out on the far side of the park he surprised me again. Instead of continuing down the hill he slowed and turned to the right onto a short, hooked spur road leading to another of the lookouts.

I tapped my brakes as I neared the turn, trying to decide what to do. The spur was a dead end. I could follow him around it or pull off the road and wait for him to come out again. The latter seemed to be the best choice and I cut my headlights and started to glide off onto a turn around. But then, over on the spur, Hornback swung past a row of cypress trees that lined the near edge of the lookout. The Dodge's brake lights flashed through the trees, then his headlights, too, winked out.

I kept on going, made the turn, and drifted onto a second tree shadowed turnaround just beyond the intersection. Diagonally in front of me I could see Hornback ease the Dodge across the flat surface of the lookout and bring it to a stop nose-up against a perimeter guard rail. The distance between us was maybe seventy-five yards.

What's he up to now? I thought. Well, he had probably stopped there to take in the view and maybe do a little brooding. The other possibility was that he was waiting for someone. A late-evening rendezvous with the alleged girlfriend? The police patrol Twin Peaks Park at regular intervals because kids have been known to use it as a lover's lane, but it was hardly the kind of place two adults would pick for an assignation. Why meet up here when the city is full of hotels and motels?

The Dodge gleamed a dullish black in the starlight. From where I was I could see all of the passenger side and the rear third of the driver's side; the interior was shrouded in darkness. Pretty soon another match flared, smearing the gloom for an instant with dim yellowish light. Hornback was not quite a chain smoker, but he was the next thing to it—at least a two-pack-a-day man. I felt a little sorry for him, and a little envious at the same time? I had smoked two packs a day myself until a year and half ago, when a doctor discovered a benign lesion on one of my lungs. I hadn't had a cigarette since,though there were still times I craved one. Like right now, sitting watching that dark car and waiting for something to happen or not happen.

I slouched down behind the wheel and tried to make myself comfortable. Five minutes passed, ten minutes, fifteen. Behind me, half a dozen sets of headlights came up or went down the hill on Twin Peaks Boulevard, but none of them turned in where we were. And nothing moved that I could see in or around the Dodge.

I occupied my mind by speculating again about Hornback. He was a puzzle, all right. Maybe a cheating husband and a thief, or maybe an innocent on both counts—the victim of a loveless marriage and a shrewish wife. He hadn't done anything of a guilty or furtive nature tonight, and yet here he was, parked alone at ten forty P.M. on a lookout in Twin Peaks Park. It could go either way. So which way was it going to go?

Twenty minutes.

And I began to feel just a little uneasy. You get intimations like that when you've been a cop of one type or another as long as I have—vague flickers or wrongness that seem at first to have no foundation. The feeling made me fidgety. I sat up and rolled down my window and peered across at the Dodge. Darkness. Stillness. Nothing out of the ordinary.

Twenty-five minutes.

The wind was chill against my face and I rolled the window back up, but the coldness had got into the car. I drew my coat tight around my neck and kept staring at the Dodge and the bright mosaic of lights beyond, like luminous spangles on the black velvet sky.

Thirty minutes.

The uneasiness grew and became acute. Something was wrong over there, damn it. A half hour was a long time for a man to sit alone on a look out, whether he was brooding or not. It was even a long time to wait for a rendezvous. But that was only part of the sense of wrongness. There was something else.

Hornback had not lit another cigarette since that one nearly half an hour ago.

The realization made me sit up again. He had been smoking steadily all night long, even during his walk along Upper Grant after dinner. When I was a heavy smoker I couldn't have gone half an hour without lighting up; it seemed funny that Hornback could or would, considering that there was nothing else for him to do in there. He might have run out, of course, yet I remembered seeing a full pack in front of him on the bar at Dewey's Place.

What could be wrong? He was alone up here in his car except for my watching eyes; nothing could have happened to him. Unless . . .

Suicide?

The word popped into my mind and made me feel even colder. Suppose Hornback was innocent of infidelity, but suppose he was also despondent over the state of his marriage. Suppose all the aimless wandering tonight had been a prelude to an attempt on his own life—a man trying to work up enough courage to kill himself on a lonely road high above the city. It was possible; I didn't know enough about Hornback to judge his mental stability.

I wrapped both my hands around the wheel, debating with myself. If I went over to his car and checked on him and he was all right, I would have blown not only the tail but my client's trust. But if I stayed here and Hornback had taken pills or done God knew what to himself, I might be sitting passively by while a man died.

Headlights appeared on Twin Peaks Boulevard behind me, then swung in a slow arc onto the spur road. I drifted lower in the seat and waited for them to pass.

Only they did not pass. The car drew abreast of mine and came to a halt. Police patrol. I sensed it even before I saw the darkened dome flasher on the roof. The passenger window was down and the cop on that side extended a flashlight through the opening and flicked it on. The light pinned me for three of four seconds, bright enough to make me squint, then shut off. The patrolman motioned for me to roll down my window.

I glanced past the cruiser to Hornback's Dodge. It remained dark and there was still no movement anywhere in the vicinity. Well, the decision whether or not to check on him was out of my hands now; the cops would want to have a look at the Dodge in any case. And in any case, my assignment was blown.

I let out a breath and would down the glass. The patrolman, a young guy with a mustache, said, "What's going on here, fella?"

So I told him, keeping it brief, and let him have a look at the photostat of my investigator's license. He seemed half skeptical and half uncertain; he had me get out and stand to one side while he talked things over with his partner, a heavyset older man with a beer belly larger than mine. After which the partner took out a second flashlight and trotted across the lookout to the Dodge.

The younger cop asked me some questions and I answered them, but my attention was on the older guy. I watched him reach the driver's door and shine his light through the window. A moment later he appeared to reach down for the door handle, but it must have been locked because I didn't see the door open or him lean inside. Instead he put his light up to the window again, slid it over to the window on the rear door, and then turned abruptly to make an urgent semaphoring gesture.

"Sam!" he shouted. "Get over here on the double!"

The young patrolman, Sam, had his right hand on the butt of his service revolver as we ran ahead to the Dodge. I was expecting the worst by this time, but I wasn't at all prepared for what I saw inside that car. I just stood there gaping while the cops' lights crawled through the interior.

There were spots of drying blood across the front seat.

But the seat was empty, and so was the back seat, and so were the floorboards.

Hornback had disappeared.

One of the two inspectors who arrived on the scene a half hour later was Ben Klein, an oldtimer and a casual acquaintance from my own years on the San Francisco cops in the forties and fifties. I had asked the patrolmen to call in Lieutenant Eberhardt, probably my closest friend on or off the force, because I wanted an ally in case matters became dicey. Eb, though, was evidently still on the day shift. I hadn't asked for Klein, but I felt a little better when he showed up.

When he had finished checking over the Dodge we went off to one side of it, near the guard rail. From there I could look down a steep slope dotted with stunted trees and underbrush. Search teams were moving along it with flashlights, looking for some sign of Hornback, but so far they didn't seem to be having any luck. Up here the area was swarming with men and vehicles, most but not all of them official. The usual rubberneckers and media types were in evidence along the spur and back on Twin Peaks Boulevard.

"Let me get this straight," Klein said when I had finished giving him my story. He had his hands jammed into his coat pockets and his body hunched against the wind because the night had turned bitter cold now. "You followed Hornback here around ten fifteen and you were in a position to watch his car from the time he parked it to the time the two patrolmen showed up."

"That's right."

"You were over on that turnaround?"

"Yes. The whole time."

"And you didn't see anything inside or outside the Dodge?"

"Nothing at all. I couldn't see inside it—too many shadows—but I could see most of the area around it."

"Did you take your eyes off it for any length of time?"

"No. A few seconds now and then, sure, but no more than that."

"Could you see all four doors?"

"Three of the four," I said. "Not the driver's door."

"That's how he disappeared, then."

I nodded. "But what about the dome light? Why didn't I see it go on?"

"It's not working. The bulb's defective. That was one of the first things I checked after we wired up the door lock."

"I also didn't see the door open. I might have missed that, I'll admit, but it's the kind of movement that would have attracted my attention." I paused, working my memory. "Hornback couldn't have gone away toward the road or down the embankment to the east or back into those trees over there. I would have seen him for sure if he had. The only other direction is down this slope, right in front of his car; but if that's it, why didn't I notice any movement when he climbed over the guard rail?"

"Maybe he didn't climb over it. Maybe he crawled under it."

"Why would he have done that?"

"I don't know. I'm only making suggestions."

"Well, I can think of one possibility, I suppose."

"Which is?"

"The suicide angle," I said. "I told you I was worried about that. What if Hornback decided to do the Dutch, and while he was sitting in the car he used a pocketknife or something else sharp to slash his wrists? That would explain the blood on the front seat. Only he lost his nerve at the last second, panicked, opened the door, fell out of the car, and crawled under the guard rail."

I stopped. The idea was no good. I had realized that even as I laid it out.

Klein knew it, too. He was shaking his head. "No blood outside the driver's door or along the side of the car or anywhere under the guard rail. A man with slashed wrists bleeds pretty heavily. Besides, if he'd cut his wrists and had second thoughts, why leave the car at all? Why not just start it up and drive to the nearest hospital?"

"Yeah," I said.

"There's another screwy angle—the locked doors. Who locked them? Hornback? His attacker, if there was one? Why lock them at all?"

I had no answer. I stood brooding out at the city lights.

"Assume he was attacked," Klein said. "By a mugger, say, who's decided to work up here because of the isolation. The attacker would have had to get to the car with you watching, which means coming up this slope, along the side of the car, and in through the driver's door—*if* it wasn't locked at that time. But I don't buy it. It's TV-commando stuff, too farfetched."

"There's another explanation," I said musingly.

"What's that?"

"The attacker was in the car all along."

"Not a mugger, you mean?"

"Right. Somebody who had it in for Hornback."

Klein frowned; he had heavy jowls and it made him look like a bulldog. "I thought you said Hornback was alone the whole night. Didn't meet anybody."

"He didn't. But suppose he was in the habit of frequenting Dewey's Place and this somebody knew it. He or she could have been waiting in the parking lot, slipped inside the Dodge while Hornback and I were in the tavern, hidden on the floor in back, and stayed hidden until Hornback came up here and parked. Then maybe stuck a knife in him."

"Sounds a little melodramatic, but I guess it's possible. Still, what kind of motive fits that explanation?"

"One connected with the money his wife claims Hornback stole from their firm."

"You're not thinking the wife could've attacked him?"

"No. If she was going to do him in, it doesn't make sense she'd hire me to tail him around. Hornback might have had some accomplice in the theft. Maybe they had a falling-out and the accomplice wanted to keep all the money for himself."

"Maybe," Klein said, but he sounded dubious. "The main trouble with that theory is, what happened to Hornback's body? The attacker would have had to get both himself *and* Hornback out of the car, then drag the body down the slope. Now why in hell would somebody kill a man way up here, with nobody around as far as he knew, and take the corpse away with him instead of just leaving it in the car?"

"I don't know. But I can't figure it any other way."

"Neither can I right now. Let's see what the search teams and the forensic boys turn up."

What the searchers and the lab people turned up, however, was nothing—no sign of Hornback dead or alive, no sign of anybody else in the area, no bloodstains except for those inside the car, no other evidence of any kind. Hornback—or his body—and maybe an attacker as well had not only vanished from the Dodge while I was watching it; he had vanished completely and without a trace. As if into thin air.

It was one thirty A.M. before Klein let me go home. He asked me to stop in later at the Hall of Justice to sign a statement, but aside from that he seemed satisfied that I had given him all the facts as I knew them. But I was not quite off the hook yet, nor would I be until Hornback turned up. *If* he turned up. My word was all the police had for what had happened on the lookout, and I was the first to admit that it was a pretty bizarre story.

When I got to my Pacific Heights flat I thought about calling Mrs. Hornback. But it was after two o'clock by then and I saw no point or advantage in phoning a report at this time of night; the police would already have told her about her husband's disappearance. So I drank a glass of milk and crawled into bed and tried to sort things into some kind of order.

How had Hornback vanished? Why? Was he dead or alive? An innocent man, or as guilty as his wife claimed? The victim of suicidal depression, the victim of circumstance, or the victim of premeditated murder?

No good. I was too tired to come up with fresh answers to any of those questions.

After a while I slept and dreamed a lot of nonsense about people dematerializing inside locked cars, vanishing in little puffs of smoke. A long time later the telephone woke me up. I keep the damned thing in the bedroom and it went off six inches from my ear and sat me up in bed, disoriented and grumbling. I pawed at my eyes and got them unstuck. There was grey morning light in the room; the nightstand clock said six fifty-five. Four hours' sleep and welcome to a new day.

The caller, not surprisingly, was Mrs. Hornback. She berated me for not getting in touch with her, then she demanded my version of last night. I gave it to her.

"I don't believe a word of it," she said.

"That's your privilege, ma'am. But it happens to be the truth."

"We'll see about that." Her voice sounded no different from the way it had when she'd hired me: cold, clipped, and coated with vitriol. There was not a whisper of compassion. "How could you let something like that happen? What kind of detective are you?"

A poor tired one, I thought. But I said, "I did what you asked me to, Mrs. Hornback. What happened on the lookout was beyond my control."

"Yes? Well, if my husband isn't found, and if I don't recover the money I *know* he stole, you'll hear from my lawyer. You can count on that." There was a clattering sound and then the line began to buzz.

Nice lady. A real princess.

I lay back down. I was still half asleep and pretty soon I drifted off again. This time I dreamed I was in a room where half a dozen guys were playing poker. They were all private eyes from the pulp magazines I read and collected—Race Williams, Jim Bennett, Max Latin, some of the best of the bunch. Latin wanted to know what kind of detective I was, his voice sounded just like Mrs. Hornback's. I said I was a pulp detective. They kept saying, "No, you're not, you can't play with us because you're not one of us," and I kept saying, "But I am, I'm the same kind of private eye you are."

The jangling of the phone ended that nonsense and sat me up the way it had before. I focused on the clock: eight forty. Conspiracy against my sleep, I thought, and fumbled up the handset.

"Wake you up, hotshot?" a familiar voice said. Eberhardt.

"What do you think?"

"Sorry about that. I've got news for you."

"What news?"

"That funny business up on Twin Peaks last night—your boy

Hornback's been found."

I stopped feeling sleepy and the fuzziness cleared out of my mind. "Where?" I said. "Is he all right?"

"In Golden Gate Park," said Eberhardt. "And no, he's not all right. He's dead—been dead since last night. Stabbed in the chest, probably with a butcher knife."

I got down to the Hall of Justice at ten o'clock, showered, shaved, and full of coffee. Eberhardt was in his office in General Works, gnawing on one of his briar pipes and looking as sour as usual. The sourness was just a facade; he wasn't half as grim and grouchy as he liked people to think.

"I've been rereading Klein's report," he said as I sat down. "You get mixed up in the damnedest cases these days."

"Don't I know it. what have you got on Hornback?"

"Nothing much. Guy out jogging found the body at seven fifteen in a clump of bushes along JFK Drive. Stabbed in the chest, like I told you on the phone—a single wound that penetrated the heart, the probable weapon a butcher knife. The medical examiner says death was instantaneous. I guess that takes care of the suicide theory."

"I guess it does."

"No other marks on the body," he said, "except for a few small scratches on the hands and on one cheek."

"What kind of scratches?"

"Just scratches. The kind you get crawling around in woods or underbrush, or the kind a body might get if it was dragged through the same type of terrain. The M.E. will have more on that when he finishes his post-mortem."

"What was the condition of Hornback's clothes?"

"Dirty, torn in a couple of places. The same thing applies."

"Anything aomong his effects?"

"No. The usual stuff—wallet, handkerchief, change, a pack of cigarettes, and a box of matches. Eighty-three dollars in the wallet and a bunch of credit cards. That seems to rule out the robbery motive."

"I don't suppose there was any evidence where he was found."

"None. Killed somewhere else, the way if figures. Like up on that Twin Peaks lookout. Hornback's blood type was AO; it matches the type found on the front seat of his car."

We were silent for a time. I watched Eberhardt break his briar in half and run a pipe cleaner through the stem. Then I said, "Damn it, Eb, it doesn't make sense. What's the motive behind the whole business? Why would the killer take Hornback's body away and then dump it in Golden Gate Park later? How could he have got it and himself out of the car without me noticing that something was going on?"

"You tell me, mastermind. You were there. You ought to know what you saw or didn't see."

I opened my mouth, closed it again, and blinked at him. "What did you say?"

"You heard me. I said you were there and you ought to know what you saw or didn't see."

What I saw. And what I didn't see.

Eberhardt put his pipe back together and tamped tobacco into the bowl. "We'd better come up with some answers pretty soon," he said. "Klein got back a little while ago from breaking the news to the widow. He says she blames you for letting Hornback get killed."

Two things I didn't see that I *should* have seen.

"She claims he siphoned off as much as a hundred thousand dollars from that interior design company of theirs. According to her, he overcharged some customers, pocketed cash payments from others, and phonied up the records. She also figures he took kickbacks from suppliers."

Several things I *did* see.

"Evidently she accused him of it earlier this week. He denied everything. She's got an auditor going over the books, but that takes time. That's why she hired you."

Add them all up, put them all together—a pattern.

"The money is all she cares about, Klein says. She thinks Hornback spent part of it on the alleged girlfriend, but she means to get back whatever's left. That kind of woman can stir up a lot of trouble. No telling what kind of accusations she's liable to—"

Sure. A pattern.

"Hey!" Eberhardt said. "Are you listening to me?"

"What?"

"What's the matter with you? I'm not just talking to hear the sound of my own voice."

I stood up and took a couple of turns around the office. "I think I've got something, Eb."

"Got something? You mean answers?"

"Maybe." I sat down again. "Did you see Hornback's body yourself this morning?"

"I saw it. Why?"

"Were there any marks on it besides the stab wound and the scratches? Any other sort of wound, no matter how small?"

He thought. "No. Except for a Band-Aid on one of his fingers , if that matters—"

"You bet it does," I said. "Get Klein in here, would you? I want to ask him a couple of questions."

Eberhardt gave me a narrow look, but he buzzed out into the squad room and asked for Klein. Ben came in a few seconds later.

"When you checked over Hornback's car last night," I asked him, "was the emergency brake set?"

"No, I don't think so."

"What about the transmission? Was the lever in Park or Neutral?"

"Neutral."

"I thought so. That's the answer then."

Eberhardt said. "You know how Hornback's body disappeared from his car?"

"Yes. Only it *didn't* disappear from the car."

"Meaning what?"

"Meaning the body was never inside it," I said. "Hornback wasn't murdered on the lookout. He was killed later on, somewhere else."

"What about the blood on the front seat?"

"He put it there himself deliberately—by cutting his finger with something sharp, like maybe a razor blade. That's the reason for the Band-Aid."

"Why would he do a crazy thing like that?"

"Because he was planning to disappear."

"Come on, you're talking in riddles."

"No, I'm not. If Mrs. Hornback is right about her husband stealing that money—and she has to be—he was wide open to criminal charges. And she's just the type who would press charges. He had no intention of hanging around to face them; his plan from the beginning had to be to stockpile as much money as he could and, when his wife began to tumble to what he was doing, to split with it. With this girlfriend of his, no doubt.

"But he didn't just want to hop a plane for somewhere; that would have made him an obvious fugitive. So he worked out a clever gimmick, or what he thought was clever anyway. He intended to vanish under mysterious circumstances so it would look like he'd met with foul play—abandon his car in an isolated spot with blood all over the front seat. It's been done before and he knew it probably wouldn't fool anybody, but he had nothing to lose by trying.

"Okay. This little disappearing act of his was in the works for last night—which is why he stopped at the drugstore in North Beach after dinner, to buy razor blades and Band-Aids. But something happened long before he headed up to Twin Peaks that altered the shape of his plan."

Both Eberhardt and Klein were watching me intently. Eb said, "What was that?"

"He spotted me," I said. "I guess I'm getting old and less careful on a tail job than I used to be; either that or he just tumbled to me by accident. I don't suppose it matters. Anyhow, he realized early in the evening that he had a tail—and it wouldn't have taken much effort for him to figure out I was a private detective hired by his wife to get the goods on him. That was when he shifted gears from a half-clever idea to a really clever one. He'd go through with his disappearing act all right, but he'd do it in front of a witness—and under a set of contrived circumstances that were *really* mysterious."

"It's a pretty good scenario so far," Eberhardt said. "But I'm still waiting to find out how he managed to disappear while you were sitting there watching his car."

"He didn't," I said.

"There you go with the riddles again."

"Follow me through. After he left Dewey's Place—while he was stopped at the traffic light on Portola or when he was driving up Twin Peaks Boulevard—he used the razor blade to slice open his finger and drip blood on the seat. then he bandaged the cut. That took care of part of the trick. The next part came when he reached the lookout.

"There's a screen of cypress trees along the back edge of the lookout where you turn in off the spur road. They create a blind spot for anybody still on Twin Peaks Boulevard as I was at the time; I couldn't see all of the lookout until after I'd turned onto the spur. As soon as Hornback came into that blind spot he jammed on his brakes and cut his headlights. I told Ben about that—seeing the brake lights flash through the trees and the headlights go dark. It didn't strike me at the time, but when you think about it it's a little odd that somebody would switch off his lights on a lookout like that, with a steep slope at the far end, *before* he stops his car."

Eberhardt said, "I think I see the rest of it coming."

"Sure. He hit the brakes hard enough to bring the Dodge almost, but not quite, to a full stop. At the same time he shoved the transmission into neutral, shut off the engine, and opened the door. The bulb for the dome light was defective so he didn't have to worry about that. Then he slipped out, pushed down the lock button—a little added mystery— closed the door again, and ran a few steps into the trees where there were enough heavy shadows to hide him and conceal his escape from the area.

"Meanwhile, the car drifted forward nice and slow and came to a halt nose-up against the guard rail. I saw that much, but what I didn't see was the brake lights flash again. As they should have if Hornback was still inside the car and stopping it in the normal way."

"One thing," Klein said. "What about that match flare you saw after the car was stopped?"

"That was a nice convincing touch," I said. "When the match flamed, I naturally assumed it was Hornback lighting another cigarette. But I realize now that I didn't see anything after that—no sign of a glowing cigarette in the darkness. What really happened is this: he'd fired a cigarette on his way up to the lookout; I noticed a match flare then, too. Before he left the car he put the smoldering butt in the ashtray along with an unused match. As soon as the hot ash burned down far enough, it touched off the match. Simple as that."

Eberhardt made chewing sounds on his pipe stem. "Okay," he said, "you've explained the disappearance. Now explain the murder. Who killed Hornback? Not his wife?"

"No. The last place he would have gone was home and the last person he would have contacted was Mrs. Hornback. It has to be the girlfriend. She would be the one who picked him up near the lookout. An argument, over the money, maybe—something like that. You'll find out eventually why she did it."

"We won't find out anything unless we know who we're looking for. You got any more rabbits in your hat? Like the name of this girlfriend?"

"I don't know her name," I said, "but I think I can tell you where to find her."

He stared at me. "Well?"

"I followed Hornback around to a lot of places last night," I said. "Restaurant, drugstore, newsstand for a pack of cigarettes, Dewey's Place for a couple of drinks to shore up his courage—all reasonable stops. But why did he go to the branch library? Why would a man plotting his own disappearance bother to return a couple of library books? Unless the books were just a cover, you see? Unless he really went to the library to tell someone who worked there what he was going to do and where to come pick him up."

"A *librarian?*"

"Why not, Eb? Librarians aren't the stereotypes of fiction. This one figures to be young and attractive, whoever she is. You shouldn't have too much trouble picking out the right one."

He kept on staring at me. Then he shook his head and said, "You know something? You're getting to be a regular Sherlock Holmes in your old age."

"If I am," I said as I stood up, "you're getting to be a regular Lestrade."

That made him scowl. "Who the hell is Lestrade?"

The following day, while I was trying to find a better place to hang the blow-up of the 1932 *Black Mask* cover I keep in my office, Eberhardt called to fill in the final piece. Hornback's girlfriend worked at the branch library, all right. Her name was Linda Fields, and she had broken down under police interrogation and confessed to the murder.

The motive behind it was stupid and childish, like a lot of motives behind crimes of passion: Hornback wanted to go to South America, and she wanted stay in the U.S. They had argued about it on the way to her apartment, the argument had turned nasty after they arrived, Hornback had slapped her, she had picked up a butcher knife, and that was it for him. Afterward she had dragged his body back into her car, taken it to Golden Gate Park, and dumped it. What was left of the stolen money—ninety-eight thousand in cash—had been hidden in her apartment. That would make Mrs. Hornback happy—sweet lady that she was—and insure my getting paid for my services.

When Eberhardt finished telling me this, there was a long pause. "Listen," he said, "who's this Lestrade you mentioned yesterday?"

"That's still bothering you, is it?"

"Who is he, damn it? Some character in one of your pulps?"

"Nope. He's a cop in the Sherlock Holmes stories—the one Holmes keeps outwitting."

Eberhardt made a snorting noise, called me something uncomplimentary, and banged the phone down in my ear.

Laughing to myself, I went back to the *Black Mask* poster. Eb was no Lestrade, of course—and I was no Sherlock Holmes. I was the next best thing though. At least to my way of thinking, and in spite of my dream.

A good old fashioned pulp private eye.

Nedra Tyre
Typed for Murder

Clearly, Uncle Roderick had no intention of dying.

And he was as rich as he was old.

During his seventies he had had various illnesses from which he emerged hale and chipper. In his eighties he had had a slight stroke and a mild heart attack, which only added to his resilience. In his ninety-fourth year he had been gravely ill with pneumonia and had had nurses around the clock and specialists from as far away as Zurich, Switzerland Yet he had survived.

So when he approached his one hundredth birthday, we gave up hope—though I'm afraid that's not a delicate way to put it, as we truly loved Uncle Roderick. Not only did he appear indestructible, but he acquired a new hobby: he began to write his memoirs. In order to do this, he taught himself to type. He was not one to dispose of his money conspicuously, and so he bought a secondhand typewriter and had Uncle Cliff get him a dog-eared typing manual at Smith's Used Book Shop.

Now, thought Uncle Roderick was in the best of health, he was virtually bedridden. He had his meals in bed and spent his entire time there, except for an occasional circuit of his room and a walk twice a day down the upstairs hall. Precisely at ten in the morning and at four in the afternoon he had what he called his constitutional. With a cane in his right hand and his nurse, Miss Bessie, on his left, he made his laborious journey, and if you had seen him teetering and tottering and swaying and trembling, you would have sworn that he wasn't long for this world. But all of our family knew better than that. Brothers and sisters and nephews and nieces and great-nephews and great-nieces had fallen along the way, abandoning in death their hope (there's that indelicate word again) that they would inherit their share of a very large fortune. For hadn't Uncle Roderick stressed that it was to be divided equally—or had he said equitably?—among his survivors?

Uncle Roderick had never married. He liked women well enough, but he despised fortune hunters or greed of any kind and he was convinced that the women who had swarmed around him were not so much nubile as avaricious. Besides, he insisted to us, he wanted every penny of his money to go to his relatives. "In my day," he said modestly, "I've contributed my share to charity. I want everything that's left to go to you all."

He didn't so much demand our loyalty as inspire it, and we were devoted to him. We really were. He insisted that we live with him. Though the house was a large one (built in 1840 in the Greek Revival style), it wasn't quite large enough for us all; that is, until death thinned out the family somewhat. Uncle Charles, before he died of a stroke at seventy-three, slept on a sofa in the library. Aunt Emma had a pallet in the butler's pantry and kept her clothes in the broom closet until Aunt Susanne died. Then Aunt Emma moved into one of the servants' rooms. Not that there were any servants. We did all the work both inside the house and on the very extensive grounds and gardens, and each of us had a specialty—though we could all more or less exchange duties in case of indisposition or death, and we willingly pitched in if anyone got behind in his appointed task.

Uncle Roderick was sweet to us. He fed us and housed us, but we didn't have any money. There was no way to get any, either, because when any one of us looked for employment in Waynesville, people thought we were joking. Uncle Lewis, who was the most enterprising one among us and a fine gardener (visitors came from everywhere to admire his box and camellias), did his best to get work cutting grass or transplanting, but people thought he just wanted to help out in a neighborly fashion and wouldn't pay him a cent. Aunt Jenny was a wonderful cook and tried to sell sandwiches and cake by the slice on the school grounds, but the officials said she was interfering with the federal lunch program.

Way back in the thirties, long before I was born, Aunt Hattie had once gotten up nerve enough to ask Uncle Roderick for a small allowance for everyone, and it had hurt his feelings so much that no one ever had gall enough to mention money again. "What on earth do you need money for?" Uncle Roderick had asked, and there were tears in his eyes. "You live here. You eat here. We share this beautiful house. What do you want with money? What do you need it for?"

I defied Uncle Roderick briefly. As he was to do later, I taught myself to type and then asked his attorney to give me a job. I thought that he, of all people, must know that we didn't have any actual cash, but he too considered it a big leg-pull. Though he indulged me, I soon learned that he paid me exactly half what he paid his other typists. No matter, I'll never forget the joy on payday of going home and distributing my money among my aunts and uncles.

Two months were all I could manage. "Now, baby," Uncle Roderick said, "I like to have the whole family home all the time. I want everybody within calling distance. There's no sense in you giving in to this whim of wanting to work. I need you here."

My relatives were all sorry for me and sympathized and said they'd miss my money, too, but there was nothing to do except what Uncle Roderick suggested. I had to resign from my job.

Finally, something had to be done (we were threadbare and down-at-heel and famished for small luxuries like chocolate bars and chewing gum) and Uncle Lewis did it, though very discreetly and not very often. Our backs were to the wall and we just had to have cash. So on those desperate occasions, Uncle Lewis would sneak something from a closet or a cabinet or a sideboard—what he took had to be portable, concealable, and disposable—and he would tuck it circumspectly into a paper bag or his pocket, hitch a ride on a milk truck to Lexington, and sell the article or *objet d'art* to an auction house or an antique shop. One of the proprietors of a shop once mentioned a frantic need for some Hepplewhite chairs and sent a pickup truck for four of them. Poor, darling, naive Uncle Lewis sold the whole set of four for one-tenth of the amount the dealer got for just one of the chairs. (All the same, the money saw us through two hard winters.) Afterward, we had to drag in chairs from the kitchen in order to have enough chairs to sit on during our meals.

No one ever wondered (though someone should have) what would happen if Uncle Roderick ever found out that the silver supply was being slowly diminished and the walls and cupboards were getting a little bare. I guess we thought that Uncle Roderick was no threat to us, since he was upstairs in his stronghold typing his memoirs and venturing no father than the upstairs hall for his constitutional. He hadn't been downstairs since V-J Day when he stumbled over the Aubusson rug in the front parlor and broke his hip. Well, the antique dealer had become desperate for an Aubusson rug and was sending a truck for it on Friday.

Half an hour after the truck had driven off, Miss Bessie, the nurse, leaned over the banister and shouted: "Your uncle wants you, Joan."

I ran up the stairs and hurried over to Uncle Roderick and kissed him. Yellow second-sheets were strewn like a patchwork quilt across his bed. The ramshackle typewriter was pulled up close on a table that straddled the bed. "Baby," Uncle Roderick said, "where is the damned 'a' on this typewriter? I've using it all day, but it disappeared suddenly."

I showed him where the "a" was.

"Thanks, dove. That's mighty sweet of you and mighty stupid of me."

"Uncle Roderick, I could do your typing. I'd be delighted to type for you, precious. Why not let me?"

"It's just like you, darling, to want to be accommodating, but I'm going to master this typewriter if it's the last thing I do. But if you want to when I've finished the memoirs, you can type a neat manuscript and have it bound. I'd love to have you do that for me, dear."

"All right, precious," I said and kissed him goodbye. We were an affectionate and sweet-talking family.

I was at the head of the stairs when he called after me: "Listen, baby, the next time you come up, will you please bring me that little Meissen tea set on the sideboard?"

"I'll get it right this minute, darling."

"You're a sweet one," he said when I came back with the set and placed it on a table in the bay window.

Things went on in their accustomed fashion for another week. Uncle Roderick kept to his writing as methodically as Flaubert or Trollope until Saturday morning, when Miss Bessie called down that Uncle Roderick wanted me. I ran upstairs and Uncle Roderick and I kissed and I called him precious and he called me dove and then he said, "Darling, whenever it's convenient, please bring the vermeil tray up here. The one with the pierced gallery. No need to hurry. I won't begin to write about it until tomorrow."

No need to hurry, he had said. I didn't sleep at all that night. I kept thinking over and over: *the Meissen tea set last week, the vermeil tray with pierced gallery today, heaven only knows what he'll ask for tomorrow.* Thank goodness Uncle Lewis hadn't been prodigal and had disposed of only the barest minimum to keep us going.

"Darling," I said to Uncle Roderick the next morning after I had set the vermeil tray on his bed where his frail hand had indicated. "I somehow never thought of you as being interested in things. People are your concern, and yet here you are writing about a tea set and a tray. I can't understand it at all."

"Well, precious," Uncle Roderick said, "that's not very discerning of you. This vermeil tray is going to evoke our family reunion in May, 1898. By looking at it and remembering how it was piled with fried chicken, I can recall the entire day."

"Honey, you mean you've just reached 1898 in your memoirs?"

"Oh, sugarfoot, I'm skipping around. I'm putting things down as they occur to me. I don't really know where I am. All I know is that there's no end in sight."

There really was no end in sight for us.

At lunchtime I had to tell my aunts and uncles what we were in for. Sharing the problem only seemed to make the situation worse, for after that they all hung around the foot of the stairs waiting for my summons from Uncle Roderick. And when it came, they all pawed about to see if the object he had requested was still in our possession. More than once the game seemed up and Uncle Lewis would wail, "I think I sold that in 1959." But Aunt Jenny or Aunt Laura would somehow ferret it out, and our torment would end until Uncle Roderick's next request.

I might have been climbing up to the guillotine for all of us when Uncle Roderick called for me again and I stumbled up the stairs.

"What do you want this time, Uncle Roderick?" I asked.

"Uncle Roderick what, precious?" he said looking hurt.

"I don't know what you mean," I said.

"Joan, baby, that's the first time in your life you haven't called me dear or darling or honey or precious. Don't you love your old uncle any more?"

"Precious lamb, I am sorry. So sorry. But please, please hurry and tell me what you want."

"All I want is a kind word from my little sweetheart and for you to sit and let me look at your pretty face for a while. I'm working too hard on my memoirs."

Life grew more hazardous every day. Our appetites were dulled. No one slept any more. We only gathered in corners to whisper desperately and to ask what we would do when Uncle Roderick told me to bring him something that was no longer in the house.

One day at lunch, as we looked at our untouched plates piled high with Aunt Jenny's delectable cooking, Uncle Jonathan, who really didn't have a dishonest bone in his body, said: "If Uncle Roderick asks for something that's been sold, we'll have to pretend we've never heard of it. Tell him we don't know what he's talking about."

Aunt Jenny said: "We can't do that. That wouldn't do any good. He'd catch us out in a minute. He'd only insist on being brought downstairs to see for himself. Then he'd find out the whole truth."

Aunt Laura cried: "It's such an abuse of his hospitality. Here we've been his guests time out of mind and we've sold the things he loves. We're thieves—common thieves."

"Now, now, it isn't as bad as that," Uncle Percy said. "In a way, the things are ours. Uncle Roderick is leaving everything to us. We've just anticipated ourr inheritance a little, and I must remind you all that we had to have the money. We haven't been extravagant. We've squeezed every penny."

"There's no way to justify it," Lewis said. "No way at all. It's all my fault and I'll take the blame. I'm the one who thought it up and did the selling. We can't live in this suspense any longer. I'll tell Uncle Roderick what's happened."

For years there must have been intimations that Miss Bessie, the nurse, was fond of Uncle Lewis, but with her outburst now, it was obvious that she loved him. "No, Lewis darling, you can't. In a way, I know Mr. Worthington better than any of you do. I'm with him almost all the time, except for meals. There's no telling what he would do if he finds out. No telling at all. And if he discovers that Lewis did the actual selling, I'm sure he'll disown him. But it's not only Lewis I'm thinking about. You've all been so patient and devoted and you're all involved in this. He'll think you've all been disloyal."

Miss Bessie was thinking of us all, but especially of Uncle Lewis. She put our predicament so nicely, so gently, while we could think only of our selfishness and dishonesty.

Just then Uncle Roderick's voice pierced our mutterings and mumblings and frenzied connivings. "Joan, baby, come up here. I want to ask a favor."

I detached myself from my panic-stricken relatives and Miss Bessie and ascended the stairs. As soon as we had kissed and called each other darling, Uncle Roderick asked for the Hepplewhite chairs.

All eight of them.

And there were only four left.

Our doom had arrived; our reckoning was nigh.

I had to brazen it out. "Yes, precious," I said and I rushed back downstairs as if I might return in a moment with every single chair.

When I told the paralyzed family, there were conferences and suggestions and counter-suggestions.

"The trouble with the Worthington family is that we aren't good liars," Uncle Jonathan said.

"Only thieves," Aunt Jenny commented tartly.

I had to act because Uncle Roderick was waiting. I took two of the chairs to him. I was overzealous and called Uncle Roderick precious and dearest in one breath, too egregious even for our ever-loving family. "Darling," I went on, "Aunt Jenny needs me to help clear away lunch. You don't mind waiting a little while for the other chairs, do you?"

"Of course not, my dove."

That saw us through more desperate conferences until mid-afternoon, when I took the third chair up.

"Darling Uncle Roderick," I said. "It's getting crowded in here. Do you actually want all the other chairs?"

"Yes, baby, I do. I can't write about that dinner party celebrating my first million unless I have every chair in front of me."

Uncle Roderick's nap gave us a slight respite and then at four thirty I took up the fourth chair.

That's all there were. There weren't any more.

My aunts and uncles decided that I had done as much as I could and that it was someone else's turn. Aunt Louise volunteered and bravely mounted the stairs. Maybe all women want to be actresses, maybe all women have to be actresses, but Aunt Louise had the looks and voice for one and perhaps could have followed that profession with brilliant success if she hadn't been born with such great expectations of inheriting part of Uncle Roderick's fortune.

"Now, Uncle Roderick, precious, what's all this about the Hepplewhite chairs?" Her voice was at once vibrant and cajoling. It was untinged by the despair she and all of us waiting at the foot of the stairs felt. "You have four already, and I must say it's a little inconvenient for us to bring the others up right at dinnertime."

Something in Uncle Roderick's demeanor made her change her tactics. "All right, darling. All right, if you insist. But I'm not about to let you see what a poor housekeeper I am. I'll wax and polish the others and bring them up the first thing tomorrow morning. Joan shouldn't have brought those others up here without polishing them."

And so Aunt Louise won us a reprieve until morning.

It wasn't a joyous reprieve. We couldn't eat our dinner and there was nothing to talk about that night. Neither scheming nor subterfuge could save us. We must meet our fate the next morning.

We went to bed early, but the house was a restless place. There was much walking about and opening and closing of doors, and for half an hour there was the rattling of Uncle Roderick's typewriter. It sounded brisk and efficient and reminded us all, not that we needed a reminder, that it and the memoirs were the instruments of our downfall.

Somehow or other we would have to account for the missing Hepplewhite chairs the next morning.

But the next morning Uncle Roderick was dead. He had died like a baby. He had burrowed into his pillows and had smothered himself.

And we were all as rich as precious, darling Uncle Roderick had intimated. Nothing is so pleasant as possessing money when you know the actual value of it. For a family of eight that had gotten through two long winters on the proceeds from four chairs, it was fantastic to have so much money. But we didn't want to live together any longer, though we were very fond of each other and never lost the close family feeling of which Uncle Roderick was so proud. None of us wanted any of the furniture or other items in the house because they reminded us of how we had been tormented by wondering what Uncle Roderick would ask for next. Avid antique dealers and curators of museums came and carried off everything except the four Hepplewhite chairs. Uncle Lewis and Uncle Jonathan tore them up with their bare hands and burned them.

As soon as we had suitably mourned Uncle Roderick, there was a wedding: Uncle Lewis married Miss Bessie, the nurse. We were all happy, yet sad that they had had to wait so many years. Both were in their late sixties, but they had been forced to postpone their marriage as Uncle Lewis had had no way to support Miss Bessie until Uncle Roderick died. "Better late than never," Aunt Jenny said philosophically, and she meant not only Uncle Lewis's wedding but Uncle Roderick's money.

Yet, whatever our ages, we were all fortunate. Each of us had a tremendous respect for money and we had so much money to respect.

Above all I wanted to do something for Uncle Roderick, chiefly because I loved him but also because he had been so generous and had died so conveniently. Bless his precious heart.

Then I remembered his memoirs and I decided to do what he had suggested one day. He had asked me to make a neat copy and have it bound.

I turned out to be a real labor of love, as his typing was atrocious and the content stupefyingly dull. That is, until I got to the last sentence of the last page. I couldn't decipher any of that page except for the final line, which had no typographical error whatever. It said simply: *Nobody would have the nerve to do it but the wren.*

That must have meant that Uncle Roderick had known about us. But who was the wren? Uncle Lewis had done the actual selling. How could wren apply to him? Wren sounded more like a woman. Uncle

Roderick called me dove, not wren. Maybe he meant Aunt Jenny because Jenny and wren somehow go together. Well, obviously Uncle Roderick wasn't as smart as he might have been, no matter how many millions he had acquired, because he hadn't suspected Uncle Lewis as the culprit.

I was especially grateful that Uncle Roderick hadn't had any suspicion about Uncle Lewis, as grief came to him so quickly after his marriage. Miss Bessie died two months later, and tragically. She was struck down by an automobile. Because of the family's wealth and prominence, there was a large photograph and a long article on the front page of the Waynesville *Inquirer*. The headline read: MRS. LEWIS WORTHING, R.N., TRAFFIC VICTIM.

I tried to comfort Uncle Lewis by telling him that she had been happy and had died quickly, but he wouldn't be comforted. "I don't think she was happy," he said. "She loved me, but she wasn't happy. Maybe she didn't deliberately run in front of that automobile, but she was confused and didn't care whether she lived or died."

I saved the article about Miss Bessie and one morning, when I opened a desk drawer to look for something, Miss Bessie smiled up at me from beneath the headline (MRS. LEWIS WORTHINGTON, R.N., TRAFFIC VICTIM). Then I saw at once that she was the wren to whom Uncle Roderick referred in the final sentence of his memoirs.

R.N.—wren.

Perhaps that's what Uncle Roderick had called her, though I hadn't ever heard him, for he had pet names for everyone. In his last remark Uncle Roderick had said she was the only one with nerve enough to do it. Surely that couldn't mean he thought Miss Bessie was guilty of disposing of his possessions. He knew quite well that she was constantly at his side, hour after hour, day by day, year after year.

Then he must have meant something else—that Miss Bessie ("the wren") was the only one with nerve enough to carry out a certain action.

I had to find out what Uncle Roderick had typed on that final night of his life. It didn't prove to be difficult once I set my mind to it. I soon discovered that in his excitement Uncle Roderick had placed his left hand one key too far to the right, so that the first sentence read: *Somryhinh dytsnhr id hoinh on hrtr* instead of *Something strange is going on here*. He had continued in that manner. However, there must have been a pause before he wrote the last sentence, for he had corrected his position by then. It took only a little ingenuity to transpose the entire passage. My shaking fingers typed and my astonished eyes read the following:

> *Something strange is going on here. I love them all dearly and have shared everything with them. But I feel they all want me dead. There's an atmosphere of murder in this house. I don't know what I've done to*

displease them and I'm not the type to be murdered. Yet this afternoon right after my nap, when the wren took my pulse and then removed a freshly cleaned dressing robe from its plastic wrapper, I saw her look at the wrapping and then at me and I remembered reading about babies and young children being smothered to death accidentally by those wrappers.

My body is certainly not what it once was, but I've been proud of my clear mind. I must be losing it, though, to think that any of these devoted people would want to kill me. They all love me and I love them. Bessie is fond of me—she's at my beck and call day and night—and she has been even more attentive and kind than any of them and she's the only one who has nothing to gain from me. I ought to have remembered her in my will, but I wanted my family to have everything. Still, I feel that she's the only one who would murder me.

Nobody would have the nerve to do it but the wren.

Later, I had the memoirs bound except for the last page. I tore that up because it was irrelevant. After all, memoirs are recollections and that page was no remembrance. A man can't remember his own murder.

As dear Uncle Roderick said, we all loved him and were attentive and devoted to him—especially Miss Bessie.

Babs H. Deal

Make My Death Bed

The phone rang at two o'clock in the morning. Bob Hudson's wife answered it, but he was awake. It was seldom enough there was a two o'clock call for the coroner in a town the size of Bellefonte. He lay quietly, listening to her voice from the next room and feeling a flood of excitement mingled with guilt. A two A.M. phone call to the coroner meant trouble for somebody—somebody he knew, at that. Still, there was the excitement.

Della came back into the room. She was a small woman with black hair and an air of competent assurance. She went to the closet and began putting on her clothes. "I reckon I'll go over with you," she said. "She'll need somebody, and her mother won't come. I'm sure she won't."

"Della!" he scolded, getting out of bed and already pulling on his pants. "Who was it?"

"I told you it'd come to this sooner or later with that country club bunch," she said placidly.

"Will you tell me what's happened!" he shouted at her, and went on knotting his tie.

"Ken Taylor's shot Bishop Darby," she said, powdering her face. "Dead as a doornail."

He cursed briefly and went on out the door, getting his hat and car keys from the hall table in the same movement of hand and eye. Della turned out the lights and followed him. They were already in the car before he said briefly, "Where?"

"Over at Taylor's, of course," she said. "You know Bishop's been staying there since his wife went home for the summer."

He said, "Oh." Then, "Light me a cigarette," turning down Laurel Street and heading out toward the lake front.

The fog was coming in off the river bottom, filling the road with its white amorphous presence, making him squint his eyes against the expected glare of an oncoming car before he thought that, of course, any car out now would probably be going in the same direction he was.

"Have they notified her yet?" he said.

"I don't know. It was Clint called. He said Ken called in himself. Said to come out there, that he'd shot Bishop, and hung up."

Bob stubbed the cigarette out in the ashtray and reached out for the new one she'd lighted. Out of the corner of his eye, he glanced at Della. She was smoking quietly, looking out into the fog.

"You reckon it was Elise?" he said.

Della snorted. "What else could it be?" she said. "What else could possibly make Ken Taylor shoot anybody?" She giggled suddenly.

"Except his golf scores. And it wasn't that. Because Bish doesn't even play golf."

"Della, it's not funny."

"I know. I'm sorry." She put her hand on his knee. "After all, you've never been immune to her yourself, have you?"

Now he snorted.

"Well you're male, aren't you?" she said. "And even we females have to admit that Elise Taylor's beautiful." Yes, she thought, she's beautiful all right, or maybe flamboyant was the word. At any rate, she didn't look as though she could possibly have been born in Bellefonte, Alabama, much less have spent her life there. She looked like one of the exotic faces that smile at us from the pages of movie magazines and TV guides, or the glossy pages of the fashion magazines. She was brunette, tall, lithe, with eyes that slanted just enough to emphasize her cheekbones, gray eyes with black lashes; her mouth curved as mouths are meant to do, and her nose was unbelievable. Noses are always so awful, Della thought. Almost everybody has an awful nose. Everybody except Elise. She thought of Jackie Darby's plain, smiling face, and sighed, wondered how Jackie would make out now that her husband was dead.

Bob made the left turn onto the dirt road that led to the lakefront, praying that no car would come barreling over the fog-covered hill, relaxing when he felt the tires crunch on gravel. "What the hell was Bish doing staying over there anyway?" he said.

"For the coroner you don't hear much," Della said. "Everybody knows it."

"Knows what?"

"That he's staying over there while Jackie goes to her mother's. I told you."

"Still doesn't explain why," he said. "Isn't that rather dumb of Jackie?"

"Bob, darling, what else could she do?" Della said. She tucked one knee under her and turned toward him. "I ask you. Your husband is making eyes at your best friend. You always go home for the summer so the children can see their grandparents. Was she *not* going to go and tacitly accuse them? *And* let everybody in Bellefonte know she accused them?"

He shook his head. "It's a shame she didn't stay, and let 'em think what they liked."

"Poor Jackie," Della said. "She'll have to come back and bury him, won't she?"

He felt gooseflesh rise on him suddenly, and rolled up the window he had cracked against the cigarette smoke. "I'd just as soon," he said, "not have to go out here."

"That's what I thought, love. That's why I came. I'm not particularly worried about Elise actually. I never knew Elise to need a woman."

"That's the first catty thing I ever heard you say," he said.

"That's not catty. That's just the truth."

And it was the truth, she told herself. Elise had never had women friends, not in high school and not since. Unless you counted Jackie. And somehow right now Della didn't feel like counting her.

Jackie and Bishop Darby had come to Bellefonte from New England, sent by the company for which he sold appliances. They were young and attractive, and very much in love. They rented an apartment just down the street from Della and Bob, and for them Della had relaxed her rule against entertaining because they were new and strangers and charming and because she thought they might want to get to know a part of Bellefonte that wasn't the country club and the endless dinner parties and fishing trips. She'd grown very fond of Jackie that first summer, Jackie with her odd ways, her faint coolness that turned into an enchanting sense of humor when you knew her. She was short and small-boned, and her two baby girls were exactly like her. Bish was the Apollo type, and Della hadn't known them long before she began to be afraid for Jackie. Because for a man to look like a Greek god and to be a newcomer in Bellefonte meant trouble, simply trouble.

Della lit a cigarette, peering out the windshield at the dark pines along the roadside. "I didn't know how much trouble," she said softly.

Bob jerked his head toward her. "What?" he said sharply.

"Nothing. Oh, nothing. Are we nearly there?"

"Couple more turns." He sighed. "Clint didn't give you any details?"

"Just what I told you. Bob, do you think we could have done anything?"

He shook his head. "Don't start thinking that, Del. People'll do what they do. That's all."

She nodded, remembering. Bellefonte's younger crowd hadn't claimed Bish and Jackie for almost a year, but of course they had eventually. Bish's folksongs that he played on the guitar and sang in a husky baritone opened the door. He joined the J.C.'s and the Lions and the country club, and after a while Bob and Della didn't see much of them any more. Because Della and Bob didn't go to the country club. "If you want to dance with somebody else's wife," Della said, "do it in private." And because Bob would rather read a book or watch TV, they didn't go to the country club.

But Bish and Jackie did, and they also went to the camps in summer and to the kitchen parties at Ken and Elise Taylor's in the winter. And after a while everybody said, "Have you seen Elise and Bish dance together?" And later, "Well, they do seem so right."

Jackie ignored this kind of talk. Jackie, after all, was Elise Taylor's best friend. They ate dinner together at least once a week; they took trips to Chattanooga, shopping and to take the Darby kids to the dentist. They even talked Ken and Bish into going shares on a boat.

Even the most persistent of the town gossips didn't dare say anything about Elise Taylor to Jackie Darby. And most certainly not I, Della thought. Most certainly not I.

They could see the lights from the house now, shining out over the point and into the road. It was a neat white ranch house like all the others along the lake, new and neat, and mortgaged. The sheriff's car was in the drive, and Dr. Clifton's, and another one Della couldn't indentify. "Probably the Taylors'," she said. "I bet her mother won't come."

"Why do you say that?"

She shrugged.

They got out and went onto the porch. Bob knocked, but no one came and he pushed open the front door and looked into the hall; then he glanced into the living room on the right. There was no one in sight.

"In the kitchen," Della said. "They all live in them all the time. I imagine they die in them, too."

He looked at her impatiently, but saw that she was serious. They walked through the living room and into the combination kitchen and den.

"Hi, Bob," Clint Hawkins, the sheriff said. He was a big man with gray hair and bifocals. He wore his badge pinned carefully to his suspenders. Bob and Della went into the room and Clint nodded toward the fireplace.

Bishop Darby lay sprawled across the hearth. He was wearing a striped T-shirt and a pair of skivvy shorts.

"What's that under him?" Della whispered.

"Say," Bob whispered back to her in astonishment, "it's his guitar."

Ken Taylor sat beside Clint's deputy on the window seat, his head between his hands. Elise was sitting at the table drinking a cup of coffee. She wore a pair of turquoise lounging pajamas, and her face was carefully made up. Ken's father and his lawyer stood beside her, talking in low voices.

Elise looked up. "Hello, Bob," she said. "You got a cigarette on you? Everybody here seems to have run out. Hello, Della."

Della pitched her pack of cigarettes onto the table and went to the stove to fix herself a cup of black coffee. Bob was across the room now with the body, but she didn't look back at it again after the first quick glance.

Elise was lighting a cigarette, her hands steady. She glanced up at Della and beckoned to her. Della took her coffee to the table and sat down across from her.

Elise looked at her and around the room quickly and back again. "They won't do anything to Ken, will they?" she whispered. "It was all my fault. I'll say so."

Della shrugged.

"It's Jackie I feel so bad about," Elise said. Della stared at her, feeling a small shock. She meant it. Elise was speaking her usual cool and exact truth. "Poor little Jackie," she went on. "What did she do to deserve this?" She glanced up at Mr. Taylor and the lawyer. "Come over here," she said to Della.

Della followed her to the stove and watched while she turned on the electricity under the coffee pot and leaned over, her hands braced on the pine edge of the stove cabinet. "It was hardly worth it, was it, Della?" she said softly. "I thought I'd die if I didn't have him. But it was hardly worth it. Jackie and the kids without any Bish. And the world without any Bish, and Bish's music, and Bish's beautiful body. I sure fouled this one up, didn't I?"

Della didn't answer her. She lit a cigarette instead.

"Of course it was the original mistake," Elise said softly. She put the palm of her hand against the side of the coffee pot, and switched off the burner. "It was the mistake of thinking Ken would put up with anything from me. That's why I married him, you know?" She looked straight at Della, and Della looked straight back.

"I could have had almost anybody in Bellefonte," Elise went on wistfully. "Bob, for instance." She didn't say it with malice, only with a sort of sad certainty. "But I thought Ken Taylor would put up with me. And, Della, just—just look at me. Was I meant for one man and one life and one dedication to the gods of Bellefonte respectability?"

"You could have got out of Bellefonte," Della said. Behind them she could hear the sounds as they put the body on the stretcher that had arrived at the back door, and the sudden twang of strings as the guitar was picked up from the hearth.

"Bish was the first," Elise said. "The first since I've been married. Just the flirting was enough ... till Bish."

"I guess the gods weren't working for Bish and Jackie when they sent him south," Della said.

She walked away from the stove and over to Bob who was writing on his report pad.

"We'll have to take statements in a minute," Bob said in her ear. "She all right?"

Della laughed mirthlessly. "She's all right," she said. "Have you notified Jackie?"

"I thought you ..."

"Oh, no," Della said, "Not me. Why don't you let her best friend?" She turned and went into the living room, the cold, useless, beautiful room with the five hundred dollar drapes and the un-sat-in chairs and the cold fireplace. She opened the drapes and stood looking out into the woodland around the house. The fog had crept up onto the road now, the wisps of white clinging gently to the pines. She shivered a little, thinking again, as she often did, how glad she was to live in town.

The door from the kitchen opened and Elise came into the room. "I feel so odd all of a sudden, Della," she said slowly. "Just odd."

Della turned, seeing Elise slump onto the edge of the velvet-covered loveseat. She was pale now, her black eyebrows and lashes standing out against her face.

"It's about time, I guess," Della said. "Why don't you get Dr. Clifton to give you something? What are they doing in there?"

Elise blinked at her. "They had us say again how it happened. How Ken came in and saw us and said, 'I waited long enough, but I got you now,' and just took out the gun. Della?" She stood up suddenly. "Where did Ken get that gun? How long do you reckon he's had it?"

Della smiled. She felt her lips curve and tried to stop them, but couldn't. She thought of Ken Taylor and his dull interminable conversations about golf and insurance and mortgages, and the thought that this negative cipher had actually had the nerve to obtain and keep and wait to use a gun still amused her. "He wouldn't have any trouble getting a gun," she said.

"We had steak for supper," Elise said. "Because Bish is dieting again. He always diets when he puts on a little weight. Jackie always laughs about it. And she thought it would be too much trouble for us to feed him diet food." She looked bewildered for a moment. "Bish is dead," she said. "I'm talking about him as if he's not."

Della sat down on a straight chair and waited.

"It was because I forgot about the J.C.'s letting their parties out early on foggy nights," Elise said. "It was the fog. Because they always come home early because so many live on the lake."

"Have they called Jackie?" Della said.

Elise shook her head. "I think Bob wants you ..."

Della went out of the room, slapping the swinging door open with the palm of her hand. They had cleaned up some of the mess, although the guitar with its crushed side and broken strings still stood against the chimney. She walked over to Bob. "What in heaven's name was he doing with that guitar?" she said.

Bob shook his head. "Had it in the other hand, I reckon," he said. "You gonna call Jackie for me?"

She shook her head. "I can't, Bobby, I'm sorry. I'd make a mess of it."

"All right." He patted her shoulder. "Say, you put Jackie on the train, didn't you?" he said suddenly. "I'd forgotten."

She nodded, and for the first time felt as if she might cry after all. Jackie had called her. She didn't see much of her any more, but sometimes in the mornings they'd get together for coffee. That morning she'd left the dishes and gone down the street to Jackie's apartment.

"I want you to take me to the train tomorrow," Jackie had said as soon as she'd poured the coffee. "Bish'll be at work with the car at train time and I don't want him to have to leave. Elise'll be busy enough getting ready for company. Lord knows, with Bish on his diet again she'll have to restock the larder." She'd laughed then, naturally and happily, and Della thought, It isn't true. It's just dirty gossip and nothing else. It's because Bish is so goodlooking and Elise is so gorgeous. Gossips would just have to pair them off because their little minds work that way. She'd convinced herself in that moment. And she'd felt a lot better about putting Jackie on that train. Because for a while she'd almost said, "Don't go." And she knew that would have been admitting she believed it, too. I wish to God I had believed it, she thought now. Because an unfaithful husband is a lot better than a dead one.

They had taken Ken away, and Mr. Taylor and the lawyer had gone with them. The sheriff still stood in the kitchen, watching the bloodstained hearth as though he might look it away. Dr. Clifton had gone in to speak to Elise. None of her family had arrived and Della thought again that they weren't likely to. They had all but disowned her when she married Ken Taylor, for all his respectability. They'd wanted her to go to college. And, Della thought, they'd been right.

Bob had picked up the phone. He was having trouble with the long distance operator. She could feel his rage and frustration mounting in the tightly controlled voice he was using.

Dr. Clifton came in. "Della," he said, "she doesn't look good. Try to get her to take these. Two now . . . two in another hour." He dropped a white envelope into her hand. "Do you think you should take her somewhere?"

"Where?" Della said.

He shrugged. "Will you stay here?"

She looked at him for a moment. Then she nodded. There really wasn't anybody else to do it.

The sheriff and Dr. Clifton went out the back door and Elise came into the room. She poured coffee again and opened the icebox and slammed the door and stirred a silver spoon slowly in her cup.

"You're drinking too much coffee," Della said automatically. "You need to sleep." She glanced over at Bob.

"Mrs. Bishop Darby," he was saying into the phone. "That's right. I'll hold on." He turned from the phone and said to Della, "Take this with me on the living room extension."

"Come on, Elise," Della said. "Let's go back into the living room."

Elise sat on the loveseat again, sipping coffee steadily. She looked worse. "I'm going to stay with you tonight," Della said.

"Thank you. I don't feel quite right. I keep thinking about a song Bish used to sing," Elise said. " 'Barbara Allen.' Do you know it?"

"I know it," Della said, seeing Bish's long fingers strumming the six strings, and Jackie, sitting at his feet on a cushion, listening, always listening. She shook her head and went across the room to the telephone on the neat cherry stand. She glanced at Elise, then picked up the phone and put the receiver to her ear.

"There's a verse to it," Elise's voice said softly. " 'Oh, Mother,

Mother, make my bed; O make it long and narrow; Sweet William died for me today; I'll die for him tomorrow.' "

"Jackie?" Bob's voice came to her through the receiver, loud and distorted in the quiet room.

"Hello, Bob," Jackie said, her voice no different, even now waked from sleep at the dead hour of the morning.

"Jackie, I'm afraid I've some bad news for you," Bob said.

"Yes?" Her voice still didn't change.

Across the room, Elise had lain down across the loveseat, the cup of coffee on the floor beside her. She was still singing softly, " 'She looked to the east, she looked to the west; She saw the corpse acoming; O hand me down that corpse of clay; That I may look upon it.' "

Della shivered.

"It's Bish," Bob said, his professional voice firming and taking over the chore for him. "He's been killed."

"All right," Jackie said. Her voice still did not change. She's in shock, Della thought. She looked out the window. The fog was creeping around the house now, its wispy tendrils catching on the tree branches just below her.

" 'A rose, a rose, grew from William's grave,' " Elise sang, " 'From Barbara's grew a briar ...' "

Della straightened and looked at her. She lay stretched out on her stomach now, her hair falling over her face.

"Do you want me to turn myself over to the authorities here?" Jackie said, "or should I come back there?"

"What?" Bob's voice exploded in her ear.

"I said who should arrest me?" Jackie said again. Her voice was still even.

Bob spoke again, less loudly. "Jackie," he said, "you're in shock. I'm trying to tell you Bish has been killed. He was shot."

"Shot?" Jackie said. "Shot?"

"Yes, Jackie," Bob said. "It was—"

"Ken." Jackie said. "Ken." She started to laugh. There was nothing hysterical in the laughter, just amusement and infinite good humor. It was the same response Della herself had felt when she'd thought of Ken Taylor with a gun instead of a golf club.

"Jackie," Bob said, "you're not yourself. Let me speak to your mother or father."

Jackie stopped laughing and for a moment there was only the sound of the humming wire, holding open the distance from south to north. Then she spoke again softly. "I'm all right, Bob," she said. "I'm fine. But if Ken shot Bish, then—then you'd better do something about the saccharin ..."

But Della had already thrown down the phone and started toward Elise. She was lying face down now, breathing shallowly. Della picked up the cup and looked into it, seeing the oily swirl where the coffee hadn't mixed with the cream. Then she was through the door and into the kitchen. Bob looked up at her dully, still holding the phone to his ear.

"Hang up," Della said. "Hang up and call Dr. Clifton. Quick."

She went to the stove and then to the cabinet, searching swiftly. It was by the cream pitcher, the small bottle of white saccharin pills that Bishop Darby used when he was on one of his diets. There were only a few pills left in the bottle now. She touched her tongue to one, but it was only saccharin. It must have been just one, she thought, or two. I don't think she meant poison for both of them. I don't think she thought at all that Elise with her figure would ever want to diet. But then, she thought suddenly, maybe Jackie thought they'd figure it was Elise who'd poisoned Bish. She shuddered, and went back into the living room. She could hear Bob on the phone now, calling Dr. Clifton.

There was no sound in the living room at all now. The slow, heavy breathing had stopped. Across the room the fog had crept onto the windowsill, curling limply against the blackness outside. She went to Elise and lifted her head, but she couldn't feel any breath or pulse.

She sat very still, holding the beautiful body of Elise across her lap, and after a while she heard Dr. Clifton come into the drive, the slamming of the back door, and the sudden discordant jangling of strings as he stumbled against the broken guitar in his haste.

John H. Dirckx

Murder on the Edinburgh-London Express

The visits of Superintendent Miller of the Criminal Investigation Department to Dr. John Thorndyke's chambers in King's Bench Walk usually portended Thorndyke's engagement—and mine—in the elucidation of dark mysteries and diabolical intrigues. Hence, when Miller put in an unexpected appearance late one midsummer morning, accompanied by a battered suitcase and a raffish-looking young man with ginger-colored sidewhiskers, Thorndyke and I with one accord laid aside the tasks upon which we had been working, made our visitors comfortable, and composed ourselves to listen to some romantic and mysterious tale.

After depositing the suitcase on the floor next to his chair, Miller opened the proceedings by introducing his companion as Mr. Philip Carmold of Leicester. "Mr. Carmold," said he, "is employed by Spiller's, a large firm of saddlers and harness-makers in the Midlands, and he has had a remarkable experience which I am going to ask him to recite to you. He has been over it three times already, and if that makes it something of a bother for him to have to tell it again, at least by now he has got all the details at his fingers' ends, and can give you an outline of the story in a very few moments."

Thorndyke arranged a noteblock on the arm of his chair and took up his pen with an expectant air. "Not too succinct, if you please, Mr. Carmold," said he. "If a mere outline of the case would suffice for its solution, I fancy that you gentlemen would not be doing us the honor of this call." At that Miller gave a wink and a nod to his companion, who settled himself in his chair and began his tale forthwith.

"Two nights since, I journeyed to London in the evening express from Edinburgh," said he. "As the train was rather crowded, I was pleased at first when I found an empty compartment. Presently, though, I regretted my choice, for I discovered that the window was stuck shut, and obstinately resisted all efforts to put it down. The day had been exeedingly warm and the compartment was as close and hot as a forcing-house. Around ten o'clock I acquired a companion in suffering—a foppish little party with pince-nez and waxed mustaches, of a distinctly foreign aspect. As nearly as I could judge by the dim light from the passage and the occasional gleam of a wayside lamp, he was about fifty years of age, and he seemed much preoccupied.

"Though he did not utter a single word in all the time we spent together, he did communicate with me once. After making an unsuccessful attempt to open the window, he intimated by a sort of dumb-show that if I did not object he proposed to lay aside his coat; and that, by way of reciprocating me for this kindness, he was content to allow me the same liberty. His absolute silence and his use of gestures to communicate with me confirmed me in my surmise that he was a foreigner.

"I must have fallen asleep not long after, and in spite of the oppressive heat, the jolting of the carriage, and the clamor of the wheels, I did not awaken until it was nearly dawn. By the faint grey light of morning I thought I described my fellow wayfarer huddled up in the corner of his seat, apparently fast asleep. But, as the light increased, I perceived that the man oppsite me was not the one who had shared the earlier part of the journey with me, for this chap was neither so old nor so slight of build as the other. Finally, when the full light of day penetrated the compartment, I made the horrifying discovery that my new companion was not only remarkably motion-less, but was likely to remain so for all time. What is more, there was a sunken purple wound just behind the crown of his head that I did not like to look at.

"As soon as I had assured myself that he was quite dead—by touching his arm, which was as heavy and lifeless as a log—I summoned the guard, who telegraphed ahead to the authorities here in London. The train was met by a police ambulance and a perfect army of detec-tives, and the passengers were required to give proof of their identities and submit to questioning before being permitted to leave the station. At least the rest of them were eventually turned loose, which has not been my good fortune, for I spent yesterday and last night in the lockup—politely referred to as 'temporary custody'—and even now Superintendent Miller is speculating on the advisability of clapping the 'darbies' on my wrists."

"Come, come, Mr. Carmold," laughed Miller. "It isn't as bad as all that, and I assure you that you are a free man and may go where and when you will—that is, as soon as you have restored a certain garment to its rightful owner. The well cut and elegant coat that Mr. Carmold is wearing," he continued, turning to us, "is one of mine, which I have lent him until his own turns up. For when he came to leave the train yesterday morning, he found that his coat was missing, and in its place upon the seat lay another. It is clear that his coat has been exchanged for that of the man who shared his compartment during the earlier part of the journey—a man whose identity and whereabouts are presently a matter of great interest to the police.

"We have been in touch with the authorities in nearly all the cities and towns through which the train passed, and particularly in Leeds and Sheffield, where it stopped between midnight and four o'clock in the morning, but no one remembers seeing a traveler such as the one described by Mr. Carmold. None of the people associated with the railway line has any recollection of him either, but that is not surprising. Railway guards and booking clerks deal with so many passengers in a day's time, without taking the least notice of them, that I believe a yellow baboon might travel by rail throughout the length and breadth of England and pass unremarked save by his fellow passengers—if there were any!"

"What of the dead man?" said I. "Can you not get some hint from his personal affairs, his associations?"

"Why, bless you, Dr. Jervis, I should give a great deal just for a hint as to his name! Not only did we find no luggage with him in the compartment, but there was not a scrap of paper on his person by which he could be identified. Of course, it is unlikely that he was altogether friendless, and in time someone is bound to report him missing, but until we can give him a name I fear we shall be able to make little or nothing of the case."

"What were the findings at the post-mortem examination?" asked Thorndyke.

"Death was due to a blow from a blunt instrument, which caused a depressed fracture of the occipital bone. He had also a very bad heart—something about a valve stopped up—and Dr. Austrin, who did the post-mortem, said that a chap with a heart like that had one foot in the grave already."

"Sounds like stenosis of the aortic valve," observed Thorndyke. "Was he carrying any medicine in his pocket?"

"None. And precious little else. Some loose silver, a cheap watch, and a latchkey—that's the lot. No papers, no letters, and barely enough money for a meal and a night's lodging."

"Taken with the absence of any luggage, surely that is highly suggestive of robbery?" I remarked.

"That is our view," nodded the superintendent in agreement. "But whether the crime was premeditated or casual, and whether it involved the theft of some particular article or merely a quantity of money, we have yet to learn."

"Merely money!" laughed my colleague. "A cavalier attitude for a police officer to take toward the coin of the realm, which happens to supply the motive for half the crimes committed in England. You remind me of the Owl and the Pussycat, who embarked on their marine peregrinations with 'plenty of money, wrapped up in a five-pound note.' But come," said he, growing serious and casting an inquisitive eye upon the suitcase that rested next to Miller's chair, "let us have a look at the mysterious gentleman's coat."

"I might have known you would guess what was in the suitcase," said Miller, grinning broadly. "You mustn't credit him with supernatural powers, Mr. Carmold. I never visit Dr. Thorndyke without bringing along some castoff article of clothing or stray bit of personal jetsam, and you will recall that I have already mentioned the coat as being in our possession." He laid the suitcase across his knees, raised the lid, and lifted out the garment in question, which proved to be in the last stages of disintegration.

"I cannot but think that our mute gentleman of the pince-nez has profited by the exchange," said Thorndyke, with a humorous glance at Carmold. "This is indeed a coat of many colors. That is ink upon the sleeve—a cheap grade, and watered at that. Here we have coffee, and this looks very much like egg. He may have appeared foppish in the semi-darkness," he concluded, "but in broad daylight the owner of this coat must have looked as shabby as a street beggar." He placed the coat flat upon the table and subjected it to a methodical examination.

"Of course, we've been all over that coat down at New Scotland Yard," said Miller, "but I know that sometimes you can find a thing that a hundred others in succession have overlooked, Dr. Thorndyke, and as our investigation is taking us nowhere, I thought I could not do better than let you have a try at tracing the owner of the coat."

"It is certainly either of foreign cut," observed Thorndyke, "or a survival from the 1860's—which, in view of its dilapidated condition, is not a wholly unreasonable surmise. There is no maker's label, nor does it appear that there ever was one." From an inner pocket of the coat he withdrew a folded linen handkerchief and spread it out upon the table. By the soiling along the creases, it was obvious that the handkerchief had been carried in that pocket for a very long time without receiving the attentions of the washerwoman. It was otherwise perfectly clean except for a number of short, curved hairs clinging to its surface.

"He has evidently been in the habit of cleaning his pince-nez with this handkerchief," remarked Thorndyke, "for these little hairs, all of a uniform length and curvature and all tapering to a point at each end, are unmistakably eyebrow or eyelash hairs."

When he had taken possession of two or three of these hairs and carefully sealed them up in a seed envelope, he replaced the handkerchief and turned his attention to the other pockets. The findings were extremely sparse. In the left-hand pocket was a worn and greasy leather case containing absolutely nothing but the cabinet photograph of a middle-aged lady, charming in a somewhat austere fashion. Though the margins of the portrait were frayed and discolored, the photographer's name—Willaerts of Antwerp—was clearly legible, and Thorndyke raised an inquiring eye to Miller.

"Nothing there," said the superintendent with a shake of his head. "Out of business for many years, records not available. The photograph is at least twenty years old."

"What have we here?" I asked, as Thorndyke produced from the opposite pocket what appeared to be a wad of waste paper.

"What we have here," he replied, "is an ounce of coarse tobacco done up in a screw of newspaper—a Dover paper, dated six weeks back. Thanks to the skill and discretion of the persons who examined this paper at the Yard, it is possible to be relatively certain that it this paper at the Yard, it is possible to be relatively certain that it was originally twisted by a left-handed person. Of course you are already looking into that?"

"We are," said Miller, "but I needn't tell you that in six weeks' time a Dover newspaper may have been to the ends of the earth and back, and if we must undertake an all-out search for a left-handed tobacconist it will be as a last resort. But we did weigh the tobacco, and it's a full ounce—in fact, a few grains over—which suggests that he had just purchased it."

Thorndyke took up a few shreds of the tobacco between his thumb and forefinger and sniffed at them before depositing them in a specimen jar. "It seems fresh enough," said he. "Did your fellow traveler smoke in the train, Mr. Carmold?"

"No, sir, and it's a mercy he did not, for I can't abide tobacco myself, and with the window shut I should have quite suffocated if he had been smoking. No, sir, he looked neither right nor left, but just sat staring at a paper in his lap, which it was too dark to read."

"I suppose you could not tell what paper it was?"

"No, but it looked something like one of those little French papers, all long and narrow."

At these latter remarks Mr. Miller had suddenly pricked up his ears, and now he gave Carmold a sharp look. "We've heard nothing of that paper before now, have we, Mr. Carmold?" he asked pointedly.

"I've only just remembered it. I told you about his luggage—a sort of portmanteau with a leather strap, and a smaller case that he placed next to him on the seat."

"The railway carriage in which the murder was committed has been taken out of service," said the superintendent. "Nothing of the slightest importance has been turned up, though our men have taken the compartment in question literally to pieces. They did find a cloth cap, which had fallen under the seat and been overlooked earlier. It is evident that the murdered man was wearing that cap when he was struck down, for it has a patch of blood and hairs on the lining just where it would lie over the lethal wound. If you would like to come and examine the carriage this morning, Dr. Thorndyke, I am sure you are welcome to do so; otherwise we shall have to let the railway people put it back into service."

"Just when I am thoroughly absorbed in his coat, you ask me to chuck it up and go look at a railway carriage," grumbled Thorndyke good-naturedly. "Very well, but first let me take some samples of the lint from the pockets. It is almost certain to be useless, for the coat has not been cleaned or even brushed for months, and it will have acquired a pretty heterogeneous collection of dust and similar particulate rubbish, but we are obliged to make the examination all the same."

In a very few minutes he had secured the desired specimens, which did indeed look like gleanings from an assortment of dustbins. Having sealed them up in a series of carefully labeled packets, Thorndyke returned the coat to Miller and signified his readiness to proceed to the railway yard.

The fatal carriage had been led off into a siding above Broad Street Station, closely adjacent to Appold Street. As we approached by a path alongside the metals, I observed two men in earnest conversation outside the door of the carriage. One of them was a policeman in uniform, who touched his helmet respectfully to the superintendent; the other presently identified himself as an official of the London, Midland and Scottish Railway.

When the official, whose name was Shorter, learned that he was talking to Superintendent Miller of the C.I.D., he expressed considerable satisfaction at the meeting. "I hope, sir, that you are going to let us put this carriage back into service," said he. "I gather that the decision rests with you, for whenever I have made inquiries of the detectives who have been prowling about the station and pulling the carriage to pieces, I have been told that they can do nothing without the approval of Superintendent Miller."

"You may have your carriage back in a very few minutes," Miller announced genially. "These gentlemen are scientific investigators who would just like to look over the compartment where the murder took place."

The railway official, now more cordial than ever, invited us with "nods and becks and wreathed smiles" to enter the carriage, and went off in the direction of the station. As we were mounting the iron stair, we met a mechanic just coming out, a grease-besmeared young fellow clutching a bulky tool chest.

"Here, you," said Miller sharply to the man, "you're not one of our people, are you?"

"It's all right, superintendent," said the police officer, touching his helmet again. "This chap is a regular mechanic of the London, Midland and Scottish line, and Mr. Shorter brought him round himself. They wanted to see to the stuck window while the carriage was out of service."

"And have you put it right?" asked Miller, turning again to the mechanic.

"Yes, indeed, sir. Only fancy, someone had dropped a penny piece into the slot behind the catch." From his slight hesitation before announcing the value of the offending coin, I judged that it was probably at least a half-crown, and I further speculated that it reposed at that moment in an inner pocket of his grimy outfit, whence it would very likely pass ere long into the hands of some jovial tapster.

The scene of the tragedy looked much like any other first-class compartment, except that the floor had been swept and the seats brushed up to a degree of spruceness not often seen by the traveler. In contrast to the spic-and-span appearance of the compartment itself, the window bore a number of oily fingermarks, for the mechanic had evidently not considered it part of his duties to clean it after making his repairs.

Thorndyke began his investigations at the window, releasing its catch and moving it up and down several times in its grooves. With his Coddington lens he examined first the dark smudges upon the glass and then some shallow abrasions in the finish of the frame just next to the catch, even scraping a few loose fragments of varnish into a seed envelope and storing them away in his pocket case.

"Thoroughness, you see, is Dr. Thorndyke's passion," remarked Miller in a bantering tone to Carmold, who stood next to him in the passage. "Even though the murder took place the night before last, the doctor wants to assure himself that this mechanic who has just been here, and who probably never clapped eyes on this carriage in his life until an hour ago, is not mixed up in the business in some way."

Without taking the least notice of these words, Thorndyke went about his work, an inscrutable and introspective smile just perceptible on his lips. Having taken a few measurements with a spring tape, he made a sketch of the compartment in his notebook. Then he went down on his hands and knees and peered under the seats with the aid of a little pocket lamp.

He next turned his attention to the luggage racks. After spreading his pocket handkerchief on one of the seats so as not to soil the newly brushed upholstery, he grasped the ornamental boss at one extremity of the rack overhead, hauled himself up, and, standing upon the seat, shone his lamp into the gloomy recess above the rack. Presently he repeated the proceeding on the opposite side of the compartment, and then signified to Miller that he had concluded his researches.

The body of the murdered man had been taken from the railway station to the mortuary at St. Bartholomew's Hospital for the post-mortem examination, and there it still lay awaiting identification. As the hospital was almost on our way, Thorndyke proposed a visit there. Miller pleaded other business, but readily assented to our examination of the corpse and its personal effects. Mr. Carmold begged to advise us that he had already seen quite enough of the deceased gentleman, and would be at his hotel if required.

Nevertheless we all set out together from the station in a taxicab. Somewhat to my surprise, Thorndyke seemed to take a profound interest in a morning paper someone had left upon the seat. Normally he eschewed newspapers—in fact, he had more than once, in moments of levity, referred to journalists and their readers as, respectively, "the Scribes and the Pharisees." But the reason for his sudden absorption in matutinal ephemera became obvious when he held up a blatant headline for us all to read: SHOCKING MURDER IN A RAILWAY CARRIAGE.

"There is a very full treatment of the case here," he said, "though I see no mention of the coat."

"Nor will you find any in the afternoon papers," commented Miller. "That is our trump card, and we have gone to some lengths to assure that Fleet Street does not get hold of it before we have played it."

For the remainder of the journey Thorndyke appeared completely immersed in the newspaper account of the murder. Before we parted from the others, he invited them to come round to our chambers again that evening, when he hoped to be able to hand Miller the solution of the shocking murder and to restore to Carmold his errant coat.

"And what about the owner of this other coat?" asked Miller, thumping the suitcase that lay in his lap.

"I think I can promise to introduce him to you," said Thorndyke. "And provided that you bring his property along and are prepared to give it up to him, there should be no difficulty about persuading him to return Mr. Carmold's coat."

Miller subjected Thorndyke to a hard scrutiny and appeared to be on the verge of asking some very pointed questions, but, evidently foreseeing that they would only receive evasive replies, he held his peace and promised to call at the appointed hour.

Thorndyke had bidden the driver to pull up in Newgate Street just in front of the General Post Office, and when we alighted he entered that sprawling edifice before proceeding to the hospital. After a preliminary stop at one of the writing tables, he handed in a telegraph form, whereupon the clerk, a peppery little man with a tic, having first raised some objections which Thorndyke speedily answered, collected the fee and went off to dispatch the message, muttering something to himself about "talking like a Christian."

By great good fortune we encountered Dr. Austrin, the police surgeon, in the Pathological Department of St. Bartholomew's Hospital. The surgeon, an old friend of ours, accompanied us into the mortuary and gave orders for the attendant to bring out the body and to unlock the cabinet in which the clothing had been placed. In response to a query from my companion, Austrin confirmed that the deceased had suffered from stenosis of the aortic valve.

"In fact, it was that which killed him, as much as the blow on the head. It is true that there is a depressed fracture of the occipital bone, but the inward displacement of the inner table is very slight, and the amount of hæmorrhage might almost be called negligible, if that word could ever be used of bleeding inside the cranium. I think it unlikely that such a wound would have proved mortal to a healthy man. Probably the shock of the blow was just sufficient to upset fatally an already deranged state of the circulation."

He drew back the heavy canvas cover from the trolley that the attendant had wheeled into the viewing room, revealing the body of a very tall, muscular, barely middle-aged man. The flesh of the face had begun to sink in, and the skin was mottled all over by far-advanced rigor mortis. Thorndyke stood for some moments regarding the body with that air of solemnity and reflection that he customarily wore in the presence of death.

"What do you make of this?" he asked at length, raising the deceased's right hand from the trolley. The surgeon and I both drew near and examined the member in question. Two fingernails were split right down to the quick, and a third appeared to have been bent back and a part of its free margin torn away. The index finger of the left hand showed a similar injury.

"He must have tried to defend himself," said Austrin with a shrug. He watched in indulgent silence while Thorndyke took some scrapings from the injured nails and carefully stored them away.

"Still," I objected, "it is apparent that he was struck from behind. And then, for all his cardiac trouble, he had the frame of a fish porter, and unless his assailant were stark mad he would be sure to take him unawares."

Austrin grunted a dubious assent. "How the deuce do you take a man unawares in a first-class compartment?" he asked.

"Why, he may have been asleep, just as the other man, Carmold, appears to have been at the time of the murder. He may even have been struck down in the passage and his body deposited in the compartment afterward."

"I wonder," came the voice of Thorndyke from across the room, "whether my learned junior can explain why a man would board a train in the middle of the night with nothing but the clothes on his back, six shillings ninepence halfpenny, a cheap out apparently brand-new watch, and a brass latchkey on a short chain adorned at its nether end with a small piece of indifferently executed scrimshaw." As he spoke he laid out the deceased's scanty effects in a row upon the table.

"The police are fairly certain that he was robbed," said Austrin. "With no luggage in evidence, no return ticket on his person, and barely enough money to exist on for a couple of days in London, that seems an inescapable conclusion. I say, Thorndyke, you seem deucedly interested in that coat."

"Yes, I fear I have rather got coats on the brain lately," replied my colleague. He made no direct reference to the one that he had examined earlier that morning—in compliance, I supposed, with Miller's tactic of secrecy on that subject. In what seemed a wholly superfluous expenditure of time and energy, he removed samples of the lint from the various pockets of the deceased's clothing and stored away each in its own seed envelope before taking his leave of Austrin and the silent occupant of the trolley.

Our lunch was rather an abbreviated affair, for Thorndyke seemed eager to return to our chambers and undertake the examination of the morning's harvest of specimens. When I reflected that Miller and Carmold were expected at eight o'clock, and that Thorndyke had practically promised to hand over the murderer to the superintendent and the missing coat to his young charge, I could not but marvel at the magnitude of the task that lay before him, and at his extraordinary confidence in his ability to perform it in so short a time.

All the afternoon Thorndyke and his familiar, Polton, were closeted in the laboratory, and though they both put in a brief appearance at teatime, they were about as communicative as a couple of undertaker's mutes. Around half-past five a telegram arrived for Thorndyke, which I had no doubt was the reply to his own of the morning. Resisting the temptation to unseal the envelope (a proceeding that would infallibly have been detected by my astute senior), I carried it up to him, and observed a smile of satisfaction spread across his normally impassive features as he perused the flimsy and thrust it away in his pocket. Though I made some effort to spy out the lay of the land by casting a sharp eye over the various pieces of apparatus set out upon the long laboratory bench, I could make no more intelligent surmise as to the overall purport of the operation than an aborigine who had blundered into a piano factory.

By suppertime Thorndyke appeared to have completed the bulk of the investigation, for both he and Polton wore contented smiles which, for sheer smugness, would have put the Cheshire cat to shame. Just as the Treasury clock was striking eight our guests appeared. After a brief and almost perfunctory ritual involving the whisky decanter and siphon, Thorndyke led them away upstairs to the laboratory floor, intimating by a nod that my presence there would also be welcome. As I ascended the stairs at the rear of the party, I noted with some curiosity that Polton remained below, ostensibly engaged in putting the sitting room in order.

I had expected to witness some elaborate demonstration, and so, perhaps, had the superintendent, for he seemed disappointed when we entered the laboratory to find only a solitary microscope set out upon the bench. Very different was the effect produced upon Carmold by the spectacle of a complete chemical laboratory, with adjacent shops and stores, in the Inner Temple. He was quite dumbfounded, and stood peering wonderingly round at the long, businesslike bench, and serried ranks of reagent bottles, and the rows of gleaming chemical glassware upon the shelves.

As Thorndyke stepped up to the bench, I noted that the instrument standing there was a comparison microscope—actually a pair of microscopes mounted side by side, with a common stage. The ordinary stage had been removed, and the instrument fitted with a warming stage and an adjustable mirror so placed as to cast light obliquely upon the specimens from above. As for the specimens themselves—one for each eye of the observer—they appeared to be mere transparent films of some viscous material spread thinly upon two glass plates.

When he had opened the valve that allowed hot water to circulate through the chamber under the stage, and taken a reading from the tiny thermometer mounted thereon, Thorndyke invited each of us in turn to peer through the twin barrels of the instrument. I know not what my companions made of the specimens, but to me their aspect under the microscope lenses was no more enlightening than when they were viewed by the naked eye. As I bent over the heated stage I was conscious of a warm, faintly aromatic vapor rising from the plates.

"What's it all about, then?" asked Carmold, taking a second turn at the instrument. "I say, though, it's different now—moving, like."

"The material is melting," explained Thorndyke. "By means of the comparison microscope Polton and I have verified that both specimens soften at exactly the same temperature, sixty-five degrees Centigrade, and that both are completely liquid at eighty degrees."

When we had all confirmed these observations, without in the least understanding their significance, Thorndyke shut off the gas jet under the water heater and carefully lifted the plates off the warming stage with a pair of tongs, placing them upon a shelf to cool. While he was doing so the laboratory bell rang sharply twice, but he appeared to take no notice. Instead, he went on with his exasperating explanations, which were no explanations at all.

"Not only can we state positively that the specimens on the two plates have identical melting points, but, taking that fact in conjunction with other observed physical properties, we can identify them both with some assurance as a resin produced by the larvae of the lac insect, *Carteria lacca.*"

"Good Lord, sir!" exclaimed Carmold in astonishment. "Is that going to lead to the solution of this beastly business, or is it just another mystery to add to the rest?"

Thorndyke made no answer but, smiling solemnly, ushered us back to the sitting room. Polton was nowhere in sight, but in the chimney corner an elderly gentleman with silver-rimmed pince-nez and waxed mustaches sat puffing his pipe in an attitude of contemplative abstraction. Miller and I paused a little awkwardly in the lobby, while Carmold stood stock still upon the threshold, his eyes fairly starting from their sockets.

Thorndyke advanced to greet the stranger and, after conversing with him for a few moments in fluent French, turned and presented him to us. "Gentlemen, allow me to introduce Monsieur Achille Lebesque, schoolmaster, lately of Ghent and presently stopping at the George Hotel, St. Albans. Monsieur Lebesque regrets that he has no English, but he will cheerfully answer questions put to him in French, German, Dutch, Latin, or Greek."

"I believe," said Carmold in an awed tone, addressing Thorndyke, "that you must be in league with the Powers of Darkness, for this is the very man with whom I came up in the train the night before last, and that is my coat that he is wearing at this moment."

At this, Miller's interest in Monsieur Lebesque became positively proprietorial. He took the chair just beside the one occupied by the Belgian, eyeing him sternly but refraining from any further display of constabulary zeal in expectation of some sort of explanation from Thorndyke.

Polton appeared presently with coffee and brandy for the newcomer and a plate of seed cakes, but these refreshments received scant attention amid the general curiosity. Thorndyke undertook to sort out the tangled strands of the affair. We all had at least a smattering of French, and although Monsieur Lebesque clung doggedly to the mistaken notion that the best way to be understood by Englishmen was to speak very loudly in Dutch—or, rather, the Flemish *patois*—we made shift to understand one another very well.

"At the outset," said Thorndyke, "it is necessary to observe that Monsieur Lebesque is not guilty of murder, not of any other crime more serious than stepping off the Edinburgh-London express at Willesden Junction in possession of another man's coat. But of that, more anon.

"The demonstration that you have just now witnessed in the laboratory showed that two specimens of material from very different sources displayed identical melting points. The specimens also behave in identical fashion in a variety of solvents. One of them consists of material that I took from under the fingernails of the body at the mortuary this morning, and the other I had collected a little earlier from the window of the compartment in which the deceased was apparently murdered.

"I say 'apparently,' for I hope to convince you that the death was entirely accidental." Miller frowned deeply, but said nothing. "As Monsieur Lebesque has told us, around one o'clock in the morning he left the compartment in which Mr. Carmold was sleeping in search of more comfortable quarters. We have heard that the compartment was exceedingly stuffy, and in case your acquaintance with French does not extend to the verb *ronfler*, I may just remark in passing that it means 'to snore.'"

Mr. Carmold, grinning a little foolishly, brushed up his exuberant sidewhiskers until he looked like a particularly jocular red fox, but made no comment.

"Some time afterward another passenger happened along. He must either have boarded the train at Leeds or Sheffield, or, like Monsieur Lebesque, have decided in mid-journey to change his accommodations. Entering the compartment occupied by Mr. Carmold, he at once perceived the desirability of opening the window. When it resisted ordinary efforts he endeavored to force it.

"We learned from the railway mechanic this morning that a coin had fallen into the catch mechanism. It seems likely that the traveler, observing that the window was not drawn up tight, attempted to unstick it by forcing it quite shut. The frame of the window was heavily coated with ordinary shellac, so that he must have had some difficulty in getting a purchase on it with his fingers. Remember that it was dark, and moreover the train may have lurched at the critical moment. He was apparently a man of great physical strength, and the abrupt loss of his grip on the window must have caused the upper part of his body to recoil with considerable violence so that his head struck the round boss at the end of the luggage rack above the seat. The size and shape of the wound as well as its location accord perfectly with that hypothesis. The state of the deceased's fingernails and the presence of material on them identical with the slightly abraded shellac upon the window frame afford further confirmation. Though powerful of limb, the deceased had a dangerous heart condition, and the force of the blow, which actually fractured his skull, was evidently sufficient to precipitate some irreversible derangement of the circulation. That is the opinion of Dr. Austrin, who performed the post-mortem, and I am entirely in agreement with it."

Miller regarded the Belgian with an eye from which the last vestiges of suspicion had not entirely melted away. "This gentleman says he left the express at Willesden Junction, does he?" he asked.

"He does. That explains why he was not found by the detectives who boarded the train at Broad Street Station. In his search for a cooler and quieter compartment, Monsieur Lebesque encountered a Frenchman who had resided in London long enough to have some understanding of the railway system. When his fellow traveler learned that his destination was St. Albans, he advised Monsieur Lebesque to leave the train at Willesden Junction."

"The Edinburgh-London express," Miller announced gravely, "does not stop at Willesden."

"It did so yesterday morning. A local train of the North London line was running late and was actually passing over the junction as the express approached. The express was obliged to stop until the permanent way was clear before proceeding to Broad Street Station, and in that interval Monsieur Lebesque and his friend persuaded a guard to unlock the carriage door and hand him out of the train. As it was a somewhat irregular proceeding, the guard no doubt resolved to keep quiet about it—especially, when he learned that the man was suspected of murder.

"But for reasons that you already know, I am confident that even when the deceased has been identified, the only conclusion that a coroner's jury can possibly entertain will be 'death by misadventure.' "

"He has been indentified," said Miller. "Not two hours ago a Mrs. Leggatt arrived from Leith and identified him as her father, Josiah Whitbread. He has not been quite right in his mind of late, according to the daughter, and has wandered off once or twice before, but never before so far astray as this. She read of the supposed murder in a London paper, and as her father had not been seen since the day before yesterday, she thought it likely that he and the body in the railway carriage were one and the same man."

"You might have told us that before," said Thorndyke in a tone of genial reproof. "You are growing positively secretive, Miller."

"Why, Dr. Thorndyke, it is generally a waste of breath to tell you anything, for you seem to know it all beforehand. And in any event, I was not so interested in the identity of the dead man as in that of the proprietor of this coat, though I see now that that was merely a red herring.

"Talking of the coat—how in the name of all that is wonderful did you succeed in tracing its owner among the eight million inhabitants of the metropolis in a matter of eight or ten hours?"

Carmold appeared positively breathless in anticipation of Thorndyke's answer, while the Belgian, who clearly sensed its purport, broke out in a broad smile and puffed his pipe with an air of ineffable drollery.

"You are not going to like the answer to that question, Miller," Thorndyke warned him. "But as in the course of time it must inevitably come to the ears of the police, you may as well have it from me. I learned the identity of the owner of the coat from that copy of the *Times* that we found in our taxicab this morning."

Amid a storm of incredulous protests, my colleague turned down a few leaves of our own copy of the *Times*, which lay upon the table, and pointed to two advertisements neatly outlined in red:

> Lost, Edinburgh-London express, Tuesday night: grey morning coat containing valued portrait photograph; if found apply Achille Lebesque, George Hotel, St. Albans.

And, directly below:

> Found, Edinburgh-London express, Tuesday night: grey morning coat containing pack of playing cards and silver penknife, initials P.C.; owner apply Achille Lebesque, George Hotel, St. Albans.

"These advertisements appeared in nearly all the morning papers," said Thorndyke, "and in the *Evening Standard* and the *Star*."

"Do you mean to say," cried Miller, "that we have had every police officer and railway guard from Dover Cliffs to John o'Groat's searching for the owner of this coat—"he bestowed a contemptuous kick upon the suitcase that reposed on the floor before his chair "—when all the while the name of the owner has been staring us in the face out of every paper in London? Snakes! It's enough to make a man turn pastrycook!"

"An instance of the devastating effect of bias," observed Thorndyke demurely. "The police were so thoroughly convinced that a murder had been committed by the owner of the coat they never imagined that he would advertise to recover it. But Monsieur Lebesque, who could not read the London papers, knew nothing of the supposed murder. Moreover, the persons to whom he applied for assistance, and who helped him draft his advertisements, could not have known that a coat had been found in the compartment with the dead man, for the simple reason that the police very carefully withheld any information on that point from the journalists."

"Snakes!" exclaimed the superintendent again. "What a sell! And are we to understand that all your mumbo-jumbo with little packets of dirt and muck from this place and that have had nothing to do with finding Monsieur Lebesque here?"

"Nothing whatever," admitted Thorndyke. "But of course I had no way of knowing at the commencement of the investigation which data would prove useless, and so I was obliged to consider them all. Have you ever seen a dog trying to follow up a scent at a crossroads? Even when he has exhausted all but one possible branching of the route, he methodically applies his nose to that one also before following it up. The dog, you see, is unencumbered by anything resembling the faculty of logical reasoning, and though that deficiency may on rare occasions place him at a disadvantage in his dealings with the species that goes upon two legs and keeps kennels, it at least ensures his absolute freedom from prejudice, preconception, and bias."

"I say—well done, sir!" exclaimed Carmold, rapping the table with his fist. "The superintendent may scoff if he likes, but I believe you are endowed with faculties that other men do not enjoy—nor dogs either! And now, if Mr. Miller will kindly return Monsieur Lebesque's coat, I shall be happy to resume possession of my own before our delightful Belgian schoolmaster—" this with a cordial smile and a bow in the direction of the gentleman in question "—spills any more of his ashes over the front of it."

There ensued a ceremony that must have appeared to one outside our little company like some grotesque species of round dance executed by a troupe of lunatics. Miller first produced the tattered and spattered coat from his suitcase and tendered it to Monsieur Lebesque. Then, with Thorndyke and me acting as *valets de chambre*, the Belgian in his turn removed Carmold's coat and restored it to its owner—whereupon that gentleman divested himself of the coat he had borrowed from Miller, who carefully folded it away in the suitcase.

When everyone was clothed again in his proper raiment, we reversed the proceedings of the wayward children of Israel, as, having risen up to play, we sat down to eat and drink.

Helen Fislar Brooks
A Woman's Work Is Never Done

Cobb Meekins sprawled in the shade of the old persimmon tree, his hat over his eyes, lifting a languid hand now and then to brush away a buzzing Junefly or a prospecting ant, as he listened to the steady whack-thud, whack-thud, which came from the hollow where his land cornered with True Bingham's.

The toe of a boot nudged his elbow.

"Who's there?" Cobb asked, not moving.

"Want to go fishin'?" Billy Bod Shaker's voice inquired.

"I been."

"Catch anything?" That was Luke Lacey's drawl.

"Cat."

"How big?"

"Twenty pound."

Silence for a moment.

Then, "Sounds like old True's workin' fit to kill over to his place," Billy Bod said, "What's he doin' now?"

"Poundin' post holes, I reckon," Cobb murmured.

Old True's already got the finest farm and the most land of anybody around, he thought, but he don't aim to be satisfied, looks like, until he's fenced in the whole valley.

"Where'd you say you hooked that cat?" Luke asked.

"Didn't."

"Twenty-two pound,huh?" Billy Bod's voice was rich with admiration.

"Twenty-five." Cobb lifted his hat briefly. "Pulled him in the other side of the river bend."

After they'd gone, he settled back and resumed his resting.

Cobb was a small man with mild blue eyes, a stubble of tawny whiskers, and hair to match, but he was large with ambition and extravagant dreams: a new roof on the sagging cabin—could he but spare the time to it; a herd of fat cattle grazing his hillside—did he but have the strength to clear off the rock, or if the price of stock would only go back to what it used to be. In his Pap's day, he'd heard tell, a good critter could be bought for seven-eight dollars. Figured out to about a cent a pound.

A good pole barn full of bottom-land hay would be mighty fine, too—if only he could call to mind where he'd laid his axe a year or so back. Couldn't cut poles or chop out brush and sprouts without an axe. And at one end, was it cleared, he'd have him a corn patch that would crop out twenty gallons to the acre and still leave enough over to feed all the hogs and chickens a man could want.

Then, if he had all that, he'd buy some store clothes and go courting. It would mean square dancing and sitting up straight, knees together, on a slat-back chair two-three nights a week, both of which were mighty hard on a man's legs and spine, but somebody would have to hoe that corn and slop the pigs and feed the chickens and such—it wouldn't be fitting a man should do a woman's work.

"Yes, sir," he murmured, "with a little luck, I could have just as much as old True—maybe more. But ain't no sense killin' myself, like he's doin'. Somethin's bound to happen, sooner or late. My Pap always said it was a long road didn't have no turnin'. I got plenty of time. I'm only thirty-two or thereabouts."

On this comforting thought, he fell asleep.

At noon, he awakened, considerably restored—but hungry. Stepping over the gaps in the broken flooring of the lean-to porch, he entered the cabin, set out the jug, and fried the catfish. It didn't quite fill the pan, but if he held back, he decided, he could stretch it enough to take care of his supper, too.

Refreshed and strengthened by the food and drink, he returned to his resting place under the tree. Then, noting the sound of True's pounding and whacking had changed to an occasional flinty ring of pickaxe on rock, he rose and wandered toward the hollow, reflecting he'd best see what True was up to. That fence was apt to be scooching over ten-twenty feet on the wrong side of the line.

True was nowhere in sight, but whatever he was up to had nothing to do with post holes. A shovel and a length of rope with a bucket tied to one end lay next to a high hill of dirt alongside a circular hole. It made Cobb tired just to look at the piled up earth.

Must have took a sight of heavin' and haulin', he thought.

Off by itself, under a hickory tree, was a small wooden box. Cobb lifted the lid. Dynamite.

He ambled over to the hole and peered in. It was a real deep hole. Heaped to one side on the bottom was a smaller mound of earth, mixed with clay. True sat astride a jutting hump of rock in the center, ankle deep in fresh-dug clods, a pickaxe held loosely between his knees. Naked to the waist, he sagged forward, staring morosely at the ground, a lock of dark hair dangling over his forehead.

Cobb hunkered down on his heels. "You drop a dime?" he inquired politely.

True jumped to his feet and looked up. Then he scowled, leaned on the pickaxe, and wiped his arm across his face. "Didn't hear you come up. Any fool can see I'm diggin' a well," he grunted, red-faced, as though it was an effort to speak.

Cobb regarded him sadly. Everything a man could want; enough money to burn a green stump in a pourdown, from what he'd heard, a tight-chinked cabin, a fine barn, fat stock eating off the best meadowland in the county and with the river running through it handy as you please, to boot, to say nothing of a good, strong woman like Ivy—handsome in the bargain, with that yellow hair and all—to wash his clothes, cook his vittles, clean the fish, and dress out the squirrels he'd bring home, did he ever go fishing or hunting—then hoe the garden, milk the cow, and still find time to work right along with him in the fields. And now, he had to have a well, besides. Bound and determined to have all there was in the world or die trying.

Which it looked like he was about ready to do, the way he was flushed up and sweating.

"Ain't you got nothin' else to do—like sleepin'?" True snapped.

Cobb let it pass. "Was it me, I'd of had a witcher," he suggested mildly.

True gave him a filthy look. "Old man Austin witched this spot, dang him. And was it you, you'd be off fishin'. Why ain't you?"

"I done been. Caught a thirty-pound cat. I'd a brought you a chunk, if I'd knowed."

"Did, huh?" For a moment True looked almost wistful, then he whacked the pickaxe against the rock. "You're a liar. Ain't been a thirty-pound fish in that river since I was a younglin'," he stated flatly.

"I've et, anyway. Ivy fetched it to me on her way to the bog. She's pckin' berries down there, today." He paused and squinted up at Cobb. "If you'd knowed what?"

"That you was fool enough to dig yourself in so deep. How you aimin' to get out?"

"Ivy's goin' to fetch the ladder when she's done berryin'," True reseated himself on the rock. "That won't be for two-three hours, though, and I'm hung on this thing. Can't do no more till I blast."

Cobb, clicking his tongue against his teeth, studied True thoughtfully. A fool, that's what he was; working so fast he finished two hours ahead of when he'd figured to—and then brooding because he couldn't go right on flailing. Honed fine as a skinning knife, his muscles knotted worse than a pieced-out fishline ... Bound and determined to kill himself.

Cobb straightened resolutely. Least he could do was lend the man a hand. After all, he was their nearest neighbor and wasn't no woman, not even Ivy, goin' to be able to run the place alone.

He fetched the dynamite. "I can haul you out with the rope, once you get it set," he said, opening the box. "You want one stick or two?" He peered over the edge inquiringly. "Now, ain't no call to act like your jaw hinges was busted."

"You been layin' out in the sun?"

"I don't hold with doin' a mule's work, if that's what you mean," Cobb replied with dignity, "but I set my mind to a thing, I can do it."

"Then you'd best set your mind to something that don't take muscle."

"You got legs to climb the sides with while I hold, ain't you?"

True considered. "Yep, I could—," he said slowly, visibly wavering. Then, "Why you offerin'? Tain't like you."

Cobb shrugged. "Neighborly thing to do, ain't it? Help a friend?"

"Tell you what." True stood up. "Let's give it a try first, just to make sure."

Cobb hesitated. Then he untied the bucket and let down the rope. Gripping his end of it tightly with both hands, he dug in his heels. "Ready."

True grabbed hold and climbed.

"By golly, I didn't think you had it in you." He was actually grinning as he scrambled over the edge. "All right, let me down again. No sense wastin' time."

Cobb thought one stick should do it, but True said to put two in the bucket.

Cobb lowered it carefully, pulled up the empty bucket, took it off, and let the rope down once more.

True whistled softly as he wedged the dynamite into a crevice under a projecting point of the rock. "Let's make tracks for your place when we get done here," he slanted an oblique glance upward. "Somethin' I want to talk over with you."

Figures it's a good time to try and deal me out of my place, Cobb thought. That's gratitude for you.

True lit the fuse.

"Now!" He grabbed the rope.

Cobb dropped his end of it into the hole and ran.

"Hey!" True's shout, though somewhat muffled, reached him clearly enough. It was a mixture of surprise, rage, and anguish.

Cobb looked back over his shoulder. Fingers appeared, clawed briefly at the edge of the pit, then vanished as it crumbled. He felt a swift stab of admiration.

For a man in True's shape, that was a mighty fine jump, he thought. Must have been close to three feet, straight up.

He'd reached the stake which marked the line between his place and True's, when the blast came, shattering the quiet of the valley. Throwing himself flat, he lay panting. When he heard Luke's and Billy Bod's voices as they came hurrying around the river bend and Ivy calling, "True?" as she approached on the run from the bog below the hill, he rose, drew a deep, sustaining breath, and reversed his direction.

They all came together at the well in a dead heat.

"True!" Ivy stared at the arm protruding from the debris. "He caved in the well," she said, stupidly.

"What was he doin' in a well?" Luke demanded.

"Never mind that. We got to get him out." Billy Bod dropped to his knees and started scrabbling at the rubble.

Cobb touched Ivy's shoulder. "Come away," he said softly. "It ain't fittin' you should see."

"Is he dead?" she whispered.

"Looks as though." Cobb pitched his voice to the proper tone of tender condolence.

By some miracle, however, True was still alive when he was dug out. By then, quite a crowd had gathered. As the word was passed, Cobb gulped and paled, but it went unnoticed. Everyone was gaping at True.

"Look! He's openin' his eyes. He's tryin' to say somethin'," Billy Bod breathed.

The women, who'd taken charge of Ivy, led her forward.

"Cobb—" True gurgled. Cobb—" his eyes closed.

Cobb somehow got hold of himself and rose to the emergency. "Stand back, ever'body," he said importantly. "He wants a last word with *me*."

The women pulled Ivy back, the men retired to a respectful distance.

Removing his hat reverently, Cobb knelt beside True and leaned down so close their noses almost touched. Under cover of the hat, he placed his thumb on True's larynx. "Yes, old friend?" he asked, tenderly.

True's lids fluttered. "Why?" he whispered. His eyes opened.

Cobb gazed back at him silently.

True raised a mangled hand and pawed the air. "She'll fix you," he wheezed in Cobb's ear. "You ain't going' to get away with—"

Cobb clamped down his thumb, under cover of his hat. "Yes, sir," he turned his head and looked at Ivy, nodded solemnly, "I sure will. You have my word on it, old friend."

True gave a final gurgle and lay still.

Cobb lifted his thumb and rose, noting with satisfaction the dumbstruck look on the faces of those present.

It had worked out better, all the way, than if he'd contrived the whole thing ahead of time, he reflected, bowing his head, his hat pressed to his heart in an attitude of silent tribute. Just proved that when a man planned on big things long enough he was primed to take hold quick on whatever Dame Chance offered when she knocked, finally. No hill woman was going to disrespect her man's deathbed wish, made before witnesses. Duty-bound, that's what she was. Wasn't going to be any might-have-been rivals come calling, neither. Not that he'd have had to fret; Ivy was lucky to get him—but this way . . .

He lifted his head, replaced his hat, and threw back his shoulders. Walking across to Ivy, he said, with quiet authority, "I'll take you home now, Ivy."

She went with him obediently, as one in a trance.

Even in a community where men of enterprise were a rarity, Cobb had easily been the most shiftless, and some of the others openly averred in his presence that the blast had scrambled True's brains, while others held that "No, sir, must be more to old Cobb here than we figured."

Cobb bore his place in the limelight with becoming modesty. "I look on it as a sacred trust," he declared solemnly.

Out of respect for the late departed, he was spared the rigors of square dancing and his sessions on a straight-backed chair were limited to a circumspect half hour, twice weekly. At these times, Ivy pieced quilt blocks and said little. In fact, Cobb decided, he'd seen cows with more sparkle than she showed, but he was well enough pleased with her. She was kind of clod-pated, even for a woman, but she smiled a lot and was easy to look at with those big, brown eyes and shimmer-shiny hair. And if she was dumb, she was also easy on the earpans. Wasn't anything in this world more wearying than a lot of witless gibble-gabble.

Everybody came to the wedding.

Although Ivy stood a head taller than he, Cobb felt they made a handsome couple as they spoke their vows; he, freshly shaved and wearing a new blue suit—bought on his lately acquired credit—his hair slicked down and his shoes polished as two apples at the fair . . . Ivy in a rose-sprigged dress which set off her fine figure, her hair brushed into curls on her neck.

That night, Cobb drifted off to sleep in the tight-chinked cabin; snug in a soft bed covered by a hand-sewn quilt, lulled by the sound of one of his calves bawling for its mother down in the meadow and by Ivy's long, yellow hair, tumbled on the pillow beside him, tickling his ear.

The next morning, after a good breakfast—the grits were hot, the side meat crisp—he rose from the table, stretched, and said, "That was a mighty fine meal, Ivy. Guess I'll go huntin'. Might get us a mess of squirrel meat."

Ivy pushed back her hair and smiled. "I had it in mind maybe you'd want to chop sprouts off your—I mean, our—bottomland."

Cobb stared at her as though she'd suggested it was a good day to burn down the barn.

"Woman, fetch me my gun," he commanded.

Ivy fetched the gun and whacked him over the head.

When he came to, she was tying on her sunbonnet.

She smiled at him, gently, kindly—and handed him the axe.

He spent the next three months clearing sprouts off his bottomland and rocks from his hillside. Then, he tore down the rickety cabin where he had lived a full and carefree life—dreaming his dreams and fishing when he wanted to—hauled the best of the boards and logs over to the barn, and built a lean-to shelter shed, cutting the rest for firewood. That done, he fenced his land on three sides, making the two places one.

He honed down fine as a skinning knife and his meager muscles became knotty as a pieced-out fishline.

Ivy worked right alongside of him and after his one try at sneaking away in the night, he gave up. She was not only bigger and stronger than he, she was rabbit-eared. And although she wasn't much for talking, she was a tornado when it came to action.

He lived in terror that someone might learn that when his woman said, "Frog," he jumped. Or that he might be caught helping with the milking and hoeing.

Then Ivy set him to digging out the well. When he'd dug so deep he couldn't climb out, she left him, finally, to work along.

"I'll fetch the ladder, come chore time," she told him with that wide-eyed, placid smile.

Cobb sat down on the bottom and thought about True. *Figured to hide at my place till dark, likely, and be long gone by the time she got this dug out and found he wasn't in it.* He sighed. *She's the devil's daughter, though, and woulda run him down, sure. I done him a favor, at that.*

"What you doin'?" a voice inquired.

Cobb jumped to his feet. "Oh, it's you." He squinted up at Billy Bod Shaker.

"I was fishin' and heard you whackin' and—"

"Look, Billy bod," Cobb said eagerly, "flag into the settlement and tell the sheriff to come get me, will you?"

Billy Bod blinked. "What for?"

"I want to give myself up for killin' True Bingham!"

It could have been purely restful in jail if it hadn't been for the keeper, who treated him like a hound dog too lacking to know the difference between a fox and a skunk.

Cobb was ready to go when the time came.

The sheriff asked if he had any last words.

Cobb looked at Ivy standing straight and tall in the front row, her yellow hair gleaming in the sun. She was smiling at the jailkeeper, who was staring at her admirinly.

Cobb shook his head.

He was smiling as they slipped the noose around his neck.

A. F. Oreshnik

Home Ground

Frank Basil got off the bus in St. Louis at two a.m. Basil was a fairly short man, only five foot seven, wearing a rumpled black suit and needing a shave. He was in his forties, and the dark bags under his weary eyes made him look every minute of it.

A small canvas satchel hung from his right hand and hit his leg as he walked toward the telephone booths. The satchel was full of paperback books and two more novels protruded from the side pocket of his wrinkled suit coat. One of them had a small strip of torn newspaper sticking out of it, showing he respected books too much to mark his place by folding a page corner. He had been connected with The Outfit in one minor capacity or another for over twenty years, but until recently books had been his chief source of excitement.

Basil stepped inside the first vacant booth and set the satchel at his feet. He dug a handful of small change from his pocket and spilled it onto the shelf beneath the telephone. He deposited a coin, dialed the operator, and placed a station-to-station call to Las Vegas. The telephone he called was on a private line in the penthouse of one of the luxury hotels along the Strip.

His call was answered by a woman who recited the number, then waited for him to state his business.

"Mr. Robben, please," he said, then added, before she could ask, "Frank Basil calling."

He had been calling that number at least twice a day for the last month, so he was well familiar with the routine.

Robben's gruff voice came on the line. "So you're still out there, are ya?"

"Yes, sir."

"Ya know ya can't run an' hide forever, don't ya?" Robben asked, as he always did.

"Yes, sir, I know that."

"Well . . .?"

"Can't we work something out, Mr. Robben? I'm real sorry about what I did. Honest, I am. I never did anything like that before. I'll make it up to you, I swear."

"Listen, creep," Robben said disdainfully. "It ain't the money; it's the principle o' the thing. You worked for me for fifteen years. You was trusted. An' what'd ya do? Ya took money what didn't belong to ya, and blew it on a horse race. It was like ya threw that fifty thousand dollars down a sewer. I gotta make an example of ya."

"Please, Mr. Robben," Basil pleaded.

"No," Robben said. "If I let ya get away with that, everyone in my organization would be tryin' somethin'. They'd have my bones picked clean in a week. My advice t'you is, take your medicine an' get it over with."

Basil hung up without replying. Take his medicine—that was a laugh. Medicine was supposed to cure, not kill. There was nothing Frank Basil wanted more than a cure for the situation his stupidity had gotten him into, but all Robben wanted was word of his death. It was as though they were speaking different languages.

Basil picked up the canvas satchel, left the terminal, then stopped at an all-night drugstore long enough to buy a cheap razor and some blades. He'd left his last room without pausing to pick up his clothes and toilet articles—and without paying the bill. He had overheard the desk clerk describing him to someone over the telephone and he hadn't stopped running until he had reached the bus station and had a ticket for St. Louis in his sweaty hand.

He had gotten out of Denver, but he knew his pursuers were close behind, and it was just a matter of time before they would be ahead of him as well.

He hurried toward the green neon sign of a hotel a block away, dragging the satchel of paperbacks. Except for his "luggage" he might have been mistaken for a derelict, and he knew it. That was why he had bought the cheap case in Denver and stuffed it with books.

The hotel had a lobby that was barely ten feet square. A self-service elevator stood open at that level, and an old man was on duty behind the registration desk. The place smelled of air freshener and decay.

"How much for a room with a bath?" Basil asked.

The clerk looked him over coldly, then gave a toothless smile. "I'll give ya the nun's rate," he said.

The room, on the second floor at the front of the building, had a view of the deserted street and the nearly empty parking lot opposite the hotel. The lot was closed and a chain had been drawn across the entrance. A drunken bum came lurching along the sidewalk on the far side of the street, and Basil watched him take a stumbling step over the chain and enter the lot. First he rattled the door of the attendant's shack, then he approached the closer of the two cars parked beside it. He walked around the car, trying all the doors, but they were locked. He had better luck with the second vehicle. One of its rear doors swung open and he crawled inside.

Frank Basil filed the scene away in his memory. If by some miracle he managed to elude Robben's killers for a few more weeks, he would probably be sleeping in parked cars, too. His cash was getting low, and he didn't dare use the credit cards he carried because of the trail they'd leave.

He went to the small bathroom and took off his clothes. He put his suit on metal hangers and hung it inside the shower stall, then turned on the hot water, checked to be sure the spray wasn't hitting the suit, and closed the curtain. While he washed his socks and underwear in the basin, hot steam took the wrinkles out of his suit.

It also took the crease out of his trousers, but he folded them carefully and spread them between the mattress and box spring on the bed. By morning, they would have a passable crease, he knew.

That left only his soiled shirt. Luckily, it was one of the wash and wear, drip-dry variety. He carried it into the shower and washed it before using the last sliver of hotel soap on his body. Then he placed the shirt on a metal hanger and hung it from the shower rod. When he finally got to bed, he was asleep as soon as he closed his eyes.

He dreamed he was being chased down a long, black tunnel by a monster with a searchlight. When the light filled every crevice, and there was no place for him to hide, he awoke abruptly and sat up in the bed. Bright sunlight was coming through the window. He rubbed his eyes and looked at his watch. It was noon.

He shaved and dressed, but by the time he was ready to leave it was still early. The check-out time posted on the inside of the door was two P.M. It was only twelve thirty. He would have to pay for that time, so he decided to use it.

He pulled a chair up to the window, found the novel he'd been reading, and settled down to wait. A truck rumbled by on the street, and he glanced up in time to see the drunk climb stiffly from the car in the parking lot. The lot was now almost filled, and an attendant was busy telling new arrivals where to park.

The derelict stretched once, then looked around with an exaggerated casualness. It was obvious he had something on his mind. At last he must have been satisfied that he wasn't being observed because he entered several cars, being careful to keep the shack between himself and the attendant, and rummaged through their glove compartments. Frank Basil figured he was hunting for parking meter change so he could buy a bottle of cheap wine.

At the front of the lot, directly across from the hotel entrance, a sedan was parked parallel with the street, taking up two parking spaces, instead of displaying its grille as the other cars in the line were doing. When the wino came to it he ducked down so the attendant couldn't see him and approached the car from the street side.

He eased the door open, then stumbled backward with an awkward, double-time shuffle as though he'd come face to face with a snake. He ended up in the middle of the sidewalk in a sitting position. Basil started to smile at his clumsiness, but the car door continued to swing open, revealing a man in a light blue suit, lying across the seat with a shotgun in his arms, and the drunk was staring openmouthed down its barrel.

The scene remained frozen for only a second or two before the shotgunner reached out and calmly pulled the door closed. The drunk struggled to his feet and scampered away without looking back. In a moment, the street was back to normal, but Frank Basil knew he was no longer being pursued—he'd been found.

Basil dropped his book to the floor and jerked back from the window. His mouth was suddenly dry. He stood motionless, but his mind was racing. If they knew he was in the hotel, they could just as easily know what room he was in. Did he dare leave it? Yes, there should be no danger there. If they had wanted to kill him in the hotel, they could have done it while he slept. Instead, they had chosen to wait for him outside. Why? Why would they do that? Of course! The hotel must belong to The Outfit, and that would explain how they had located him so quickly after he arrived.

He grabbed his satchel of books and left the room. The elevator stood open, invitingly, but he passed it up and took the stairway to the lobby. The old clerk from the night before was still stationed behind the desk. Even if Basil hadn't seen the waiting shotgunner, this would have been a tipoff. The man was there long after he should have been relieved because he would be able to recognize Basil quickly and give some kind of signal to the man or men waiting outside. To add more substance to Basil's suspicions, the clerk became far more startled and nervous at Basil's sudden appearance than he should have.

"Call me a cab," Basil ordered.

"Uh . . . there's a cab stand just a block north of here," the clerk said. "You'll—uh—be able to get one there without any trouble."

"I'd rather have the cab come here," Basil said. "Call one for me."

Reluctantly, the clerk turned to the ancient switchboard beside him and began to dial. Basil reached across the desk and put a hand on his shoulder. "It'll work better if you plug into an outside line," he said. One of the jobs he'd had as a teenager had been as night clerk in an Outfit hotel in Baltimore. He was familiar with switchboards.

"Oh, yeah, that's right," the clerk said.

Basil stood where he could see the street through the glass door and also keep an eye on the clerk without seeming to do it. As soon as the taxi pulled up at the curb, he dashed out, climbed into the back seat, and said, "Take me to the airport." He waited until the car was moving and the driver had dropped the flag, starting the meter, then added, "Try to make it fast, will you? I have an upset stomach and I think I may be sick." Basil knew that the one thing a cabbie dreads most is having to clean up after a sick passenger. That one line would make him drive faster than a fifty dollar bribe.

The cab picked up speed, and Basil turned his head in time to see the parking attendant get into the sedan beside the shotgunner. As long as they didn't know he knew they were this close to him, he figured he still had a chance. They would hold their fire, hoping for a clear shot at him when he was alone. Just as he wouldn't think of going to the police for help, they would avoid, at all costs, killing an innocent bystander. Hunters and hunted, they both had rules to follow.

As Basil predicted, the cab broke all speed records getting to the airport. The shotgunner and his companion were lost somewhere behind in the traffic. When the cab pulled up at the passenger terminal, they were nowhere in sight. Basil had no doubt they'd be along soon, though. They must have guessed where he was headed before the cab got away from them.

Basil paid the driver, grabbed his satchel, and rushed inside. He studied the arrival and departure times on display at the airline ticket counters and saw there was a flight leaving for Chicago in half an hour. He quickly bought a one-way ticket, then hurried through the metal detector into the safety of the departing passengers' lounge. No one with a weapon would be able to get near him.

He had time to smoke two cigarettes before his flight was called. As he left the lounge, he saw the shotgunner standing empty handed on the other side of the barrier, pretending to be looking somewhere else. Basil hid his nervousness and hurried to the waiting plane.

Basil knew the shotgunner hadn't been able to get on the flight because he'd been too far behind and hadn't known which one Basil was taking; but the man knew which one it was now, and he was probably already on the telephone. If there wasn't someone at O'Hare when he landed, there would be someone there soon afterward.

Basil swore under his breath. A fat lot of good it had done him to read crime and mystery novels most of his life. Not one of them had helped him. Not a single fictional hunt or chase had furnished him with a useful idea. The characters in books always got caught. Hiding in faraway places or big cities was never the answer, and the hunted were always conspicuous when they stopped in a small town. What was left? Nothing that Basil could see. Every avenue open to him seemed to have a dead end, literally.

The flight to Chicago was surprisingly rapid. It was a distance of less than three hundred miles, and it seemed the plane had no sooner left the ground at St. Louis than it was entering the traffic pattern at O'Hare. Basil was one of the first people into the terminal and since he had no luggage to claim, he left it immediately. All he had was the canvas satchel, and he was carrying that with him.

He found that a flight was leaving for New York City in a little over an hour. Because Robben's people knew where he was, he didn't have to worry about leaving a trail. He was able to purchase his plane ticket with a credit card that had been issued to one of Robben's business enterprises. He picked up his ticket and fled behind the shield of airport police and metal detectors, as he had done in St. Louis.

The thought of Robben's expression when he learned he was paying for his travel expenses might have made Basil smile, but it didn't. He was too busy trying to discover which of his fellow passengers might be following, to make identifications easier at the other end and to be sure he didn't give them the slip again. One thing was certain, they

would have plenty of time to arrange a reception for him at La-
Guardia. Basil's stomach was tight with apprehension.

The plane was already descending toward Buffalo when he discovered it wasn't a nonstop flight. It would be on the ground at
Buffalo for thirty minutes before continuing to New York City.

Buffalo, New York; he'd been running back and forth across the
country for a month and hadn't even thought of Buffalo. He had been
born there, had lived there until he was fifteen—perhaps the happiest
years of his life. He suddenly decided he wanted to see it again before
his life ended.

As soon as the plane was on the runway at Buffalo, he ignored the
stewardess's admonition to remain seated until the plane came to a
complete stop at the terminal. Instead, he crossed the aisle and took
a vacant seat next to the emergency door. When the plane slowed
to a crawl and began to turn onto the taxiway, he pulled the release
handle and jumped out onto the broad wing. He ran along it until he
saw grass, not pavement, beneath him. Then he slid down the shiny
surface to its trailing edge and jumped.

It had been like jumping off a building, but there must have been a
recent rain. The ground was exceptionally soft. He rolled once and then
got to his feet, paying no attention to the pain in his ankles. He knew
nothing was broken or he couldn't have stood.

One quick look around and he knew exactly where he was. He had
spent almost every weekend of his thirteenth summer at the airport.
Jets were just coming into use at the time, and the airport pigeons were
a hazard to the new aircraft. One small bird sucked into one of the
engines was enough to do thousands of dollars' damage and cause the
costly rescheduling of the flights. The airport was too near the
populated areas for firearms to be used, so a bounty of twenty-five
cents was placed on each bird and boys were encouraged to hunt them
with slingshots. Frank Basil had been one of them.

Basil began to run. He looked back once and found faces pressed to
the windows of the plane he had just left, but no one was attempting to
follow. Ahead was the Buffalo Aeronautical Corporation, the service
facility for small private and company-owned aircraft at the airport.
There were dozens of small planes parked to the east of the red brick
building, and a road and parking area was along the northern side.

Basil was in luck. He could see a taxi letting out passengers at the
entrance to the B.A.C. operations office. He tried to run faster, but he
was nearly out of wind. He slowed to a trot as the cab was turning
around, then he put on a burst of speed to get to the end of the building
before the cab reached it and was gone.

He was just in time. He waved it to a halt and scrambled into the
rear seat, heaving and gasping for breath.

"Where to, buddy?" the driver asked.

"Take me to . . . the . . . main passenger terminal," Basil said, then settled back to get his breath and compose himself while the cab took the rundabout route necessary to get him there. His right hand was clutching the worthless satchel of books.

His breathing quickly returned to normal, and he wiped the sweat from his face and brushed the grass from his suit. When the cab stopped, he climbed out and paid the driver. He stepped inside the terminal and went directly to a car rental desk. He figured The Outfit had surely known about the stop at Buffalo, even if he hadn't, and there had probably been someone on the plane with him as well. Right now, the last place anyone would look for him was inside the terminal building. After all, he'd risked a pair of broken legs to avoid it.

He surrendered a credit card and his driver's license to a young blonde girl at the rent-a-car desk. While she was making out the papers and having a sedan brought to the entrance, he went to a nearby booth and called Las Vegas.

"Hi, creep. Still runnin', are ya?" Robben said.

"Yes, sir."

"But not for long. Believe me, not for long."

"Can't we work this out, Mr. Robben?"

"It's bein' worked out," Robben said.

Basil returned to the car rental desk and was given a copy of the rental agreement and a key. The girl walked to the door with him to point out the sedan.

Two men went past, walking rapidly, as Basil was climbing into the car. One of them glanced at Frank Basil, looked away, then his head spun around in a classic double take.

Basil slammed the car door, started the engine, and pulled away, all in one unbroken motion. He went around the traffic circle and sped out Airport Drive toward the main road. As soon as he had seen the man's reaction, he'd realized he had made a blunder. Just because no one would be looking for him at the airport terminal didn't mean no one would see him. He had arrived before his pursuers had an opportunity to reorganize and take up the chase again—and he'd run right into two of them.

The traffic light was with him when he reached the highway. He made a right turn toward Buffalo and shot a quick glance at the road behind him. A yellow Corvette was speeding down the drive, passing the other cars as though they weren't moving. Basil didn't need three guesses as to who was in it.

He slammed his foot to the floor and kept it there. Half a mile later he flashed across Union Road and looked back to find the sports car was gaining on him. Some cars were blocking both right-hand lanes, so he crossed the double line and passed them with his horn blaring. There was a turnoff for the thruway, but he kept going. The quickest way to get fouled up would be to get on a road he didn't know well. He decided to stick with ones he'd ridden on his bicycle as a boy.

The sun was low on the horizon, and he was heading directly into it. That didn't help his ability to judge distance or anticipate traffic conditions. The glare on the windshield kept him from seeing other cars as well as he would have liked, so he made it easier for them to see him. He turned on his headlights and drove with his left foot tapping the floor switch from low beams to high and back to low again.

He traveled the mile from Union Road to Harlem Road in less than a minute, but traffic was getting heavier. He made a skidding left turn onto Harlem Road against the light and went back to standing on the accelerator. Behind him, the Corvette tried to follow his lead and got caught in a minor traffic jam.

At Walden Avenue he found a huge plaza had been built on the swampy marsh where he'd once hunted frogs, but the Corvette had taken up the chase again and was gaining. He was too busy looking for a way to lose his pursuers to think about the changes that had occurred since his youth. The road ahead went over several New York Central Railroad lines and Broadway Avenue, which ran parallel to the tracks. This looked like it might provide a chance to give the Corvette the slip. If he could make the sharp right turn at the far end of the overpass and double back before his pursuers reached the top, they might think he had turned at one of the streets farther along. By the time they learned otherwise, he could be on Broadway, putting some real distance between them.

Basil slammed on his brakes halfway down the overpass and managed to make the turn at the bottom, but he wasn't quite quick enough. The yellow Corvette came leaping over the top of the overpass while he was still in sight.

Basil floored his gas pedal again and his wheels spun wildly on the loose gravel of the exit road, causing the rear end to swing sideways. He had enough sense to let up on the accelerator until he gained traction, then straightened out the car and sped away. At Broadway the light was with him and he turned left, toward Buffalo. The Corvette was too powerful a car for him to lose on the open road. If he were going to do it, he knew, it would have to be on crowded streets with which he was familiar.

He soon had the rented car barreling along at sixty—seventy—eighty! But the Corvette not only kept up with him, it steadily closed the gap between them. Broadway was straight as a bullet, with railroad tracks running parallel to it on the right. Any turn was therefore limited to the left, but his speed and the dense flow of oncoming traffic ruled that out.

Then Basil remembered the underpass. Not far ahead, he recalled, Broadway dipped down abruptly, made a ninety degree right turn under the New York Central tracks, then made a sharp left on the other side. It was impossible to negotiate that dogleg turn at speeds above twenty-five mph, as numerous drivers had discovered. The center support for the railroad trestle had brought many speeding cars to an abrupt halt.

As soon as he remembered the hazard, Basil took his foot off the gas. The Corvette was directly behind him now, and the driver pulled out to pass. The second man had rolled down his window and Basil could see a shotgun barrel protruding. Then the road dipped, and the underpass was coming up fast.

Basil jammed on his brakes and the Corvette flashed by so quickly the men in it had no chance to shoot. They must have interpreted Basil's action solely as a tactic to evade them. The driver touched his brakes, causing his taillights to flare briefly, but he had to have been looking at Basil in his rear view mirror. He didn't use the brakes in earnest until the Corvette was less than ten yards from the turn—and it was far too late. The sports car smashed into the concrete retaining wall at sixty mph.

Basil managed to slow to thirty-five and, amazingly, it was enough. He was able to make the turn without wrapping the sedan around the center support. He kept going for a few hundred yards, then made a left turn and parked in a lot behind a long, red transit-company garage. He got out and walked back to the underpass.

On close inspection he saw that the turn had been improved a bit since he was a boy, but it was still formidable. Several cars had pulled up and the people from them were milling around the wreck. The entire front end was pushed in, compressing the car's length about three feet. The engine, the fire wall, and the seat were all mashed together in one dripping mess.

The condition of the dead men was bad,but Basil spotted something that was worse; a small radio antenna was sticking up out of the center of the trunk lid. The car had been equipped with a radio transmitter.

Basil turned away just as the police arrived and walked slowly back to his rented sedan. He sat in it for a while, thinking about the close call he'd had. The sun set and it got a little cool. He had no way of knowing whether the men had used their radio, or what the may have said if they did. He didn't know what he should do next.

Finally, he started the car and left the lot. He drove past the transit garage and kept going. The intersection at Broadway and Bailey was changed. The brownstone police station was gone from the southeast corner, and the large lot where the circuses used to pitch their tents was now occupied by a huge, white supermarket.

He turned onto Bailey and headed north. A fine rain—almost a mist—began to fall. Basil turned on his windshield wipers and drove slowly, comparing the stores and offices he passed with his quarter-century-old memories. There had been changes, a lot of them. He decided he might as well drive out to the Kensington section and see his old neighborhood. He might not get another chance.

He was half a dozen blocks from the Kensington Theater when an oncoming car slowed suddenly and made a U-turn behind him. He knew the chase was on again. The two men earlier must have used their radio after all, giving out a description of his car and its license number.

Basil turned the first corner he came to and raced down the residential street, using every ounce of power he could wring from his engine. As soon as he saw the other car turn behind him, he swung around another corner and continued to watch his rear view mirror. The car appeared behind him again, and he turned another corner, only this time he slammed on his brakes instead of speeding away. He pulled to the curb and backed up so that his license plate was concealed by another parked car. The rented sedan was a common make, model, and color. There was one like it on every block. He was sure his pursuers would think he had reached the next intersection and turned. He lay across the seat and waited.

He heard the car turn the corner. Its lights swept past him and someone yelled. He didn't wait to find out what had given him away. He pushed open the curbside door and ran into the nearest driveway before they could get out of their car.

Coincidence, luck, fate, whatever—the home beside him was the one in which he'd been born. When he turned the corner of the building he ducked his head, as he always had, to avoid the low steel cable his father had strung up to replace the clothesline that was always breaking. It was too dark to tell if the cable was still there, but he'd soon know. There were running feet close behind him.

An exterior stairway was attached to the rear of the building. He located it by touch and began to climb just as someone rounded the corner of the alley and let out a strangled cry. The cable was still there, all right, and it must have nearly torn his head off. The man was making gurgling sounds, and he'd stopped advancing.

Basil moved as quietly as he could to the second landing and waited. He heard the cautious scrape of feet aong the driveway, then a voice called softly: "Tony? Are you all right, Tony?"

There was no answer.

Lightning flashed far to the south and it must have reminded the man of his cigarette lighter. He clicked it on, and the long, blue flame lit up the yard. The first man was flat on his back with a shotgun beside him. His face was purple. He had hit the cable with enough force to crush something in his throat. The second man set his weapon down and went to him.

There were three potted plants lined up along the railing in front of Basil. He picked up the largest one, took aim, and let it fly at the back of the man's head. Fear and tension forced a nervous laugh from his lips as he let it go. The man heard him, started to turn, and the pot smashed into the side of his face, knocking him cold.

Basil flew back to his car and saw that his tire tracks on the wet street were what had given him away. He jumped into the front seat and drove off as fast as he could. He returned to the airport, put the car in a crowded lot, and checked into the airport motel.

He'd learned something: he'd learned that he'd been trying to hide in all the wrong places. Instead of heading for strange cities, he should have sought out familiar ones. He decided to return to Las Vegas in the morning. He knew that city far better than he knew Buffalo. He would know where he could go, and he would know which places to avoid. Rather than run blindly about, he decided to stay on home ground.

The next day he gave Robben another call, but it didn't follow the same pattern as their earlier conversations.

"I didn't know ya knew karate," Robben said with a touch of wonder. "Tony Mead's throat was crushed. Ya busted a bunch o' little bones an' stuff, an' he choked to death. An' they tell me the Morrow brothers are gonna hafta be buried from closed coffins. They're a real mess."

Basil couldn't tell him it had been a combination of luck and coincidence. Robben was a professional gambler—he didn't believe in either one—so Basil just said, "Yes, sir."

"An' Ernie Boyer sez ya laughed before ya broke his jaw. Is that right? Did ya laugh?"

"Yes, sir," Basil answered.

Robben paused for a long, reflective moment. Then he said, "Ya know, Frank, you've always been a stand-up guy. An' ya never got out o' line before." His tone conveyed a new respect he never could have faked. "Why don't cha come on back t' Vegas? I think we can work something' out, don't you?"

"Yes, sir," Basil answered, and picked up his satchel of books. For the first time he was certain he'd be able to read them.

Kathryn Gottlieb
The Letter Carrier

To celebrate his seventh anniversary Bill Lasker bought himself the biggest and best-looking Red Delicious he had ever invested in. He stuck an apple in his mail sack every day, but this apple was really something. It cost thirty-five cents.

It was not a family anniversary he was celebrating. Bill Lasker had no wife, no family, and, for that matter, no friends. For seven years to the day he had been delivering the mail along Route West in the little suburban town of Folsom, New Jersey, a day to be marked. The weather blessed him—a bright October sun, a cloudless sky, and, gliding past his ears, the many-colored autumn leaves.

He had been, as always, first man out, as soon as the sorted mail had come up in the truck to the Folsom substation. He wanted to put the little Main Street commercial section behind him before people began to arrive at the shops and offices along the way. Otherwise it was Good morning, How are you?, Nice day! (or How do you like this rotten weather?). Enough to drive a man crazy.

He kept a fast, steady pace through the crowded uphill residential streets beyond: a section of no particular interest. It was out beyond the end of Hightop Road that his own world began. There, in the narrow neck of woodland that slashed his route in two, lay his own private estate, and in the winding, pleasant streets beyond lived those he thought of as his family, although he had spoken not a word to any of them.

He covered the early part of his route in record time, pressing forward to reach his kingdom in the woods—a brook, rocks, solitude. There he would rest, read, and eat that magnificent apple. Then, luck permitting, he would catch another glimpse of the young woman who had moved into 119 Folsom Road three weeks before.

One-nineteen Folsom was the only rental house in the neighborhood. It was painted a drab bluish grey and had the look of a place where people know they are not going to stay. No one had ever put in a garden there. She—he still didn't know her name—had moved into the dismal place alone. There was no man about the place when he passed by on Saturday mornings. On that day husbands were usually in evidence, putting up the storm sash or raking the leaves.

He had first glimpsed the new occupant of 119 as a dim figure moving across the rooms beyond the then uncurtained windows. A slender back, a drift of dark hair to her waist, a sense of quick and vital movement, and that was all. Beauty. He had been dropping a flyer from the local Shop-Mart into her box when he had caught that fleeting vision, and he had not seen her since. In three weeks she had received

no mail. Plainly, she had left no forwarding address. He had concluded that she was, so to speak, on the run.

Marching down Hightop, he saw Mrs. Campbell and Mrs. Parker
chatting away on the sidewalk in front of 93—waiting there to trap him
with questions. It was meanness to begrudge them the brilliant day,
but Mrs. Parker would say good morning and Mrs. Campbell would
demand his opinion of the weather. His response, he knew, would be a
jerky nod, flaming ears, and a burst of speed. And it was.

The old ladies watched his progress down to the cul-de-sac end of
the road. Mrs. Parker spoke first. "What a handsome head of hair that
young man has! My Joey had a mop of fair hair like that before he
began to go grey."

"He's not what I'd call a young fellow," said Mrs. Campbell. "He
must be close to forty."

"Half my age. I like to think that's young."

Mrs. Campbell grunted. "Have you ever seen him smile? Has he
ever said good morning? When I say good morning I want good
morning back!"

"Ah, well," said Mrs. Parker. "Maybe he has trouble at home."

Bill Lasker's path through the woods was leafstrewn and quiet.
From time to time little animals scuttled across it, quaking at his
thunderous approach. "Hey there," he called out to them softly.
Chipmunks were easy to talk to. He thought, smiling, of the others,
the night animals fast asleep in their burrows; garbage pail raiders.
Under the trees grew clutching brambles and shrubs whose names he
didn't know, and ferns in all the puddled spots. Through the neck of
woods ran a curving brook in a stony bed—in the spring, and after
rainstorms, a noisy torrent. The footpath crossed the brook by means of
two planks laid side by side that tilted under his feet. Someday he'd go
into the water—if any—mailbag and all!

Once across the makeshift bridge, he left the path and followed his
own beaten track along the far side of the brook, deeper into the
woods. There, out of sight of the path, he made himself comfortable on
a kind of rocky sofa, where a boulder supported his back and a flat
slab of stone made a seat at a convenient height above the ground. The
autumn had been dry, and that morning there was no water running
in the bed of the brook, which was filled instead with a river of yellow
leaves. Bill Lasker stared down into it from his rocky perch. How pretty
it was!

He reached into the depths of his mailbag, drew out his anniversary
apple, and polished it on his sleeve. He then emptied the pouch and set
the mail snugly down on the rock beside him; letters for Ramsay and
Oak and Folsom Road, and Harrison to its junction with Main. His
interest in the affairs of their recipients—on whom, when they met, he
turned that unconsciously forbidding gaze—was benign and, until
now, unflagging.

He picked up a handful of mail, took a bite of his apple, and read.

He scanned all postcards, picture and message; studied the return adresses on envelopes; and peered into those that were unsealed without disturbing their contents. And—lucky day!—slipped the Kolgers' *Playboy* carefully out of its wrapper, looked it over, and slid it carefully back. An overdue notice (purple) winked at him through its glassine-fronted envelope: the Second National wanted its money from the his-and-her Jaguars on Ramsay Place.

For the Wildes, next house after the spendthrift Jags, there was a nice postcard of Westminster Abbey from Jennifer Wilde, who was studying in England. Fabulous, she wrote. Good. She was a nice kid—always used to wave at him and never, never spoke. He was sorry for the Groleys, whose kid never sent them a line. Be fair, Bill told himself; maybe he calls up. But that wasn't what he called keeping in touch.

As he leafed through the mail he replaced it in neat order in the sack at his side.

The corner of Ramsay and Oak supported the Organization to Revive Prohibition. He went on hastily past their monthly newsletter. (His beer!)

Mrs. Wiggram, on Oak, would lurk behind her draperies in vain, darting out to the box as soon as he reached the sidewalk. There was still no check from Mr. Wiggram, who lived in Tucson, Arizona. Short of money, poor lady. Which could not be said of her neighbors, into whose mailbasket he dropped little showers of dividend checks. It would be nice to play God sometime and do a little rearranging.

What would his own life be, he wondered, deprived of this route, these people, his place in the woods? How people stood to be shuttled around, like those families that whipped in and out of 119 Folsom, he simply couldn't imagine. What chance was there, in only a year or two, to get acquainted with a place? Here the bumpy tree roots and sidewalks and cobblestone curbing were as well known to him as the stairs in his house. He could have delivered the mail blindfolded. His route; his home. They'd never take it away from him. He was a steady and devoted worker; he showed up in the worst weather, ready to protect his mailbag with his life.

And so on that brilliant day he celebrated his anniversary. The apple was a treat, the *Playboy* another; but later, passing 119 Folsom, he caught no glimpse of its new occupant.

Three days later, he did.

He was walking past the orphaned-looking house, wondering if he would ever catch sight of her again, when she sprang to her feet on the far side of the hedge that bordered the sidewalk. She was clutching a garden trowel and her face was streaked with earth. She looked as pretty as a picture.

"Good morning!" she said.

The miracle shocked an answer out of him. "Good morning!"

"I've been putting tulip bulbs in," she said. "You don't think it's too late in the season, do you?"

"Of course not—they'll do fine." Her eyes were as blue as the sky; *today's* sky. "My mother never put bulbs in until the real cold weather. She—" But there he stopped. Long years ago she had told him, laughing, that she was punishing herself for her extravagance. Someday he might be able to tell that to this extraordinary young woman, who now shrugged her shoulders in a mock-guilty gesture and said, "I mustn't keep you from your appointed rounds, must I?"

Over so soon. "I guess not."

She gave him a little wave of the trowel and sank back to her knees. He marched down the street, his heart pounding. She was the prettiest woman he had ever seen, and the kindest. Had he not *spoken* to her?

And speak to her he did, day after day, as he plodded up and down the streets of that familiar route. True, he had yet to see her again, but the conversation, once begun, went on and on in his head. You know, he told her, there's nobody around here would believe the way you and I were talking about those tulip bulbs. And it's the God's truth, I'm not the local chatterbox. But I don't mean to be unfriendly—you know what I mean? She always knew what he meant, of course. Never any doubt of that.

And I'll tell you another fact—he was at the moment dropping Mrs. Wiggram's check into her box—nobody would believe what a talkative kid I was at one time. One door past the Wiggrams' he stopped still—the name of his mother's favorite tulips had just popped into his head. General de Wet! And the day they had planted those bulbs—it must have been November, cold enough to burn your ears off. Imagine remembering General de Wet, bright orange, after all these years. That girl at 119 must have opened some magic door in his head.

A week passed and he caught no further glimpse of her. On Tuesday, and then again on Thursday, there was the sight of her car in the driveway to console him—she was *there*—but when the driveway stood empty his heart flapped in panic. Suppose she had gone away? Nonsense. She had to go down to the Shop-Mart sometimes, didn't she? Or the bank, or the library—or maybe she'd taken some kind of a job. People didn't just stay shut up in their houses day in and day out. Still—he frowned, thinking about it—she still hadn't gotten any mail. Nothing personal, that is. He had put a soap sample in her basket and more flyers from Shop-Mart, all addressed to Occupant.

Occupant. He still didn't know her name.

The conversation went on in his head, confiding. When I first started to get really quiet, he told her, was after my mother died and I got sent to live with my Aunt Ethel. You're probably wondering about my father. He wasn't dead or anything like that, he just wasn't around. I hardly remember him. Aunt Ethel was really my mother's aunt. She seemed like a hundred years old to me then and I'll tell you the truth, the poor old lady didn't know what hit her, getting this thirteen-year-old boy dumped in her lap. She was a real old maid, if you'll pardon the expression, and just the sound of my footsteps crashing around in her house must have been enough to drive her crazy, let alone the sound of my voice.

At that point he was climbing the steps to Mrs. Parker's porch, and he turned off the conversation until he was back on the sidewalk again. I have to admit it, there was no reason for that woman to love me. I was kind of a homely kid and I never could think of the right things to say. So after a while I just shut up. My mother and me, we used to talk about stuff and make jokes together, and I was *somebody* in our house. I could change a faucet washer before I was ten, and I mean so it didn't leak or shriek when you turned the water on. But with Aunt Ethel the talk just went out of me.

On the next day the fine weather broke, and the postcards began. Bill Lasker woke to an overcast sky—the exact color of the house at 119—and a smell of rain on its way. Seated on his rock in the woods, dampness beading his hair, he pulled the mail out of the sack, looking for 119 Folsom. His interest in all the others—on Ramsay, on Oak, all along—belonged to a time that no longer existed. And there, sandwiched between bundles of mail for 117 and 121, he found a picture postcard of Los Angeles, view side up. Sorter's error. It was a nighttime view from someplace high up—a lot of black and little dots of lights. He stared at like a man in a trance, and then he turned it over.

Mrs. Jean LaBarre. He repeated the syllables like a man reciting a poem. Jean. Jean. Jean LaBarre. He read the message, and read it again. "Found you!" it said. The writing was ugly; a triumphant scrawl that almost filled the message space. "Found you," he said aloud. What would be the proper tone of voice? *Found you!* The card had been mailed from Los Angeles. It was unsigned.

Her car was not in the driveway when he slipped the card into the box.

Two days later he found another postcard addressed to her. It had been mailed from Flagstaff, Arizona, and held a one-word message: "Closer." No signature.

Closer? It was a good thing, Bill Lasker told himself, that she was hearing from somebody after all this time; it was no kind of a good thing for her to be living alone and apart from people—*his* kind of life. But what kind of a friend wrote cards like this? He leaned back against his rock and closed his eyes. A picture came into his head clear as day: a man driving a car with California plates, headed for Folsom, New Jersey, face a blank, character and intentions unknown.

The next card was postmarked Albuquerque. Bill Lasker read it and

it slipped from his hands, like a leaf, onto the ground. "My darling."
Damned fool! Damned fool! That let him out, didn't it? Mr. California
Plates and Mrs. Jean LaBarre were none of his business. They had had
a lover's quarel. Lovers quarreled and made up. He picked up the
card, replaced the mail, and got to his feet. The sack weighed a ton. He
felt old and hollowed out. All the same, on his way home in the late
afternoon he stopped at Pringle's Stationery and bought a road atlas of
the U.S.A. He looked for Albuquerque and found it; east of Las Vegas.
"Closer."

On Sunday he sat home and watched TV and drank beer and the
day was a thousand years long. Monday there was nothing in the
mail. On Tuesday a card arrived from Amarillo, and it was different
from the others. The message was so long that, though the writing was
very small, it reached the bottom of the card and then continued,
curling up and around twice, crowding the address space illegally.
"Oh my darling," he read. "Each day draws me nearer to you and my
heart is renewed with gladness. Soon we will join hands and you will
believe with me that we never should have parted. Oh my love, why
did you leave me? Whom God hath joined together! Joined together! But
I will not repeat it. I patiently explained to you His holy command and I
know in my heart that you repent. It is that knowledge that draws me
to you—I love you, I forgive you. Oh my Jean, never again—" At that
point the message began its long tailcurl around its own body and Bill
Lasker stopped reading and looked away from the card. Not three feet
away a chipmunk sat at the farthest edge of the slab of stone and
stared back at him. "I don't know," said Bill. The chipmunk ran away.
He looked at the card again. The man was out of his mind. Or was he?
Maybe he was just very religious. Bill shut his eyes. He could see the
car bouncing down the dusty desert roads.

He would knock on her door, put the card in her hands, and say, "If
you're in trouble, Mrs. LaBarre, I'll protect you from this man—" and
he heard her voice, shocked, angry: "You've been reading my mail!"
And then God knows what. They'd take him off the route—no, they'd
fire him—and then he'd sit alone in his room day after day until he was
as crazy as the man in Amarillo.

He jumped to his feet and threw his half-eaten apple in the direction of the chipmunk. He had time. Texas was far away. But of course
the man was traveling ahead of the cards. Never mind. He'd work
something out.

For three days there was no message, and then two cards arrived
together, both posted from Colorado—some town named Trinidad.
One card read "Jean"; the other, "Zigzag." That night, frowning over
his atlas, he found Trinidad—small print, small town, "Zigzag" described it: the place was north and west of Amarillo. And then, for days,
there was silence. Maybe California Plates had given up and was
heading back to L.A.

On a day of pouring rain he delivered half a ton of shampoo samples, one in every box: to Mrs. Campbell, *no* hair; to the Prohibitions. "Drink it!" The very next day, Jean LaBarre was outside on her lawn, facing away from him, grubbing the leaves out from under the decrepit shrubs in front of the house. Today of all days there were no samples, no flyers, no postcard. Could he hand her somebody else's mail? He stared at the long slender back and the shining dark hair, then trudged on down the road. "I've been reading your mail." How could he say it? For the rest of that day he even stopped talking to her in his mind. The situation was impossible.

The week ended. Sunday passed. On Monday morning, under a sky as hard and grey as any November would bring, Bill found another card in his hands. The fellow was back in Amarillo, and he sounded just as ordinary as the guy next door. "Damn this car. Broke down again. Half the time I don't know where I am!" She wasn't home for him to put the card into her hands, and she wasn't home two days later when a card came from St. Louis. That tiny handwriting again, the message curling around and around. This one he read to the end. The ending was obscene. His hands shook when he put the card into her mailbox. If her car had been standing in the driveway he would have rung the bell and told her everything—that he'd read every word. Let the sky fall on his head! "You'd better get out of here," he'd say. "I'm telling you, you've got to get out!" And then a voice whispered in the back of his head. You do and she'll get out, all right—out of your life.

The next day, when he was just two doors past her house, she backed the car out of the driveway and shot off down the street, waving a friendly hand as she passed. He waved back vigorously and continued to confide in her, tramping down the sidewalk, everything that went on in his head. He complained in a good-humored way about the old ladies who sprang conversation traps on him. I deliver their mail, he said. Do I have to give weather reports, too? He smiled at her, and the Jean in his head smiled back. He told her the plots of the programs he watched every evening, and she agreed with his opinions, absolutely. "Dumb stuff!" "Isn't it though? Why on earth do we watch it?"

Two days after the ugly message from St. Louis a card arrived from someplace he couldn't make out in Kentucky. "I don't know what comes over me," wrote the man who never signed his name. "But don't be afraid of me ever again. *Please.* Don't run away from me. You are my only friend."

Oh, you're safe, he told the card. She's not running. Runners don't plant gardens. She'd be right there to face him when he came knocking on her door. But which man would stand on her doorstep—the pathetic pleader of Someplace, Kentucky, or the madman of St. Louis? Oh, God help me, thought Bill, what can I do? Talk to the guys at the post office? But he never talked to them. They'd think he was the crazy one.

For the first time in his life he wished a man dead.

He still went each day to his woodland place. The weather had turned cold, with the bite of winter in it, but he was sturdy, and indifferent to the change of season. He looked at no mail but hers. Out of habit he continued to carry an apple in his mail sack but, distracted, half the time he forgot to eat it. On a day of pallid sunshine he found the next message in his hands. "Soon." The postmark was Akron, Ohio. Akron! The man might *be* here!

He stepped along Ramsay Place at a pace that left him gasping. The mail sack weighed at his shoulders and every damned house on the block had mail. The same on Oak, where he had to slow down; the pain cut right across his shoulders. When he reached the top of Folsom Road he stared in terror down the sloping street to her house. Peace and quiet. No one on the sidewalk, no strange cars.

He went on at a human pace and got his breath back. Her car was not in the driveway.

It wasn't until he had rounded the downhill corner and got halfway down Harrison to Main that he spotted the car parked in front of the empty lot past 168. Dark plates; out-of-state plates—Jersey is black on cream. It was a beat-up Chevy, he saw, coming abreast of it, and the plates were yellow on navy blue. California. The driver was sitting in the car. Passing, Bill glimpsed an oil-stained khaki sleeve. The man's hands rested on the wheel, holding something—some piece of paper, too small to be a map. Big hands, a long arm: more than that he couldn't have seen without stooping to peer into the window. He forced himself on, one foot in front of the other, up one walk and down the next. He wanted the strength to turn back but the habit of his route, of his perpetual silence, held him in its grip. What would be say? How could he say it? Jersey was full of out-of-state plates, and that empty lot was for sale. The man could be some stranger looking at the lot to buy it.

He finished his route and went home.

That night he slept badly. He dreamed of a man at the wheel of a car. The man had no face but spoke to him all the same. "You wanted me to drive into a ditch," he said. His voice was reproachful. "But you don't get what you want in this world. Don't you know that?"

The last postcard came the next day. A picture of the Folsom War Memorial, a Folsom postmark. It was addressed to Mrs. Jean LaBarre. There was no message.

He fled from his place in the woods, the mailbag jouncing against his hip. He delivered the mail on Ramsay and Oak at a run, groaning for breath, pushing at a task he hadn't the strength to abandon. He rounded the corner of Oak to the top of Folsom Road.

"No," he said aloud.

A knot of people had gathered out on the sidewalk in front of her house.

"No." All the way down the hill he delivered the mail. "No!" The word tolled in his head like a bell. When at last he stood in front of 119, Mrs. Parker from 93 Hightop looked at him and spoke. "That poor young woman." Her lips were trembling. "Poor child! She was beaten to death last night.

"A package came from United Parcel this morning and the driver found the door open and—" the old voice faltered "—they found blood just inside the door. She must have struggled to get away. Poor child! They say she was only twenty-five."

He was standing like a man turned to stone.

"Are you all right?" asked Mrs. Parker. "Are you feeling all right?" She was looking at him anxiously.

"Yes," he said. "Thank you." He moved to go on, and then he saw the stranger standing at the edge of the crowd, staring at the house. A tall man, young, with a deeply tanned and rather coarse complexion, and sun-bleached hair cut very short. He was wearing the khaki shirt with the oil stain on the sleeve. Bill Lasker moved on, stuffing mail into every box—*Time, Newsweek*, dunning letters, love letters, hate letters— he didn't know what was in his hands. What was the use of any of it? Why did anyone want it? Rubbish. Heartbreak. Trouble. Sorrow.

When he turned the corner into Harrison, he saw the Chevy with the California plates. It was parked in front of the empty lot, just as it had been yesterday; as though it were yesterday. He threw his mail sack to the ground and ran up the street. At the end, at Main, he thrust himself into a telephone booth and dialed the police; reported the watching stranger, the waiting car.

He had expected a reprimand for a task abandoned, a mailbag thrown God-knows-where, but instead he found himself congratulated for his quick thinking and fast response. The California driver, a man named Frank LaBarre, had been picked up at once for questioning. He had admitted readily to the murder of Jean LaBarre, who had once been his wife. It was something, he stated, that he had had to do.

The abandoned mailbag was retrieved, its contents apparently intact. The letter carrier received his commendation without response. He asked to be transferred to another route. The request was refused. He was the hero in the neighborhood.

Kept from his little kingdom in the woods by the deep snows of winter, he did not return to it in the beautiful days of spring. He took no apples with him in his mail sack, and never read the mail any more.

Late in April the tulips bloomed inside the hedge at 119. When he saw them he cried like a child.

Penelope Wallace

The World According to Uncle Albert

My uncle was mad about Sherlock Holmes.

Sometimes I thought he was just mad.

He had this enormous magnifying glass and, when he wasn't rereading The Master, he was cantering around the ample grounds of his country estate, waving it around. "A big dog's been through this thicket," he said.

"Yes, a Great Dane called Hound. *Your* Great Dane. You walked him through here this morning."

His embarrassment was fleeting. "I'd have known anyway, from the paw marks," he said scathingly.

"If you use that great thing in the afternoon sun, you'll start a fire," I told him. I'd just snagged my pantyhose and I reflected for the hundredth time that the proper apparel for a stroll through Uncle Albert's underbrush was slacks.

Uncle Albert was against slacks. Women should look feminine and behave in a feminine way—preferably in high necks and long skirts as in dear old Sherlock's day. He didn't want an Irene Adler in the family.

I'd once pointed out to him that there were other crime writers. It was like telling a religious bigot that there were other churches.

I always explain to any visitors who my uncle means when he speaks of The Master. We'd had a nasty interlude when one of my old school friends thought he was referring to Noel Coward.

I should, perhaps, explain that I live by myself in London, but Uncle Albert is my only living relative and, despite what he calls my aggressive modernity, he seems to like me, so I come down most weekends.

This Friday afternoon was particularly hot and, after my remarks about starting a fire, he reluctantly agreed that we retrace our steps.

He always wears an inverness for these walks—just like you-know-whose—and he stowed the magnifying glass away in a large pocket. "About the party—" I began. But he bent suddenly over a thorny bush, dragging out his "eye of God" and peering intently.

"That's not Hound's hair," he announced. "It's some fine shreds and—yes, by Jove, it's blood!"

"Group O," I told him. "Rhesus Positive."

He turned, amazed.

"How—?"

I pointed to my leg. "My blood," I told him. "And shreds of my pantyhose."

He put away the magnifying glass and walked with me, rather huffily, back to the house.

I wondered whether I should apologize for scratching my leg or if I should have left a little notice: "Here lies the fine blood of Frances Stephen—wounded while on lawful pursuits."

Uncle relented when we were back in the drawing room. "Tea now, I think," he said, and rang the bell by the fireplace. "After tea I think I'll dip into *The Hound of the Baskervilles*."

The Great Dane uncurled himself at the sound of his name and ambled over to see if he was missing anything—like tea, I thought, the way that dog eats.

Poor Uncle. Mrs. Hubbard, the housekeeper, had refused to let him buy a mastiff, and although Hound was large enough, he didn't have at all the temperament of his namesake.

Once I'd pointed out to Uncle Albert that the Great Man hadn't owned a dog and had, on occasions, employed a tracking dog called Toby, who was an ugly lop-eared mixture of spaniel and Labrador. Uncle had become frosty and Hound had looked sad. He wasn't actually the kind of dog who carries the burglar's torch—he was too lazy even for that.

"Uncle," I said firmly. "Not too much reading after tea. Remember, you're giving a party; the guests will start arriving about seven."

Uncle mumbled crossly, but I knew that he actually liked parties. It gave him a chance to quote The Master and recall a few occasions when he himself—in his humble way, as he put it—had made some startling discoveries and deductions.

"You're giving the party for me," I reminded him. "My nineteenth birthday party—although I'm not actually nineteen until the week after next. Roger and his wife will be coming from London. They'll be staying the weekend, and John Canning will be here for the night."

"Where's he coming from?"

"Six miles away, but you asked him when you met him last May. You said he was an unusually sensitive and perceptive young man."

"Oh, yes. I remember the boy. Reads The Master and congratulated me on some of my own achievements. Who else is coming?"

"Don's driving down from London with his sister and various others."

"Long-haired layabout."

"He's not a layabout; he works at the BBC."

Uncle Albert muttered something about Lord Reith and inquired whether they were all staying the night.

"They'll drive back to London after it's over," I told him.

"So few people," he said mournfully.

"I thought *you'd* ask some guests as well."

"The vicar and his wife and Dr. Spence and the Paynes and Mrs. Caxton, but they won't stay long after dinner. Oh, yes, and an author fellow I met last weekend—he lent me one of his books—I can't say I think much of it, but he seems a decent chap. Quite young, too.

"I've got your mother's jewelry in the safe—you will wear some of it, won't you? I remember when your mother wore it at her parties."

He'd said the same at my last birthday party and the one before and the one before that. Then, as now, I agreed.

"I'll get it out now," he said, and I followed him through the connecting door to his study—an indescribably untidy room, since Mrs. Hubbard was allowed to do no more than vacuum the carpet. The safe was large, solid-looking, and very old. Uncle Albert started spinning dials. Usually he supported himself on the top while he did so, but on this occasion he kept well clear, with his left hand behind his back.

"Is it that dirty?" I asked him.

He hesitated. "Not dirty exactly," he said gruffly and I went forward to investigate. "Don't touch the door!"

I looked carefully at the safe door. "It's shinier," I said. "What have you done to it?"

"I suppose I might as well tell you. In fact, I'm rather proud of the idea. It's covered with a special fine grease. For fingerprints," he explained. "Of course, there are burglar alarms at the windows and doors and there's Hound, but someone might gain admittance by day when the alarms are off."

I recalled that they had been, at one time, left on by day—until one memorable occasion when the vicar, waiting for my uncle in the drawing room and presumably stifled by the heat, had flung open the french windows—and all hell had broken loose. Mrs. Hubbard, relating the event, said that even Hound had entered into the spirit of the thing, and fascinated villagers had seen the vicar running down the main street with his hands clapped to his ears and his bony legs clearly visible through the rips in his cassock.

The safe was filled with envelopes and packages—rare first editions and what Uncle referred to as "memorabilia and ephemera." My jewelry was in a strong cardboard box on the top shelf. Normally, covered with oceans of sealing wax, it was held at the bank. Only for my birthday was it brought to this temporary home. As usual I chose to wear a small diamond pendant and, also as usual, I refused to bedeck myself with various rings and bracelets or to take the box back to London to "bring an aura of gracious living," as he put it, into my bed-sitter.

I had referred to my "birthday party" because that's how Uncle Albert thought of it, but it was really his evening. Some of his cronies, some of my more respectable friends—the others couldn't afford the fare or petrol from London—came in for a few drinks, dinner, and the birthday cake. Then, after a decent interval for coffee and recovery, the older guests would depart and Uncle would take himself off to the study and, as he said, "Leave the young people to enjoy themselves." Not surprisingly, the proceedings which followed lost spontaneity.

I was dutifully dressed, wearing the pendant, and downstairs by six thirty. Roger and Jane arrived a few minutes later. Roger's father had been a friend of my father's; they were in their late thirties but deter-ined to be young or, as Roger said, "with it." Jane was small and slim, but Roger's spread was definitely middle-aged. I had a standing invitation to visit them in London and felt rather guilty that I so rarely did. Roger's publishing house was reputedly going through a difficult time. Soon after they joined me in the drawing room for a drink, a tap on the door revealed John Canning. Apparently he had arrived when I was changing and had been shown to his room by Batty Annie, who came from the village to help Mrs. Hubbard on special occasions.

I had only met John Canning twice before, and he didn't improve with the third meeting. He had impressed Uncle Albert with his knowledge of Sherlock Holmes and, when he heard that Roger was a publisher, he launched into the Meaning and Significance of the Modern Novel and the particular significance of Roger's publications.

Roger was puffing up nicely when Betty Annie flung open the door and let in the vicar and Mrs. Vicar and Mr. and Mrs. Payne. The Paynes were in their seventies; they had known my mother when she was a child and I was very fond of them. I couldn't say the same of Mrs. Caxton, who followed them in. She was a predatory forty-fiver, a widow whose target, I felt sure, was Uncle Albert. I didn't think she'd have any luck, noticing that when he joined the throng he had the wary look he usually has when she's around.

Dr. Spence arrived next, as untidy as usual, with his neat sparrow wife. I wondered where Don had got to, and then Batty Annie brought in Uncle Albert's author—who turned out to be Simon Lantern—and I rather forgot about Don. I could see John Canning bestowing himself on one group after another and, during lulls in the conversation, I heard him discussing heart surgery with Dr. Spence and God with the vicar. Predictably, he soon turned his attention on Simon.

"Mr. Lantern," he said. "You have given a new dimension to crime fiction."

Simon gave an enigmatic smile and I hoped the subject would change because although, of course, I'd heard of the great Simon Lantern I'd never read any of his books. In fact, I don't like crime books, although it seems terribly disloyal to Uncle Albert to mention it.

I was saved by Batty Annie announcing dinner. She wasn't really mad—I should explain—but had acquired the adjective as a result of a passing interest in spiritualism.

Uncle Albert had the problem of rudeness to my friends from London if we started dinner without them and offending Mrs. Hubbard if we didn't. I assured him that Don's car had probably broken down and we certainly shouldn't wait.

Dinner was somewhat formal, with Uncle Albert at one end of the long table and myself at the other. I firmly put Simon on my right, the chair on my left was tacitly left empty for Don, and a block of four were left empty below Simon. It turned out they weren't all needed, because Don arrived soon after the soup with apologies—they *had* broken down—and with him were only his sister Susan and one other. Susan was wearing a scarlet blouse and purple slacks; I could see Uncle shuddering in the distance, but he should have seen the jeans she normally wore. With Susan was a new friend of hers named Sammy—I hadn't met him before, but Susan believed in variety. Sammy had a scrubbed look and I suspected that Susan had bathed him for the occasion; my suspicion was later confirmed when I passed to windward and was rewarded by the unmistakable smell of Pink Lilac tale.

"Only the three of you?" asked Uncle.

"Yes," said Don. "The other two fell out at the first roundabout."

There was a stunned silence, and I feebly explained that Don was joking. Nobody laughed.

Simon asked Don what kind of car he had and they immediately entered into the kind of dialogue which is common to males of all ages and races—I suspect it's when they beat out on African drums, and maybe those streams of little flags my naval friends refer to as "making signals" don't actually carry stirring messages about "England expecting" or instructions to "Form line of battle," but really read, "I'd just been passed by this Lotus Elan—"

Anyway, it gave me a chance to look around the table. Uncle Albert was debating, as usual, with Dr. Spence. Mrs. Spence was chatting demurely with the vicar. Susan and Sammy were holding hands, which meant that Susan had to hold the soup spoon in her left hand. And John Canning was using what he thought was charm on Mrs. Caxton, who was smiling and nodding. He certainly worked hard. Jane was working hard too, conversing with Sammy, but whereas I thought John Canning had ulterior motives, I knew that Jane was just pursuing her affection for, and hopeful affinity with, the young.

The car conversation seemed to have petered out, or maybe Don and Simon had remembered whose party it was. "So how are you, Frankie?" asked Don.

I hoped Uncle hadn't heard—and I loathed it, too. "I'm fine, thank you, Donnie."

I was happy to see that he winced slightly.

Dinner proceeded smoothly with Mrs. Hubbard, as always, giving of her best. Her crowning effort was the birthday cake. The lights were turned out as she brought it in, firing on all nineteen candles, and put it in front of me with a large cake knife. Uncle Albert always insisted on champagne for my birthday dinner and, as the candles flickered, I began to wonder if I had let my glass be filled rather too often.

I stood up and thanked Uncle and Mrs. Hubbard before starting to blow at the flames and it was while I was leaning forward, puffing, that someone remarked on the beauty of the pendant—I couldn't tell who it was in the dark. I heard a murmur of assent, and by the time the candles were out and the lights back on, Uncle Albert was holding forth about the beauty of my mother's jewelry and my inexplicable behavior in refusing to take it to London and wear it. There were assents and reminiscences from the older members of the party and a tactful silence from the younger until Sammy, whom I had thought incapable of conversation, suddenly said that he thought I was right; that the trappings of wealth were no longer acceptable.

He didn't actually say, "Come the Revolution," but I could see Uncle Albert heating up—he has a low boiling point—and then Simon Lantern was coming to my rescue by pointing out the responsibility involved with valuable jewelry and the risk of theft. Someone mentioned the recent loss of a film star's emeralds and soon the conversation had generalized into talk of burglaries in general and of jewelry in particular, with Uncle quoting The Master's cases at appropriate moments.

Uncle Albert had a hankering for the port-and-nuts-for-the-boys segregation but I had talked him out of it the preceding year, so after we had finished the cake we all trooped into the drawing room for coffee.

By about ten the locals started to leave—but not, I was happy to see, Simon Lantern.

At ten thirty, Uncle Albert retired to his study and the rest of us sat around talking—except for Susan and Sammy, who sat on the sofa still holding hands and apparently oblivious of all but each other. It was when Don got into a political argument with Jane and Roger—with John Canning agreeing with both sides—that Simon said, "You haven't read any of my books, have you?" I admitted that I hadn't and apologized for the fact that I never read crime fiction. "There's one I think you would like," he told me. "May I send you a copy?"

I said I'd be delighted and he wrote down my London address, adding, as an afterthought, that perhaps I could dine with him the next time he visited his publisher and he could give me the book in person.

He was an undeniably attractive man—mid-forties, I thought, with black hair greying at the temples. It occurred to me that perhaps I should keep the diamond pendant because I was sure he'd take me to dine at that sort of place. While I was telling him that I'd like that, I thought how part of his charm lay in the way he actually listened when people were speaking, his head held slightly on one side.

When the telephone rang about eleven thirty, I didn't bother to answer it because I knew that Uncle Albert had an extension in the study and would deal with it there. It was a call for Simon, and Uncle invited him to take it in the study. Don took advantage of his absence to remark unkindly on him and suggest that he practiced his air of attentive listening in the mirror each morning.

Simon wasn't long on the phone. We heard him speaking to Uncle Albert and Uncle saying, "Nonsense, my boy, no trouble at all," then he returned to explain that the call was from his sister. All the lights had failed and the electricity people had told her it was a cable fault that couldn't be mended until the following day. She was going to spend the night in the nearest hotel and advised him to do likewise but Uncle Albert had pressed him to stay the night here.

I thought his sister was talking rather drastic action but I only said that I had no idea he had a sister and asked why he hadn't brought her to the party. He replied that his sister wasn't good at parties, whereupon Don gave a baleful look at Susan and Sammy and said, "Nor's mine."

Around midnight Don said they'd better start back. It was a warm night and we all went out to wave them goodbye.

It was a dead loss, waving goodbye, because the car wouldn't start, and although Don and Simon both poked around under the bonnet it appeared that the problem couldn't be repaired without spares from the local garage. That meant three more besides John Canning, Roger, and Jane staying the night.

Proprieties had to be observed and Don and Sammy were given a twin-bedded room, Susan a smallish single room down the corridor. Uncle Albert doled out toothbrushes and pajamas, and I gave Susan a nightdress. Uncle Albert then took the reluctant Hound for a short walk while I busied myself with sheets and towels and offers of help in making beds.

While I was thus skivvying, I heard Uncle return and the clanking of bolts as he locked up for the night. He always locked the doors from the passage to the drawing room and study and took the respective keys to bed with him. When I heard his footsteps on the stairs, I left Don to finish making his own bed. Uncle Albert has some old fashioned ideas, and I hate to shock him unnecessarily.

My bedroom was in the middle of the corridor and there was a certain amount of traffic during the night which I took to be guests en route to the bathroom or Sammy en route to Susan. I didn't sleep particularly well and sometime in the early hours I remembered that I should have given the pendant to Uncle Albert so he could lock it away in the safe. Instead, I had left it on the dressing table by the window. Remembering the tales of robbery earlier in the evening, I got up and actually leaned out of the window to check for drainpipes and other furtive access to my room but I couldn't see anything that would help a would-be thief. My room overlooked the drive and I peered anxiously at the trees which flanked it but I didn't see any suspicious shadows. I could hear owls hooting sadly and, somewhere to the front of the house, a faint hissing. For a moment I thought it was rain; then I remembered the Speckled Band Uncle Albert had insisted I read about in my early youth—but neither seemed applicable, so I went back to bed and, finally, to sleep.

When I woke, it was half-past nine and there was a lot of noise outside my window. I looked out and saw Don and the man from the local garage peering into the guts of Don's car while Simon sat in the driver's seat using the starter when requested. The car burst into noisy life for brief periods while the garage man poked about with an enormous screwdriver and Don watched anxiously.

I had a quick bath and dressed. My final look at the scene outside showed Don at the wheel—and no sign of Simon. I hoped he hadn't left.

I was halfway down the stairs when I saw Uncle Albert at the open study door.

"Frances," he called to me, and I followed him in. Simon was there. "I said I'd show Mr. Lantern some of my treasures," Uncle told me darkly, "and when I opened the safe, I found that all your jewelry is missing. We've had a burglary."

I wasn't particularly upset for myself. I seldom wore it and had no doubt that it was well insured. But Uncle Albert was very unhappy.

"Come and see this, Frances," he said, and Simon and I followed him to the drawing room.

The french windows were open—apparently Mrs. Hubbard had assumed that Uncle had opened them before she cleaned the room, since the alarm seemed to be switched off. "However," said Uncle, brightening visibly now that he could start deducting, "the alarm was *not* switched off, someone disconnected it. And look there"—he pointed to the earth outside the window, which bore strange marks, fairly deep and spade-shaped—"You will remember," he said, "how in 'The Adventure of the Priory School' The Master realized the cow hoofprints were actually made by horses?"

Simon said he remembered it well.

"*I* deduce that those prints were made by a man walking on his toes."

"Why?" I asked.

"Because," he explained, "it would give less guidance to the man's size of shoe then would a full footprint. You can see the tracks he made coming in—and going out."

"So," I said with some relief, "it could have been any thief for miles around."

"I'm afraid not, Frances. I told you the alarm on this window had been disconnected. That could only be done from inside the room. And it was done yesterday because I tested the alarm on Thursday evening when I brought your jewelry home from the bank."

"Anyone could have come in yesterday. The windows were open and we were out on the grounds. We wouldn't have seen anything."

"One thing we do know from the size of those footprints is that the robber returned to force open the french doors after it started to rain: the ground was very wet, which made the prints wide and deep."

"But," said Simon, "it didn't rain last night—or, if it did, it was a very light shower. I've been out in front trying to help Don with his car, and the ground's bone dry."

"Have you called the police?" I asked Uncle Albert.

He looked hurt. "Simon persuaded me to do so. I've called the C.I.D. at Midhampton. I think I'll just go and have a quick look outside before they arrive. They have to travel sixteen miles." He scooted through the open french windows, more or less avoiding the footprints, and disappeared behind some nearby bushes. He didn't ask Simon to go with him; maybe he just didn't see him as an obedient Watson.

We saw Uncle Albert emerge from the bushes holding something white, and as he came back through the windows we could see it was a pair of gloves.

"Look," he said proudly. "The fingers of the right glove are covered with grease. The burglar was left-handed. The left glove is quite clean and is obviously the one that came in contact with the dial." He turned to Simon. "Who else aside from you is left-handed?" he asked.

Simon looked surprised. "I'm right-handed," he said.

Uncle was disappointed. "You picked up the telephone receiver with your left hand last night."

"I'm deaf in my right ear," Simon told him.

Uncle turned to me. "Your friend Susan," he said. "She held her soup spoon in her left hand at dinner."

I explained that Sammy had been holding her right one, and Uncle tutted a bit. "Anyway," I pointed out, "who's to say it's one of us? There are probably hundreds of left-handed burglars in the county."

A local bobby arrived at that moment. P.C. Brown was a keen gardener and, after one look at the footprints, opined that something funny had been going on because it hadn't rained for three weeks and if someone had been using a hose it was strictly illegal.

"Of *course*," I said. "The hissing noise last night—it was either the hose or the garden sprinkler!" I explained why I'd been looking out of the window and Uncle Albert beamed at me.

"Excellent," he told me.

Don came in at that moment to say goodbye and P.C. Brown explained that Don and his party must wait for the inspector from Midhampton. Uncle told Don about the burglary. P.C. Brown frowned at Uncle and Don swore. Reluctantly, the P.C. allowed him to telephone his excuses to London.

"Who else is staying in the house," Mr. Brown asked us afterward, "and where are they?"

Don had seen Roger and Jane heading toward the village, Sammy and Susan were packing—packing what? I wondered—and nobody had seen John Canning. "His car's still outside," offered Don.

P.C. Brown could never have played poker. Over his face there flitted the go-seek-and-round-up-suspects look, closely followed by a baleful stare at Uncle laced with the obvious thought—based perhaps on previous experience—that if he left the room Uncle would be off clue-hunting and Midhampton would be very displeased with the results. To his evident relief, Midhampton itself showed up at this point. The party consisted of a rather elderly and cynical inspector, a sergeant who reminded me of a vicious terrier I'd once had, and a horde of experts who proceeded to search the grounds, take photographs, make casts of the footprints, and dust surfaces with grey powder.

The inspector turned to Uncle Albert. "Have you found any evidence?" he asked in a sad voice. Evidently Uncle's fame *had* spread. Uncle pointed out the footprints outside the french windows. The inspector peered out, looked for rather a long time at those on the periphery, and opined that Mr. Holmes would have used a mat.

A convert!

Uncle beamed. He realized he couldn't always be as perfect as The Master. With a flourish he produced the white cotton gloves. The sergeant yapped, whipped a polythene bag out of his case, and dropped them in.

P.C. Brown, who was being upstaged, told the inspector of the hissing noise I'd heard in the night.

"Not the Speckled Band," I interrupted and got a half smile from the inspector and a rather hurt look from P. C. Brown, who battled on and was then sent to round up those of the party who could be located. The sergeant left with him, and Mrs. Hubbard appeared with coffee and biscuits, followed by the still-clasped Sammy and Susan, who sat together on the sofa.

We all heard a sharp yelp through the french windows. It wasn't the call of Hound. I suspected it was the terrier-sergeant hot on the trail. The inspector departed in its direction and Uncle Albert said he must wash his hands. He reappeared some ten minutes later with a smug expression, a pair of binoculars, and Hound.

He hadn't been able to observe much from the downstairs loo—cloakroom, as he insists on calling it—even with the binoculars, because the window glass is opaque and the window is small and high, but he'd had a good view of the sergeant's back and heard him refer to faint scuffmarks at the foot of the drainpipe and yelp a second time when he spied some threads of material caught partway up the pipe.

A man had been dispatched for a ladder and Uncle had had to step away so that the climber wouldn't see him.

"It's definitely an inside job," he said. "Someone in the house climbed down the drainpipe after everyone was asleep, forced open the french windows—having earlier disconnected the burglar alarm—opened the safe, took the jewelry, and climbed back up the drainpipe to his room."

"Clasping the jewelry," I asked, "until such time as the police would arrive to take it from him?"

"He may have had an accomplice on the grounds," said Uncle, "or he may have concealed it in the house. In 'The Naval Treaty'—"

Jane and Roger came in that point and Jane, wearing a well cut trouser suit which had Uncle tutting under his breath, helped herself and Roger to coffee. Uncle brought them up to date on the facts and on his deductons. Midway through his dissertation John Canning came in and explained that he'd been reading in his room until the police had turned him out to conduct their search. I gave him a cup of coffee.

Uncle moved to the window, his binoculars in hand.

"They've found something!" he said.

And Hound, who'd been lying peacefully on Sammy and Susan, obeyed some atavistic call, leaped to his feet, bounded through the windows, and was off at a speed I'd never credited him with. I could see that Uncle was as surprised as I was, but he was very loyal.

"They've found something!" he repeated. "They're holding it up—some sort of bundle—and Hound—yes, Hound's got the scent!"

I suppose I was the only other persion in the room who knew that Hound could no more follow a scent than I could fly to the moon. Uncle retained his optimism.

"Yes," he cried, "and now he's coming back here!"

Hound came bounding back and sank, panting and exhausted, at Uncle's feet.

A few minutes later, the inspector came in with a rolled-up bundle tied with garden twine. From it he drew a pair of loud check trousers. I'd always thought they were hideous since the day Uncle bought them.

"These are yours also?" asked the inspector, holding up a pair of overshoes. "And the gardening gloves?"

"Yes," admitted my uncle. "I keep them in the garden room for when I do the garden."

"The garden room," I explained, "is the one with the cracked sink and the broken lawnmower next to the—the cloakroom."

"And the room is not locked?"

My uncle looked sad and shook his head.

"I assume," he said, "that the thief wore my clothing to protect his own whilst climbing up and down the drainpipe—and then threw it out of the landing window."

"It would be one hell of a throw," I pointed out.

"Yes," agreed the inspector. "It seems more likely that your uncle's clothes were hidden in the bushes sometime later, possibly early this morning."

"And why the hose?" I persisted.

"You will remember," said Uncle Albert, "that The Master could calculate the weight and possibly the height of a man from his footprints, but a man standing on very wet ground in someone else's overshoes—" A faraway look came into his eyes and I knew he was on the track—or, as he would have said, "deducting."

I tried to pull him back to the present. "Surely it would have been even more difficult if the ground had been bone dry."

Uncle responded with a proud smile. "I always keep that patch of ground slightly wet," he said. "Damp enough to hold footprints in the event of a burglary."

I saw Don looking at Uncle Albert and then at me. Well, I'm not the only person in the world with an eccentric relation.

"It's very interesting," said Don. "But may I ask when we shall be allowed to leave, inspector?"

"You're all free to go now" was the answer.

Don galvanized Susan and Sammy and then his car into action. In minutes, they were speeding dangerously down the drive. Then John Canning made his polite departure, followed by Simon Lantern.

Our weekend guests, Jane and Roger, remained.

The inspector agreed to join us for a pre-lunch drink. Uncle Albert looked portentous and frustrated until both Jane and Roger decided to tidy up before lunch. As the door closed behind them, Uncle launched into his theory.

"Of course it was them," he said. "Very sad, but Roger's firm is in need to money and the jewelry would fetch a very good price." He shook his head sadly and continued. "They are both familiar with the house. They knew where I kept my gardening clothes and where the hose was. They went out for a walk quite early, hiding my clothes in the bushes on the way. They're great walkers, so on one would remark on the fact that they strode out to the village. No doubt they met an accomplice there. Of course it was Jane who came down the drainpipe—Roger's a little stout for a maneuver of that sort—and she had to make the ground really wet to disguise her lack of weight and inches. It all fits," he added. "And I hope that you will be able to apprehend them and trace the jewelry before the accomplice sells it."

He said it with a look which would have made Lestrade quail, but it didn't have that effect on the inspector.

"We certainly hope to recover the jewelry," he said. "My men are watching the thief at this moment and they will see when he makes contact with his accomplice. In fact, we pretty well know who that will be becaues he usually works with the same man."

"Usually?" My uncle was shocked. "You mean this isn't their first offense?"

"It won't be the thief's first offense—but the thief is neither of your two friends."

"I'm glad of that," I said with feeling, "but who is it?"

"I'll tell you that as soon as we're able to make the arrest," the inspector promised.

It was a sticky weekend, with Uncle having to admit failure to himself and pretending like mad he'd never suspected Jane and

Roger—who didn't make the situation any easier by constantly asking Uncle for his opinion on the theft. It was quite a relief when they left on Sunday afternoon, and even more pleasant when the inspector rang in the evening and asked if he could call around. I'd refused a lift from Jane and Roger and decided to stay over and take an early train in the morning in case there was any news.

The inspector brought my jewelry along for formal identification.

"Who was it?" I asked.

"Mr. Canning."

"How did you know?" Uncle asked.

"It was quite simple. Canning had several convictions under other names and it was his style. He fit the general description. His fingerprints clinched it. Of course, the fact that he is a jewel thief didn't prove he'd stolen Miss Stephen's jewelry—we had to wait until he collected it from his accomplice."

"But how could you know?" I asked. "How could you know his style, what he looked like, who his accomplice was?"

"I didn't need to, Miss Stephen. Scotland Yard has a fine Criminal Records Office. A man with a police radio has a great advantage over a man with a magnifying glass."

Uncle Albert was very unhappy in the hours that followed the inspector's departure and I was considering phoning the office in the morning to say my uncle was ill when he suddenly perked up.

"It was entirely solved by the fingerprints," he said. "Entirely. And, of course, The Master was one of the very first to realize their importance."

T. M. Adams
Requiem for Three Sharks

Found among the papers of Hiram Daugherty, editor from 1870 to 1904 of the Hardluck Messenger, of Hardluck, Nevada. The few revisions of spelling and punctuation are those of Mr. Daugherty.

Mr. Daugherty's Introduction:
The manuscript enclosed herein is the confession of one Scott Trefoil, who was hanged in Hardluck on May 9, 1882, for the murder of a dry-goods drummer named Clem Sampson the previous month. Mr. Trefoil, a quiet-spoken man in his early thirties, had come to Hardluck only a few days before the shooting in the company of a "Major" DeWitt, whose subsequent demise was apparently the source of the fatal quarrel between Trefoil and Sampson.

At his trial, Mr. Trefoil declined to defend himself or, indeed, take much interest, save at one point to call the late Sampson "a welsher, a cheat, and an accessory to murder." His main preoccupation in his last few days was the total expenditure of what money he had. After purchasing at some cost an elaborate headstone for DeWitt's grave, he arranged for an unmarked plot for himslf, perpendicular to DeWitt's and, as it were, at DeWitt's feet. His remaining funds, minus one dollar, were spent on a lavish meal the night preceding his execution and on the attendance at that meal of two loose women, procured, I regret to say, by the deputy sheriff. The following morning, shortly after completing the confession that follows, he ascended the scaffold. His last dollar went as a tip to the hangman.

I had asked Mr. Trefoil to set down his story, along with whatever religious reflections occurred to him and perhaps a few admonitory words to Youth, as such testaments from notorious murderers are always very popular with the readership. He obliged me, and I considered the result literate enough, despite lapses, but after much internal debate I forbore to print it. It is a moral statement of a kind, I grant, but of *what* kind?

The Confession of Scott Trefoil:
I, Scott Trefoil, being of sound mind and body, wish to attest in my last hours to the existence of a Divine Providence that shapes our destinies and brings harm upon the heads of all who do wrong. That there is no corresponding Power to protect the innocent is the other lesson of my tale, for it is my duty to here set down the true story of the death of Major George Washington DeWitt, the kindest, wisest, and noblest man I have ever known.

Had I more time, I could devote a volume to the superior qualities of my late friend and partner. As it is, I can only attempt to sketch a few representative incidents in his life.

As near as I can remember, it was five years ago that we were in Denver. It was mid-morning. Since ten o'clock the evening before, the major had been playing poker at the Long Chute Emporium with a bunch of silver miners up from Custer County. He had about seven hundred dollars in front of him and his opponents looked hard-pressed, but he excused himself for a drink and took me aside. "Scotty," he said, "get me three hundred."

He was like that. He knew just exactly how the game was going to go, even when he was not dealing. Many's the time when he'd seem to be far ahead but would somehow know there was a rough patch coming up and say to me, "Scotty, get me a hundred," or "five hundred," or, in tough cases, "Scotty, get me a gun." This time it was three hundred dollars.

I walked outside, squinting at the bright sunlight, wondering what I was going to do. Three hundred dollars is a sizable piece of change, even in a mining town, and it cramped my style considerably to have to raise it in broad daylight. I drifted along and finally fetched up at the railroad station.

In Denver you can see pretty near all the trains there are in Colorado. You have the Denver Pacific coming in from the north, the Kansas Pacific from Ellsworth and Abilene, the Denver and Rio Grande running down to the Atchison, Topeka, and Santa Fe in the south, and various spurs off west and south to Boulder, Golden City, and all those other boomtowns. So you have trains coming in constantly, five or six times a day and even at night, and the people on them have money. I stood there, twirling my watch chain, waiting for marks.

The train from Pueblo came in and I watched the people getting off, the women lifting their skirts above the dust and them men looking for a drink—and I noticed an interesting thing. There was a big clock on top of the train station and as the men got off most of them set their watches by it. There was nothing unusual about that; I guess local time in a town usually goes by the biggest clock in it. But I had never given the matter any thought before. Just suppose, I thought, I had a nickel for every man who set his watch by that clock.

At this point some hayseed bumped into me, not looking where he was going because he was setting his watch.

"That'll be a nickel, please," I said to him.

"Pardon me?" he said.

"You just set your watch by the company clock, colonel. Now can I have my nickel, or must I call a constable?"

The hayseed apologized, gave me a nickel, and departed.

I cadged a few more nickels in this manner, more to pass the time and keep my hand in than anything else. As the major always told me, if you want to land a fish, you have to get your feet wet. A nickel a mark was nothing of course, but sure enough, those three hundred dollars came in with the tide.

The hayseed had reappeared at my shoulder. "Yes?" I said, wondering if he had tumbled to my game.

"I been watching you," he said, suspicious-like. "Seems to me you don't rightly collect from ever'body."

It was like the sun coming out. I hadn't heard him speak a full sentence before, but now I knew I had myself a live one, a bona fide open-plains yokel of the old school.

"You're right, colonel," I said. "It's my bad leg, I just can't keep up with them all. I'll tell you something, a young fellow like yourself would make out a sight better in my job. I take in only five to ten dollars a day, but there's a good twenty dollars more that escapes me."

"You're talking about thirty-five dollars a day?" he hayseed exclaimed.

"I can see you're quick," I said. "Yes, it's quite an opportunity. But let's not talk about it here in the hot sun."

We retired to a nearby beanery, I remembering to limp, and there I set the mark to talking about himself. A trailhand up until a few days before, he had been paid off in Dodge and had taken it into his head to invest his stake in the mines and make a fortune. He was as green as the watch he'd bought from some peddler on the train.

As a cowboy, the was used to being flat broke most of the year, getting paid off big at the end of a drive, and then blowing it all in town. He suspected mining might be much the same. But the idea of having his fortune doled out to him forever at so many dollars a day, while he did nothing more strenuous than standing around in his new suit looking grand in front of the ladies as they got off the train, had a certain appeal.

So he kept nosing around my "business."

"You own that clock, now, do you?" he asked, and there was still a trace of suspicion in his manner.

"No, no, of course not," I assured him. "Look here, you can read, can't you?" Before he had time to admit he couldn't, I whipped out a detailed hotel bill the major and I had failed to settle in San Francisco and held it under his eye. "As you can see," I said, "this is a Clock Correction Franchise from the Denver and Pacific Railroad Company. It authorizes me to collect a fee from every man who sets his watch by the clock in their station, in exchange for which I insure that the clock keeps correct time."

"That's the hard part, is it?" he said.

"Not a bit of it. Every morning I go down to the telegraph office, not a block away from the station, and ask the time. I get that free. Then I carefully set my own watch—a very accurate naval chronometer—to telegraph-corrected time, walk to the station, and hand it over to the station master. He sets the big clock, if it needs it, I tip him a nickel, and that's all. The rest is just a matter of collecting my fees. I think I do pretty well for a man who's been limping ever since Gettysburg." And indeed, I kept up a very good front in those days, with a suit and hat from St. Louis and a silver-headed cane.

The hayseed allowed as how it might not be as hard a job as some, but wasn't it rough on my bad leg? I had only said as much half a dozen times, but I said it again and admitted that if only I could sell the franchise I had a place waiting for me in the Assay Office at Boulder where I could just sit and count money all day.

The hayseed could hardly stay still in his seat by this time. He wondered what the qualifications were for my position. I said there wasn't much to it. A fellow had to be in good health, and of course the Company would expect him to pay a good price for the franchise, just to show he was a gentleman of substance. I said I didn't suppose that a boy like himself could meet my figure, but if he could—no, but I'd forgotten, he had to have a good watch, too—

"I've got a watch, remember? I showed it to you," he said, hauling out the brass wonder again. "Bran' new!"

"Why, that's right," I said. "I guess it's just a question of price, then."

I had to ask for seven-fifty to make it look good, but I finally let him have the franchise for three hundred dollars. Funny coincidence—that was very nearly its face value, less a few dollars the hotel had tacked on for breakage and missing silverware.

The point of all this is, a lot of people wouldn't have thought to go to so much trouble for money when the major was far ahead of the game and didn't seem to need it. But I swear that the moment I walked in and handed him the roll, he tossed it in the pot. There was nothing but small change left in front of him. He had known he would need it, he had known I would get it somehow—he never did ask me, afterwards, and I never bothered him with details—and he had known he would win the pot and be three thousand ahead at the end of the day. If anyone ever asks you, that is what Genius is.

I don't want to leave the impression that the major depended heavily on me. He had inner resources, as perhaps the following incident will demonstrate.

Two years ago, on a Mississippi packet to New Orleans, the major was on deck playing draw poker for more than nominal stakes. It was a beautiful day; the orchestra was playing and the sun was high. I was standing by and fetching drinks, as usual. The major had been a big winner all morning, but his cards had been slacking off since noon and the game was too public to permit skill to make up the difference.

Betting was brisk, pot limit and table stakes, and the major was keeping the opening bets high so he could bring to bear the full weight of his earlier winnings later on, as the luck of the draw dictated. He had a decent hand in any case, drawing one card to the three, four, five and six of diamonds. Since two of the other players were drawing two cards apiece and one was standing pat, either the low straight or the diamond flush might have been in trouble.

But if the long-shot straight flush came in against good cards, the already considerable pot might multiply twelvefold before falling to the major.

At this critical juncture, the dealer erred. He was one of these sticky-fingered fellows who has to reach your card over to you hand-delivery, snapping the last corner down with needless punctilio. Too often, this sort of dealer is feeling for a pinprick mark, but this had been a fairly honest game, for poker. Anyway, this fellow was too clumsy to be cheating. As the major sat there with his sucking-straight four-flush, admirably concealing his anticipation, this so precise dealer judged his fancy snap wrong. The upper half of the card was exposed to the major's eyes for some small fraction of a second, then the card flitted off the table, over the rail, and into the river.

The major shouted, sprang to his feet, pointed at a fleck of blue in the dirty brown river, and said, "Scotty, get me that card!"

I didn't hesitate an instant. I had never jumped from a steamboat before, but at one time or another I'd had reason to give the problem serious thought, and I knew that my first concern had to be getting clear of the paddlewheel, which would jolt me like a chicken if I got caught up in it. Accordingly, I ran not to the stern of the boat but to the bow, got up on the rail, and pushed off as hard as I could to the side.

The steamboat passed me as I oriented myself, although there were already cries of "Hold up, man overboard!" The major was leaning over the rail, bawling directions, and with his help I got a bearing on the card. The exploit would hardly have been possible had we not been in one of those long shallow S-bends where the river is more mud than water and so slow that sometimes straight new channels—chutes, they call them—cut through to bypass. The steamboat had been making way slowly and the card had not been left too far behind. Swimming in that muck had a lot in common with ditch digging. I was soon exhausted and my suit was ruined, but when the steamboat stopped and I'd been reeled in on a float, I had the card tucked into my pocket.

I handed it to the major first thing and I'm sure that if my jacket had been dry he would have clapped me on the back, he was that pleased. While the captain and the pilot dressed me down, the major returned to the card table, announcing that he was raising the last bet—they had started the bets during my recovery—by the sum of the pot. He cursed when he looked down and saw that in the excitement he had put the rest of his hand on the table face up; it was evident to all players that the card I'd risked my life for must have filled a straight flush, and one by one, with rueful smiles, they folded to the major's raise.

Just as well, as the major said later. You can't fill a low diamond straight flush with a nine of hearts, wet *or* dry.

That was a lucrative week—and fortunately too because I came down with pneumonia and we were out of action for a while, the major looking after me.

I had not always had someone to see to my welfare. Indeed, it is one measure of the major's great heart that he took me in when he did.

That was during the War of the Secession, at Gettysburg. The major and I were both in the 20th Infantry, Maine Volunteers, under Colonel Chamberlain. The major was not a major at the time; he had been broken all the way down to the ranks during the Mexican War. (I never asked him why, or why he re-enlisted so much later.) I was just a kid, a regimental drummer boy, but I wasn't drumming that day. I was terrified out of my wits, and on top of that I had a freshly killed chicken hidden inside my drum, a little something I'd picked up on the march from Maryland. We were tucked up there on a hill, Little Round Top, whose name we didn't then know. The easternmost extension of the line, we weren't allowed to break or fall back lest the whole Union line be flanked.

As we were in danger of being flanked ourselves, Chamberlain drew part of the line back perpendicular to the rest to guard our left. A few attacks later, with dark coming on and our ammunition gone, he gave the order to fix bayonets, moved that perpendiuclar edge back around front like swinging a gate, and led everyone in a downhill charge, the last cast of the dice. The Rebs, as exhausted as ourselves, broke and ran and were captured in the hundreds by men with empty rifles.

That's the story everyone knows, but the major's part in the battle has never been recorded. It was the penultimate moment. The Rebs were coming up the slope and we had no rifle balls with which to meet them. "Fix bayonets!" came the cry, and two hundred men were poised atop the slope of History. From there they went on and down, to the easy capture of those Alabama boys and, farther, to the bloodshed at The Wilderness and Petersburg and Five Forks, to Appomattox, to Glory, or to the death camp at Andersonville. And as the sergeants yelled "Charge!" and we moved from cover, I suddenly felt a hand grasp my shoulder and heard a voice above the tumult—just four words, but to my mind the pivotal speech of the war: "Not *that* way, boy."

The great tide of Destiny had broken against the major. Chamberlain charged down the hill, but we charged the other way.

I never knew my father, having met him just one time less than my mother did. From the first, the major took his place. What had caused him to single me out as his protege I'm not sure, although he once made a comment of sorts about that.

"I took one look at you," he said, "and immediately noticed two things. One, that you had a good head on your shoulders, and two, that you had a chicken."

The major raised me. I had been taught to read and write at the orphanage, but the major taught me grammar, spelling, and the love of literature, mainly by forcing me to keep a journal, and keep it in English. It's true that I still tend to write the language as she is spoken instead of stodging it up and shifting it around to make it look as though I were translating from my native Latin, but otherwise I think I can pass as educated. In addition to French and Spanish, the major also taught me about whores: to stay away from them, how not to catch anything from them, and what to do when you caught something—three times as much as I'd never been taught on the subject before.

Most importantly, he taught me to love what he called "the action" for itself, not just for the money it brought in.

"You have to like what you do, as well as what you have," he would say, "or else everything goes sour."

I have very little time left and cannot list all the major's accomplishments. However, his contributions to the growth and develoment of the Republic should not go unmentioned. In the late sixties and early seventies, he was instrumental in forming railroad companies all over the Southwest, and almost all the railroad lines he proposed were later constructed, although people did object to having to raise the money a second time. And I think that the spread of Law and the increasing effectiveness of Enforcement throughout the territories have been in some small part a response to the major's unflagging efforts.

Unfortunately, poker is performed in the most soul-deadening surroundings of all Man's highest arts. The decades of dark rooms, bad whisky, and worse cigars finally caught up with the major, and in the last few months of his life he lost the enthusiasm he used to preach to me. His skill had begun to wane—not the mechanical aspect, for he was as dexterous as ever, but his nearly supernatural ability to "grasp this sorry scheme of things entire" and predict beforehand the ebb and flow in human affairs.

Without this ability, he was nearly rudderless in a poker game. He became just another cheat and, as he taught me, a cheat is at a disadvantage among players of skill. Instead of bending his full powers of concentration to the hand in play, he would be gathering discards for bottom-dealing, only to see no real money fall on the next stacked hand. Other hands, quite trivial, would seem great crises to him, and these misapplications of energy were a soure of nervous strain.

Had I surmised the gravity of the situation, I might have tried to keep him from playing, but I doubt I would have succeeded.

He saw his last game here in Hardluck. It began in the small hours of the morning, May ninth of the present year, continuing through the day and the evening. The major's luck held through the daylight hours, but he was exceedingly wary of the other strong player in the game. This was a traveling salesman named Sampson, who I thought had the cheeky, no-account look of a welsher. I consoled myself with the thought that this was a no-credit game.

Since his playing had become worse, the major was increasingly unwilling to have me watch over his shoulder. I contented myself with checking in every hour or so with a weak drink for him. I know now that the major had invested his heart and soul in this game, but at the time I could detect on extra effort on his part. He always took his poker very seriously.

At eight o'clock in the evening he said he had been having a bad time but was rallying. "The Ohio boy is dealing seconds," he reported. "Sometimes thirds, too, but I don't think that's deliberate."

At nine o'clock, he told me that the key to this game was the drummer Sampson. "If I can drive him out," he said, "the rest will be like picking berries."

At ten o'clock, he said that by the grace of God he had prevailed. Sampson had a few hundred left in front of him and the major was confident that that was the last of his cash. He permitted me to stand by and watch for the next hour. A lot of money changed hands among the small fry and Sampson seined his share of it, but every time he seemed likely to get ahead the major would bet into him, uncovering and punishing every bluff.

At eleven came the *coup de grace*. Sampson had worked his way up to a balance of seven hundred dollars and lost it all bluffing with a four-flush against the major's trifling pair of tens. The major was happy but weak, clearly played out.

Then the blow fell. Sampson reached into his pocket and produced his wallet. Although he was out of cash, he had a deed of property, and from the comments I heard I gathered that it would be admitted to the game at a valuation of five hundred dollars. I walked out under a dark cloud. There was nothing to stop the major from winning that five hundred, too, but somehow I knew he wouldn't. He was spent, and he wouldn't admit it by quitting, either.

He came back to my hotel room shortly after two in the morning. He had lost all but a few hundred dollars. I had seen him play like a loser once or twice before, but at such times he had always known enough to quit before too much damage was done. Now he worried me. He was all blue in the face and he made little whistling sounds as he breathed.

I took him to his own room and camped out there after putting him to bed. When I could tell he was asleep, I lit a candle and browsed through a penny newspaper I'd bought during the day. Around three, I heard his breathing become very agitated. I thought of calling for a doctor, but the major hated doctors and I was afraid that the strain of cussing one out would carry him off. He quieted down finally.

I next heard from him at three thirty. He called out to me in a clear but low voice. He said he'd had a very strange dream. "We were back on the hill, Scotty, only you were all grown up. We were back on the hill and this time we went down with the others, through all the smoke and the noise and the boys falling—but when we got to the bottom, all there was . . . there was a long table and everyone was lined up to it and as we passed by they gave us our mustering-out pay . . . just paid us off . . . that was at Puebla, reinforcements came in and I was mustered out . . . and I said, 'Wait, I have two years' officer's pay before that other.' But they said, 'No, private . . .' 'No,' she said to me, '*tu pecasste . . . tu pecasste*', she said . . ." Then he said someone's name—a foreign lady's, I think—but it was hard to catch.

At four o'clock he was dead.

I didn't tell anybody. I just went back to my room and slept for fourteen hours. When I woke up, I still had the same feeling. Why this town? What would be the point in burying the major in this particular town? I couldn't see much point in anything else, either. I went to a saloon, ordered a drink, and spent a few hours trying to finish it. Then I chanced to overhear a conversation about the poker game of the night before.

Someone with a sour-grapes voice suggested that the big winner, Sampson, had bought his way back in with a forged deed that wasn't worth a cent. I didn't listen to the argument that followed. I was thinking about that piece of paper Sampson had produced at the last moment. There was no doubt in my mind that that document, more than anything else, had killed the major; he had broken his heart against it. Had it been worthless? Had Sampson been attempting to welsh out of five hundred dollars? It was something I had to see to.

I had never killed anyone before, but I had come close a number of occasions, and had a pretty good idea of how to go about the job. Just a year past, for instance, I had put four bullets into a drunken lawyer who had tried to rob us at gunpoint, and it was only by a miracle that he had survived to run for governor that fall.

I went back to my room and took a pistol from my valise. It's a real antique, an 1849 Colt .28 pocket pistol with a three inch barrel and most of the stock removed, which I hereby bequeath to anyone wh can still find ammunition for it. It's troublesome to load and it's only single-action, with a trick trigger that doesn't pop down until you've cocked, but I've found it very useful as a sort of five-shot derringer. As usual, I slipped it inside a folded-up newspaper and cut a slit to work the trigger through.

There were only a few hotels in town and Sampson, a traveling man, figured to be in one of them. I found his room at about eleven o'clock that night. He opened the door to my knock.

"Yes?" he said. He had no reason to remember me.

"Mr. Sampson," I said, "people have been dropping remarks about your behavior last night, and I thought perhaps you might like to set the record straight."

He opened the door wider and asked, "Just what are you talking about, old horse?"

"That deed you bought back into the game with last night," I said, poking him in the stomach with my newspaper, as if for emphasis. "Folks are saying it's no good. I'd like to have a look at it."

He gave a little snort, saying, "And I'd like you to go to hell!"

"After you," I said, working the trigger.

He fell inside his room. I followed him in and closed the door. The noise having been louder than I expected, I took his pillow from the bed and used it to muffle the second shot. Goose feathers sprayed everywhere. The newspaper had caught fire; I dropped it to the ground and stamped it out.

I rolled him over and went through his pockets. Aside from a great deal of cash, there was only the one deed. I would have known it was the same one anyway, from the glimpse I'd gotten the night before. It was a gaudy thing, all gold ink in curlicues, two columns of find print, and a fancy seal on the bottom—as worthless as its owner.

I just sat there. Something awful had just been revealed to me, and I needed time to think. Someone came looking for Sampson and raised a cry. I could have gotten away—by morning, I probably would have—I know I'd try now, if I could see a way. But it's best as it is. Once things go sour, as the major taught me, they stay sour. I could never live happily in the world knowing I had killed the major. And I did. I had killed him five years ago without knowing it, and the proof was the paper in my hand.

It was a Clock Correction Franchise for six towns on the Union Pacific Railroad.

How many like Sampson are there, I wonder, who heard tell of my Denver invention and determined to work it? Very few, I suspect, or the word would be out and the game ruined. Quite likely Sampson was the only such in all the state.

There is a God, then, as in my gloomiest moments I always half suspected. Sampson He took for welshing, me He'll take for killing the major, but I think the major himself was just struck down in passing. There was no Divine justice in his death, not unless the psalm-singers and the pew-buyers and the finger-pointers are right and it's their Temperance God who runs things—and I know more about how things run than they do. I've made my peace with Whomever, anyway.

I guess that's all.

Jack Ritchie
When the Sheriff Walked

"Joey Lee is—or was—about five foot ten, had short brown hair, a small scar right under the left earlobe, and weighed a hefty one hundred and seventy pounds."

Hefty? I regarded one hundred and seventy pounds as lightweight.

The counterman continued. "But I suppose L. K. gave you a snapshot?"

"No," I said. "And I don't even know who L. K. is."

He smiled wisely. "Joey Lee's father, L. K. Williams."

So Joey Lee's last name was really Williams? I had thought it was Lee.

The counterman refilled my mug of coffee. "L. K. has this New South Cafe in Cumberdale. That's about sxity miles due east, where Joey Lee originally come from." He looked up as the door behind me opened, quickly wiped the counter, and moved away.

The sheriff of Staceyville was a small, immaculately uniformed man wearing a white hat. He took the stool next to me. "I hear you been asking a lot of questions, especially about Joey Lee."

I put down my coffee. "I have not asked anyone at all about Joey Lee. On the contrary, ever since I set foot in this town, people have been asking *me*."

He regarded me stonily. "You wouldn't be one of them private eye investigators?"

"Do I look like a private investigator?"

"Nowadays you can't tell. They run from Mannix to Cannon. Just what is your line, mister?"

I have a tendency to bristle when harassed. "I am an admiralty lawyer."

He was not at all convinced.

"We got no water around here except for Lake Jubal A. Early and that's only twenty-six acres when it rains. Why did you come here, mister?"

"I consider that my personal business and nothing short of a court order will unseal my lips. Am I the only stranger who's ever stopped in this delightful town?"

"Just about. For the last two years, anyway. Ever since Amtrak took away our daily train we been pretty isolated." He seemed to give that some dark thought and then frowned. "The situation don't make much difference to the men, but the women complain a lot."

He studied me for another moment, then turned and went back out into the night.

The counterman returned. "I guess I was the last person to see Joey

Lee alive. Except maybe for ..." He glanced signficantly in the direction the sheriff had taken.

"Are you telling me that Joey Lee is dead?"

He shrugged elaborately. "There are some of us who think so. Joey Lee disappeared one week ago and there's nothing to show for it except the mud on the patrol car tires."

Mud on the patrol car tires? I was about to ask about that, but he continued.

"When a thing like this happens, it splits the town in two." He mulled that over. "Come to think of it, when *anything* happens, it splits the town in two. Anyway, half the people are in favor of keeping this thing quiet and local and the other half would like to bring it out into the open."

"Why don't they?"

"The sheriff's got a rotten temper and you hate to cross him. Especially in something like this." He leaned a bit closer. "You got a badge?"

I closed my eyes. "I am an admiralty lawyer."

He chuckled. "Just what is an admiratly lawyer supposed to do?"

"At present I am representing the last living survivor of the *Lady Diana* ship disaster of 1893."

"Of 1893? You mean it's been dragging through court for eighty-one years?"

I smiled. "My dear fellow, if you knew anything at all about law, especially admiralty law, you would know that these things can not be rushed." I glanced at my watch. It was nearly nine. "Am I being optimistic when I ask if there is a hotel in this town?"

"The Beauregard. Got lots of room these days. Rafe Covert owns it and he's a cousin of the sheriff, so don't let him give you the Ulysses S. Grant room. It's number 222."

I went back to where I'd parked my car and carried my suitcase the half block to the Beauregard. When I entered the lobby I had the distinct impression that everyone there knew about me, or thought he did.

The man behind the desk seemed a touch hostile as he watched me sign the register. He took a key off the board. "Your room number is 222."

I smiled generously. "I am psychologically allergic to number 222. It is a long story and someday when I have more time, I will tell it to you. Another room, please."

Reluctantly he produced another tagged key.

My room appeared quite clean and comfortable. I turned on the TV set for half an hour and then went to bed.

In the morning, just as I finished dressing, there came a knock at my door. I found a small, elderly woman in maid's uniform with sheets and pillowcases draped over her arm. "I come to change the bed linen."

She began stripping the bed. "I'll bet L. K. hired you."

"L. K. Williams?"

She nodded. "Do you think Joey Lee is still alive?"

"Why does everybody think that Joey Lee is dead?"

She slipped a pillow into a fresh pillowcase. "We're all concerned citizens—or at least half of us are—but we got to be careful what we say in front of the sheriff and his relatives. I guess I was the last person to see Joey Lee alive."

"I thought that distinction belonged to the counterman at the Staceyville Cafe?"

She sniffed. "Alex saw Joey Lee last at nine thirty Monday night. I saw Joey Lee *and* the sheriff at nine forty-five. Right behind the jailhouse. And they were arguing."

"About what?"

"I couldn't rightly make that out. They stopped when they saw me and didn't go to it again until I was well past. How do you like our town?"

"Charming."

She unfolded a sheet. "Staceyville is heaven for men and dogs, but hell on women and horses. Ever since they took away our train, we women have been cut off from the world."

"Can't any of you drive automobiles?"

"We're mostly a one-car-per-family town. Have you ever tried to pry the car away from your husband just to take an innocent shopping trip to Montgomery?"

"Then you are isolated and desperate?"

"We got TV and the library's open Tuesday and Thursday afternoons, so that takes care of culture. But we're people who are isolated. If you don't get out and meet new people now and then you get provincial and inward-turning in your thoughts for the day."

When she was gone, I went to the window and looked down at Main Street. According to the information I'd gathered, Staceyville had —among other things—two drugstores, four cafe-restaurants, five churches, two doctors, three dentists, and one chiropractor.

There was another knock at the door.

This time I found a large young man, blue-jeaned and T-shirted. I gauged his age at the senior level in high school.

He glared at me menacingly. "Mister, I'd advise you to take the first bus leaving Staceyville."

"Staceyville doesn't have a bus."

He flushed slightly. "I mean take your car. Anyway, leave town."

"Why?"

He flexed a conspicuous *biceps brachii*. "Because I say so."

I showed my teeth. "I warn you, I have a brown belt in karate." Actually, however, I cannot distinguish a karate chop from a hibachi casserole.

He hesitated. "I got a white belt myself. My coach in phys ed says I'm pretty good."

I chuckled menacingly. "You must be aware that people with white belts simply do not mess around with people who possess the superior brown belts, except if they are heavily insured. Just what rash impulse brought you here?"

He shifted nervously from one foot to the other. "The sheriff is my uncle and he's been good to me, like at Christmas and birthdays. So I thought maybe I could help him out in his hour of need—no matter what he's done—by leaning on you a little."

"Did he send you here?"

"No. He doesn't know anything about it."

I shook my head sadly. "Mr dear young man, in your career of television viewing, have you *ever* seen any detective frightened out of town by threats or even by violence itself?"

He frowned in retrospect. "Now that I come to think of it ..." He eyed his wristwatch with sudden discovery. "Gee, just look at that time. I got to get moving or I'll be late for chemistry class." He picked up a stack of books he had evidently deposited beside the door before knocking and quickly disappeared down the stairs.

I went out to the nearest restaurant for breakfast.

The waitress serving me had the name Billie Gee embroidered over her uniform pocket. She smiled. "Good morning, Mr. Collins."

I had never seen her before in my life.

She winked. "We don't see many admiralty lawyers around here."

"And I doubt that you will in the future."

"How do you like our town?"

"Interesting."

She shrugged. "It's heaven for men and dogs, but hell on women and horses."

I stared at her. "Do you have many horses around here?"

"Well, no. That was just an expression. But we got lots of women."

I glanced out of the window. The sheriff had parked his patrol car across the street and now he stood beside it, ostentatiously inspecting his shotgun.

"The sheriff just loves hunting," Billie Gee said.

"What does he hunt?"

"Rabbits, mostly."

The sheriff noticed a dust mote on his otherwise spotless car and dusted it off with a handkerchief.

"The town lets the sheriff use the car for his own personal use, too," Bille Gee said. "He takes real good care of it." She smiled slyly. "Except for last Tuesday when he walked."

She took my order and departed.

When I finished eating and left the restaurant, the sheriff stopped me. "Who hired you?"

"How does L. K. Williams sound?"

"Don't give me that. It was somebody in town, wasn't it? Or maybe they formed a committee?" He glared down at three pre-school children who gingerly sidled past him. "I know what everybody in town's thinking. But not a single one of the them has got the guts to come right out and say it."

"Say what?"

"Never mind. I just don't want no outside interference."

I went on to the drugstore a short distance down the street.

The proprietor scowled at me. "I'm not answering any of your questions. "You'll get nothing out of me."

Another one of the sheriff's relatives?

"I just came in for some cigars."

He regarded me coldly. "All right. I'll tell you this and no more. Ask Randolph." He moved to the rear of the store.

"What about my cigars?"

He disappeared into a back room.

I sighed and bought cigars at the town's second drugstore where the clerk was friendly. I walked back down Main Street, past the courthouse square which featured a Civil War cannon, pointed north. I went back up to my hotel room.

A chubby, beard-stubbled man sat on my bed. His suit was considerably off-white and his Panama somewhat crushed.

He ventured a smile. "The door was unlocked, so I just walked in when nobody answered my knock. Besides, I didn't want to be seen here by anybody. You never know who you can trust."

"Just who the devil are you?"

"I'm Randolph Wister." He ran his tongue over his lips. "You don't happen to have a little drink around?"

"No. But I assume you have looked?"

He nodded. "I just thought you might have something on you."

"Sorry."

He philosophically accepted the situation. "You pay for valuable information, don't you?"

"I suppose you're going to tell me that you were the last person to see Joey Lee alive?"

"No. That was Mrs. Whittaker over at the hotel. But I seen something else."

I checked the contents of my suitcase. Nothing seemed to be missing.

"I was in the jailhouse Tuesday night," Randolph said. "That's sort of thing happens now and then. Anyway, the sheriff put me in a cell to sleep it off."

I closed the suitcase and locked it.

Randolph continued. "I woke around seven Wednesday morning when I heard this water running just outside in back of the jailhouse. I looked out of my cell window and there was the sheriff washing his car down with a hose."

"He's never washed his car before?"

"I mean there was *mud* on the patrol car tires. Dried mud. How could he get mud on his tires when we haven't had any rain around here in two weeks?"

Randolph tried the glass of water on the night table. "On Monday night at nine forty-five, Mrs. Whittaker saw the sheriff and Joey Lee arguing. That's the last anybody saw of Joey Lee. and then early Wednesday morning, the sheriff cleans mud off the tires of the patrol car."

"You seem to have skipped over Tuesday entirely."

"On Tuesday the sheriff was in town all day. Walking."

"Why should that be so significant?"

"When the sheriff arrested me on Tuesday night, he *walked* me to the jailhouse. When I asked him why I didn't get a ride like always, he just got mad and told me to shut up."

He put down the empty glass. "When I got out of jail I heard that Joey Lee was missing. I also heard that nobody saw the patrol car all day Tuesday. The sheriff was in town all right, but he tended to all his business on foot. And when anybody asked him about the car, he'd get testy and say that it was in the garage being repaired. But there's only two garages in town and neither one of them did any work on the sheriff's car on Tuesday. Now why would the sheriff lie about something like that unless he had something to hide?"

"I haven't the faintest idea."

"Suppose that on Monday night the sheriff killed Joey Lee during that argument. Right off he didn't know what to do with the body, so he hid it in the trunk of the patrol car and left the car parked in his garage all day Tuesday while he was thinking it over. And then Tuesday night he got rid of the body. Now if I were looking for a body, the shores of Lake Jubal A. Early might be a good place to start. The water's receding because of the dry spell and the shores are muddy."

"If that is what you people suspect, why hasn't any one of you gone to the state authorities?"

"I guess everybody was waiting for somebody else to do something and nobody did. I suppose L. K. hired you?"

I picked up my suitcase. "No."

He frowned. "You leaving town?"

"Yes." I smiled, opened the door, and left.

On the way back to my car, I met the sheriff again. His eyes went to my suitcase. "You leaving town?"

"Yes. I've enjoyed your hospitality, but the time has come for me to move on. I have accomplished what I came here for."

I left him standing there, mouth slightly open.

I drove out of Staceyville, spent some time in both Newcourt and Portertown, and reached Cumberdale by three in the afternoon. My eyes took in the shops and stores and the window of the L. K. Williams Cafe.

I hesitated a moment, then parked and went inside. At this time of day I was the only patron. I took one of the empty booths along the wall.

The waitress who came to take my order was a tall woman who seemed to be nursing a tragedy. She dabbed at red-rimmed eyes.

She stood about five foot ten, had short brown hair, and a small scar below her left earlobe. I estimated she weighted a hefty one hundred and seventy pounds.

Yes, hefty.

A sudden, incredible thought came to me. "*Are you* Joey Lee Williams?"

She seemed a bit surprised at the recognition. "Joey is for Josephine. Like in Joey Heatherton, the famous actress whom I admire from afar. Williams is my maiden name, but I'm married now. Do I know you?"

"You've got all of Staceyville in a dither," I said. "Nobody knows what happened to you."

The mention of Staceyville brought forth new tears. When she managed to control herself, she was in a mood to talk. "It all started just because I took the car to Montgomery for a little shopping."

"That doesn't seem like such a heinous crime to me."

"To me either, and I don't know why Clyde got so excited about it. After all, he has the town's permission to use the car for personal transportation, too."

"Who's Clyde?"

"My husband. The sheriff in Staceyville."

I blinked. "You took the patrol car to Montgomery on a shopping trip?"

"Clyde hasn't chased anybody with it in months and I didn't think it would make any big difference if I borrowed it for just one day. But I couldn't make Clyde see it my way and we had a big argument."

"On Monday night? Behind the jailhouse?"

She nodded. "So Tuesday morning when Clyde was still asleep, I took the keys and just took off. I wore one of Clyde's caps and a dark coat and nobody thought anything of it, especially in Montgomery where they got women's lib."

She dabbed at her nose. "On the way home I had carburetor trouble and then I got stuck for a while in the mud on a town road in Autauga County. And what with one thing and another, I didn't get back home until well after midnight. Clyde was simply furious."

The memory was quite painful to her. "The things Clyde said relative to my intelligence were just awful. So I just phoned Daddy and he came and got me at three in the morning."

"Your husband *knows* you are here?"

She nodded. "And he hasn't phoned even once to apologize."

Obviously the sheriff was a prideful man who chose not to confide in anyone that his wife had, in effect, stolen the patrol car, gone to Montgomery on a shopping trip, and then left him.

He must have been aware that the town knew his wife was gone, but did he know that half of it—if not really all of the town—suspected that he had killed her?

I sighed. "Have you ever thought of doing the big thing by phoning your husband and telling him that you forgive him."

She seemed to need only the slightest encouragement. "Do you really think I ought to call him?"

"Of course. And besides, you can always hang up if he gets nasty again."

"I'll do it," she said emphatically. She left me abruptly and went to the public phone booth at the end of the room.

I watched as she got her number. She used her handkerchief profusely as she spoke, but from her general expression it appeared that she would soon be back in Staceyville with Clyde—a husband forgiving, if not forgetting.

I am not an admiralty lawyer. Neither am I a detective, private or otherwise.

I work for the South Central Bus Line and it is my job to survey possible new bus routes, especially in those areas no longer serviced by railroads.

Another waitress appeared to take my order. "How do you like Cumberdale?" she asked.

"Amusing."

She sighed. "It's heaven for men and dogs, but hell on women and horses. I haven't been to Montgomery in three months."

I made a note that in addition to Staceyville, Newcourt, and Portertown, I might just as well add Cumberdale to the new route.

Al Nussbaum

Korda

I was sitting on an empty wooden crate in front of my father's workshop, a converted store, waiting to help him unload the truck when he got back from Chicago. He had driven north early that morning to pick up some used jukeboxes, and it was now after six in the evening. He was due back any time.

I was probably the first person in town who gave Leonard Korda any notice, except, of course, the sheriff. Korda strolled toward me from the direction of the bus station, swinging a small canvas satchel from his left hand. He had a head of bushy, reddish-brown hair and a short full beard. It made him look something like Lon Chaney, Jr., in his Wolf Man makeup on the Late Late Show. There was a lot of spring in his step.

Korda was about my size. I had just turned fourteen, and I stood five foot seven and weighed one-fifty. Even today when I've reached my full height of six foot one, I don't think of Korda as small. Compact would be a more accurate word. A year ago I saw a Japanese gymnast on television and immediately thought of Lenny Korda.

He had almost reached the sidewalk in front of me when the sheriff's patrol car glided silently to the curb and stopped beside him.

"Hey, you!" Sheriff Masters called, stepping out of the car and adjusting his wide-brimmed hat to sit squarely on his head. He wore khakis and a pearl-handled revolver rode high on a wellpadded hip.

Korda stopped and turned toward the sheriff. His beard split in a broad grin. He seemed relaxed and pleased to see the policeman, but his eyes were narrow and wary. "Yes?"

"You jus' got off the six o'clock bus?"

Korda allowed the satchel he was carrying to drop and looked at the watch strapped to his wrist. He confirmed the time and said "Yes" again.

He had to tilt his head back to look the sheriff in the eye His smile held steady.

"Where d'ya think you're goin'?" the sheriff demanded.

Korda hesitated a moment.

"New York," he answered. Then added, "Eventually."

"You got a ticket?"

"Uh-huh."

"Let me see it. And some identification."

Korda reached for his hip pocket, and Sheriff Masters put his hand on his pistol butt. Korda must have been watching the sheriff out of the corner of his eye because he slowed perceptibly and twisted his body so the sheriff could see it was a wallet he was taking from his pocket. He opened it and handed a few papers to the sheriff—a folded string of tickets like the bus company issues, a brand-new Social Security card, and an out-of-state driver's license—California, I think.

"This license has expired," the sheriff said.

Korda shrugged.

"What's that supposed t'mean?"

"I don't need an up-to-date license if I'm not driving."

Sheriff Masters handed back the papers. "We don't need any wise guys around here, Korda. Where d'ya think you're goin' now?"

"For a walk. The bus driver said there'll be an hour's stopover here, so I thought I'd work some of the kinks out of my spine. I've been riding for over ten hours."

"Okay, mister, but let me give you a tip—be on that bus when it pulls out. You smell like trouble to me, and I don't want you around."

The sheriff climbed into his cruiser, made a U-turn, and headed back toward the bus depot. He always kept a close personal eye on the bus station because most of the crime in Livingston involved people who were just passing through.

Korda stood with his hands on his hips until the car was gone. He saw me watching him and smiled. "Your sheriff's a hard man, kid."

"But a good one," I answered, echoing something my father always said.

Korda nodded. "That's probably so."

Right then my father arrived. He stopped in the street, then backed his beat-up truck over the curb to the front of the shop. He had two old but still serviceable jukeboxes on the back. They were all chrome, glass, and colored plastic. They looked a lot like the two that had been wrecked a few days before.

"Come on, Bobby," my dad called as he dropped the tailgate and started putting a pair of planks into position for unloading the machines. "And ask your friend if he'll give us a hand."

Korda was standing with his back to him, so all my dad had to go on was his size. He couldn't tell that Korda was twice my age.

We slid the jukeboxes down the planks and into the shop. They were weightier than they looked. Dad and I stood there breathing heavily while Korda glanced around the shop, taking in the bending brake, metal shears, and other tools Dad used for fabricating heating ducts and storm gutters out of sheet metal.

"I thought you were one of my son's school friends," Dad said, noticing the full beard. He offered his work-scarred hand and Korda took it.

Korda smiled, but it was warm and real, not just something to hide behind as it had been with the sheriff.

"We just met. I'm Leonard Korda. Call me Lenny." He gestured to indicate all the equipment and tools, and raised his eyebrows inquisitively. "The music machines seem out of place in here," he said.

"The machines are for a new business I'm starting," Dad told him in his quiet way. "My boy wants to be a doctor, and that's going to take a lot more money than I'm earning now."

Korda pointed to the *Man Wanted* sign in the front window. "I'd like to apply for the job," he said.

"Do you know anything about working with sheet metal?" Dad asked.

"I used to," Korda said. "And I can probably still calculate setback and bend allowance for most materials."

I laughed. "That's more than the last four guys could do," I said, then stopped myself, knowing I shouldn't have said anything about the others.

Korda picked up on it right away. "You having trouble keeping a helper? Why's that?"

"Well, first there's the pay. I can't afford to pay very much. Then there's the new business I'm trying to start. I'm having some trouble."

"What kind of trouble?"

"I thought placing vending machines and jukeboxes in this area would be a good way to earn the money my boy will need to see him through school. But because I don't have union stickers on my machines, businessmen are being told not to use them. Every time I've hired a helper, he's quit after a few days. I guess someone threatens them, scares them. A few days ago a couple of hoodlums smashed two of my jukeboxes with crowbars. I bought these machines to replace them."

"Why don't you join the union and save yourself a lot of headaches?" Korda suggested.

"I tried. They told me I couldn't join, said this territory has already been taken by a man named Clyde Anderson who lives in Bradyville, the next town west of here. Then I learned he's head of the union."

Korda scratched the side of his face, making the beard fluff out. "That'd make a good plot for a TV show."

"I need a helper who knows sheet metal," Dad said. "If you want the job and don't scare easy, you're welcome to it."

"I scare as easily as anybody else," Korda told him. "but I don't let it get in the way of anything I want to do."

My dad drove Korda back to the bus station in time for him to get his footlocker off the bus before it pulled out. He cashed in the rest of his ticket and returned to the pickup, balancing the trunk of his houlder. He put the footlocker in back, then climbed into the cab with me and Dad. Across the street Sheriff Masters watched from behind the wheel of his cruiser.

My dad and I were living in an apartment behind the shop. My mother died when I was four, so there were just the two of us. We had a spare room, and Dad offered it to Korda until he could find a place of his own or for as long as he liked.

The next few days Dad worked on the used jukeboxes to see that they'd work properly, and Korda proved that he knew his way around a sheet-metal shop. There didn't seem to be anything he had to learn; he could read blueprints and his work was a match for my dad's.

The Saturday after the machines were cleaned up, I went out to the shop in the morning like I always did when there was no school. Dad and Korda were already there, loading a machine onto the truck. I helped with the second one, then Dad locked the shop and we all got into the cab on the truck.

The two places where the machines had been smashed were out on the highway, a pair of truck stops about a mile apart. When we got to the first one, Dad parked in front and we all went inside, planning to have breakfast before unloading the machine.

The first thing we saw was a brand-new jukebox against the right-hand wall. We gave our orders to the girl behind the counter, then Dad asked, "Is Mr. Allen around?"

"Charlie!" the girl called at the opening to the kitchen. "Someone here to see you!"

A thick-waisted little man in a spotless apron appeared. He had a round face with pink cheeks. The laugh lines around his mouth showed he was the kind of person who is always cheerful, but his smile faded when he saw Dad.

"I thought you were going to use my machine, Mr. Allen," Dad said.

"Yeah. Well, that's right, I guess. I did say that, but—but I was without music for a week. Then a guy showed up and offered to put in a new machine with two hundred songs on it and give me the same split on the money that you were going to give me."

"We had a deal, Mr. Allen," Dad said reasonably.

"Yeah, sure we did, but those thugs weren't part of it. I'm a businessman—I'm not fighting a war. This machine has the union sticker and won't cause me any worries."

"Okay," Dad said, accepting defeat. "I guess I can't expect you to put yourself in the middle. I don't want trouble with those people either."

Our order arrived and we ate in silence. Allen came back when we were nearly finished. "Let me get you folks some more coffee," he said and returned with the Silex. He started to fill my cup, then stopped, staring past me out the front window.

We all swung around to see what he was looking at. A new sedan had pulled up beside the pickup truck and two men were getting out. They both wore dark suits with wide lapels. One pointed to the truck and said something. The other walked around the sedan and joined him.

Allen's voice dropped a little more than a whisper. "Those are the guys who smashed your machine," he said.

Dad got up without a word wipping his hands on the front of his work shirt, and went outside. I got up and followed him, but Korda hung back. I figured, like Allen, he didn't think it was his fight.

"You men looking for something?" Dad demanded.

"That depends," the larger of the two said. "This your truck?"

"Yes, it's mine."

"Those ain't union machines. My friend an' me, we don't like machines that don't have union stickers."

"Haven't you caused enough trouble already?"

The second man had climbed onto the truck and was tugging at the tie-down ropes. Now he stopped and joined the conversation. "You accusing us of somethin', buddy?" It was as though he were playing a game he'd played many times before.

"You're the ones who've been wrecking my machines."

"You shouldn't go around saying things like that. You need a lesson. Just t' show you how wrong you are, we're gonna dump these two pieces of junk off the truck."

I didn't see Korda approach. Suddenly he was between the men and my dad. He threw a handful of pepper into the big man's face. Then, while the man clawed at his eyes, trying to get his vision back, Korda hit him below the belt buckle with a looping right hand. The man dropped to his knees, howling in pain. Tears streamed down his face.

The second man jumped down from the truck and roared toward Korda.

Korda stood his ground and waited for him. My dad moved to help Korda, but he wasn't fast enough. The man swung his right fist and Korda stepped inside the arc. He grabbed the man's right wrist with both hands and walked under the upraised arm to stand behind him, twisting the arm and forcing the man to his knees. Korda kept twisting until the man's face was pressed to the asphalt of the parking area.

"Let go! Let go—you're gonna break my arm!" the man screamed.

I thought it was over then, but it wasn't. I thought Korda would let him up, and the two men would drive away, but Korda kept the pressure on the man's wrist, holding the arm straight so he couldn't bend his elbow, then he kicked him in the armpit as hard as he could. There was a loud crack, like a piece of dry wood breaking, and the man's scream ended abruptly. He was unconscious, and it was obvious from its position that his shoulder had been dislocated or broken.

Korda walked back to the first guy. His tears had washed most of the pepper from his eyes. He was kneeling, sitting back on his heels as he looked up at Korda. "Now," Korda said, "go pick up your partner and get the hell away from here."

We watched them drive away, then got into the pickup and headed for the next truck stop, where we also found a new machine had been installed and the owner of the place no longer wanted to use one of my father's.

The next day the sheriff stopped in while Dad and I were getting ready for church. Dad gave him a cup of coffee in the kitchen. The sheriff said he'd heard Dad had been involved in a fight out on the highway and that Korda had hurt a man badly enough to cause him to be hospitalized.

"The highway is outside your jurisdiction, isn't it, sheriff?" my dad said. "Has someone made a complaint?"

"No, no complaints; and you're right, it didn't happen in my jurisdiction."

"What's the problem, then? You didn't show much concern when my machines were wrecked."

"I'm sorry about that, but this is different."

"How?"

"It looks like your troubles with Clyde Anderson are goin' t' be dragged back here. I don't want that. I'm paid t' see that we don't have trouble aroun' here."

Korda came out of his room and joined us in the kitchen. Dad and I were in our Sunday clothes, but Korda wore Levis and a faded T-shirt.

"I see you don't plan on goin' t' church," Sheriff Masters said with disapproval in his voice. He finished his coffee and stood up. "From what I've been hearing about you, a little prayer wouldn't hurt you. Unless you're one of those people who don't believe in it."

Korda smiled. "Oh, I pray all right, but mostly on airplanes."

At seven on Monday morning a deputy sheriff parked an old camper in front of Dad's shop and walked away. He didn't return for it until after dark. He did the same thing on Tuesday and Wednesday.

It was there again on Thursday morning when I left for school, but it was gone when I got home.

Dad and Korda were in the kitchen. Dad was fixing spaghetti. I could smell our favorite sauce from the supermarket being heated on the stove. Whenever it was Dad's turn to cook, he made something that was hard to ruin. He was a far better tinsmith than he was a chef, and he knew it.

"The camper's gone," I said. Dad and I had been wondering why it was there, but Korda hadn't seemed curious.

"It turns out the sheriff has been sitting out there, giving us police protection these last few days," Dad said.

"Why did he leave?"

Dad and Korda exchanged looks, then Dad said, "I guess he figured we didn't need him any more."

I was burning with curiosity, but I knew better than to push it. I figured he'd get around to telling me about it in his own good time.

After dinner, while Korda went out for a walk, Dad turned to me. "An odd thing happened today. Lenny and I were working in the shop when two men I'd never seen before started to come in. They had the door open and one of them was already inside when the other one swore like he'd been surprised, grabbed his partner by the arm, and pulled him back outside again. They were hurrying away when the sheriff climbed out of the camper and took them in for questioning."

"What does it mean?"

"I don't know," Dad said.

The doorbell rang, and we could see the silhouette of the sheriff, easily recognizable because of his wide-brimmed campaign hat, through the curtain on the door glass.

"Maybe the sheriff'll be able to tell us," Dad said and went to let him in.

"Is Korda here?" Sheriff Masters asked.

"He went for a walk," Dad said. "Can I help you?"

"Maybe," the sheriff answered, stepping inside. "I want t' talk t' him about those two men. I couldn't hold them for anything, but I think they were workin' for Clyde Anderson. I knew he wouldn't like the way his other two flunkies were treated and would bring in a couple more. Their car had Michigan tags on it. An' they had very little luggage, so they didn't plan t' stay, jus' do whatever they'd been hired t' do an' then leave."

"Aren't they in jail?"

"No. I couldn't hold 'em. They hadn't broken any law, an' I can't prove they were intendin' t' break one. I was able t' make 'em identify themselves though. An' they didn't waste any time gettin' out of town. If that kind can't be anonymous, they don't do anythin'."

"It looked to me," Dad said, "that they were planning to leave even before you showed up."

The sheriff nodded. "I had that thought myself. That's what I'd like t' talk t' Korda about."

The sound of power shears came from the shop. "That must be him," Dad said.

"I thought he wasn't here."

"He wasn't. He must've let himself into the shop with the front door key I gave him."

"You gave him a key t' your shop?" the sheriff asked, shaking his head in disbelief. He motioned for Dad to lead the way.

We all went out into the shop and found Korda hard at work, making a length of heating duct. He looked up when we came in and wiped his hands on the front of his shop apron.

"Why d' ya think those fellas were in such a hurry t' leave this afternoon?" the sheriff asked him.

"Maybe they suddenly remembered something else they had to do."

"That's your best guess, is it?"

Korda shrugged.

"In that case, maybe you won't mind comin' down t' my office for a few minutes."

"Why?"

"I'd like t' take your fingerprints, Mr. Korda. I'm not all t'gether satisfied with you. You don't mind givin' me your fingerprints, do you?"

"No," Korda answered slowly, "I don't mind. But I'd like to clean up first." He held out his oily hands.

"Sure, go ahead," the sheriff replied.

Korda walked back to the utility sink to wash his hands. I saw him reach up and take a brown bottle off the shelf above the concrete basin. I didn't realize anything was wrong until I heard the bottle crash against the bottom of the sink and he called, "Bobby, help me quick! Turn on the cold water!"

I didn't pause to wonder why he didn't do it himself. He sounded urgent, so I ran over and did it for him. Then I looked at the hands he plunged into the rushing stream. They were a mess.

Instead of taking down the bottle of hand cleaner, Korda had grabbed the sulfuric acid Dad used to prepare metal seams for soldering. The two bottles were similar. Korda had poured about an ounce of it into one palm, then brought his hands together, rubbing the acid over them until the odor and sudden pain made him realize he'd made a mistake. Anyhow, that's the way I think it happened.

Dad wrapped a clean towel around Korda's hands and the sheriff rushed him over to Doc Bryant's office in the cruiser. Dad went too, and I stayed behind and watched the shop.

It was almost two hours before Dad and Korda came back. Korda's hands were both bandaged—he looked like he was wearing white boxing gloves. The sheriff dropped them off in front of the shop and then sped away.

"He's angry," Dad said. "He thinks Lenny may have burned his hands intentionally to avoid being fingerprinted."

"That's crazy," I said. "He'll be able to get them as soon as Lenny's hands heal."

"No, he won't. The doctor said the burns had reached the third layer of skin. Whatever fingerprints Lenny had are gone forever."

Now that Korda couldn't work, it became more necessary than ever that I hurry home from school afternoons and spend a good part of the weekends in the shop, too. But although Korda couldn't use his hands, there was nothing wrong with his head. As I worked, he taught me more about sheet metal than I'd thought there was to learn. Dad was a fine craftsman who knew all there was to know, but he wasn't the teacher Korda was. In one afternoon Korda taught me how to estimate material for the more common jobs, and he soon began instructing me on the fine points of design. I knew then that if I didn't become a doctor, I'd still be able to make a living anywhere in the world.

You might think Dad would have been jealous with a stranger teaching me all the things he hadn't been able to pass along, but that wasn't the case. He worked right beside us, listening to every word. Whenever I looked his way, he'd nod his head in agreement with what Korda was saying and tell me, "That's right. You listen to Lenny, Bobby."

Six weeks after the accident, the small ad my dad had in the telephone book paid off. Someone called about having him install a jukebox in a new restaurant. He drove over and talked to the man, and a couple of days later the two of us loaded the machine onto the truck and took it to him. Korda's hands were now only lightly bandaged, but he still couldn't use them for any heavy work.

A week later, Dad got another call about a jukebox and went out to see if he could place the last one. A few hours after he left, Sheriff Masters came by to tell us Dad was in the county hospital. He'd been found beaten and unconscious outside a vacant building.

We rushed to the hospital and were allowed to see him. His nose was broken and so was his left leg. He didn't know who had done it. They had been two strangers armed with clubs made from cut-down baseball bats or pool cues. That's all he knew.

Korda didn't say much while we were in the hospital room, but as we walked back to the pickup truck he began to swear. I'd heard most of the words before, but I'd never heard them spoken with such venom, and it frightened me.

"Do you have a camera?" Korda asked. He was driving despite the fact that he had no driver's license.

"Yes."

"When we get home, you get it."

He parked in front, and we entered the house through the back. I headed for my room to get the camera and he went directly to his. It took me a few minutes to locate the camera and put a fresh roll of film into it, and when I came out Korda was waiting by his door with his footlocker beside him.

"Give me a hand with this," he said, and I helped him. We took it out to the truck and put it in the back. His hands were still very sensitive, and he couldn't have handled it alone. We got back into the cab and he started to drive.

"Why did you pack your trunk?" I asked.

"Because I have something to do, and I won't be able to stay here when I've finished."

He took the state road south, then turned west toward Bradyville. I didn't have to ask where we were going.

The Bradyville main street was only half a dozen blocks long and it was dominated by a long flat building that covered most of one block. Across its face was a plastic and neon sign proclaiming *Clyde Anderson's*

Amusement Center. It had a restaurant, a bar, a pool hall, and a theater for showing X-rated movies.

Korda parked across the street and went to a pay phone. He was back in a minute, but he didn't get into the cab. "Come on," he said, heading toward Anderson's, "and bring your camera."

I followed Korda through the entrance of the pool hall. It was a deep narrow room with a line of eight billiard tables extending back to a low counter where a fat grey-haired man sat guarding the telephone and cash register. There were half a dozen men playing on the tables farthest back and an equal number sat on high benches along the wall, watching them.

Korda fumbled in his pocket until he found his penknife. It had a thin two-inch blade not much good for anything except sharpening pencils. He went to the first table, jabbed the blade through the green baize covering, and slit it the entire length of the table. When he got to the second table he did the same. And at the third, too. The blade was penetrating all the way through the pad to the slate base underneath and as it slit it made an agonized sound, like chalk on a blackboard. By the time he reached the tables that were in use, the players watched his progress with their mouths open. He continued to slash and walk rearward until the fat man shouted an order to two tough-looking spectators who ran forward and blocked Korda's path.

Korda swung at the first one with what looked like an awkward slap, but the lower half of the man's face was driven to one side and he dropped like a sack of cement.

The second man had a cue stick in his hands. He reversed it so he could swing the heavy end like a club and aimed it at Korda's head. Korda crouched and raised his left arm to protect himself. I heard a bone snap when he was hit, but it didn't stop him. He straightened up and fired a billiard ball at the center of the man's forehead. His eyes rolled back and he fell forward, hitting his head on the edge of a table and smashing an ear on his way to the floor.

Korda picked up the fallen stick and stuck the thin end into a table pocket. He leaned on it until it snapped, leaving him with the weighted end in his good hand, and advanced on Anderson. The fat man was pressed against the wall, his eyes darting right and left, searching for a direction to run.

"Sit down," Korda ordered, jabbing him with the jagged end of the broken stick. The fat man started to sputter and protest, but Korda pushed him. He stumbled backward and fell into his chair.

"I'm an old man," he whined.

"You may not get any older," Korda said. Then to me, "Bobby, take this guy's picture."

I aimed my camera at him and snapped the shutter. The bulb flashed and the fat man blinked his eyes.

"Take another," Korda said.

I advanced the film and took the fat man's picture again.

"Now give me the film."

I gave it to him.

The room was so quiet I could hear the fat man's breathing.

Korda casually swung the stick in a short chop to his nose.

"I'm leaving this area," Korda said, "but I'm taking this film with me. If my friends have any more trouble—any kind of trouble—I'll send someone around to see you."

We walked back to the truck and drove away. No one tried to stop us.

Korda pulled up at the bus station, and I helped him carry his footlocker to the next bus heading east.

Weeks later the sheriff visited Dad and me. He had a pair of wanted posters and a newspaper clipping. One poster told about a man named Coffey who was an escapee from Folsom Prison. He fit Korda's description and had been a syndicate enforcer serving a life sentence. The picture showed him clean-shaven, so he didn't look much like Korda.

The second poster offered a reward for help in locating a missing war hero who had walked away from an army hospital. He, too, fit Korda's description and his face might have been the one Korda had beneath his beard.

The newspaper clipping was from the Los Angeles *Times*. It told about an aircraft design engineer named Leonard Kaiser who had killed his wife's lover in a fit of rage and disappeared. His physical description matched Korda's.

Any of these men might have been Korda, but I don't believe any of them was.

But whoever he was, I'll never forget him.

Jon L. Breen

Silver Spectre

Want to hear a ghost story? Come on, listen to this. The next drink's on me. You don't like ghost stories? Well, call it a detective story then, with yours truly as detective. I can't prove I was a detective, but then nobody can prove there was a ghost either. You don't like detective stories? Well, it's also a racing story—and I know you like racing, because you have today's program from Santa Anita sticking out of your jacket pocket. Pretty good, huh? I told you I was a detective.

I heard this story years ago, in a bar. It wasn't a sleazy joint like this one, though. It was much cosier, sort of like a friendly English pub. It was back east, in a place called Blakemore Village, an Atlantic resort town. It doesn't exist any more—it hardly existed then. But there was a racetrack there, Blakemore Downs. It went bankrupt about the time racing was booming all over the country. The whole operation was snake-bit from the first, they say, though it managed to stay in business quite a few years. At the time I got to Blakemore Village, the wrecking ball was only a week or two away from that pretty grandstand. The track had been closed for a couple of years. My paper had assigned me to do a piece on the track—a nostalgia piece, they'd call it today.

I wasn't too thrilled with the assignment, but I always tried to do my best. In the middle of the day I went out and looked at the track. I talked to the caretaker, the only human being on the premises, an old ex-jockey named Billy Duff. He rode around the grounds on an aged grey gelding, the only horse left at a place where so many crashing hooves had thudded their way to glory or disaster. Yo can laugh all you want, but sportswriters had to write that way in the old days.

It turned out that nearly everything at the track was still intact. Even the jockey room had racks and racks of bright-colored silks hanging there. Everything was a little dusty and the infield was overgrown with weeds, but you had the idea they could have started racing tomorrow if there'd been any horses to race or any suckers to watch them. No offense, friend. I'm sure you're a scientific bettor and regularly show a profit on your investments. But I'm sure you'll agree that most of your brethren lack whatever sense they were born with.

I got what I could from Duff, but he was a closemouthed oldtimer without many stories to tell, and it began to look as if I'd be writing a dull piece. Over the forty years of Blakemore Downs' existence, some really fine horses had run there. But I wanted to turn in something more than just a walk through the old newspaper files and racing manuals.

That night I went into the local travern, sat down at the bar, and ordered a drink. In those days, I did that for information, for color, not just because I wanted to drink away the evening. Now I don't have that excuse, but back then when I walked up to a bar I was working.

There were a few regulars sitting there shooting the breeze, and they were cordial to me. By that time in the history of Blakemore Village they weren't seeing many visitors and much of the conversation was devoted to figuring out why their town was dying. They were philosophical enough about it. Just one of those things—boom today, bomb tomorrow.

At a corner table, away from anyone else, was a gaunt and gloomy-faced man of about sixty. He didn't join in the conversation, but devoted himself to serious drinking. The bartender would provide him with a fresh drink periodically in response to some practically invisible signal, and the other regulars would cast a voyeuristic glance his way every so often.

Promptly at eight o'clock, Billy Duff came in for what was apparently a nightly quick one, something you could set your clock by. He was friendly enough but no more talkative than he had been with me that day at the track. He too cast an interested glance at the man at the corner table. Obviously he knew him but he made no move to go over and say hello. I offered to buy Billy a drink but he assured me that one was his permanent limit, and he left at a quarter past eight.

I hung on, chatting with the regulars. I was enjoying the conviviality and had a hunch that if the man at the corner table ever got up and left the tavern an interesting story might come my way. It might or might not have any bearing on my story about Blakemore Downs—but by that time I didn't much care.

Sure enough, about ten o'clock, the man at the corner table lurched to his feet, made his way to the bar with wobbly dignity, wordlessly paid his tab, and made his way out the door.

As soon as he was out of earshot the bartender said, "Old Stu. I haven't seen him around here in years."

The other regulars nodded or grunted in uninformative agreement. Finally I had to ask. "Who is he?"

"Stuart Gallon. He used to be a trainer of racehorses. He led the trainer standings at the Downs for years."

"He must be sorry to see the place torn down," I remarked.

One of the regulars snickered. "I don't know," he said.

I smiled. "Come on, you guys. There's a story to tell about this guy. So tell it."

"You may not be able to use it. It's sort of a ghost story," said the bartender.

I shrugged. "I don't believe in ghosts—but some of my readers might."

"Okay." The bartender looked over my shoulder toward the window with a slight smile. "Fog's rollin' in," he said. "Sometimes it gets so thick here you can't see your hand in front of your face."

"Save the atmosphere," I kidded. "Don't try to scare me. Just tell me the story, and I'll provide the whistling wind or the cold chill or whatever's called for when I write it up. And—" I added as an afterthought "—set up a round on me." I didn't want to lose the story, whatever it was.

"We do get a lot of fog here, though," the bartender said. "It's one of the things that didn't do the Downs any good. Sometimes it would be so foggy in the afternoon they couldn't even do a full chart of the race. It'd just say 'fog' and give the positions at the finish. Along the backstretch, the jockeys could have been wrestling or shooting pool or kissing each other and nobody in the stands'd know it.

'But that's getting away from the story. Not too far, though. The man who just left, Stu Gallon, was not well liked in these parts. Whether it was justified or not, I don't know."

"It was justified all right!" snapped one of the regulars, a smallish old man with leathery skin. Another ex-jockey? I wondered.

"I know you think so, Fred. All I know about it of my own knowledge is that he believed in racing his horses a lot. He thought a race wasn't much harder on a horse than a workout—and he might as well go for the money as just run 'em around the track for no reason. Some folks said that was inhumane, but I don't know."

Fred said heatedly, "It wasn't just that, Charley. A lot of good trainers believed in racing their horses a lot. But Stu Gallon was a hard man. He hated horses—that's the long and short of it. He'd race them when they weren't right and he'd take a whip to them if they looked cross-eyed at him. And he didn't treat people much better. I'd have gone over and punched him one tonight when he came in, but I guess he's been punished plenty already for what he did."

"Anyway," said Charley, the bartender, "for purposes of the story let's just say Stu Gallon was not a popular man around the racetrack. People who worked for him never seemed to stay long. But he was a successful trainer.

"Now about the best horse Stu Gallon ever trained was a grey stallion named Silver Spectre. Ever heard of him?"

I shook my head. And I knew most of the good horses in those days.

"It was thirty or more years ago, of course, and the Spectre never got to show what he could really do. But he was a good one—right, Fred?"

Fred nodded solemnly. "He could have been a great one. He was a beautiful thing, too. His coat was nearly white, and that was a time when grey horses were a novelty on American tracks. I remember folks used to say that grey horses were bad luck, but I never bought that."

The bartender, who had established himself through the evening as the best raconteur of the group, took up the story again. "Well, Silver

Spectre became a real favorite of the track patrons, for his style as much as for his color. He won four straight races at the Downs that year, beating a rougher field each time he went to the post. And every single time he'd enter the first turn at the rear of the field, and on the backstretch he'd sometimes be fifteen or twenty lengths behind the leader, but on the far turn he'd suddenly start to get himself in gear and make his move. As they turned into the stretch he'd be picking up his opposition one by one, and by the finish line he'd have his grey neck in front one way or another. He was a real crowd pleaser, I can tell you. I won some money on him in my day."

Fred allowed a suggestion of a smile to crease his grim face.

"You were lucky, Charley. I just ate his dust."

"Well, came the week of the Blakemore Handicap—that was a real big race in those days. Horses used to ship in for it from all over the east. One year Equipoise was supposed to come—"

"And another year," Fred added, "Seabiscuit was supposed to come."

I laughed. "But who did come?"

"A lot of big horses came," said Fred. "It really was a big race."

"Sure it was," I said. "I remember."

They seemed mollified. Charley went on. "Well, this particular year everybody was talking about Silver Spectre and whether he was good enough to challenge the great field that would be going to the post that Saturday. He'd beaten the best horses stabled on the grounds, but he hadn't yet faced any horses as good as some of the ones shipping in. I remember on Tuesday of that week there was a rumor going around that he had hurt himself in his stall and it was doubtful Stu Gallon would run him. All week it was touch and go. But on Saturday, sure enough, his name turned up in the entries.

"Well, the weather that day was typical of the kind of luck that dogged the Downs all the years it was in business—"

"Dogged this whole town, in fact," another of the regulars amended.

"That's right. The fog rolled in. The folks in the grandstand—I wasn't there, I had to work the bar that day—could only see the stretch run. Beyond the turns, around the backside, you couldn't see a thing. All in all it was a crummy day to have to run the Blakemore Handicap, but they had a big crowd just the same. And sure enough, when the bugler played 'Boots and Saddles,' there was Silver Spectre going to the post with Ike McCann on his back."

Fred tilted his glass in a suggestion of a toast. "A great rider," he said.

"Some of the folks that were there that day swear that Silver Spectre looked lame in the post parade."

"If it were now," Fred put in, "the vet would have scratched him on the spot. They weren't as careful in them days."

"Did you think he looked lame?" I asked Fred.

"I wasn't there—I had a mount in New York that day. I'm glad I missed it."

I looked around at the other regulars. "Were any of you there?"

None of them had been. I sighed. This was a second- or third-hand story I was getting. And when was the ghost coming into it?

"I've seen pictures," said Charley. "And I know from the pictures that he had one foreleg wrapped going to the post—the right, I think. And we all know that any kind of front bandage makes a bettor wary. But to have just one leg bandaged! You might as well hang a sign reading UNSOUND around the horse's neck.

"It was a big field for the race—fifteen. They started from behind the webbing—that was before the days of the starting gate, you know. It was a mile-and-a-quarter race, so they went all the way down the homestretch once, in front of the crowd, then all the way around again. Silver Spectre broke with his field, but as usual he dropped quickly to the rear of the pack. He looked to be running okay though, and his fans were yelling encouragement to him and Ike McCann as the field passed the stands. If anything, the Spectre was closer to the pace than usual, even though all fourteen others had him beat going to the turn. Then the field swept past the clubhouse and out of sight into the fog."

Charley paused a beat for emphasis, then gave me the next bit dramatically.

"My friend, fifteen horses entered that fog, and only fourteen returned. It was much later before most of the spectators were to learn that Silver Spectre had gone down on the backstretch, his right foreleg broken. The vet put him down on the spot. What was worse, Ike McCann had fallen on his head, and after a couple of days in a coma he was dead, too."

"It was a terrible tragedy," said Fred. "They buried Silver Spectre in the infield at the Downs. Ike's family had him buried in a regular cemetery but, knowing him, I think he'd have liked to be buried alongside the Spectre. He loved that horse."

"And he hated Gallon," said Charley.

"Sure. The two emotions went together."

"Everybody figured Gallon ran the horse when he shouldn't have," said Charley.

"And everybody was right," said Fred. "He did."

"Up to then, Stu Gallon was unpopular only with people who knew him. Now he was hated by a world of horse lovers who had never met him. Stu Gallon had become the most despised man on the American turf."

A touch of hyperbole there, I thought. I'd never even heard of Stu Gallon until that evening.

"For a while at least," Charley went on, "it didn't seem to make that much difference to Gallon's career. As I say, he was a good trainer, nasty as he was, and his horses won their share of purses. But then things started to go bad for Stu Gallon. We ought to tell you about a certain morning in October, some thirty years back. It was during the morning training period out at the Downs, and it was pea-soup foggy. You were there, weren't you, Fred?"

The ex-rider nodded his head. "Yeah, I can give you this part first hand. It was a terrible morning, but the business of training horses went on as usual. The clockers had to keep a close watch on horses going on and off the track. They didn't want any expensive pieces of horseflesh running into each other in that treacherous fog. Oh, I guess they didn't want any of us jockeys getting ourselves killed either, but that wasn't uppermost.

"I remember I was sitting on a brown two-year-old filly. I don't remember her name—she wasn't much. We were at the gap on the backstretch where you could go from the stable area onto the track to work out. The ground crew had been renovating the track, so no one had been allowed to go out for several minutes. The filly's trainer and I were about to take her onto the track—the chief clocker had given us the nod—when all of a sudden this big grey stallion comes charging out of the fog, hell bent for leather. He was hugging the rail, and the boy on his back was pumping him for all he was worth. As he streaked past us, the chief clocker was sputtering about how he hadn't let any horse on the track and where the hell had the grey come from. He told his outrider to go after the horse and rider, but the outrider, who'd turned downright pale, said to him, 'Not me, boss. I ain't chasin' no ghosts.'

" 'Ghosts!' the clocker roared at him.

" 'Yeah, ghosts,' he said. 'You can laugh at me if you want, but that was Silver Spectre, with Ike McCann on his back.'

"We did laugh at him, but not for long. Because nobody ever found that grey horse or his rider. The only other interval on the track is on the front side where the horses come out in the afternoon, and there was a maintenance man working there who said no horse went through that interval all morning. So, as far as anybody could tell, that horse and rider didn't ever exist at all except along the backstretch rail from out of the soup and back into it.

"And it was that same morning that Stuart Gallon's little girl was drowned."

"Somebody drowned his daughter?" I asked.

"No, no, it was an accident," said Charley. "Hell—nobody, no matter how much they hated Stu, could have wanted a terrible thing like that to happen. It happened in the swimming pool at Gallon's hotel. It was a sad thing. The death of a child always is. And Stu Gallon was really devoted to her, too. Nobody's all rotten, I guess. Gallon was only mostly rotten."

"Did you ever see the ghost again, Fred?" I asked.

"No, not me."

"He *was* seen again, though," Charley said. "Several times. Always on foggy mornings. People I know have seen him—people who used to come in here."

I looked around at the gathered regulars. Again, no witnesses.

I think Charley sensed I was losing interest. He leaned across the bar and looked me in the eye. "And every time that grey phantom made his appearance, something else terrible happened to Stu Gallon, as if Ike and the Spectre were getting their revenge from beyond the grave. The second time the ghost ran, Stu Gallon's wife died. The very same day. Then his house burned down. Then he lost his job with Lakehills Stable and really went on the skids."

"I was surprised to see him in here tonight," said Fred.

"Yeah. He hasn't been in here in years."

I had a feeling I'd had enough for the evening, enough to drink and enough ghost story. Not that they'd scared me—I wondered if they were making it all up. As I swayed to my feet I asked Fred, "After all the terrible things that happened to him, did most people come to forgive him for the things he did in his earlier days?"

"Well, I never heard that his misfortunes made Stu Gallon any nicer. And some of the things he did back when I knew him are the kind of things you just don't forget."

I said good night to the assembly, paid my bill, and made my way carefully through the fog back to Blakemore Village's last remaining excuse for a hotel. There I saw the former trainer, Stu Gallon, sitting in the lobby, just staring into space. He did seem to have an oddly haunted look in his eyes.

I have to confess, though, I slept well that night. No nightmares. And if I had had one, it probably would have been about confronting my editor without a good story.

I slept late into the morning, as is my custom. When I was out on the street at eleven, the fog had cleared and it was a bright, sunny day. I was debating whether to try to gather more material for my article or just go back to the city and do my best with what little I had. As I passed the tavern, Charley was just opening up. "You keep long hours," I said.

"It's my place and there's not enough business to hire anybody to help pour. You heard what happened at Blakemore Downs this morning?"

"No. Something happened and I missed it?"

"The town cop came by a few minutes ago and told me. Stu Gallon is dead. They found him out at the Downs. In the infield."

"What was he doing there?"

"The guys that found him are from the wrecking company that's going to tear the place down next week. They said he was lying on the grave of Silver Spectre. They say he had a shovel. It seems he was digging."

I must say that gave me more of a shiver, there in the bright sunlight, than anything I'd heard in the foggy, theatrical gloom of the night before.

"You know what I think?" said Charley. "I think Silver Spectre and Ike McCann made one last appearance this morning."

And as I've thought about it over the years I think that's what happened too—in a manner of speaking.

Stuart Gallon died of a heart attack, they found. And it could have been brought on by the strain of his crazy digging. Or he could have been frightened to death by something he saw.

A ghost horse and rider coming at him out of the fog? Maybe.

But I thought of that old ex-jockey, Billy Duff, who took care of the place. And I thought of his old grey gelding, the only horse on the grounds. And I thought of that jockey room with the silks still hanging there ready to wear, surely including the silks worn by Ike McCann when he rode Silver Spectre. And I wondered if what scared Stu Gallon to death might not have been a flesh-and-blood man streaking out of the fog on a flesh-and-blood horse, participating in a quite deliberately deadly masquerade. It could have been an act of durable, burning hatred. Or it could have been an act of mercy.

Or it could have been a ghost.

William Bankier
The Prodigal Brother

The ceramic mug on Norman Harper's kitchen table was in two shades of blue with a streak of sunshine yellow. Norman pulled out his chair and sat down opposite Karen and his daughter, Anita. Before he took his first sip of coffee, he said,

"This is new, isn't it?"

"I got it yesterday at Peter Jones', " Karen said. "To replace your old favorite that got broken. Do you like it?"

"Nice. It's all sky and light. It's the way I feel."

"That's why I picked it."

Never in his life had Harper been so inclined to say how happy he was. Back in Montreal before he moved to England, when he was locked into the public relations business, a sense of well-being was a rare thing. When it happened, he hesitated to mention it for fear it would go away. But here in Wimbledon, out of the P.R. rat race and being well paid to do a job he would have performed for nothing, he found himself continually talking about his good fortune.

"What's on for you today?" Karen asked.

"Not much. I'll walk over to the office and answer a couple of letters." Simply by meeting and impressing some key people and by being the right man at the right time, Harper had landed the plum job of publicist for the All England Lawn Tennis Club. This meant his main job was to provide the news media of the world with material about the annual prestige tennis tournament known as Wimbledon Fortnight.

"See this?" Anita Harper was holding up the morning paper, indicating a grainy photograph on the business page. "That's the computer section, and that's me."

Harper took the paper and saw his daughter with a couple of male colleagues huddled around a printout. She looked cute and business-like with her feathery short-cut hair and her tinted spectacles down her nose. On arrival in London three years ago, Anita had taken a job with an American petroleum company now busy drilling for offshore oil in the North Sea. With no experience or training but with diligence and a quick brain and a charming sense of humor, she had managed three promotions and was now sitting very prettily indeed.

"Great picture," Harper said. "Must be trick photography—you look as if you're working."

"Daddy!"

Harper finished his coffee and held the new mug, still warm, in both hands. There was something very nice about it; he liked this mug. "How about you, Karen? Can you meet me for lunch?"

"I was going to tame the garden," she said. "But for lunch, I could be persuaded to change my plans." Lunch with Norman meant a good feed at one of their favorite restaurants in Knightsbridge. And then they usually went on to drift through the Victoria and Albert or the Natural History Museum, as bemused by the vast halls and pillars and the exquisitely made cabinets holding the exhibits as by the bones and paintings and cameos themselves.

"If you want to take advantage of the sun to do the garden ..." Norman began.

"That's all right, I can garden tomorrow." Karen's confidence came from an awareness that England was experiencing its second consecutive summer of drought. "It never rains in sunny Southern Counties," she said.

Anita got up and took her handbag from the top of the refrigerator. "If you guys are going to start doing song titles," she said, "I'm getting out of here."

"I'll see you out." Karen pushed back her chair.

"No need."

"I want to make sure you're really gone."

Alone at the table, Harper turned the new mug in his hands, enjoying its smooth slide against his skin, enjoying the easy feeling in his stomach. He would never take this lack of tension for granted. There had been fifteen years of the other life, the chemical taste in his mouth, the sudden awareness that he had been sitting rigid for an hour and the ache in his muscles when he forced himself to relax. Now, at forty-three, he felt like a well fed lion basking in the sun. Was this the way everybody else lived or was he now one of the lucky few? He suspected he was one of the lucky few.

The mug had something etched on the bottom of it. Harper turned the base around and saw the words, "Hand Made in England by Chelsea Crafts." Then he saw the initials, TH.

He recognized those initials, the way they were formed. The T was joined to the H by a coiled line like a little length of electric wire. Norman's big brother Tom had invented this logo for himself years ago when the two boys spent all their time together. Norman had made one too, a more obvious symbol using a common upright line between the initials. But Tom had made a big thing of the coiled wire. They were reading *Tom Swift and His Electric Rifle* at the time and this symbol of power was important to him.

Karen was back in the kitchen. "What's the matter?" she said, sounding concerned.

"Look at this."

"I know. They make a lot of ceramics there."

"I mean the initials."

"TH?"

"Tom Harper."

It was all he needed to say to her. Karen knew all about her husband's missing brother. Perhaps missing was too dramatic a word but they both agreed it had gone beyond the point of a man being too lazy to answer letters. Four years ago, when they were still in Montreal, their Christmas card to Tom had come back marked "Not at this address."

"Is it Tom's sign? That's incredible," Karen said.

"It's even the way he makes the letters. It has to be him."

Harper was feeling a surge of excitement. If Tom was here in London, it would be too much. He had been blaming himself for losing sight of his brother, although the truth was that Tom had been the one to let the correspondence lapse. Still, Norman had seen Tom coming apart, the drinking, his resignation from the teaching post at Kitchener High School, then the failed marriage and separation from his wife and sons. It was not enough for the brother with the stable life to write letters and sit back waiting for replies. He should have gone to Tom, spoken to him, taken hold of him, helped him, instead of leaving him to sink or swim.

Now it looked as if Tom was just down the road in Chelsea. What a fantastic break. It was not too late—he could find him and they could get their lives back together again after all these years.

"Let me have the telephone directory, will you, Karen?" Harper said.

There was a compact, contained look about his big, greying head and the boyish lips were firm as he ran his finger down the column of names. The ceramic mug was at his elbow. "Here it is," he said. "Chelsea Crafts, 25A Wellington Mews."

"Do you want me to dial?" Karen reached for the telephone.

"Too early." Harper was reading his watch. "There won't be anybody there before nine thirty. Anyway, it would be better if I go and see them."

When he was shaved and dressed and at the front door with Karen, she said, "If you run into Tom you won't feel much like meeting me for lunch."

"This could have been made last year." Harper hefted the mug in a plastic bag. "He might have quit and moved on."

"Still, why don't we make lunch another day?" She could see the excitement in his eyes, could imagine the anticipation he was feeling. "Concentrate on what you're doing."

"What I'll do is phone you as soon as I know," Harper said. "We might lunch late and go see that new Bogdanovitch in Leicester Square."

Harper walked to Wimbledon Park underground station and caught a District Line train to Sloane Square. Here, not exactly sure of the streets, he hailed a taxi and gave the driver the Wellington Mews address. Then he sat back and stretched his legs in the spacious spanking-clean interior of the cab and thought about Tom. Was it possible he was going to see his brother here in London after so much time? The coincidence of finding his initials on the mug was incredible, but such things had happened to him before.

When had he last laid eyes on Tom? This was a difficult question. A flood of memories came rushing in on Harper—Tom dribbling in and scoring a jump shot for the school basketball team; Tom entering the house, tanned, dusty, and exhausted after a day's labor in the railway yards; Tom in his cassock and surplice waiting confidently for the organ to introduce the processional hymn so he could fill the church with his soaring tenor.

The taxi rocked around a ninety degree turn and Harper held on. None of these images, he knew, related to the last time he had seen his brother. That was in Baytown railway station. He and Karen were on their way back to Montreal after a holiday weekend at home. Tom had driven them to catch the train and was waiting to see them off. His two boys were doing something pointlessly energetic around the platform pillars. The brothers stood silently watching and only now, years after the occasion, did it occur to Harper that they could have been watching themselves as children.

"Here we are, mate," the driver said. "Sixty pence, please."

Harper paid and as the cab drove away he looked around Wellington Mews. The paving was uneven brick, oil-stained in places. It was a narrow laneway lined on either side with former garages and stables converted now to dwellings and businesses. There was a lot of shiny paint in evidence, doors with brass fittings, and flowering trees in tubs stood incongruously beside overflowing dustbins. A sign pinned to the door of Chelsea Crafts said "Ring and Enter" so Harper rang and entered.

He saw a modern desk with a typewriter and a telephone on it and an attractive blonde girl behind it. When she saw him, she began to stand up, then frowned and sat down again. A glassfront cabinet held a display of mugs, pots, vases, and ashtrays. A flight of wooden steps led to the floor above where sounds of activity suggested to Harper that work was being done.

"Can I help you?" the girl caroled, each word on a different note. She loved her work, loved life, loved everybody who came through the doorway. Looking as she did, she probably got it all back with interest.

"Yes, I bought one of your mugs and I have a feeling I know who made it." Harper unwrapped and showed the mug. "TH. I think I know who did that."

"Those are, in fact, the initials of the craftsman," the girl said, "but I'm not supposed to identify our people. You'll have to speak to Mr. Gorman."

She pressed a button on her telephone and soon Mr. Gorman appeared from a doorway near the foot of the stairs. He was younger than Harper, bearded, very natty in tailored denim. He looked at the base of the mug as he listened to Harper's story.

"You're Canadian yourself, I expect," he said.

"Yes, I am."

"A Canadian made this mug. He was quite good, he could have been very good. Tom Harper."

Harper felt the floor slide back and forth under his feet. "He's my brother," he said, his own voice echoing inside his head. "Is he still here?"

"Afraid not." Gorman was looking at Harper in the way television doctors look at the relatives of dying patients. "You resemble him, you know. You'd better come into my office."

The office was small and crowded with filing cabinets and shelves of ledgers. Gorman's desk was littered with papers; his job was clearly the grubby side of the business, ordering materials that kept going up in price, trying to get customers to pay.

When he had cleared a seat for Harper, he sat on the edge of his desk and said, "As I told you, Tom Harper could have been one of our best people; he could have made a lot of money. But he just wasn't reliable. I had to let him go."

"Alcohol?"

"Yes. And badly, not just the occasional Friday afternoon. As soon as he got some money ahead he'd vanish. we might not see him for a week. And after that, his work would suffer."

"Not just his work," Harper said. Gorman's holy attitude was getting to him.

"What?"

"He was suffering too," Harper said. "My brother was suffering."

"Oh, I dare say." English courtesy—I forbid you to have an argument with me.

"When did Tom finish up? When did you last see him?"

"What's today?" Gorman turned his desk calendar. "It'll be two weeks on Friday."

Harper felt the dizzy sensation again. Such a near thing! Tom had been walking back and forth on these premises less than fourteen days ago. "I don't suppose you have an address for him?"

"Nothing. He gave me an address for tax purposes once, but when I tried to contact him there they'd never heard of him."

Harper left Gorman in his office. The disappointment must have registered on his face because the girl behind the desk said as he went by, "Is everything all right, Mr. Harper?"

"Not really. I thought I'd found somebody but I guess I haven't."

"You're Tom's brother Norman, aren't you?"

Her knowledge made sense. Unless Tom had been lobotomized, he would find it mandatory to go after any woman as beautiful as this one.

"He talked about me?" Harper said.

"We talked at times, yes." She gave a cryptic smile, some pride in it, some pain. "He thinks a lot of you. He kept saying you were the only member of the family to amount to anything. When he'd had a few beers he always got back to that."

"Thank you for telling me." It was worth a try. "Can you tell me where I might find him?"

She was fumbling inside her handbag. "I have an address." She took out a slip of paper and handed it to Harper. "He told me I could look him up there if I ever got the chance."

Harper looked at the scribbled address. "Montreal?" he said.

"That's right. He seemed to think London was going to become a problem for him. He said he was going home."

Harper copied out the address and gave the paper back to the girl. At least it was a place he could write to—not that Tom would ever reply. "Thanks a lot. This may help."

"I hope it does. If you see him or talk to him, tell him Gillian was asking. Gillian Mill."

"I will." It was hard to turn away from her. They were both smiling.

"I'd know you were Tom's brother even without an introduction. The resemblance is striking. You even dress the same."

"When we were kids, people thought we were twins." He tucked Tom's address in his pocket. "Well, thanks for the help."

"My pleasure. Ciao."

Outside, the sun was hammering down into the mews, reflecting from glass and painted brick, hurting Harper's eyes. He walked down the cobbled paving, the soles of his shoes slipping on the uneven surface.

From the shadowy doorway of an open garage, a voice said, "Harper?"

He turned and faced the darkness. "Yes?"

"Come here, me boy."

He took half a step forward and then instinct stopped him, a curtain of cold fear touched him and stopped him. A man stepped forward, put his hands on Harper's shoulders, and dragged him into the garage. Harper saw a freckled face and a lot of red hair parted on the side and combed wet. The man was in suit trousers and a striped business shirt, no tie, the sleeves rolled up. His ankle was bothering him—he limped.

Somebody else was in the garage. A fist hit Harper in the stomach and he almost passed out. The redhead was supporting him from behind as punches struck him on the chest and in the face. Harper had never been beaten up before and he was astonished to discover it didn't hurt. Not yet, anyway. He could smell motor oil and rust and the thought flashed through his mind that he would never inhale that sharp tang again without remembering the shock of fists smashing into him.

It was over and two men were sitting him on something hard, propping him against the wall. Now a face came close to his in the darkness, close enough so he could smell a pungent lemon aftershave. The voice against his ear was husky and confidential.

"Harper, me boy. We're letting you live because you did help. But don't try to disappear again. We may need you. And we can always find you."

When he felt strong enough to stand, Harper limped out into the light. The mews was peaceful and deserted and disavowed all knowledge of the nasty experience he had just undergone. His first inclination was to find a policeman, but something told him this was not the thing to do. He thought it out as he walked slowly towards the main street.

First of all, the police could do nothing for him except to look for unknown assailants. But the second point was the important one. This was obviously a case of mistaken identity. Harper had no enemies; the bullies were after Tom. And from what the voice said, Tom was involved with them. He had helped. So if the police got lucky and found the men, Tom might be the loser.

No, the thing to do was to make himself presentable enough to show up at home without terrifying Karen, and then to decide calmly the next move.

Harper's battered face made little impression along the street. Most people didn't notice him and the few who did glanced away instantly. He found a pub with a grotty washroom and a sliver of mirror in which he could see that he was not too badly off. One eye was swollen, his nose had stopped bleeding, the side of his jaw was bruised. He would check beneath his shirt when he got home, but he pressed his ribs now and decided none were broken.

As he washed in cold water, a surprising sense of well-being came over him.

No, better than that; it was a feeling of triumph. This beating had been intended for Tom, but Norman had absorbed it in his place. He had done something for his brother at last, and if his body was aching his soul was soaring.

The cleanup worked wonders—he had seen tennis players with hangovers who looked worse. Before he left the pub, Harper sat at an oak table splashed with colored light from a stained-glass window and drank a pint of ale. He let his mind go and by the time he went to catch the train home he knew what he had to do and what he had to say to Karen.

"It shouldn't take more than a couple of days," he said. They were sharing the same folding reclining chair in the garden, Karen stretched out in her bikini and Harper seated on the footrest section. The concrete birdbath beside them was dry and so was the hard grey earth and the drought-scorched grass. "If Tom isn't in Montreal I can take the next plane back. But I have a feeling he'll be there.'

"Never mind the plane back," Karen said. "Stay at least a week. Enjoy yourself."

"If we're talking about a holiday, you ought to come too. Anita's old enough to take care of herself."

"It isn't a holiday. It's you finding your brother and having some time alone with him."

So Harper got on the telephone and booked a flight the next afternoon. Then he went around to his office at the tennis club and cleared himself for a week.

Dinner that evening was an intense affair for Harper. The heightened awareness he had felt after the beating was undiminished and he found himself valuing the company of his wife and daughter more than ever before. Karen made a banquet of it with four tall candles on the table, red wine in crystal goblets, and a massive joint of beef. She was a girl with a great sense of occasion and whenever Harper had reason to take a trip she always managed things so he felt he was a character in a film drama.

On this night, the sensation was one of a successful enterprise well and truly begun—yet his throat ached with the tug of potential tragedy just below the surface. He had concealed from Karen and Anita the facts of the attack upon him in the garage, his knowledge that the punishment was meant for Tom, and the implications this held if his brother was involved in something criminal. The way he told it, a couple of Chelsea football supporters had gone at it in a pub and Harper had made the mistake of mixing in.

Anita's boyfriend showed up after dinner looking mandarin-like in his slim mustache and silken shirt. He shook Harper's hand and wished him a good trip, then he and Anita were gone to The Grapes and Karen could raise what was troubling her.

"What happened at the ceramics place today, Norman?" she said. "Did you learn something you haven't told me?"

"I learned Tom worked there until two weeks ago, that they sacked him for drinking, and that he's probably gone back to Montreal." Harper never invented a lie for his wife, but sometimes the truth he told her was incomplete.

"But something is troubling you. I've sensed it all evening."

"Nothing. What do you think?"

"I think they told you something bad. Maybe Tom was very ill. Or maybe he stole from the company. I'm sorry—anything. Whatever it was depressed you so you went and got drunk and got into a fight."

"That's a marvelous scenario but there's no truth in it whatever." This was why he encouraged her to invent her own version of what happened; it pleased him to be able to reassure her by dismissing it out of hand. "Now come here," he said, "so I can eat your earrings. *Je suis le croqueur de diamants.*"

She left her chair and sat beside him on the settee. "Remember Zizi Jeanmaire?" Karen said. As newlyweds, they had seen a film featuring the leggy French dancer in an exotic ballet about a girl who ate diamonds.

Wine and candlelight and the recollection of that sensuous dance put Harper in just the mood for Karen, who could match legs with Zizi or anybody else. Anita came home in the early hours of the morning and smiled to find some of her parents' clothing abandoned in the living room. They were not like other mothers and fathers. They were like kids themselves.

Not appreciating farewells at airports, Harper kissed Karen at home and then journeyed out to Heathrow by himself. It was another fine day and the airplane took off right on time. His bruises and swellings were looking better but the ridge of eyebrow visible above his right eye was a reminder of Tom's situation and Harper thought about it as he sat in the plane drinking rye whisky.

The key to the mystery was that whispered statement, "We're letting you live because you helped." Obviously they were criminals of some sort and Tom had taken part in their activities—he had been useful. And he might be useful again; the voice had said, "We may need you." But what was the crime? Harper could not imagine Tom involved in anything as sordid as narcotics. But he had no illusions. With the same confident spirit in which he tried to score with anyone in skirts, Tom would knock over a bank or smuggle currency.

The whisky was doing its job. Harper closed his eyes and lapsed into a sort of half dream. He and Tom were crouched behind the garage beside the old house on Standard Street in Baytown. Before them on the ground lay a heap of burnt-out cones and cylinders, the collected residue from last night's fireworks activities. Yesterday had been the twenty-fourth of May, Firecracker Day. The cardboard shells in their colorful wraps, pungent now with the smell of burnt gunpowder, deserved a more spectacular end than just to rot on wet lawns or in garbage heaps. The funeral pyre was Tom's idea and he had stolen a handful of matches from the box in the kitchen.

But before the stuff was properly ignited, their mother was among them and the blows she delivered were devastating because she had never struck the boys before. They ended up trembling in bed while she raged and wept below them.

Years passed before Harper began to understand his mother's exaggerated reaction to what was only a boyish prank. He himself began to experience periods of her grim Irish depression, which he would control, when the mood became unbearable, with a couple of red and black capsules. But Moira Harper had it all to do by herself, living in those dangerous years before such medication was developed. Now, as the airplane carried him swiftly back to Montreal, within a couple of hundred miles of where his mother and his childhood were buried, Harper wondered how much of that Gaelic propensity for doom had been passed on from Moira to Tom, and perhaps even to himself.

After the plane landed and the limousine ran him in and dropped him on Peel Street outside the Mt. Royal Hotel, Harper did what he had done over twenty years ago when he first moved from Baytown to Montreal; he walked over to the Central Y.M.C.A. on Drummond Street and got a room. It was cheap and neat and uncomplicated there. He needed only a few minutes to unpack the single bag and as he put his things away in the musty chest of drawers Harper had an overpowering sense of being alone in the world. It seemed to go with the tiny room and its history of young displaced souls in residence. His cosy home in Wimbledon, his perfect job at the tennis club—he was not alone.

But Tom might be alone at this moment, facing all kinds of trouble from the mews attackers—or, worse still, unaware that the danger existed.

Harper found the slip of paper with the address given him by Gillian Mill and went outside to hail a cab. It was less than ten minutes away, an apartment block on Lincoln Avenue. The somber maroon brick walls were coated with grime and the marble vestibule made Harper think of a grand lavatory.

A row of buttons, one for each apartment, was set in the wall near the inner door. The button for Number 7, Tom's according to the address slip, had no name card beside it. Anonymous to the end, Harper thought as he pressed and waited. A buzzer snarled inside the lock and he was able to open the heavy door and go inside.

The hallway smelled of soup and stained upholstery. Harper went up a short flight of marble steps and found the door marked 7 just off the landing. He knocked once and the door was opened immediately.

She was silhouetted against pale light from the room behind her and even before she spoke Harper recognized her.

"Surprise, surprise," Gillian Mill said. "Come in."

He followed her into a kitchenette no bigger than a telephone booth. A kettle was steaming on a gas fire. "Tea's up," she said, getting down a second mug to set beside her own. She was obviously alone, Tom was not here. Harper felt a mixture of disappointment and racing excitement.

"Just like home," he said.

They carried their tea into the lounge and perched across the room from each other on cheap furniture. Out of the office setting, Gillian Mill looked younger and more vulnerable.

"Tom gave me a key as well as the address," she said. "I didn't tell you that."

"We have to hold back something."

"We're very close, Tom and I. It worried me when you came in looking for him the very next day after those two men."

"Redhaired chap?"

"With freckles. Then there *is* something going on." The mug trembled as she raised it to her lips. "Tom was worried those last few days. When he said he had to get out of London I thought he just owed money. But this is worse, isn't it?"

"I think so."

"Don't you know? You're his brother."

Harper touched his jaw where the swelling was almost gone. Beating be damned, he had still never knowingly done anything to help Tom out. But that was why he was here.

"Where is he?"

"I don't know. I let myself in when I arrived this morning. I'm waiting for him to show up."

"You were quick off the mark."

"I told Mr. Gorman there was illness in my family in Cornwall. He gave me a couple of days off."

"Will that be time enough?"

She began to look more sure of herself. "Depending how things are with Tom, I may never go back at all."

The dim room in the dying building began to spook Harper. He gave the girl his telephone number at the Y and she promised to call as soon as Tom showed up. Then he fled into the sunshine and walked quickly downtown.

There was polished wood and a fine smell of beer inside The Shamrock. Haper took his customary stool at the end of the bar and began to drink Guinness from a fat black beaker. The bartender who served him left his post for a minute and disappeared through a doorway at the far end of the bar. A moment later he returned, followed by the aristocratic presence of Pat Leary, and the two of them stood together looking Harper's way like visitors at a zoo.

Leary put his arm around the bartender's shoulder and said something to him. Then he came towards Harper with a smile on his lacquered face and his right hand extended through cuffs of blue mohair and white lines. Harper could never be sure if Leary painted himself a little, but his skin had the rich tones of a cheap oil painting and you could count the individual hairs in his glistening black eyebrows.

"Norman, it's you," he said. "What a grand surprise. My boy just told me my old friend Tom Harper had showed up, but I'm equally glad to see you."

"I'm looking for Tom myself," Harper said. "How goes it with you, Patsy?"

"We're making money hand over fist. To tell the truth, it's embarrassing. The streets are full of wealthy American visitors, God save the troubled economy."

"Have a drink with me, Pat."

"I will. But it's on the house." Leary smiled at the bartender who bent to his refrigerator cupboards and opening bottles. "So you're looking for your wandering brother," he said. "Last I heard, Tom was searching for you."

"Oh? I never heard that. The fact is, Patsy, I haven't laid eyes on my brother in years, and that's the hell of it." It was uncanny, and just on the verge of being comic, but whenever Harper entered The Shamrock, and especially when he talked to the owner, he found himself sounding progressively more Irish.

"I remember when Tom first came in here over a year ago," Leary said. "Thinking it was you, I was all ready to go up and say I knew you'd hate England. Then I saw that interesting variation in the Harper eyes. Have you ever marked the difference, Norman?"

"It's easier for someone else to see."

"Yours have a look of holy self-assurance in them. You've never done anything wrong in your life, have you, no need to answer, so who can face you down? But Thomas, poor doubting man, he's part of the great imperfect mass and he knows it. He's got the look in his eyes of the scavenging animal, always afraid he's about to be caught."

"You make him sound pathetic," Harper said, feeling some resentment. There was a different quality about Pat Leary today; time had soured him.

"Your brother is not pathetic, he's just the normal stuff of the human race," Leary said. "You'd never understand that, Norman. You're one of the angels."

The bar became busy and Leary went away to see to things in other areas. Harper had three more beers, enjoying the sensation of getting a little high with the Montreal summer streets waiting for him outside. Just as he was readying himself to leave, Leary reappeared at his side.

"I'll keep an eye open for Tom, though I haven't seen him for months. He has a way of disappearing, your brother."

"I know. He showed up in London for a while but I missed him. They told me he was coming back here."

"Then he'll arrive sooner or later. Where can he find you if he comes in?"

"I'm registered at Central Y. Humble Harper, they call me."

"Fair enough. And Tom, I suppose he'll book himself a suite at the Queen Elizabeth. Nothing but the best."

"No, he has a place on Lincoln Avenue. But he wasn't home when I looked in earlier."

Harper left The Shamrock, walked on down to Dorchester Boulevard, and sat on a bench in the sun. Endless traffic streamed in six lanes in both directions in front of him and as he stared and blinked he felt the effect of jet fatigue. Sooner or later he would have to sleep. Looking left, he saw the gleaming black glass tower where he had spent fifteen years as a P.R. man, being straight-faced-serious about the most ludicrous projects. Clouds moved in the glass prism.

He must have dozed for a while because he felt his head come off his chest with a snap. The sun was a degree or two farther down the sky. He thought of Gillian Mill and wondered whether, if Tom was still absent, she might come out with him for dinner. He got up and stepped to a taxi waiting in traffic, opened the door, and got in. Ten minutes later he was in the marble lavatory ringing the Number 7 bell. There was no reply.

Harper tugged at the inner door. It swung open and he went through. Up on the landing, as he knocked at Number 7, the door creaked inwards. Harper took a step inside and encountered the same cold net of fear as when he entered the dark garage in Wellington Mews. He froze and held his breath. There was a slight movement in the dim room to the left, a scuffing noise, a thump. Then silence.

His right hand found a light switch. The sound had been Gillian Mill trying to pick herself off the floor. Her blood was soaking into the threadbare carpet.

Harper knelt beside her and turned her over. They had done a much more thorough job on her than on him—her pretty face was grotesque. He tried to translate into words the sounds she was making. It sounded like, "I didn't tell them."

"Don't try to talk," Harper said. "Just move your head yes or no." He was holding her against his knee, feeling the rhythmic shuddering in her body.

"Were they after Tom?"

She nodded.

"Do you know where he is?"

Again her bloodied head moved up and down.

"I have to know. I have to get to him and warn him, or help him. Can you tell me where he's gone?"

The single word was like a moan, but he understood it clearly. Home. Tom had gone home.

"All right. Now listen, Gillian. I'm going to leave you. I have to go, I'm in danger too. But I'll call the police and they'll be here within minutes with an ambulance. They'll fix you up and give you protection. Okay?" She was silent in his arms. He lowered her gently, and crept out of the room.

On the street, he kept his head up, looking for men trailing him while he walked as fast as he could east along Lincoln. At the first call box, he rang the police and gave them the address of Tom's apartment, saying a girl had been beaten up.

Half an hour later, safe in his room at the Y, Harper lay on the bed and with his eyes closed could almost see sleep rolling towards him like a tidal wave. He had time to realize that his call to the police might get his brother into trouble. If they apprehended the brutes who were doing the hitting, Tom could end up being linked to them. But it couldn't be helped. Gillian needed immediate care and Harper was in no position to ferry her to the hospital.

His last image before he slept was of the redhaired man and his invisible, whispering companion following himself or Gillian across the ocean on the trail of the missing Tom Harper, probably on the same airplane. It had to be that way. How else could they have located her so quickly?

He slept eighteen hours. It was ten o'clock on the following morning when he sat up in bed, his next move clear in his mind. Taking towel, soap, and room key, he walked down the hall to the communal bathroom where he showered and shaved. Again the years fell away and he was a young journalist newly arrived from the sticks, delighted with his low-paying job on a tabloid that was about to fold.

Those were the years when he strode around the magnificent city at night, splendidly drunk and speaking exuberantly inaccurate French to waiters and cab drivers and bar girls, climbing the stairs time and again to Ciro's to hear the Joe Holliday Quartet, sobering up at dawn in distant parts of town, and then walking home within view of great bridges. Karen's inviting face across a crowded restaurant was still two years away.

Spruced up and with his packed suitcase in hand, Harper checked out of the Y and walked to the Avis office on Dominion Square, where he rented a sedan. By midday, he was speeding down Highway 401, passing Dorval, heading for the Ontario border.

It was incredible the way Baytown never changed. As he drove in, Harper saw new people walking on Front Street but many of the same shops were there. Teddy Marcus was probably inside his book store—but how could he be? He was fifty when Harper left over twenty years ago. And inside Sullivan's Barbershop, old Sweets Cameron was probably still clicking his scissors and breathing through his mouth.

Driving past the high school, Harper swallowed hard against the rising sob in his chest as he saw the windows of classrooms he had inhabited for all those golden, glorious years. Tom had carried the football well on the broad playing field, taking the lumps as usual while his young brother stayed out of it on the sidelines, organizing clever rhyming cheers in safety.

"No more of that, Tom," Harper said aloud in the car. "I'm coming this time."

The house on Standard Street looked unchanged, too. That was the think about a collapsing porch and peeling stucco, Harper realized. It stayed the same because it had no place to go.

Tapping twice with the brass oak leaf knocker, he considered opening the door and walking in as he would have done when he lived here. But that would have been unfair to Mary, might have frightened her. It was bad enough showing up unannounced—he really should have telephoned from Montreal.

"Hello, Mary," he said as his sister opened the door.

She denied him the slightest show of surprise. "I knew it would be you. When Tom showed up this morning I said, you wait, Normie will be here before supper."

She stepped back to let him in, her cloudy eyes expressionless in her round beaming face. Her hair was the straight, styleless shag of a woman who could hardly see. Failing sight would also explain the two crayon strokes of her lipstick.

She led the way through the dark hall and into the dining room, moving expertly amid familiar surroundings.

Tom's voice sounded from the kitchen. "Is that Norm?" He walked into the room with a beer bottle in one hand and an empty glass in the other.

"Found you at last, you bastard," Harper said. The handshake, brief but firm and achingly familiar after so many years, said much that the brothers would be unable to put into words.

Tom poured the beer. "Here, drink ye all of this in remembrance that there are twenty-three others in the case." He handed the full glass to Norman. "How's your drink, Mary?" he said as he went back into the kitchen.

"Fine, I'm coasting." Just a passing, mystic wave of the hand as she found her glass.

Harper sat down at the dining room table, the oak dropleaf job with rounded corners. He remembered wartime Sunday afternoons when Mary was dating the lads from the air station. Table-tennis matches were played then on this table and the uniformed boys would start as what they were, champions of Vancouver or Toronto or wherever they came from. But those missing corners soon got to them as did the glass-front china cabinet waiting to receive their backswings with a smash, and they ended up embarrassed amateurs, losing to girlfriend, mother, father, both little brothers, everybody but the dog.

"Cheers," Harper said, and he drained most of a very necessary beer.

"You sound unchanged," Mary said. "England must agree with you. How's Karen? How's Anita?"

"Fine, all fine. They send love." He went on for a minute about the glories of the job plugging the tennis tournament, an easy set piece he was used to delivering. But as he talked and Mary smiled, he sensed her isolation and the way his presence in the room was nibbling away at it already. It was painful to realize that the check he sent her in the mail each month was not good enough. She was a person and she needed people.

Tom came from the kitchen with a full glass and two full bottles, one of which he set beside his brother's glass. Tom was blocky now, almost barrel-chested, so solid he could not slump. He sat on the straight-backed chair just the way Harper remembered their father sitting—legs apart, feet planted firmly, thick chest rising from a curved abdomen encased in a balloon of grey flannel. Harper felt if he looked under the table he would see the old man's shiny black high-laced boots.

"How very nice," Tom said. There was the shy glancing aside, the half smile that the experienced Harper family member could read as a show of great affection. "What brings you back here?"

"Just an impulse. With Wimbledon Fortnight over, I get to take some time off. Actually it was Karen's idea I get on a plane and come." Harper had decided not to mention the trouble in front of Mary. He and Tom would find time sooner or later.

The time came sooner. Mary insisted on preparing supper without help; she knew the kitchen and had been managing for years. The brothers ended up in the overgrown garden, sitting on a gliding swing that was immobilized in grass a foot tall. Irises run wild bloomed around them and late afternoon sunlight glistened on the jewelled wings of a hovering dragonfly.

"Okay," Harper said. "What's happening? I know all kinds of things, Tom. What's going on?"

"How much do you know?" The insolent confidence persisted from long ago.

"That you worked in London for Chelsea Crafts, making ceramic mugs. That you came and went, and they had to let you go."

"I'm a boozer. And a loser."

"Maybe worse than you realize. When I was in Wellington Mews two guys gave me a controlled beating. They thought I was you. No question about it from what they said."

"I believe that. What did they say?"

"That they'd let me—you—live because I'd helped. But I was not to disappear because they might need me again."

Tom Harper frowned. "They'd had their last from me."

"Last what? What did you do for them?"

Tom got up, stood in the tall grass, spilled half a bottle of beer onto a patch of earth behind the old garage. "Remember the famous bonfire, Norm?" he said. "Better late than never. No chance of burning the wall now. Mum would be pleased."

"What is it?" Harper persisted. "What sort of foolishness were you into?"

"Not foolishness, little brother. Patriotism. Unless they're one and the same."

"I don't follow."

"I did. I listened to long stories about how the English came and took over the land. How they tried to dominate and suppress us. And then the famine, with our women and children literally starving to death in cold huts by tens of thousands."

"What are you talking about?"

"I'm talking about freedom for Ireland after all these years. About the I.R.A." The sheepish expression on Tom Harper's face did not exactly mark him as a true believer.

"You don't buy that madness any more than I do. Who tried to sell it to you?"

"Patrick Leary. Sitting in the back room of The Shamrock early in the morning over jars of smoky whisky." Tom sat down again, facing his younger brother on the old swing with all its paint weathered off. The wood looked natural, as if nature grew swings. "It's really your fault, Normie. I came to Montreal following in your footsteps. You seemed to have the magic touch, or else you knew the way to go. That's why I went to England, too. My life was bloody murder, boredom and drink and failure. I thought if I could duplicate your moves I'd be a winner too."

Harper wanted to say something encouraging to Tom about his life but there was nothing that would ring true. "But how come the I.R.A. at Leary's place? This is Canada. There's nothing going on here."

"Only the raising of money. They need cash for gelignite. And alarm clocks."

"But you haven't any money."

"No. I was the courier. Sort of a delivery boy. Leary would get together a bundle of cash—they don't like checks or bank accounts—and I'd shoot across to London and make the delivery. My fine Canadian face and voice made excellent camouflage."

Mary's voice rang out from the kitchen informing them that supper was ready.

The brothers got up and stepped off the swing, then stood for a moment in the path facing the back of the house. Behind them, a slanting post intended to anchor a clothesline served as a platform for a homemade birdhouse. Somewhere in a tattered photo album was a snapshot of the two boys in high school cadet uniforms standing just this way with their arms entwined. The young Norman was holding a slice of bread with a crescent bite out of it and Tom had a small Union Jack on a stick protruding from his belt.

So that was it, Harper thought. Tom had helped, and they let him live. Now they might want him again and he was trying to disappear. Once in, never out.

"You might wonder why they'd be after me, a low-class messenger. But you see, I did a silly thing. I volunteered."

"For what?" Harper's heart was sinking.

"To go on active service. I showed up with my cash delivery just when a major blitz was to be carried out. A whole mess of bombs in the Oxford Circus area. But one of the lads who was to make a drop fell downstairs and broke his ankle. A very Irish thing to do. So I asked to be allowed to take his place. And Healy said I could."

"Let me guess," Harper said. "Healy has a soft husky voice and he calls you 'me boy'."

"That's right."

"And the lad who broke his ankle has red hair and freckles."

"Right again. Sean Culkin." Tom squinted at his brother. "Ah, the lads who thumped you. Sorry about that."

"Never mind. What happened?"

"The inevitable unexpected. I took one of the plastic bags and left it on the first floor landing of an office building near Bond Street underground. They were all timed to go off after midnight. No casualties intended—just a demonstration of how devastating we can be."

"Oh, God," Harper said. "I read about those bombs."

"Yes, and about the cleaning lady. Set down her mop and bucket and picked up the bag just as it went off. Fifty-three years old and a very youthful and pretty grandmother, according to the press."

They moved slowly towards the house. "So you packed it in," Harper said.

"Or so I told Mr. Healy. He laughed and said there was no such arrangement in the I.R.A. I promised I'd say nothing to anybody, but he pointed out you can't run an army on that basis. So I changed bed sitters and went out of sight."

"Why Chelsea Crafts?"

"To save money to come home. I'd learned ceramics teaching a class at Kitchener High. But the cash kept going on drinks so I ended up working my way back on a freighter. Anyway, it looks like I just got out in time, with Sean and Healy gettig so close."

Through dinner, Harper wondered when to inform Tom about Gillian Mill. He would have to know. But there was no telling what he might do as a result. Harper ate while his sister and brother did most of the talking. The style of cooking on Standard Street had not changed. The sausages were charred black, the mashed potatoes had lumps, and there was lots of that unique salad—chopped cabbage and onion mixed together with mayonnaise and liberally dosed with salt and pepper. It was the best meal he had tasted in years and he cleaned his plate.

Mary insisted on washing up alone so Harper had Tom to himself in the living room for a while. He said, "You know about Gillian Mill?"

"Sure. She showed up in Montreal yesterday and told me you'd been looking for me. And she described my Irish friends who came in before you. That's why I faded to Baytown."

"They found her."

"Who did?"

"The redhead and the other. I came by not long after, in time to call an ambulance."

Tom Harper stared at his young brother, the expression in his eyes so level he looked almost stupid. It was an animal look. It suggested he knew exactly what he had to do, but doing it would be hateful and dangerous. "I'd like to borrow that rented car, Normie," he said flatly.

"Stay out of Montreal, Tom. They're trying to find you. Gillian didn't tell them you came here."

"I have no choice. I'm going after Pat Leary."

"Why him? He can't be behind your trouble in London."

"No. But he must have set them on Gillian. They'd never have found the apartment without help."

Harper had a terrible recollection of the moment in The Shamrock when he mentioned Tom's address to Leary. The man had been probing, he could see that now, so Gillian's suffering was his fault.

"Tom," he said, "listen, I'll go to Montreal and talk to Leary. I've got enough friends in London, he won't dare mess with me. I'll make a bargain with him. He calls his thugs off you and I forget what I know. Let them go on killing each other, but leave the Harper family alone."

"What about Gillian?"

"That was bad but she'll mend in time. Meanwhile, will it be better for her if you get killed by Leary? Or if you kill him and go to jail forever?"

Tom was silent, his face sullen.

"Then I'll drive back in the morning," Harper concluded. "You sit tight here and by this time tomorrow your troubles will be over."

Harper spent a restless night in his old room, aware of the calcimined wallpaper surrounding him and the same distant railway sounds clanking in the dark outside the screened window. In the morning, Mary made him Fried Eggs Baytown, their edges burned crisp as bacon rind. He relished them, swabbing the greasy plate clean with toast. Tom was still in bed when he drove away at ten.

Passing Dorval on the way in to Montreal, he thought it would make sense to go to the counter and book the soonest flight out that evening. The girl at the Air Canada desk put his name down for a seat on the plane departing at half past nine. Then, leaving the terminal, he passed a bank of phones and decided to ring home. There was nothing to report yet, but suddenly it seemed very important he should call.

He dialed direct and Mary answered, her voice a subdued howl. "Hello?"

"It's me, Mary."

"Oh God, Normie. Tom is dead! They killed him."

"What?"

"Two men. They came to the door and I said he was in the garden. They went through and I heard shots and then running in the lane."

Harper almost asked her what they looked like before he remembered she couldn't see them. Anyway, he already knew. He felt himself sinking in a sea of anguish—this was how he had helped his brother, by leading the killers to him. Mary was asking him a question. He said yes, he would be home as soon as he could make it. That was true enough. But in the meantime he had more reason than ever to visit Pat Leary.

Behaving responsibly out of habit, he turned in the car at the rental office.

Then he walked to The Shamrock, went inside, saw no sign of Leary, and headed for the door at the end of the bar.

A bartender he had never seen approached him but Harper smiled and said, "A package for old Patsy. Not to worry, he's expecting me."

There was a short passage and then another door, padded with green leather and brass studs. Without knocking, Harper opened it and walked into the office. Pat Leary swung around in his swivel chair and so soon as he saw the visitor's face his hand went for the side drawer in the desk.

The hand was in the drawer when Harper slammed it shut with his knee. As Leary screamed, Harper seized his mouth in one hand, twisting the flesh shut while his other hand grasped Leary's throat. In seconds he had Leary out of the chair, across the desk, and onto the carpet where he knelt on his arms, both hands around Leary's throat now, squeezing, but not hard enough yet to cut off the air.

"I'm going to kill you, Pat. Your people tried to beat Tom in London and got me by mistake. Then you battered that poor girl—you did that. And now you've killed my brother."

"Norman," Leary managed, "this is war. The cause is just. A lot of people are dying but it can't be helped."

"Bullshit, Pat."

"We'll win. Someday we'll win. But right now the enmey is strong and determined—we must have security. Tom left us, he knew us—he had to die."

"And now it's your turn."

"That's crazy. You've got a life to live, Norman—family, success in England. Kill me and you throw it all away. That's insane."

"Of course it is. Who ever said revenge is anything but insane?" Harper tightened his fingers and saw Leary's eyes bulge from the pressure and the realization it was actually happening to him. "But you forget, Patrick," he said. "I'm as Irish as you are."

When Leary was dead, Harper got up and picked up the telephone. A buzzer on it was labelled "bar." He pressed it and when the bartender came on he said, "Leary doesn't want to be disturbed. We're discussing business."

"Right."

"But when Sean and Healy come in, he says send them right through."

He put down the phone, found the revolver in Leary's desk drawer, and placed himself in the swivel chair facing the leather door. He decided that when it opened he would kill the redhead first. But now his job was to wait, and to force himself not to think about Karen or Anita, or about his blind sister who would now live even more alone in Baytown. Stubbornly, he would keep his mind on his brother Tom.

Kenneth Gavrell

Death in the Barrio

We had arranged to meet for lunch. She'd said she would feel most comfortable talking about it that way. She didn't like offices and thought it would be an imposition to ask me to drive out to her place in Bayamon.

That was all right with me; I had to eat lunch anyway. But I wouldn't have chosen this place: phony-looking wood paneling, plastic flowers on the snow-white tablecloths, and waitresses in cutesy aproned skirts. The kind of restaurant you'd expect to find in Disneyland rather than on San Juan's Condado. Unfortunately it fit into the Condado all too well these days.

I was nursing a Corona beer when she arrived–ten minutes late.

"I'm sorry," she said. "I couldn't find a place to park."

I smiled my that's-all-right smile and held her chair for her. She was about thirty-five would have been pretty if she weren't so overweight. Eggshell-blue eyes, hefty breasts, and hair as fine and golden as a doll's.

"You aren't what I expected," she said.

"What did you expect?"

"Someone frumpier, tougher-looking. Maybe older. It's hard to tell anything from your telephone voice."

"You want a drink?" I asked.

"No. I don't like to drink."

I signaled for one of the waitresses–Mary Poppins in a miniskirt–and ordered a ham sandwich. Mrs. Holling ordered a meal that would stuff a Victorian sofa. That explained the weight problem.

She smiled sheepishly. "I know I eat too much. It seems to be my way of coping since Jay died."

"It's better than drinking, I suppose." I was being Mr. Affable today. When the food arrived she ate quickly and nervously, and it looked like she was going to finish it, but by then she'd gotten down to business. On the telephone she had said little beyond reawakening my memory about the case. It had been in the papes. About two months ago her husband, a computer programmer with IBM, had been driving down to Lake Loiza to go fishing. It was around two o'clock on a Saturday afternoon. As he'd rounded a turn up in the hills in the vicinity of a few houses and stores, a gunman had fired two shots through his windown, one of which had killed him.

The police had been working on it ever since, without turning up a clue. They'd checked all the houses in the area and come up without a gun or a likely suspect. They'd also checked into Mr. Holling's past and present with no results. It appeared to be a completely unmotivated killing by a sniper.

The people in the area had heard shots but couldn't provide any other information. They hadn't seen a thing. A search of the probable location of the sniper–arrived at from a study of the car marks, bullet angle, and local testimony–produced nothing except some crushed vegetation and a grimy Winston cigarette butt.

"It sounds like an impossible case," I said.

"I don't trust the police," Mrs. Holling said. "I'm told they're not very efficient."

"On a case like this that's an understatement," I said. "But their conclusion seems the most likely: some nut who had to get something out of his system. It happens in the States all the time."

"Does it happen in Puerto Rico all the time?"

"No," I admitted. "It's pretty damn rare, actually."

She was getting into the dessert now–a chocolate sundae that would have made Sydney Greenstreet blanch.

"You want coffee?" I asked.

"Yes, please."

I ordered some from Mary Poppins.

"You're supposed to be good," she said. "I've been asking around. I want you on the case."

"I can't promise you a thing," I said. "The odds are I won't come with anything."

"Well, I can't go on like this," she said, her voice rising surprisingly. "I've got to know something. Look, Jay and I loved each other. We were married eight years and we still loved each other. I amy be able to adjust to living without him, but I'll never adjust to not knowing why he died. I've *got to know!*"

"You've had over two months to think about it," I said soothingly. "Don't you have any idea yourself?"

"Jay had no enemies," she said. "There was certaininly on other woman."

"Was he involved in politics?"

"He cared about politics as much as I care about fishing."

"So you haven't the slightest."

"That's what's so *maddening.*"

"I'll have to check into your pesonal lives," I told her. "Bank accounts, friends, people at his office, how he spent his time–that sort of thing."

"I don't care," she said. "What will it cost?"

"I can't say. That depends on how many hours I have to put in."

"I have over ten thousand dollars in the bank," she said.

"It won't come to anything near that," I said.

The waitress brought the coffee. I had to reach to another table to supplement our sugar bowl.

I called my friend Robert Burgos at Homicide. He was out, but got back to me about four o'clock.

"I'm taking up the Holling case. Mrs. Holling just hired me."

"And she seemed like such an intelligent woman," Roberto said.

"Ho ho."

"What is that, your Santa Claus imitation?"

"Look, seriously, do you really think it's hopeless?"

He gave a grunt that sounded like a verbal shrug. "If you can find a connection it's not hopeless. If there's no connection–which is what we think–" he left the sentence dangling.

"You'll give me what you have?"

"*Por que no*? We don't have much of anything."

"You don't mind my horning in?"

"I'm getting used to it. Anyway, we've given up on it," Roberto said. "But that's just between you and me.

"When can I come by?"

"Any time. I'll get out the file."

"I'll be around in fifteen minutes."

He was right: there wasn't much of anything. A lot of photos of the car, the body, even one of the crushed vegetation and the cigarette butt. Statements from the people in the neighborhood, all pretty useless. The most interesting part was the personal stuff on Holling. He had been with IBM in San Juan for six years. Originally from Joliet, Illinois. Spent time working in Chicago and New York. A good company man, generally well liked. There was a bank account at Citibank, smaller than you'd expect, and a checking account, same place, with a little over twelve hundred dollars in it at the time of his death. Two newish cars–a red Camaro, which he had been driving that day, and a Datsun. A sixty thousand dollar house in Bayamon. No unusual debts for a peson of his income bracket and life style. No bad habits beyond an occasional overindulgence in alcohol. No known enemies.

His photo showed a man of forty-two, fair complexion, grey eyes, nondescript-colored hair (slightly balding), glasses. You'd never notice him in a crowd. There wasn't much of the face left in the photos taken at the murder site. I copied down the data about his office, bank, and friends.

"Your men aren't very good at Easter-egg hunts," I said to Roberto. "No bullets, not even the cartridge cases."

"You know what it's like trying to find bullets outdoors," Roberto said. "The killer apparently picked up his spent cases."

"Leaving you with no information about the gun except what little the wound provides."

"We're assuming it was a rifle," Roberto said. "He fired from about twenty yards. We can also assume it was probably a semi-automatic since he had very little time to get off two rounds with a moving target."

"Obviously no amateur with a gun," I said.

"He may have used a scope."

"Even so."

"The bullet shatteret the right side of Holling's head on exit. I'd guess a high velocity, maybe a spitzer."

"Caliber?"

"Entrance wound suggests something like a .308."

"And that's it."

"That's it. I thought you liked them tough."

"I'm getting old and soft," I said.

"You'll be older by the time you solve this one," Roberto said.

That evening I looked up Holling's close friends. There were just two of them. Both worked for IBM. It turned out to be a waste of time—neither of them could provide anything I hand't learned already. I hinted rather pointedly at a possible extramarital affair, but it was no go. Jay and Christine had had a very close marriage. Their friends envied them. They hadn't been able to have a child and had been considering adopting one at the time of his death.

The next morning—after phoning my secretary at the office, who told me nothing very important was happening—I went to the IBM headquarters in Santurce. It was the same story: no one could think of the vaguest reason why somebody would want to kill Jay Holling.

After lunch I got into my Toyota Corolla and drove out to the scene of the killing.

It was one of those marvelous Puerto Rican afternoons: clear, high sky, almost painfully bright sunlight, and—once I got out of town—air that smelled of fresh vegetation and baked earth. Route 176, south of San Juan, is a typical narrow country road that winds among green hills. As in all the island, you are never very far from people; at every other turn there is a house, a restaurant, or a gas station. Girls in bright dresses, cows and chickens, abandoned ancient cars, flowering trees, loud music, dirty puddles, stands of bamboo. I reached the murder scene at about two o'clock—oddly enough, at the same time Jay Holling had reached it the day he died.

There were a gas station, a bar, three houses, and a colmado sitting in a cluster at a high point on the road just after a curve. I swung over onto the dusty gravel in front of the bar and cut the motor. Ednita Nazario was belting one out on the bar jukebox or radio. A couple of kids were playing in front of one of the houses and two guys lounged outside the gas station, one of them cradling a can of beer. Traffic along the road was sparse. I went into the bar. A big T-shirted kid in his late teens hung over the jukebox, studying it instead of his schoolbooks. Aside from him there were only the bartender and an old man on a stool who wasn't drinking.

The bartender looked at me pregnantly.

"Corona," I said.

"*Schaefer o India, nada mas.*"

"*Schaefer esta bien.*"

He dug a beer out of his icebox under the bar. He was an old guy too and looked like he had made that motion a million times.

"*Que calor,*" I said. "It's hot out."

He made an indifferent gesture.

The kid came over from the jukebox and stood in front of me.

"You a cop?" he said, surprising me.

I looked him over. The kind of kid who'd probably seen a lot of cops in his short time.

"Funny question," I said.

"Not so funny. We get cops out here all the time lately."

"Since the 'accident'," I said.

"I thought so," the kid said. He spat on the floor. The two old men just watched quietly. I took a sip from my beer. It was well chilled.

"Can't you creeps leave us alone?" the kid said. His features had congealed into a permanent snarl at an early age.

"Actually I'm not a cop," I said. "I'm a private detective."

"Big deal," the kid said.

"Who hired you?" the old bartender asked, leaning on the bar.

"*La viuda del norteamericano.* The American's widow."

"We don't know anything," the bartender said. "The police have been here many times. We've told them all we know."

"Did you hear the shots?" I asked.

"No, I can't hear anything with that." He pointed to the jukebox. He was right. I could barely hear him.

"What about you?" I turned to the other old guy on the stool. He looked like everybody's grandfather: about sixty-five, deeply tanned, whitening hair, healthy-looking for his age.

"Yes, I heard them," he said slowly. "There were two."

"Where were you?"

"In my house across the street. I thought it was a car backfiring."

The kid pulled a cigarette from the pocket of his over-tight T-shirt and lit it, eyeing me hostilely through a smoke cloud.

"Now what would your mama say if she knew you smoked," I said.

He replied with an obscenity directed very personally at me. I smiled. I enjoyed this kid.

"You hear the shots?" I asked him.

He carefully took the cigarette from his mouth, turned his back to me, and walked out. I made a mental note to check my hubcaps when I left.

"I'd like to see where the car crashed," I said to the bartender.

He pointed in the opposite direction from which I'd come. "It's about a hundred yards past the colmado on this side. You can't miss it."

"Why not?"

"He knocked over a couple of small trees. You'll see it."

I thanked him, paid for my beer, and strolled out into the dazzling sunlight.

I found the two trees without any trouble–small, green-trunked palms. But aside from there there was very little evidence of a car wreck only two months earlier. Nature comes back fast in Puerto Rico. This area was pretty heavily grown on both sides of the road. The two trees were about fifteen feet downhill of the road, and on the other side of it the terrain rose very gently toward some cleared land surrounding a big house built at the top of the hill.

I tried to guess where the car might have left the road, assuming it was traveling about forty miles an hour as witnesses had said, and then I tried to calculate about where Holling had been hit and where his killer would probably have been hiding. The police could have told me exactly. So could any of these cooperative country folk. But it didn't make much difference: any place on that side of the road where the killer could have been hiding was heavily overgrown and well past the last house of the barrio. It was wonderful terrain for a sniper with a good rifle. One who knew how to us it, as this fellow had.

jI walked back and sent into the colmado. It was very dark inside after the sunlight-a dank wooden place with shelves of canned goods from floor to ceiling, barrels and sacks on the floor, and a turn-of-the-century cash register that any museum would have given its right arm for. The place suddenly shot me back thirty years to my childhood in Salinas. A Puerto Rican mother and a gringo father, a childhood spent half in Salinas and half in New York–I sometimes wasn't quite sure who I was myself.

Behind the counter stood a dowdy middle-aged woman in a pink blouse and black skirt. What looked like a mother and her son were buying rice and bacalao. The boy was maybe twelve or thirteen. The mother completed her purchase rapidly and they went out, giving me a wide berth.

I told the woman at the cash register who I was and why 1 was there. She took it all in without comment. "I wondered if you could help me with any information," I said.

She smoothed her skirt against her lumpy body–or perhaps she was wiping dust from her hands. "I was in Ponce all that day," she said distantly. "I'm afraid I know nothing."

"Who do you think *would* know something?" I asked.

"The police have already been through all this," she said. "We do not need private detectives as well. We live quietly here."

"Well, who do you think shot the norteamericano?"

"I have no idea. Perhaps an enemy. Perhaps just a loco."

"A loco from around here?" I asked.

"*Mira,*" she said, "*estoy ocupada. Yo no se nada.*"

"What about the man who runs the gas station?"

"Did you want to make a purchase?" she said. "If not, I'm very busy."

"I think I'll try the gas station," I said.

"*Bueno,*" she said. "Try the gas station."

She turned a stiff back on me and started to arrange cans on a shelf. Apparently it took more than my natural charisma to warm up these people.

The gas station owner was a hulking brute in his early thirties, the sort of guy you expect to have hair growing on his teeth. The butt of an S&W .38 was sticking out of the back of his pants, a practice becoming more common among gas station people, I'd noticed.

Business was slow. He was talking to a younger man of much slighter build in jeans and an open shirt. They both watched me walk up in the way people watch you who are doing their damndest to act as if they don't know you're around.

I pulled out my card and showed it to them. No reaction—it might as well have been my birth certificate. I leaned against a pump and studied the hills across the road.

"I'm investigating the shooting of the norteamericano a couple of months ago," I said.

No reaction. The hulk kicked an empty beer can toward the garage. It was a good kick—the can landed about a foot from the wall.

"What kind of name is that?" the younger man said finally. "Carlos Bannon. You a hybrid?"

This one has dome education.

"My father's from the States," I said. "The full name is Carlos Bannon Santiago."

"Assimilation," said the younger one. He made a face.

"I had very little to do with it," I said. "You don't like norteamericanos?"

"No. The island's too small for them. And for all the others who come here to live off us."

"He's an independentista," said the bear indifferently. I got a look at his teeth: there was no hair on them.

"Shall we speak English?" said the younger man sarcastically. "I afraid I no spik the inglish very good."

Some clouds were beginning to build over the hills.

"It looks to me as if the norteamericano was shot by somebody from around here," I said quietly. "But the police couldn't find the gun. Are there many guns around here?"

"As far as I know only this one," said the big guy. He pulled it out suddenly and pointed it at my stomach. I froze. Then he laughed, his fleshy blue face corrugated like the roof over his pumps.

KENNETH GAVRELL

"You have a wonderful sense of humor," I said. "Have you got a permit for that?"

"I don't see how it's any of your business." He didn't lower the gun.

"Did the police check it out?"

"The norteamericano was killed with a rifle," he said.

"Oh? How do you know?"

"I may look stupid," he said, "but don't you believe it."

"I'd put that away," I said. "Or I may be tempted to wrap it around your thick neck."

"Mierda," he said, and showed me his hairless teeth again.

"Put it away," mumbled the independentista.

The bear just looked at him. Then he lifted the barrel of the gun. But he didn't put it back in his belt. "We're not answering any questions for private detectives from the big city," he said. "Now get off my property."

"I have some friends in Homicide," I said. "I'll check on that gun."

"I wouldn't push him," the younger man said. "If I were you I think I'd go, hybrid."

What the hell, I wasn't going to get anything out of them anyway.

"By the way," I said as I turned, "how did you know about me?"

"A little pig told me," the big man said. "He told the whole neighborhood. I think you better get in your car and go back to San Juan."

"I may be around a while longer," I said. "If I need any gas, I'll let you know."

"Mierda," he said.

I walked back toward my car. What next? Check out the houses? I didn't see the point. The old man who'd been in the bar was coming out as I approached the car.

"Are you still here?"

"As you see."

"I think you're wasting your time."

"You may be right."

"The people here are fed up with all the notoriety."

"I can understand that," I said.

"You want a cup of good coffee? My wife makes very good coffee. I'll show you we are not really inhospitable to strangers."

"All right," I said.

"I live over there." He pointed to the first house on the right: flat-roofed, cheap, hot, concrete. There were flowerpots lined along the porch.

"Thank you," I said as we crossed the street together. My soul needed a little friendliness just then.

"What's your name?" the old man asked.

"Carlos."

"Mine's Ricardo."

"*Mucho gusto.*"

He led the way into the open doorway of the house.

We sat in his rather baroque living room while his wife made coffee in the kitchen. As old people will often do, he took out an album of family snapshots. He was especially proud of his grandaughter.

"How old is she?" I asked.

"Four."

"Very pretty," I said, which was true.

"Yes," he agreed. "She is the person I love most in the world."

A young woman appeared at the doorway. One look at her and I realized she was the child's mother.

"Oh, come in, Alicia. This is my daughter," he said to me.

We exchanged *encantados.* She too was very pretty. She seemed embarrassed and excused herself to join her mother in the kitchen.

"Here's a picture of me when I was young," Ricardo continued.

The photo showed a handsom man in his late twenties wearing an army uniform. A black mustache and a smile that would have charmed the ladies. "I was in the infantry during the war. I was in Italy."

"The war: for him, World War II.

"I was in Vietnam," I said. "When it was just starting."

He nodded.

There were other pictures of him in uniform and several with his wife, who had not weathered the years as well. But most of the pictures were of his daughter and granddaughter. Not many of the son-in-law.

I wondered if the daughter was divorced. While I was wondering, she came in with the coffee.

"You bore everyone with those photographs," she said.

"He's not bored. Are you, Carlos?"

"No," I said. "After all the hostility I've met here, it's a pleasure."

"We're all tired of the police," Alicia said. So she knew who I was, too. I noticed what a fine figure she had as she leaned over the coffee tray.

"What happened after the car crashed?" I asked. "Did anyone try to find the killer?"

"No one had any idea where the shots came from," she said.

"There were no strangers around that day?"

"No one remembered any strangers," she said.

The old man excused himself and went to the bathroom. Alicia was clearly uncomfortable about being left alone with me.

"You have a beautiful daughter," I said, trying to put her at ease.

"Yes, she was."

"Was?"

"She died some months ago."

I understood then what is meant by an eerie feeling.

"My father spoke as if she were alive?" Alicia said.

"Yes."

"He does that. My father is getting old. It is not so easy to accommodate yourself to changes when you get old."

It rained most of the way back. The weather does that in Puerto Rico: a beautiful day suddenly dissolves in a downpour.

I pulled into San Juan at about five o'clock, feeling tired. Enough for one day. Plenty to think about. I took a shower, ate, and went out to a movie.

The next morning I was at the office by nine. Maria was typing up a report for a client—the usual divorce stuff. I told her to get Burgos at Homicide on the phone.

He came on, sounding abnormally cheerful. "Well, how's it going, Sherlock Holmes?"

"I'm not sure yet."

"Did you go out there?"

"Yes. You would have thought I had the plague."

He chuckled appreciatively.

"Look, Roberto, I want you to do a couple of things for me, and get back to me as soon as you can."

"Depends what the 'things' are," he said. "Let's have it."

Mrs. Holling had called my office and invited me to lunch again. She was going to be in San Juan anyway. The 'anyway' made me feel less flattered by the invitation.

We went to the same restaurant. Once again she ordered enough for two of me.

"You don't each much," she remarked.

"No. I drink."

"On the phone you sounded as if you might have learned something."

"I think I have."

"Well, tell me," she said anxiously.

"I can't. Not yet. I have to go out to that barrio again. Right now all I have is a hunch."

"How do hunches become facts?"

"I'll let you know when I get back."

"You think someone out there shot Jay?"

"It seems the only reasonable assumption at this point."

"But who? Why?"

"I know this is bad for you," I said. "I hope that by later tonight I'll be able to tell you."

"Why later tonight?"

"I'm not going out there till six o'clock."

"Is there any danger?"

"No," I lied.

"Shall I come with you? I have nothing to do this evening."

"No," I said. "I think I'd better go alone."

The small group of buildings looked pretty under a wine-colored sunset, like something from a Haitian painting. In twenty minutes it would be dark. I pulled over in front of the bar.

There seemed to be nobody around except my gun-toting friend across the street at the gas station. He made a show of watching me as I climbed out of the car. I went into the bar for a beer.

"Still only India and Schaefer?" I asked the bartender.

"Si."

He pulled a Schaefer out of the icebox and pushed it across to me.

"You have a good memory."

"You're easy to remember."

"I like your place a lot better without that damn thing going." I motioned toward the jukebox.

"Yo tambien," he said. "So do I. But most of my customers like music." He switched on the lights and leaned against a shelf behind the bar. "So you're back."

"Yes. I stil lhave some unfinished business here."

"Have you discovered anything?"

"I think so."

"That's more than the police did."

I finished off the beer and got up to leave.

"You were thirsty," he said. "Where are you going now?"

"I thought I'd walk around a bit. I want to take another look at the spot where the shooting took place."

"It's almost dark."

"I have a light."

"What do you expect to find there?"

"Now *you* sound like the private detective," I said.

He almost smiled. I counted that as a victory of sorts in this barrio.

I walked out, took my big lantern flashlight from the car, and started up the road. I walked slowly, out in the street where I'd bve conspicuous. The bear in the gas station watched me. I already felt that other people were watching me. In a tight little place like this, people seemed to develop a sixth sense when there were strangers around.

But they hadn't noticed any strangers that day.

The door of Ricardo's house was open, but I didn't see him or his wife or daughter. The woman in the lighted colmado noticed me as I passed. She followed me with her eyes. Just past her store I ran into the juvenile delinquent: he was strolling with his arm wrapped around a bombshell of a girl of about seventeen, the two of them looking like they'd stepped out of *West Side Story.*

"Well, well," I said. "Why aren't you helping your mother with the dishes like a good boy?"

He snarled in his inimitable style. The girl looked me over curiously. She had jet hair and eyes, *cafe-au-lait* skin, a face and figure to make a man's palms sweat.

"When the hell are you going to leave us alone?" the kid said.

"When I've solved this case," I said amiably. "Which I think I may do this evening. When are you going to change your T-shirt?"

I chin-pointed toward the girl friend. *"Que linda,"* I said. "Beautiful girl."

I knew that would do it. The punch came high and fast and I just caught it with my right forearm, holding the flashlight, while I drove my left deep into his stomach. He doubled over and I caught him with another left, almost straight up from below, and his head snapped back as he went down. I felt pretty good; I hadn't even dropped the flashlight. He was a big kid and I'd known it would take at least two to put him down. The girl crumpled beside him, making little distress noises, punctuated by curses at me. She'd picked up some of his vocabulary. I stepped around the two of them and continued up the road. Thekid was holding his stomach and the girl was begging him to tell her he was all right.

Her voice faded behind me as I reached the spot where I surmised the sniper had fired from that day. I turned up several yards into the brush and began poking around in the area. By now it was almost dark and I had to use the light. It cast a good strong beam, very little of which came back on me. I moved a bit farther up the incline and then began working in a circle. The heavy brush came up to my waist and grabbed at my clothes. Quite a few trees of different varieties dotted the slope. Once in a while I bent down as if studying something. It was getting darker every second. As the darkness deepened, I held the light farther out from me.

It would take a little time for him to get into position. Unless I was all wet. I hoped I was. A few minutes more should tell me–us. Anyway I kept on the move, bending over frequently, the light well out from my body. I suppose I've been more scared in my life, but I don't remember when. If they didn't get him first, this might be my last walk on this planet. I didn't see or hear anything unusual, but it was hard to hear much above the din of the *coquis.*

With the falling of darkness it had cooled, but I was still sweating through my light jacket. I'd had to wear the jacket to hide the gun. The hand holding my flashlight was trembling. What the hell was he waiting for? I'd certainly given him time enough by now.

At that instant it came: I heard the report and went down as the bullet sang past my chest. He hadn't shot from very close. I wrenched my revolver out and heard him crashing away through the brush. I also heard the yelling of Roberto and his men in pursuit. The chase was taking place on the other side of the road. Tehre was another shot, more running and yelling, and then two more shots. Then there was just the yelling of Robert's men. They all seemed to have converged at one point about fifteen yards below the road. I walked down, my hands still trembling.

The three of them were gathered over him. He lay, eyes closed, in a pool of light from Roberto's flashlight. My only feeling then was one of sympathy for him. I didn't see any blood.

"Is he dead?" I asked.

"No," Roberto said. "He's passed out–he's not a young man."

"Why did you have to shoot at him?"

"He was shooting at us. Did you want him to get away?"

"I don't know," I said.

Roberto put his brown paw on my shoulder. "He's got one in the back, but I don't think he'll die."

"He's deranged," I said. "You knew that."

"If someone shoots at my men, they have to shoot back," Roberto said. "I'll go call an ambulance."

"I'll wait here with him and your goons," I said. "If you'd found him before he started shooting, this could have been avoided."

"You're the one who's crazy," Mrs. Holling said. "How *could* you use yourself as a decoy.

"It was the only way I could think of to bring him out into the open. I had no proof, nothing at all. Those people up there certainly were'nt going to help me get any.

"They all knew," she said bitterly.

"Maybe not. But it wouldn't have made any difference: it's a tight little community."

"It's so insane," she said. "Just because Jay was driving a red Camaro."

"And for all we know it might not even have been a red Camaro that killed Ricardo's granddaughter," I said. "Perhaps just a car that looked like it."

"How did his wife and daughter take it?"

"They'd expected something like this. The old man's had a history of mental illness, and he was getting worse. At times he actually believed his granddaughter was still alive. That day he saw your husband's car stop for gas. He ran home and got his hunting rifle and lay in ambush beyond the houses. His wife told me he'd qualified as a sharpshooter in the army and has hunted all his life."

"Do you think he intended to hit you out there or just scare you?"

"I don't know. I'd like to believe the second."

"And how come the police couldn't find the gun?"

"Guns," I corrected her. "He had three of them, all hidden in a space under his porch."

"It's so sad," Mrs. Holling said. "Now that I know the truth I don't feel any better. I think I regret having hired you."

I didn't say anything.

"Just one more question," she said after a bit. "How did you know that the granddaughter had been killed by a hit and run driver?"

"It was just a hunch that seemed to fit. I asked a friend at headquarters to check on any hit and runs in the area during the last year. The little girl was killed three months before your husband."

"They'll probably commit him," she said tonelessly.

"Yes," I said. "That's what they usually do."